IMPASSIONED

Book 2

DARCY BURKE

ZEALOUS QUILL PRESS

IMPASSIONED

Society's most exclusive invitation...

Welcome to the Phoenix Club, where London's most audacious, disreputable, and intriguing ladies and gentlemen find scandal, redemption, and second chances.

In nearly two years of marriage, Sabrina Westbrook has barely spoken to her husband and shared a bed even less. Both activities would require they actually live together. As it is, the Earl of Aldington attends to his seat in the House of Commons, while she and her crippling social anxiety tend to his country house and gardens.

Their arrangement is quite civilized, and their letters are painfully polite. Their twice-yearly visits are...awkward. But, if Sabrina can muster the necessary courage, all of that is about to change. Starting tonight.

Heir to a dukedom, Constantine Westbrook knows his duty: to country, to family, and to the shy, retiring wife whose beauty stole his breath the moment they met. Whose arousing, enticing body he's never seen in the light of day. Or any light at all.

However, there's something different about the woman who shows up in London unannounced. For the first time in their marriage, Sabrina has a request. No, a *demand*. But wanting and having are two different things. And to give Sabrina her heart's desire, they'll both need a few lessons in love...

Don't miss the rest of *The Phoenix Club*!

Do you want to hear all the latest about me and my books? Sign up at Reader Club newsletter for members-only bonus content (including the prequel short story for The Phoenix Club!), advance notice of pre-orders, insider scoop, as well as contests and giveaways!

Care to share your love for my books with like-minded readers? Want to hang with me and see pictures of my cats (who doesn't!)? Then don't miss my exclusive Facebook groups!

Darcy's Duchesses for historical readers
Burke's Book Lovers for contemporary readers

CHAPTER 1

March 1815, London

*C*onstantine Westbrook, Earl of Aldington, slid the
key into the lock. Apprehension overwhelmed any
anticipation he might have possessed. He glanced over at the
beautiful woman he'd hired for the evening and doubted his
actions.

Don't. Plenty of gentlemen take a mistress.

Constantine, however, was not plenty of men, and his
arguments for tonight's activity were not entirely persuasive.
He prided himself on being a man of integrity and principle.
He was also a man of needs, and he was weary of being alone
every night, despite having a wife. If one could even call her
that when she avoided his presence and behaved as if he
were either repulsive or terrifying. Or both.

Barbara slid her hand beneath his coat and curled her
arm around his waist. Sidling closer, she brushed her large,
round breast against him. "Come on then, love."

His body reacted, quieting the doubts. The key clicked, and Barbara pushed the door open with her hip, giving him a saucy smile.

She turned from him and sucked in a breath. "What in the devil is going on here?"

Constantine immediately took in the scene. The Earl of Overton stood close to a young woman—his bloody ward, whom Constantine had met and who was a close friend of his sister's—and both were undressed. Overton scrambled to pull on a shirt and responded to Barbara, though Constantine didn't hear what he said over the cacophony of distress in his head. This was supposed to be a private assignation —*secret*.

Horrified at being seen, and seeing Overton with his ward, Constantine pivoted. His feet were somehow rooted to the floor despite his brain screaming at him to leave as quickly as possible. Damn, Overton was coming toward him. Constantine glanced in the man's direction before stalking away from the room, quickly retracing his steps to the back staircase that he and Barbara had used to ascend to the second floor of the Phoenix Club.

Apparently, they should have gone to her lodgings instead. But Constantine had asked his younger brother for assistance with carrying out his scheme in a more discreet location so as not to be seen entering or leaving Barbara's. As the owner of the Phoenix Club, Lucien had enthusiastically provided Constantine with a key to a bedchamber on the second floor of the club, saying he and Barbara would be completely undisturbed.

Not only had that been untrue, but Constantine now found himself in the infuriating position of having his behavior known. Hopefully, Overton and his ward would say nothing. That seemed likely since they wouldn't want their assignation to become public knowledge either.

Then he heard Overton coming after him. "Aldington, wait! Why are you here?"

Constantine did not turn as he gritted his teeth. In fact, he hastened his pace. "This was a mistake. Please don't follow me out." He opened the door to the backstairs and slipped through, closing it firmly behind him.

Thankfully, Overton did not continue his pursuit. Still, Constantine hurried down to the ground floor and made his way out of the back of the club into the garden. Sounds from the club's assembly, the first of the Season, carried to him from the ballroom. Constantine had never been to an assembly at the club because he wasn't a member. His brother and his mysterious membership committee hadn't invited him.

Tonight's scheme had been ill-planned. Lucien should have warned him that both the gentlemen's and ladies' sides of the club would be teeming with ball-goers.

Eager to put this entire event behind him, he found the almost unidentifiable door in the wall along Bury Street where he and his companion had come in. He opened it just enough to slip outside and made sure it was latched before he rushed away, head down, toward St. James where he would be far more comfortable.

The thought nearly made him laugh. Was he ever comfortable? Yes, when he worked on the matters that he was most passionate about in the House of Commons, despite the fact that his seat there was yet another duty his father had insisted upon, like his marriage. But while his service in the House of Commons had actually brought satisfaction and even given him a sense of purpose, his marriage was another story entirely.

As he approached the entrance to White's, Constantine cast his head back and took a deep breath, inhaling London's scent of coal smoke and horses. Sometimes he envied his wife and the time she spent at Hampton Lodge, the home they'd chosen as their country residence about fifteen miles outside London, with its country air and open spaces.

Residence? Hers, certainly, but not his. Constantine visited twice a year—in the summer for a few weeks and over the holidays. Yes, he envied Lady Aldington and the fact that she had a place where she felt at home. Since moving there after they'd wed, she'd refurbished several rooms and planned to redesign the gardens. Her enthusiasm and dedication were impressive. Inspiring even. It seemed to be her passion, just as his work in the Commons was his. Notably, they had no passion for each other.

"Good evening, Lord Aldington." The footman greeted Constantine as he entered the familiar space.

"Evening," Constantine said as he walked into the main room where Brummel sat in the bow window with his acolytes surrounding him.

Constantine strode past without pausing and was immediately intercepted by one of his colleagues, Mr. Horace Brightly. Short and fit, Brightly was a fellow member of the Gentlemen's Phaeton Racing Club.

"Evening, Aldington. May I have a word?" Brightly asked pleasantly.

Relieved to turn his mind to something other than the mistake he'd nearly committed and would surely have regretted, Constantine inclined his head. "Certainly."

They moved to a relatively quiet table in the corner where a footman brought them glasses of port. Brightly took a sip before setting his glass down and fixing Constantine with an intense stare. The man was tireless in his work and saw the gentlemen's clubs as an extension of Westminster— places where he could present his arguments and hopefully persuade others to his side. Like Constantine, he had no interest in gaming, placing wagers in the betting book, or drinking to excess.

"The Importation Act is gaining ground," Brightly noted with grave concern. "I'm hoping we can count you among our supporters. To oppose the law, that is."

Constantine tensed. "I haven't yet decided, but I promise I am giving it careful consideration."

"Without your father's input, I pray." Brightly gave him a direct, sincere look before abruptly changing the subject. "Has Lady Aldington arrived in town yet?"

"No. I don't expect her for a few weeks." That was a lie. Constantine didn't know when to expect her, if at all. She'd written a few letters since he'd returned to London in mid-January, all of them about the newly refurbished drawing room and the spring plans for the garden. He'd responded in kind, discussing his activities here in London. Their correspondence was polite and respectful and utterly devoid of anything personal. Once upon a time, he'd hoped that would change, but after nearly two years, he accepted their marriage was one of extreme convenience.

He supposed she'd probably come sometime this month. Last year, she'd arrived in mid-March. Really, he should write to her and ask. Perhaps he'd do that tomorrow.

"Well, when she's in town, you must come for dinner," Brightly said. "Mrs. Brightly thoroughly enjoys her company."

"I'm sure Lady Aldington would be delighted." Because she would. During the few dinners they'd shared with the Brightlys last Season, Sabrina had been at her most animated. Most Society events seemed to terrify her.

"Excellent, we'll look forward to it then." Brightly finished his port. "And I won't harass you about the tariff until next week." He winked, then rose and took himself off.

Constantine smiled faintly into his port before sipping.

Then he promptly drank the liquid down the wrong side of his throat as his father walked into his line of sight.

Coughing, Constantine set his glass down with a bit too much force. Or perhaps, in his agitation, he gripped the stem too tightly. Whatever the reason, the stem snapped, and the glass fell over onto the tablecloth, spilling what remained of his port. The jagged edge of the broken glass tore into Constantine's palm. Blood welled on his flesh, and he turned his hand over to keep it from spilling onto the tablecloth.

"Good Christ," the duke muttered before waving for a footman who hurried to the table. "Bring his lordship a cloth for his hand and tidy this mess."

"Yes, Your Grace." The footman rushed to carry out the older man's bidding.

Constantine looked up at his father, into the familiar dark eyes that seemed to detect everything in Constantine's mind and soul. He hoped his father hadn't seen that Brightly had just been sitting here.

That was, however, far too much to hope for.

The duke's cool gaze flicked to the chair Brightly had vacated. "Why were you speaking with that upstart? I really should ensure he's cast out. He has no business here and should keep to his kind at Brooks's."

His kind. Constantine winced as he pulled the glass from his palm. He set it on the tablecloth, staining the fabric with his blood. "Because he has Whig tendencies."

"Because he *is* a bloody Whig." The duke spoke in a low but irritated tone.

The footman returned to the table, accompanied by another. The first one handed Constantine a small towel while the other gathered up the tablecloth and broken glass. The latter hurried away, and the former spread a fresh, clean cloth over the table.

"Can I fetch anything else for you, my lord?" he asked Constantine.

"No, thank you." Constantine gave him a reassuring nod, knowing how intimidating his father could be and understanding the footman was likely anxious.

"A glass of claret," the duke barked before sitting in a chair that hadn't been occupied by Brightly. Which put him directly to Constantine's right. The footman quickly departed, and the duke glowered after him. "I do think I'll see what I can do about having Brightly expelled. He doesn't belong here."

"Why not? His father was a member." Besides, nearly everyone liked Brightly. He was an enjoyable verbal sparring partner, regardless of whether you agreed with him.

The duke's eyes glittered with annoyance. "His father is deceased and can no longer recommend him."

Constantine held the towel to his wound, pressing hard to staunch the flow of blood. "Do you plan to have Lucien expelled too?" His brother also had "Whig tendencies." Frankly, so did Constantine. "Or is he exempt from such action because he's *your* son?"

"Don't be clever." The duke glowered at Constantine before lifting his gaze to the footman who arrived with the claret. "Thank you." His brief show of gratitude eased some of the tension in Constantine's shoulders. His father was in quite a mood this evening. He wasn't a genial sort at any time, but he wasn't always this surly either.

"If you'll excuse me, I need to go home and bandage this." Constantine's palm stung and was still oozing blood. But more importantly, he wasn't of a mind to suffer his father's interrogation about Brightly, which was surely coming.

"Yes, you should. I hope that doesn't affect your racing grip." He said that because he liked to wager on Constantine's coach races. That Constantine had formed a racing club with a group of gentlemen a few years ago was a point of pride for the duke.

"Good night, Father."

"Good night." He inclined his head before sipping his claret.

Before leaving, Constantine gave the stained cloth to a footman. A few moments later, Constantine stepped into a hack, which he directed to his house on Curzon Street. His hand was still bleeding a little, so he removed his cravat and wrapped it around his palm.

By the time he arrived home, he was exhausted, aggrieved in a myriad of ways, and he realized his wounded right hand wouldn't allow him to ease at least a part of his frustration. Smiling at the absurdity, he greeted his butler, Haddock, at the door. "You're up late. Did one of the footmen take ill?"

"Good evening, my lord." Haddock's wide brow furrowed beneath his severely combed gray-black hair. Constantine knew right away that something was amiss.

The tension he'd just managed to push away in the hack returned, shooting a pain down his spine. "What's the matter?"

Haddock's pale blue gaze dropped to Constantine's wrapped hand. "Did you injure yourself, my lord?"

"A broken glass at the club. Are you going to tell me what's going on, or do I need to go in search of Mrs. Haddock?" His housekeeper was the wife of his butler, and she would likely be abed by now. As Haddock typically was. Or at least not at their posts. Constantine had no idea what they did when they weren't performing their duties, and it was none of his concern.

Haddock stiffened, his shoulders squaring as he met Constantine's stare. "Lady Aldington arrived earlier this evening."

The pain in Constantine's spine sharpened, overtaking the wound in his hand. "I see. Thank you, Haddock."

"Shall I have some bandaging and poultice brought up to Peale?"

The valet would offer to dress the wound, and Constantine supposed he should let him. "I'd appreciate that." He started toward the stair hall but paused and looked back at the butler. "The countess's arrival surprised you."

"Yes, my lord." Faint color rose in Haddock's cheeks. "Perhaps you mentioned it to me, and I forgot."

Constantine nearly laughed at the preposterousness of that occurrence. "You know that didn't happen. I'm surprised too. Did she say why she arrived unannounced?"

"She did not."

"I'm sure I'll find out in the morning. Good night, Haddock." Constantine left the entry hall and climbed the stairs. Passing the drawing room, he made his way to the sitting room that served as a sort of antechamber to his and his wife's bedrooms.

Upon entering, he stopped cold. Seated in a chair before the fire was his wife.

Sabrina Westbrook was the most beautiful woman in England. Or so many had called her during her debut Season two years ago, including him. With her red-gold hair that made one think of honey glistening in the sun, her brilliant sky-blue eyes, and warm cream complexion, she was an ideal. To Constantine, she was the only woman who'd taken his breath away the moment he'd seen her. That she was the young lady his father wanted him to wed had seemed an impossible dream.

Too bad his dream wife had tried to avoid marrying him and was clearly filled with so much loathing that their union was damned from the start. Oh, she could be pleasant and polite, but there was no question that she detested being forced into this marriage and despised his nearness and his touch. Constantine had done a fair job of burying the hurt he'd felt then. So much so that he could almost forget it. Almost.

"What happened to your hand?" She came toward him, jolting him from his reverie. The skirt of her dark green dressing gown swirled about her ankles. Without waiting for his answer, she reached for him.

He took a step back, shocked by her approach. "I think the more important question, madam, is what are you doing here?"

CHAPTER 2

Sabrina froze, her mind arresting on the fact that she'd almost touched him. They only ever touched in her bedchamber, on the rare occasions that he'd visited her in the not yet two years of their marriage. She hadn't even realized she was going to touch him, and if she'd thought about it, she would not have tried. But she'd seen that he was hurt, and her instinct to care for him—for anything or anyone who needed help—had taken over.

"I live here." She met his gaze with a haughtiness she'd never managed before and was proud that she'd been able to do it. Her anxiety with people, particularly strangers—and her husband was little better than a stranger—had always been crippling. But no more. She needed to emerge from the shadows, to claim her role as countess, both in public and in private.

His expression flickered with surprise, and she felt a flare of satisfaction along with her pride. He was expecting the shy, malleable wife he'd married.

"You could have sent word that you were coming so that the household was prepared."

She really should have, particularly since she was in need of a new ladies' maid. Hers had married last year and was now expecting her first child. She'd resigned her employment before Sabrina had left for London, and one of the upstairs maids here at Aldington House had been unceremoniously thrust into the position upon Sabrina's arrival.

"My decision to come was made rather hastily." Once she'd decided to make a change, she'd moved quickly before she could lose her courage. "I apologize if I've upset you or the household." She used a neutral tone just as he had.

"You could never do that," he said.

Sabrina wasn't sure how that made her feel. On the one hand, she liked to be amenable and would hate to cause trouble for anyone. On the other, her husband's easy insistence that she would never be a bother made her *want* to be. If only to prove that he barely knew her.

Except he was right. Did that mean he *did* know her? At least a little?

His valet, Peale, entered the sitting room bearing a tray with what looked to be supplies to care for Aldington's wound. Summoning the bravado and steel she knew she needed for this entire trip, Sabrina strode toward him and took the tray. "I'll take care of his lordship. Thank you, Peale."

The valet's auburn brows arched briefly before he inclined his head. "Of course, my lady. May I say what a pleasure it is to see you."

"Thank you. I'm glad to be back in London." She clutched the tray in front of her.

Peale flicked a glance toward Aldington. "Just ring if you require anything further." He bid them good night before departing the sitting room.

Sabrina set the tray on a nearby table and went back to her husband. Her gaze dipped to the triangle of dark ivory flesh that was exposed at his throat due to his lack of cravat.

She wasn't used to seeing him like that. Her mouth suddenly felt a bit dry, so she licked her lips. "May I see your hand?"

As he unwrapped the cloth, she realized what had happened to his cravat. Moving toward her, he held his hand out, palm up. The uneven gash was midway between his thumb and forefinger. Dried blood clung to his flesh.

"This needs to be cleaned first." She lifted her gaze, passing over that taunting triangle of his exposed chest. She'd barely seen him without clothing. When he came to her bedchamber, he wore a banyan, then closed the curtain around the bed so that they were always cloaked in darkness. "Do you have water in your chamber?"

"Yes." He turned his body and waited for her to pick up the tray. "After you."

She'd never been in his room. Decorated in a rich, vibrant blue and accented with golds and browns, it was surprisingly warm. She wasn't sure what she'd expected, but perhaps she'd assumed his bedchamber would be cool and austere, like his personality much of the time.

Aside from the bed, which she studiously avoided looking at, there was a small desk, a pair of dressers, and a cozy seating area with two wingback chairs in front of the hearth. The latter drew her attention as she wondered who would join him there. He'd certainly never invited her.

He went to one of the dressers and poured water from a pitcher into the basin beside it. Picking up the basin with his uninjured left hand, he carried it to the small table near the door and set it down. It was as if he didn't want her coming too far inside.

She nearly said so, but her newfound courage failed her. Setting the tray beside the basin, she plucked up a small piece of cloth and dipped it into the water. "Your hand, please," she murmured softly.

He extended it again, palm up. Now she *had* to touch him.

Keeping her gaze averted from his, she put her palm beneath his hand and gingerly clasped him. The connection made her breath stall in her lungs. She dabbed at the dried blood, working as quickly as possible but gently too, lest she cause him further harm.

"What happened?" she asked.

"A glass broke in my hand at White's."

"Bad luck." She finished cleaning his flesh and set the soiled cloth back on the tray, letting go of his hand. At last, she exhaled as she reached for the small jar of poultice.

"I can apply that," he said, his voice neither rising nor falling. He nearly always spoke to her in a monotone. *When* he spoke to her, which wasn't often. That required them to be in the same physical vicinity.

"Yes, but I'm going to do it," she asserted.

She glanced at his face, just catching the arch of his brow and the flash of surprise in his eyes. Busying herself with her task instead of looking at him, she took the lid from the jar of poultice and set it onto the tray. She dipped a fingertip into the salve, then clasped his hand again to smooth the medicine onto the cut.

The barest intake of breath—his—prompted her to look back to his face. Faint lines fanned from his hazel eyes, marring the perfect planes of his countenance. He was an exceptionally handsome man, with his aquiline nose and sharp jawline that looked as though they'd been chiseled from granite to be displayed in a palace somewhere. A face for people to look upon and admire but that masked an empty shell.

Only he wasn't a statue, even if it was easier for her to think of him as such. He was a man, and he was her husband. For better or worse.

Forever.

"It hurts," she noted, as she carefully applied the salve.

He barely nodded in response.

"I'm sorry," she added.

"It's fine." The words were low and clipped, and they irritated her. Everything was always fine. Except that it had never been. Perhaps for a short time after their betrothal, when he'd been charming and attentive. Then, just before the wedding, he'd seemed to grow more distant, less charming and far less attentive. As if he regretted their engagement. She assumed he had. Then her mother had told her quite plainly that Aldington didn't care for the union but that he would see his duty done.

That had set the stage for a thoroughly awful wedding night and subsequent marriage. It was bad enough that Sabrina suffered from an excess of nerves and anxiety. Add in a husband who had no desire to marry her, and the result was a union of polite detachment. She supposed it could be worse, that they could openly despise each other. Yes, she was grateful for polite detachment and hoped they could move beyond that, if only to do what was necessary to have a child—something she wanted and he *needed*.

She exhaled as she took the bandaging from the tray. "Do you think we could try to be pleasant?" Her gaze fixed on the small area of his exposed chest once more, and a peculiar heat flushed her neck.

"Am I not pleasant? Ow!"

She'd begun to wrap his hand and realized she'd pulled the cloth too tightly against the cut. "My apologies."

He frowned, his brow creasing. "Should I call for Peale?"

"No." She continued, moving more slowly and gently. "Do not call for Peale. And no, you aren't pleasant. You are… dispassionate."

His hand twitched, and she feared she'd struck a nerve. She finished wrapping his wound and tied the ends of the cloth together. "There." She put her hands around his, holding him for a moment as she looked into his eyes.

There was a wariness in his gaze. Not quite vulnerability, but that seemed…not far off. Her breath snagged again.

"I don't mean to be," he said softly. "Dispassionate."

"I know." Did she? How could she know anything about him? "Actually, I don't know, but I'll give you a chance to prove it." This was the moment.

He took his hand from between hers and stepped back. His wariness intensified, and it was as if he'd stepped back behind the wall he kept around himself. "What do you mean?"

"I wish to share your bedchamber. Or we can share mine. However, yours is larger."

His jaw tightened. "I told you when we wed that I expected us to retain separate bedchambers. I have not changed my mind about that."

He'd stated that quite clearly not long after the ceremony. It was not a strange request—many married couples, including his parents and hers, slept separately. "Then I would like you to visit mine more often. Starting with tonight." She sounded so bold, so confident. She prayed she could maintain that attitude when he actually arrived at her bed. In the past, she'd shrank from him, her anxiety and apprehension getting the better of her. Their wedding night in particular had been ghastly, a dark, quick encounter during which she'd lain practically immobile, paralyzed with fear. After which, he'd apologized and hadn't visited her again for some months—not until they'd gone to Hampton Lodge later in the summer.

He held up his hand with a grimace. "I'm afraid I'm indisposed."

She'd been prepared for prevarication—this was a dance

at which they were both very accomplished. It was time, however, to change the steps.

Sabrina moved toward him so that they were as close as when she'd tended his hand. "You need an heir. We've been married almost two years. My mother is certain there's something wrong with me, that I can't bear children, and I know there is speculation as to my...ability to give you a child. The sad fact is that I daresay we haven't tried enough to ascertain if any of that is true."

A small burst of exultation at having made it through saying all that resonated in her chest. It was short-lived, however, since his face had turned ever increasing shades of white until he looked like the alabaster bust of David in her father's library.

"Er, well, we will keep trying." He pivoted slightly, his gaze focused on the hearth and the low fire burning in the grate.

It was time—past time—to make her mission clear. Perhaps then his attitude would change. *If* he could bring himself to want her, and Sabrina wasn't sure he could. Nothing he had ever said or done had led her to think he found her desirable. Her shoulders twitched with the discomfort she'd come to accept, that her husband would never be pleased with her. When she had a child to love, none of that would matter. She wouldn't be lonely anymore. "I've come to London to get with child, and I'm not leaving until I am."

His head snapped toward hers, his eyes goggling. "What has happened to you?" His shocked reaction was at least better than one of disgust. She hadn't been sure what to expect.

"Nothing has happened to me. I am merely trying to be a proper countess. You need an heir, and I want a child."

He continued to stare at her, and it took him a moment to respond. "That will come. In time."

Not disgust then, but apathy. Which was worse? "We've had plenty of time. I expect you to visit my bed every night until I'm certain I'm with child."

He didn't meet her gaze. "I can't commit to every night. I'm a very busy man."

"What are you doing when you should be sleeping? Have you taken a mistress?"

"No!" He answered quickly and vehemently, a look of sheer horror arresting his features for the barest moment. The reaction was so stark and so swift that she was certain it had to be a lie.

And why wouldn't he have a mistress? That's what men in his position did, particularly men who weren't remotely interested in their wives. At least, that's what she'd been told. It made no difference to her how he spent his time, so long as he gave her a child. Mistress or no mistress, he had a responsibility as a husband, and especially as a future duke, to produce an heir.

Irritated that he didn't seem to see the urgency, she fisted a hand on her hip. "I'm not asking you to be a husband, just to do your husbandly duty. Do you think you can manage that?" Now she was shocking even herself. She'd planned to confront him; it was her entire purpose for coming to town. However, she hadn't expected to lose her temper. She hadn't even realized she had one to lose.

"You—you…," he sputtered, his forehead furrowing with deep lines as the muscles of his jaw worked. "Who *are* you?"

She straightened her spine, rising to her not unimpressive height of five feet and five inches. He might have a mistress, but she was his *wife* and only *she* could give him an heir. "I am the Countess of Aldington, and I demand my marital rights."

"Good God," he muttered, walking away from her toward the fireplace. He gripped the back of a chair, then immediately lifted his right hand while whispering something else. A curse perhaps, because that likely hurt his wound. After a moment, he faced her, his features tightly drawn. "I will do my duty, but I will visit you in your chamber, as usual."

"When?" She crossed her arms over her chest.

"When my hand is better." He scowled at her.

"Didn't you marry me in order to carry out your duty to produce an heir?" She knew it wasn't because he'd fallen in love with her. Or even that he *liked* her. And he certainly didn't desire her.

His jaw clenched again, and she swore she could almost hear the grinding of his teeth. "I did."

The temper she'd just realized she possessed took rein once more. "Don't take too long, because I'm going to have a child whether you participate or not."

His eyes darkened, and he stalked to her, standing even closer than when she'd bandaged his hand. "Did you just threaten to allow another man into your bed?" Oh, this was new. It seemed he had a temper too.

She ought to be frightened—and part of her was, the part that was still reserved and soft-spoken, afraid of her own shadow, no matter how badly she didn't want to be. This new part of her, however, the one that was tired of being alone and desperate for someone to care for, wasn't scared. She was emboldened. Or perhaps even…excited. A reaction from him meant she was gaining ground. She hoped so anyway.

She arched a brow and gave him what she hoped was a saucy look. "Would that encourage you to do your duty?" How she hated that word. As if she were a required task instead of a woman. His wife.

But wasn't a wife—and a husband—merely a duty personified? Her mother would say so, and everything her husband had said and done led her to acknowledge that he would believe the same.

He frowned. "I don't find your attempt at lightheartedness or flirtation remotely amusing or enticing. Indeed, I am shocked by this change in your behavior. Where is the woman I married?"

"Gone." She leaned forward and inhaled, catching his scent—an elusive combination of cedar and spice. The heat she'd felt earlier returned, climbing into her face but also spreading lower and making her body...tingle.

He jerked back from her. "If you'll excuse me, I need to retire. I have an early morning appointment."

Sabrina's body, taut with apprehension and expectation, relaxed. The battle was over for now. A draw, which was better than a defeat. Uncrossing her arms, she turned and left his chamber, closing the door gently behind her.

Now that she was gone from his presence, all the bravado slipped from her body like jelly sliding from a spoon. She gripped the doorframe of her chamber as she staggered inside. She swung the door closed, more forcefully and loudly than she had her husband's.

Then she slumped back against the wood, closing her eyes and taking deep, rapid breaths.

Slower.

It was a mantra she'd often repeated since the first time her breathing had become too fast, her head had gone dizzy, and her chest had felt as if a horse were standing on it. She'd collapsed to the floor, terrifying her mother. That had been the day before she'd been presented to the Queen two years ago.

Regaining control, Sabrina opened her eyes and moved into her bedchamber. Smaller in space and in the size of furnishings, her room was soft and pale when compared with her husband's. A palette of light pinks and greens soothed and comforted, reminding her that she was a delicate flower, as her father called her.

The young woman who'd been promoted to act as Sabrina's lady's maid came in through the dressing chamber. Charity Taylor was perhaps a year or two older than Sabrina, with dark, chocolate brown hair and wide, tawny eyes. "I thought I heard you come in. Can I offer any further assistance, my lady?"

"No, thank you. I do appreciate you stepping in to help me this evening."

"It is my privilege," she said with a bob of her head. "I may not be trained to be a lady's maid, but I could learn if you decide I suit you. My sister is a lady's maid to one of the patronesses of the Phoenix Club. In fact, she's the one who was able to secure this position for me."

"And how did she do that?"

"I suppose it wasn't her specifically. Her employer, Mrs. Renshaw, and the owner of the club assist people—sometimes with employment and sometimes with other matters. If you need help with something, you go to the owner of the Phoenix Club."

That was Lord Lucien Westbrook, Sabrina's husband's younger brother. This new information clung to Sabrina's mind even as she focused on the young woman in front of her. "I'd be delighted to have you train to be my maid, if you are inclined." Finding a lady's maid was not something Sabrina wanted to spend time on. Besides, Charity seemed a pleasant and eager sort, so why bother looking? However, that didn't mean Sabrina knew her or what type of person she truly was. Summoning her newfound courage, she forced herself to say, "I do have one requirement. I don't tolerate gossip of any kind. Anything I say to you or that you overhear must not leave your lips. Is that understood?"

Charity's eyes widened briefly as a shadow of apprehension flashed within them. "Yes, my lady."

Sabrina offered her a smile. "Please don't fret. I'm sure you'll be discreet. I just find it's best to communicate expectations at the start." If only she and her husband had done that. But then she hadn't known enough about anything to do so and still didn't. Except to demand a child. That was the single expectation they both shared—or should anyway.

Shoulders relaxing, Charity nodded. "Thank you, my lady. Good night." With a curtsey, she departed the chamber.

Staring after her, Sabrina's mind went back to what the maid had said about Lucien. He helped people with "other matters." Sabrina certainly needed help if she was going to make the changes she wanted to.

The heaviness of her thoughts pulled her mouth down as she strode to the bed and cast her dressing gown to the floor. Responsibility told her to pick it up and lay it carefully across the end of the bed, but she tore the coverlet back and flounced onto the mattress instead.

She reclined against the pillows and stared up at the canopy, reliving the encounter she'd just had with her husband. The look on his face when she'd demanded a baby... A devilish giggle burst forth, and she clapped her hand over her mouth.

That was most uncharitable of her. Did he even deserve her charity? He'd been nothing but condescending and aloof since just before their marriage. Yes, she'd been reserved, but would it have killed him to try to reach out to her? Her mother had said that her new husband would guide her, that she need only follow his direction. How could Sabrina do that when he gave her none?

You haven't really tried either. No, she hadn't, but how could she when she was utterly ignorant of marital relationships, particularly in the bedchamber? Not just ignorant, but afraid.

She wasn't going to be afraid anymore. Or shy. No more "Wallflower Countess," the nickname some had called her last Season. She couldn't be any of that if she wanted to entice her husband into her bed and have a child. And since he had a mistress, she was going to have to work even harder to gain his attention. She only hoped she could.

It would require the drastic change she planned. A complete rejection of the woman she'd been, one who lived in the shadows and clung to propriety, wielding it like a shield against, well, everything.

The new Lady Aldington would be witty, charming, and daring. She would garner attention and admiration, even if it didn't come from her frigid husband—and she would have a child to love.

CHAPTER 3

The crisp, late winter air bit at Constantine's cheeks as he thundered down Rotten Row. He'd slept horribly, his mind and body awash with thoughts of his wife's demands.

She'd actually *demanded* he visit her every night until she was with child. He still didn't recognize the woman who'd arrived at his house unannounced.

And the thought of bedding her—every night—made him twitch with anxiety. The act was dull and dutiful, and every time he did the deed with her, he felt...empty. Especially when he compared the occasions with the times he'd been with a woman before he was married. Those nights had been filled with joy and sweat and rapture.

Constantine could imagine *his* wife's reaction—horror, revulsion, and perhaps even tears. Not that he recalled her crying on any occasion. She had, however, seemed close a time or two, particularly on their disastrous wedding night. Just thinking of that made him cringe.

No, he couldn't envision her appreciating a passionate

advance from him. She'd never once given any inkling that she wanted him or felt any attraction or desire toward him. If she had, what would he have done?

There was no point in wondering. They were currently faced with a duty, and they would meet it. Perhaps now that she was *demanding* him to visit her, she would be more amenable to the act? He simply couldn't imagine it. But then he never would have imagined her behavior last night either.

He had to admit he wanted to shut his father up about having an heir. The duke had recently begun to badger him about whether his countess was capable of giving him a son. He'd also noted that she and Constantine didn't spend enough time together to give the matter the appropriate attention and effort.

Oh hell, was the duke behind Lady Aldington's sudden change of behavior?

Constantine slowed his mount as he reached the end of the track. His father was an overbearing, meddling authoritarian. Of course he was behind this. Constantine should have seen his manipulation straightaway. He'd simply been too astounded at her sudden arrival. And by the way she'd cared for him. Seeing her never failed to steal his breath, and her touch had driven a stake of keen yearning straight through him.

He'd been too long without a woman. If only he'd been able to alleviate his needs last night with the courtesan.

Scowling to himself and eager for another bruising ride along the track, he turned his horse only to see his brother riding toward him.

"Morning, Con," Lucien greeted with a wide smile that always seemed genuine, no matter the time of day or occasion.

"I'm exercising." He sounded terse, and he didn't care.

"As genial as ever. I'll race you to the other end then."

They'd been competitive about a great many things throughout their lives, but riding was something at which neither was better than the other. Sometimes Lucien won and sometimes Constantine did. "Yes."

The word barely left Constantine's lips before Lucien raced forward.

Muttering a curse, Constantine kicked his horse into a full gallop. It took him nearly the entire length of the track, but he ultimately overtook his younger brother and emerged the victor.

"Feeling better?" Lucien asked after they'd walked their horses for a few minutes.

"Yes, thank you. It always feels good to win."

Letting out a sharp laugh, Lucien cast him a sidelong look from atop his horse as they walked beside each other. "I let you win to improve your mood."

Constantine snorted. "You never let anyone win, not even for the sake of someone's mental state."

"Do I need to be concerned about your mental state?"

"No." Despite the fact that his mind could *not* fully comprehend his wife's sudden change in behavior. Or that she wanted him to bed her every night. For the purpose of having a child—he mustn't forget that was *all* she wanted.

This predicament wouldn't confound Lucien. Hell, it never would have happened in the first place. Lucien would have successfully seduced his wife on their wedding night, if his reputation as an accomplished and sought-after lover was to be believed. Constantine tried not to pay too close attention. Such things should be private.

Aside from his reputation, Lucien was known for helping people. Constantine knew that from personal experience since he'd been eager to provide assistance when Constantine had decided to take a mistress.

"Are you certain I needn't be concerned?" Lucien asked, keeping his voice low, since there were other riders about, not that any of them were close enough to overhear them. "I heard what happened last night. I apologize for the confusion."

"Confusion? You promised me secrecy and absolute discretion. Now I must worry whether Overton or his young ward will tell anyone they saw me."

Lucien shook his head with a half smile. "You're daft if you're worried about that. Why would they endanger their own reputations?"

While Constantine assumed they would not, the encounter still didn't sit well with him. "I don't like that they know I was there. It will make things extremely uncomfortable. Especially since I saw what they were doing. I can't believe Overton has fallen so far as to take advantage of his ward."

"They are in love, actually," Lucien said with more than a hint of exasperation. "And currently on their way to Gretna Green where they will be wed." He pinned Constantine with an expectant stare. "Don't you possess even a tiny shard of romanticism in your cold, black heart?"

His heart wasn't cold or black. It just wasn't terribly... alive. Not since he'd lost the only person who'd ever loved him fifteen years ago.

"I do," Constantine said defensively, even as he felt the tiniest tinge of envy for Overton and his ward. "Lady Aldington arrived last night." He blurted the revelation without any thought.

Lucien blinked in surprise. "I didn't realize you were expecting her."

"I wasn't." Constantine sealed his lips together lest he share anything else without thinking, such as the reason for her arrival.

"You don't seem enthused," Lucien observed. "Would you rather she'd stayed at Hampton Lodge?"

"Of course not. She should be in London for the Season."

"I should think she ought to be in London to be with her husband." Lucien spoke lightly but with an edge of concern that only dredged up Constantine's sour mood. He hated when his brother tried to meddle—it was bad enough when their father did.

"Mind your own business," Constantine muttered.

"There's my surly brother." Lucien laughed. "One of these days I'm going to wedge that stick out of your ass, and you are going to feel so much better."

"I need to get to Westminster." Constantine turned his horse.

"Have a splendid day!" Lucien called after him.

As he rode from the park, Constantine pushed his brother's cheerfulness out of his mind. For a man who'd fought in Portugal and been sent home after being injured, he was particularly pleasant. And that was in spite of their father's badgering. The duke looked for every opportunity to question why Lucien wasn't still fighting, since his injury hadn't caused any lasting effects.

Constantine guided his horse into the mews and dismounted. "Excellent ride, Zephyr," he murmured before declining the groom's assistance. He generally liked to care for his horses when he had the time, which wasn't often when he was in town. Since his encounter with Lucien had cut his riding time short, he took advantage. Brushing Zephyr soothed Constantine's agitation, and by the time he walked into the house, he was feeling better than he had all day. He'd just go upstairs to change before heading to Westminster.

Haddock met him in the foyer. "Good afternoon, my lord. Your gig will be ready shortly."

With a nod, Constantine started toward the stairs. "I'll be back down directly, Haddock." He looked over his shoulder to see the housekeeper, Mrs. Haddock, walk into the foyer, her gaze on her husband. Haddock pivoted, his brows arching slightly before his features softened.

Constantine had never noticed the butler doing that before, but then they didn't realize he was watching. Their mutual attention was entirely focused on each other as they spoke in low tones that Constantine couldn't overhear. Were they discussing a household matter or something more... intimate? Constantine was reminded of how his marriage didn't have similar moments.

With an abrupt turn, he climbed the stairs and at the top nearly collided with the countess. As usual, he was momentarily stunned by her beauty. Because he didn't see her regularly, he reasoned. Her honey-gold hair was only visible under the front brim of her bonnet, and a rather plain, pale walking gown draped her figure. She was just pulling on her gloves.

He swept his hat from his head. "Are you on your way out?" Constantine was surprised, for she didn't often venture from the house, and certainly not the morning after she'd arrived.

"I have errands." Her voice carried that haughty edge he'd detected briefly last night.

"What sort of errands?"

She narrowed her eyes slightly, and he wondered if she'd ever done that in the history of their acquaintance. "The sort that would bore you."

Constantine straightened. "I see."

Her gaze dipped. "How is your hand?"

"It still hurts. More than I would have expected, actually." It didn't really, but if he could postpone the resumption of his marital duties until he'd sorted his thoughts, he would seize the opportunity.

That was prompting his delay? Sorting his thoughts?

"Perhaps you should not have gone riding," she suggested. "You might put more salve on it. That would ease the pain. Unless you prefer to be uncomfortable." Did she think he was using the wound as an excuse?

Which he was, dammit.

He did *not* know what to make of this woman. "I'll do that before I go to Westminster."

"Will I see you later this evening?" Now she gave him an expectant look, her hands clasped before her.

"I will likely be late."

"Of course you will," she murmured before summoning a slight smile and then abandoning it. "I'll wait up. Should you find your...*disposition* improved."

Before he could reply—and really, what the hell could he say at this juncture without sounding like a *complete* ass— she'd started down the stairs. He stared after her, wondering again who this new Lady Aldington was and what had happened to provoke this stark and bewildering change.

Perhaps he *should* visit her tonight. If she was so changed, she might be different in their marriage bed. She certainly didn't seem to be anxious or tense around him as she had before. Was there a chance she *wanted* to participate?

Making his way to his chamber, Constantine stopped abruptly in the sitting room as he caught the scent of apples and vanilla. His wife smelled like that, he realized.

For a moment, he tried to think of doing things to her that would make her scream with pleasure. He couldn't envision it. All he saw was her pale, mortified face.

He should speak with her plainly—ask if she was still going to quiver with apprehension and turn rigid until he left her. But to speak of such things gave *him* tremors of anxiety. And she thought him dispassionate. Her description had pricked him, made him question whether it was true.

Of course it was.

For fifteen long years, he'd worked hard to keep every emotion bottled tight. Before that, he'd only revealed them to one person, to the mother who'd loved him and assured him his father did too. Constantine wasn't sure he believed that. The duke was proud of him, but that was not the same thing.

How he wished he could talk to her now, ask her what he should do and whether he was completely wrongheaded about his wife or, hell, about everything. Since he could not, he went into his chamber and carried on with his day.

$\approx$

*T*he thrill of saying exactly what she'd wanted and the resulting expression of shock and uncertainty on her husband's face was still thrumming through Sabrina when she met Charity downstairs. Together, they left the house and went to the coach, where a groom helped them inside.

"Where are we going, my lady?" Charity asked with an edge of excitement. This was her first time leaving the house as a lady's maid, and she'd confessed that she was a trifle nervous.

"Just a few errands," Sabrina said vaguely. Though she'd received Charity's assurance that she wouldn't gossip, Sabrina wasn't going to freely offer information about certain things. And their first stop was one of those things.

When the coach entered Piccadilly, Charity asked if they were going shopping.

"We may." That depended on what happened next.

A few minutes later, they rolled into St. James Square and

then onto King Street, where the coach stopped in front of a small terrace house.

Sabrina turned her head to the maid who was staring out the window. "Now, Charity, you are going to remain in the coach while I pay this call. I shan't be long." With a brief smile, Sabrina left the vehicle and stopped short when she encountered the person she'd come to see.

"Lady Aldington?" Lord Lucien Westbrook squinted briefly as he came toward her. He removed his hat and offered her a bow. "What a delightful surprise."

"I hope I'm not interrupting," she said.

"Not at all. I am just returning from the mews after riding in the park. I saw your husband there, in fact."

Sabrina did not react to him seeing Aldington. "May we go inside for a few minutes?"

"My apologies. I should have invited you straightaway." He indicated for her to precede him to the door where the butler admitted them inside.

Lord Lucien's house was much smaller and less opulently decorated than his brother's or father's. Which wasn't to say it was spartan. The entry hall was compact, but the white marble floor gleamed, and a painting of a cloudy sky graced the wall.

"It's an odd painting for an entry hall, I'll grant you," he said. "It reminds me of the sky in Portugal. I would lie on my back and stare up at the clouds, wondering where they'd been and where they were going. Sometimes, I fancied reaching up and catching a ride."

She turned her head from the painting to see him smiling. "How do you possess so much charm compared to the other males in your family?"

Lines creased across his forehead as his smile dissipated, and a slight grimace pulled at his mouth instead. "Shall we adjourn to the library?"

He led her from the entry past the stairs and into the room at the back of the ground floor. It was a library but also a parlor with a comfortable seating area. Her gaze fell on a large desk in the corner, which was stacked with papers, and she realized it was also his study. It seemed Lord Lucien was an economical man, at least when it came to space.

"Can I offer you refreshment?" He stood in the center of the room, perhaps waiting for her to choose a place to sit.

"No, thank you." Her bravado faltered for a moment. It was one thing to boldly face her husband and another to approach her brother-in-law, whom she didn't know all that well. Then again, did she really know her husband well either? Perhaps not, but her frustration with him and their marriage provided an excellent fuel for her audacity. "I came to, ah, ask for your assistance. I understand you do that. Provide assistance, I mean."

One of his dark brows ticked up. "I see. Tell me how I can help."

Sabrina moved to a chair and perched on the edge of the peacock blue cushion. Lord Lucien set his hat and gloves upon the desk and took another chair nearby.

Gathering her courage, she laid out precisely what she required. "I am in need of a new wardrobe, and I should like to receive invitations to the best events the Season has to offer. You may wonder why I'm coming to you for this, and the truth is that I don't know where else to go. I can't ask my mother. She thinks my wardrobe is fine, and she'll only tell me that as the Countess of Aldington, I already have everything I need and shouldn't desire anything more."

"How unhelpful," he murmured. "I am sorry about that. Are there no other women with whom you may confer?"

Sabrina shook her head, feeling the old, familiar heat in her cheeks. Anxiety floated up her throat, and she struggled to swallow.

"I know just the person who can help you," he said warmly. "Mrs. Renshaw is one of the patronesses at the Phoenix Club. She has excellent taste and is well-versed in the latest fashions. I'm not entirely sure how to help you garner the 'best' invitations, but I do have an idea that will vault you to the inner circle of London gossip and intrigue."

That sounded troublesome. Sabrina didn't care for gossip *or* intrigue. "Oh dear, do I want that?"

"Yes, because it will prompt people to invite you to everything." He grinned and leaned back in his chair.

"Well, then I suppose I must. What is your idea?"

"I'm going to present your name to the membership committee of the Phoenix Club."

She leaned forward and forgot she was already quite close to the edge of the seat. Gripping the arm of the chair, she resettled herself more firmly on the cushion. "Is Aldington a member?" She didn't think he was, but she was hardly informed as to her husband's activities.

"He is not."

"Then how could I be a member?"

"Membership has nothing to do with a husband—or wife. We have several members whose spouses have not been invited and will likely never be."

"Aldington would hate that," she said softly, thinking it was the most wonderful idea she'd ever heard. She met Lord Lucien's dark—and suddenly curious—gaze. "What a lovely offer, thank you."

He rubbed his hand against his jaw a moment, studying her. "I don't wish to intrude, but if you're comfortable sharing, I wonder what is prompting this?"

There was no reason to say anything other than the truth. "I wish to be more like a countess." It was her hope that Aldington would be more inclined to give her the attention she required if she better fulfilled her role. She lifted her chin and stiffened her spine. "I'm weary of being overlooked and ignored, of being shy and afraid."

Lord Lucien blinked, a look of admiration flickering in his gaze, his head cocking to the side, as if he were regarding her in a new light. "I am delighted—no *thrilled*—to help. I can only imagine what Con thinks of this."

"He doesn't exactly know. I didn't expect he could help me with any of this."

"Ah, that makes sense." Lord Lucien winced, as if he'd stepped in a thorny shrub. "I take it the state of your marriage is as sad as it looks."

Sabrina was mildly surprised by his bluntness but didn't find it unwelcome. "I don't know how it 'looks,' but since we spend most of our time apart and I couldn't tell you what he likes for breakfast or whether he is a member of the Phoenix Club, I would say sad is an accurate description."

Now, he shocked her by swearing under his breath. "My apologies, Lady Aldington, but my brother is a colossal ass."

"I won't disagree with that assessment. However, in his defense, I have been less than amenable. I *have* been shy and…afraid."

His eyes took on a dark intensity. "Not of him, I hope."

"Not like that. He's…intimidating. Or he was before I decided I wasn't going to perceive him that way anymore. Honestly, *you're* intimidating."

"Am I?"

"I suspect it's the Westbrook way." Or the fact that nearly everyone intimidated her. *Used to* intimidate her.

"That sounds like some sort of rule that my father and brother would like. Hence, I hate it." His tone was breezy and charming, and in that moment, Sabrina decided not to be intimidated by Lord Lucien either. Their father, however, was another matter. Hopefully she'd only have to suffer his company once or twice before she was able to return to

Hampton Lodge where she would delightedly await the arrival of her child.

But first she had to entice her husband to create that child.

Would this transformation snare his attention? Joining the Phoenix Club would. It could also make him very angry. She'd seen a glimpse of his temper and wasn't sure how far he could be pushed.

"I'm not going to be intimidated by you either, Lord Lucien," Sabrina said, circling back to where they'd left off before thoughts of a murky but hopeful future had distracted her.

"Please call me Lucien. We are brother and sister, even if only by marriage."

"Then you must call me Sabrina. I admit I find it odd that you and Lady Cassandra refer to Aldington by his Christian name."

"How do you refer to him?"

"I don't, really."

"Of course you don't," Lucien muttered, wiping a hand over his forehead. "What is your end goal here, Sabrina? Are you trying to make this marriage into something more than it is?"

"Since it is currently next to nothing, yes. I'm not ready to ignore it. Certainly not until after I have a child." Once she was no longer alone, she didn't particularly care what happened.

His dark brows shot up. "That is your goal then—a child?"

"Yes."

He massaged his temple. "You aren't asking for help with that, are you?"

"No." She would not rule it out, however. Perhaps Mrs. Renshaw could be of assistance. She was a widow, after all.

Lucien sat forward in the chair, his hands braced on his

knees. "I am going to pledge my assistance—and that of Evie, Mrs. Renshaw, I mean—to you. My brother might be the most uptight, remote jackass in England, next to our father of course, but I love him and want to see him happy, even if he doesn't know what that means."

"Do you think that's true?" Sabrina didn't know or understand her husband at all.

"Sometimes, yes. It's been ages since I can recall a time when he seemed genuinely joyful, and I'm sorry to say it wasn't when he married you." His brow furrowed, and he looked past her. "I think it was before our mother died."

"I've often wondered about that. He's never spoken of her."

Lucien's gaze snapped to hers. "Never?"

She shook her head, and he sat back, extending his legs out while he adopted a pensive expression, his cheeks elongating as he tightened his jaw.

"Perhaps jealousy would unseat the giant stick up Con's ass," Lucien mused.

"I beg your pardon?"

Lucien sat straight and waved his hand. "We need to provoke a reaction from your husband, and your transformation will do just that. I'll do everything in my power to ensure you're admitted to the Phoenix Club with due haste. That way you can attend the assembly next Friday. That will drive him mad, I'm sure. Especially when you are the toast of the ball." His mouth spread into a wide, cat-like grin. "Come, let us go see Mrs. Renshaw." He jumped to his feet and offered her his hand.

Sabrina took it, rising slowly to her feet as a mixture of excitement and trepidation washed over her. "Now?"

"There is no time to lose. The new enigmatic and devastatingly charming Lady Aldington awaits." He waggled his brows at her, and Sabrina's insides turned over. She hadn't imagined such enthusiastic support.

Gratitude, along with a myriad of other emotions, welled within her. "Thank you." She only hoped she could become the things he said. She'd give anything to be that woman.

CHAPTER 4

$\mathcal{A}$ s Sabrina and Lucien stepped outside, she looked askance at him. "My maid is in the coach. I should bring her to Mrs. Renshaw's." He'd already explained that Mrs. Renshaw lived just a short walk away on the other side of St. James Square.

Lucien inclined his head. "I'll direct the coach to meet you there."

While he went to converse with the driver, Sabrina reached for the door to the coach, but the groom beat her to it. Smiling, she thanked him, then explained to Charity that they would be walking to their next destination.

"We're just going to the other side of the square," Sabrina explained as Charity joined her on the pavement. As Charity glanced toward where Lucien was speaking with the driver, Sabrina added, "That is his lordship's brother, Lord Lucien. He's helping me with, er, a surprise." That wasn't exactly a lie. "Remember, Charity, no gossip."

"Not a word, my lady." The maid shook her head solemnly even as her tawny eyes glimmered with excitement, as if she were thrilled to be included in something.

Lucien joined them and offered his arm to Sabrina who introduced him to Charity.

"My sister works in a house on Charles Street," she said.

He glanced toward Charity. "That is where we are going, actually."

Sabrina suddenly recalled that Charity had said her sister worked for Mrs. Renshaw. "My goodness, Charity, we are going to your sister's employer's house." She glanced toward Lucien. "I'd forgotten that. Her sister is Mrs. Renshaw's lady's maid."

Lucien's brows climbed as he looked to Charity. "You must be the other Miss Taylor. I arranged for your position in my brother's home. He was in need of an upstairs maid, and you were in need of employment—and now look at you, promoted to lady's maid." He winked at her, and Charity's round cheeks turned bright pink.

"I can't thank you enough, my lord." She dipped a curtsey, her bonneted head bobbing as she looked toward the ground.

"It is my pleasure to help whomever I can," Lucien said smoothly. "Now, let us be on our way." He led Sabrina toward the square, and Charity followed behind them.

"Does Aldington know you did that?" Sabrina asked. "I can't imagine he has anything to do with the hiring of servants or that he's even aware when his household needs a new upstairs maid."

"He does not. As with most men of his station, he leaves that sort of thing to their butlers. I have a network of people who contribute to my cause."

"Haddock is part of that network?" she asked in surprise.

Lucien winked at her. "Don't tell anyone."

She tipped her head to the side and peered up at him. "What is your cause?"

"Helping people with whatever they require. Everyone

deserves to have comfort and security and even to have their dreams come true."

"Is that what you do?" Sabrina found herself smiling. She couldn't imagine two brothers who were more different. "Fulfill people's dreams?"

"I don't know that I achieve that, but I do help where I can. Just as I'm going to help you." They reached the other side of the square and started along Charles Street. At the second house, he stopped and pivoted. "Here we are."

They continued up to the door where a rather young, and frankly attractive, man opened the door. Was he the butler?

"Good morning, Foster," Lucien said cheerily. "We're here to speak with Mrs. Renshaw."

Foster opened the door wide. "Come in, my lord. I'll take you up to the drawing room and fetch Mrs. Renshaw."

The house was similar to Lucien's in that it was a small terrace, but it had a distinctly feminine air with the paintings of flowers adorning the walls. They followed the butler into the stair hall and up to the first floor. Situated at the front of the house, the drawing room was most definitely decorated by a woman, with peach and ivory floral wallpaper and an array of furnishings in those colors in addition to russet and a pretty blue that was just a shade darker than Wedgwood. Sabrina had never been in a more stunningly appointed drawing room, and she knew immediately that she would wear whatever Mrs. Renshaw recommended.

A few moments later, their hostess swept into the drawing room. "What a lovely surprise!" Her gaze immediately landed on Charity, who smiled broadly at Mrs. Renshaw's warm welcome. "Charity, your sister would love to see you. If you go back downstairs, Foster will direct you to the kitchen. That is where you'll find Delilah presently."

"Thank you, ma'am." Charity curtsied, then looked to Sabrina who nodded.

She'd no sooner left the room than Mrs. Renshaw approached Sabrina. "You must be Lady Aldington."

Sabrina clasped her hands, nervous as usual when meeting someone. "I am."

Lucien stepped closer as if he sensed her discomfort. "She's here to make your acquaintance and obtain some assistance that you are perfectly suited to provide." He gave Sabrina an encouraging smile which helped ease her trepidation.

Mrs. Renshaw possessed the most intriguing eyes Sabrina had ever seen. The color of lapis lazuli, they were rounded but turned up on the outside corner, almost like a cat. With her sculpted cheekbones and plump lips, she was a model of beauty Sabrina could never achieve with her too-pale skin and too-sharp chin. Her mother had always said her coppery blonde hair was her best feature, but Sabrina found herself envying the rich russet hues of Mrs. Renshaw's. Perhaps because there seemed to be some gold and red intertwined with the dark locks, as if she'd been kissed by the sun—which carried over to her skin, for it held far more color and vibrancy than Sabrina's.

One of Mrs. Renshaw's dark brows arched as she glanced toward Lucien, making her eyes look even more captivating. "Indeed? I am eager to help however I may. Shall we sit?" She flashed a smile at Sabrina as she indicated a seating area with a settee and two chairs near the windows that overlooked Charles Street below.

Sabrina had to blink and stop focusing on Mrs. Renshaw's attractiveness. Comparing herself to other women was a bad habit she would blame on her mother, for she had constantly done that during Sabrina's one and only Season two years ago.

"I'm not going to stay. You don't need my intrusion," Lucien said with a smile. He directed his dark gaze at

Sabrina. "Tell her exactly what you require and don't withhold a thing. Evie will know exactly what to do." He winked toward Mrs. Renshaw.

Mrs. Renshaw's lips curved up. "I can already tell this is going to be a delightful association."

After bowing to them, Lucien took his leave. Sabrina went to the settee and managed to sit despite the anxiety teeming through her. It had been difficult enough to find the courage to seek out her brother-in-law, and now she had to do it all over again with a complete stranger. A beautiful stranger, who was gazing at her with kindness and compassion.

Suddenly it was all too much.

Sabrina's throat constricted and tears welled.

Mrs. Renshaw had sat in a chair opposite Sabrina, but now she leapt up and joined Sabrina on the settee. Putting her arm around Sabrina's shoulders, she gave her a squeeze. "Cry, scream, rail, do whatever you must," she said softly but with an edge of steely determination that was perhaps more soothing than anything else she was doing.

"I don't really want to do any of those things," Sabrina managed as she wiped at her eyes and drew in a deep breath. Horror rose in her chest. How had she exposed herself so easily—and readily—to a complete stranger?

Mrs. Renshaw patted her back. "There's no shame, and whatever you say or do here will be kept completely confidential. How can I help?"

A comfort Sabrina rarely experienced settled over her. Mrs. Renshaw had put her immediately at ease with her kindness and authenticity. She had to be the first person Sabrina had met who'd done so. Taking a breath to quell her remaining nerves, she repeated what she'd told Lucien about needing a wardrobe and invitations.

"Lucien was correct in saying that I'd be delighted to

assist with your wardrobe. We will begin immediately this afternoon." She smiled brightly at Sabrina, her eyes dancing. "We are going to have such fun."

A weight lifted from Sabrina and was replaced with a burgeoning excitement. For the first time since she'd conjured this far-fetched scheme to come to London and reinvent herself, she felt as though it was actually possible. "Thank you. I'm doing this to gain my husband's attention. I've come to London to get with child." The inevitable heat rose in her cheeks.

"I see. Is your marriage as estranged as Society thinks it to be?"

Hearing Mrs. Renshaw say what Sabrina had suspected was rumored about them stung, but she was not surprised. "Yes. We rarely spend any time together."

"Do you mind telling me about it? Your marriage, I mean."

Sabrina wasn't sure where to begin. The story of their marriage started well before the ceremony. "We met during my first Season, but I felt as if we were already acquainted."

"You struck an immediate accord?" she asked with a smile.

"No. I was terrified when I met him. Though my parents had spoken of him for over a year, he was still a stranger." And Sabrina didn't like strangers—until today. "They'd already communicated with Aldington's father—the duke— about a potential marriage. It was all but arranged by the time I came out."

"I didn't realize that." Mrs. Renshaw took her arm from Sabrina and angled herself toward her on the settee. Sabrina did the same so that they were facing each other. "Were you in favor of marrying him?"

"Not particularly," Sabrina whispered. She'd never admitted that to anyone outside her immediate family. Why would she when they'd reacted so poorly? Her father had threatened to send her to a nunnery if she didn't wed Aldington. *"He is the heir to a dukedom!"* her father had raged. "I was not given a choice in the matter."

Mrs. Renshaw's answering grimace was tinged with sympathy. "Women seldom are, particularly young ladies being used to further a family's social position."

"He was not in favor of the marriage either."

"How unfortunate for you both. I can imagine things did not progress well after you married."

"Not at all. We barely knew each other, and I was content for things to remain that way—at least until I grew more comfortable with him."

"And did you?"

Sabrina shook her head. "That's difficult to achieve when you are scarcely together. I spend most of my time at Hampton Lodge, a place I have been fortunate to call home and in which I find comfort. But it's lonely." Her throat burned to say the word. She *was* lonely. She longed for a connection, a family. "Aldington only visits twice each year, and when I came to London last Season, we rarely attended events together. He is always busy at Westminster or with the business of it. And as I said, I didn't mind because I was still growing accustomed to being a countess."

"Are you now?" Mrs. Renshaw asked. "Used to being a countess."

Sabrina pressed her lips together in frustration. "Only at Hampton Lodge. Here in London, I still feel like I'm an imposter."

"You are *not*. You are a countess, so let us make sure you act like one. That is what you want?"

"It is. Along with a child. That is what I want the most," she added softly.

"Forgive my candor, does your estrangement extend to the bedchamber?"

Despite an edge of discomfort, Sabrina was surprised to find she wanted to share this with someone, and Mrs. Renshaw seemed to genuinely care. "That is where we are least suited." Sabrina clasped her hands once more, squeezing them together as she worked up the nerve to tell her everything—she felt in her bones that this woman could help her, that this woman was a friend. "He rarely comes to my bed and when he does, it's dark and quick, and utterly unremarkable. I understand that is how it's supposed to be, but neither one of us wants to endure the ordeal."

Mrs. Renshaw leaned her shoulder against the settee. "Oh dear. You think it's an ordeal?"

"That is what my mother always called it." Sabrina mimicked her mother's higher tone. "You must suffer the Ordeal whenever your husband insists upon it, my dear."

Staring at her wide-eyed, Mrs. Renshaw murmured, "How dreadful. And you say Aldington is uninterested?"

Sabrina unclasped her hands and flattened them against her lap. "He seems to loathe the prospect and can't get through the event fast enough. I don't think he finds me desirable. When I demanded my marital rights last night, he used an excuse to avoid coming to my chamber."

"What is *wrong* with your husband?"

"We are simply not well suited."

Mrs. Renshaw pressed her lips together. "It doesn't sound as if you can know for sure. When you've shared a bed with Aldington, has he found pleasure in the act?"

Sabrina tried to think of his behavior, but it was difficult. She was typically too engrossed in her own anxiety to pay attention to how he felt. But then her anxiety was partially due to his dispassion for her. "He doesn't seem to."

"Does he orgasm?"

Sabrina blinked at her. "Does he what?"

"Orgasm. Come. Find his release."

"Oh, yes, he releases his seed."

"Men generally find pleasure when that occurs, to varying degrees. I'm assuming you don't realize there is a feminine version of that where you feel pleasure?"

Frowning, Sabrina tried to understand. "I don't have any seed to spill."

"No, but you can still find pleasure—astonishing pleasure —and any good husband will ensure you do. I've half a mind to knock some sense into Aldington." Her brows knitted angrily as the muscles in her jaw clenched.

"Can that still happen if their wife is shaking in fear?" Or if the husband has no desire for the act?

Mrs. Renshaw grimaced. "Perhaps not. In that instance, he may just do what he must in order to get things over with. This *is* a conundrum."

"Why? Is pleasure necessary to have a child?" Perhaps that was why she hadn't conceived.

"Sadly, no, but it's better, is it not? Otherwise, it's just a dull and terrible duty."

Yes, that was *precisely* what it was.

Mrs. Renshaw straightened. "You only need to show your husband that you are no longer afraid, that you welcome his advances—that you *desire* him."

Did she though? Sabrina had always found him attractive. She recalled the sensation that had stolen through her when she'd smelled his scent the night before. Was that akin to desire? "I'm not sure I know what that feels like," she whispered, hating to admit it but somehow knowing this woman wouldn't shame her.

Mrs. Renshaw's gaze shone with understanding and warmth. "Oh, Lady Aldington, we shall ensure that you do."

"Please, call me Sabrina. This is such an intimate conversation." Again, her cheeks flamed. "Surely only friends can speak in this manner."

Smiling, Mrs. Renshaw nodded in agreement. "Just so. You must call me Evie."

"Assuming I can feel desire for him, what will I do if he is still reluctant? What if he doesn't desire me in return?"

"I'm willing to bet that he will. However, his behavior is puzzling. There could be any number of reasons for his reluctance, including your fear." She pressed her palm to her jawline and glanced away. When she pulled her focus back to Sabrina, she returned her hand to her lap. "There is one possibility regarding his reluctance, and if that's the case, there is not much that can be done about it, I'm afraid."

"This doesn't sound good. What is it?"

"Perhaps Lord Aldington prefers a male partner in bed."

Sabrina clapped her hand over her mouth. "I hadn't considered that." And likely wouldn't have if she lived five hundred years. How she loathed her naïveté. "I believe he has a mistress. Perhaps it's not a woman."

"It's more common than you realize." Evie said this with a certainty that made Sabrina incredibly curious. Despite that, she couldn't bring herself to ask how Evie knew. Perhaps when they became closer friends, she might summon the nerve. "How do you know about his mistress?"

"I asked if he had one and he immediately denied it. *Too* immediately to be believed. You can confirm it?"

Evie shook her head. "This is the first I've heard—there are no rumors that he has a mistress. Aldington is an extremely private person. Does it concern you?"

Sabrina leaned back. "Not particularly. I know men like him usually have mistresses. Given the state of our marriage, I think I'd be more surprised if he *didn't* have one. However, if it's a man, I'm not at all sure how to proceed."

Perhaps she would have to do what she'd brazenly—and without thought—threatened the night before: have a child without him. The thought of that only filled her with more anxiety, which she absolutely did not need. She considered retreating to Hampton Lodge to perhaps hide under a blanket.

No, the old Sabrina would do that. New Sabrina wasn't going to sit by and let life happen to her. "What can I do to feel less apprehensive?"

"It doesn't sound as if you know each other at all," Evie said.

"We don't," Sabrina whispered, feeling as though she faced an insurmountable obstacle.

"Perhaps that should be your primary objective before you can get to the pleasurable creating of a child. Get to know him and make him get to know you. Then, you'll seduce him. Assuming he doesn't prefer men and can be seduced by you, are you up to the challenge?"

"Of seduction?" Sabrina feared she'd ended the word on a squeak. "I suppose I shall have to bluntly ask if he is aroused by men or women." The thought of doing so made her feel as if she were riding a runaway horse, but she worked to rein in her nerves. "I think I must. The time for prevarication and avoidance is past. I am on a mission."

Evie laughed and reached over to briefly clasp Sabrina's hand. "You aren't at all what you think, at least not what I've seen today. You possess a steel inside you, Sabrina. I hope you realize that. I also hope you never forget it," she added with a soft smile.

Sabrina *hadn't* realized that, and of everything Evie had said today, it might be the thing that stuck in her mind the longest. She'd certainly be thinking about it for some time— whether it was actually true and how she could learn to use that steel.

"Let us discuss the fun part of this, shall we?" Evie's gaze held a mischievous sparkle. "In order to conduct a successful seduction, you should experience an orgasm—or several."

"How do I do that before seducing him?" Sabrina feared her naïveté was once again rearing its head.

"By pleasuring yourself."

Sabrina gaped at her. "How on earth would I do that?"

"You'll have an orgasm," Evie explained. "What I was telling you about before. You don't need a man to give you one. You can do all this by touching yourself—your breasts, your sex, whatever feels good."

Sabrina brushed her hand over her forehead. "Please forgive my ignorance. It's quite maddening, if I'm to be honest. Why would I touch my breasts?"

Evie exhaled and pinched the bridge of her nose. "Aldington has never touched your breasts."

"Why would he?"

"Because it feels lovely." Evie resituated herself on the settee, turning even more toward Sabrina and bringing her thigh slightly onto the cushion in the process. "You definitely need to have an orgasm—or three—before you attempt seduction. Tonight, I want you to touch yourself until you find release. It will take some effort, but I promise you'll enjoy it."

Sabrina didn't understand any of this. "How do I do this?"

"I'm going to explain, and I'm going to give you a book from my library. It has drawings and descriptions." Evie gave her a wicked smile. "They will, hopefully, arouse you."

"Oh." Sabrina remained skeptical.

"Trust me. You are going to be amazed at what you have been missing. And when you learn to find and experience pleasure you will wield a power that will give you a singular confidence when dealing with your husband. When he comes to your bed, you will know what you want and what to ask him for. Rather, what to *demand* from him."

Sabrina put her fingers to her lips, imagining this power and using it to demand…pleasure from Aldington. It almost seemed impossible, but she'd already demanded he visit her bed. This would be easy after that, wouldn't it?

Evie abruptly rose. "I'm going to fetch the book so we can have a nice, in-depth discussion. I'll also have Foster bring sherry—you'll thank me for it. Then, after we have finished your education, we'll go shopping." Eyes glowing with enthusiasm, she took herself from the drawing room, leaving Sabrina to stare after her in wonder and perhaps a bit of mental paralysis.

This was not at all what she'd imagined when she'd gone to Lucien for help. She'd never considered all that she was missing. How could she? It seemed, however, this was precisely what she needed.

She only hoped she was up to the challenge of seduction, especially in the face of a man who didn't want to be seduced.

CHAPTER 5

*C*onstantine didn't stay out quite as late as he'd planned. Through the course of the day, he'd convinced himself that he needed to visit his wife tonight. The sooner he got her with child, the better. Perhaps they might even enjoy it. But to do that, she'd need to be open to such a thing, *if* her newfound courage actually extended to the bedchamber.

There was only one way to find out.

Garbed in loose-fitting breeches and a banyan, he went to her chamber and rapped lightly on the door.

"Come in," she called.

Every muscle in his body tightened as he opened the door and stepped inside. She rose from the single chair in front of the hearth, and Constantine nearly choked.

Her slender frame was draped in a dark pink dressing gown that hugged her…curves? Yes, she had curves—a rather lush flare from her narrow waist to her rounded hip and a surprisingly full bosom. How had he never noticed this before?

Because she'd never dressed like this before. The gown

formed a deep vee leading into her cleavage. His mouth went dry as his gaze followed the trail, and he realized he could just detect her nipples through the thin silk.

Holy hell. This was not the shy, terrified wife he knew.

"I'm pleased you came to visit," she said. "However, given the state of your hand, I think you're right that we should wait until tomorrow or perhaps the following night to resume our marital duties."

Marital duties. His brain was having a hard time reconciling that last word in particular while he tried—in vain—not to stare at her breasts. As his cock grew hard and lengthened, he acknowledged there would be nothing dutiful about taking her to bed tonight.

Except there is, his mind argued. Marriage was nothing if not duty, and begetting an heir was at the top of the list of duties.

This was a moot debate—even inside his head—since she was turning him away. The irony that he would have eagerly tumbled her, and that last night she'd asked him to and he'd refused, was not lost on him. He took a deep breath in an effort to cool his arousal.

"I'm surprised at your change of…mind." Had he been about to say heart? There were no hearts involved in this union—of that he was certain.

She gave him a placid smile. "I want to be a supportive wife. How was your day at Westminster?" Her hands were clasped at her waist so that her upper arms were pressed against her breasts. As if he needed more help in directing his attention to them.

He forced himself to focus on her question. Westminster… "It was fine, thank you. Productive, I think."

"Indeed? What were you working on?"

"The apothecaries act," he responded without thinking.

"I don't think I know about that. What is it?"

Constantine blinked, his brain catching up with the conversation. He didn't typically discuss his work with her, but then she'd never asked about it before. "I'm, ah, working on a law that would require apothecaries, and other medical practitioners, to be regulated."

She tipped her head to the side, her gaze trained on his. "Why do you think that's important?"

"The current system is dangerous. Apothecaries are conducting surgeries and chemists are dispensing medicine —there needs to be order and regulation to ensure these practitioners are trained and educated. Many apothecaries are illiterate. The College of Physicians are demanding changes to the bill, as is the Society of Apothecaries. We met today to try to find some compromise."

"And you think you were successful?" Her interest seemed…genuine.

"Perhaps. You can't possibly find this interesting?" It was of particular import to him—if not for a rogue apothecary who'd also called himself a surgeon, his mother might be alive today. But his wife couldn't know that.

"I do, actually. My mother's chemist prescribes a dizzying array of tonics and medicinals. I can't imagine she needs half of them. She may not need any of them, in fact."

"That is troubling." An overzealous apothecary was the reason Constantine's mother had died. He'd bled her repeatedly, which Constantine's father had allowed, and his mother hadn't survived. "Have you tried to talk with your mother about the matter?"

Surprise flashed in her eyes, but it was more than that. There was fear, yes, that was it. This was the wife he recognized.

"I couldn't ever do that," she said quietly, her gaze moving to the coals glowing in the hearth.

He hadn't meant to cause her distress. "How was your day?" he asked, hoping to divert her thoughts.

"Lovely, thank you. I'm afraid I spent all my quarterly allowance as well as some of your money."

He'd thought he supplied her with enough funds, but perhaps he didn't. "Do you require a larger allowance?"

"Probably not. I needed several new items for my wardrobe. I didn't add anything last Season."

"You don't need to justify the expenses. I'm sure they were necessary. I'll increase your allowance. I don't want you to feel as though you can't have what you need. Or want," he added, because why shouldn't she? His gaze moved over her dressing gown once more, and again he felt a strong, undeniable attraction. "Is that new?" He vaguely gestured toward her.

"Yes. Do you like it?" Unclasping her hands, she turned—she *turned*—and the gown gently flowed as she slowly spun about. With the movement, he could see her legs and thighs, and the enticing curve of her posterior. Every bit of moisture left his mouth, and he struggled to swallow.

"I, ah, do." He had to cough the cobwebs out of his throat. "Yes. It's very nice." *Nice?* It was bloody tantalizing.

She took a step toward him, and he wondered if perhaps he wouldn't leave after all. She was incredibly tempting, and right now his hand didn't hurt in the slightest. In fact, he wasn't even sure he still had hands. She did, though. And arms and smoothly sloping shoulders, and a captivating collarbone, along with a gorgeous neck he suddenly ached to kiss.

She'd gripped her hands together again, rather tightly this time, as evidenced by the paleness of her knuckles. "I need to ask you something, and I hope you won't find it gauche. Do you prefer the company of men?"

He gaped at her. What on earth was she asking?

As if she'd heard his thoughts, she clarified, "In bed, I mean."

Constantine couldn't think of a single word to utter. Instead, a garbled stream of nonsense stole past his lips. "Er, buh, no, why, I, just, ah, erh, argh."

"I think I heard a no in there?"

Who was this woman who looked like a siren and possessed a confidence he'd never once glimpsed in her?

"Yes," he managed, sounding as though he was being choked—and really, he felt like he was too. "I mean, *no*. Of course I don't prefer men. I bid you good evening."

He spun about and left her chamber, closing the door more forcefully than he meant to as he rushed to get away from her. When he was back in his room, he latched the door and leaned back against it.

What the absolute bloody hell had just happened? Why had she asked him that? How had she even known to ask such a thing at all? What was going *on* with her?

He pushed away from the door and stalked toward the hearth. Once there, he pivoted and marched right back. He completed this circuit several times, his mind tumbling.

She thought he wanted to bed men? Absolutely not. He'd honestly never given that any thought—it just didn't apply to him. From even before the time his father had purchased his first sexual experience at the age of fifteen, he'd firmly fantasized about women.

Fantasized? Did he actually do that? Yes, on occasion, but he was admittedly not as driven by lust as most gentlemen. He'd attributed that to his extreme sense of propriety and sensibility. He refused to be ruled by his baser instincts, and he was a model of self-control. While other gentlemen suffered the negative effects of gambling, drinking, and all manners of excess, Constantine was not beleaguered by such vulgar impulses. It was why he hadn't taken a mistress.

Lucien would argue Constantine suffered from an excess of self-righteousness, and perhaps he was right. He would also insist that Constantine was lifeless and tedious, and in desperate need of excitement.

Perhaps he was right about that too.

Constantine looked toward his wife's bedroom. He imagined her doffing the beautiful dressing gown and slipping between the bedclothes. Had she been nude under that gown or was the undergarment simply so filmy and slight that he'd been able to see her form?

Suddenly, Constantine *was* excited. And eager to demonstrate to his wife just how much he desired a woman in his bed. Not just any woman—*her*.

He stalked into the sitting room. A moment later, he stood in front of her door, his hand poised to knock.

A soft sound carried to his ears, making him lean forward so that he nearly pressed himself against the wood. Was she…moaning?

Oh God. She wasn't…?

Sucking in a breath, he stood motionless as he strained to hear. The bed creaked and there was another sound—a deeper moan. Good Lord, he couldn't—

Constantine sealed his ear to the wood, desperate to make out the slightest sounds. There. Moaning, a whimper, another, a soft cry. At some point in the last few moments, his cock had gone painfully and irrevocably hard. But she couldn't be pleasuring herself. Could she?

At last, a louder cry engulfed him, making his body shudder with want. He finally drew a breath, now panting because he'd gone so long without. Pushing away from the door, he braced his hand on the frame, his head bowed as he fought to regain his infamous and currently absent self-control.

When his breathing was finally regulated, he stood

straight. He heard something new. Laughter? Yes, pure joy, from the sound of it.

Constantine stared at the door for a long moment before returning to his room. His life suddenly seemed upended, unrecognizable, untethered. Why hadn't he gone into her bedchamber as soon as he realized what she was doing? It seemed she was not at all the meek woman he'd thought her to be. She'd changed. But how?

Perhaps you never really knew her. Perhaps everything you thought you knew about her—about marriage—is wrong.

What if he was the one who was afraid? And if that was the case, what in the hell was he afraid of?

One thing was certain: he was still painfully erect and if he didn't frig himself, he would be sorry. Wounded hand, be damned.

~

*A*fter a mostly sleepless night, Constantine found himself at his brother's house the following morning. He paced in Lucien's library as he waited for his brother to join him so he could ask for help.

Constantine stopped pacing and stared at the window that looked out to the small garden at the rear of the terraced house. Was he really so desperate as to seek his brother's counsel? There would be no end to Lucien's taunts.

Starting toward the door, Constantine stopped short as his younger brother appeared in the doorway. An inch taller and with dark hair that matched their father's, Lucien was the more handsome, more charming, and, overall, more liked brother. He was always surrounded by friends and admirers, while Constantine preferred solitude and anonymity.

Dressed in a dark red banyan over black pantaloons,

Lucien prowled into the library with a subtle smile quirking his mouth. "Shouldn't you be at church?"

"I wanted to see you, and there's no chance you would be there," Constantine retorted.

"You know me well. I can think of much better things to do on a Sunday, such as sleep." He yawned. "But you've forgone church to seek me out, so this must be an important errand indeed. I can't remember the last time you paid me a surprise visit." He cocked his head. "Have you ever?"

"Just sit down." Constantine sat in a chair and balanced near the edge with a nervous tension that would send him from the room at the slightest provocation.

Arching a brow, Lucien lounged in another chair. "How can I help?"

Constantine flinched. He *was* here for help, and Lucien had saved him the pain of asking for it outright. Somewhat. Having to come to his brother still burned. Constantine could barely push the words out. "I need—" His tongue dried up, and he clenched his jaw.

"You seem distressed." Lucien sat forward, losing the air of nonchalance. "Tell me how I can help, Con. I'd like to if I can," he added gently.

"I don't know why I came here. You aren't married. You wouldn't understand."

"You're having marital problems?"

"Er, yes."

"You're correct. I am not married, nor do I plan to ever be. Which makes me think you came to me because it's not necessarily due to your marriage—"

Constantine interrupted him. "But it is. It's everything to do with my marriage, and the duty that's required. I need an heir, dammit."

"Dammit?" Lucien cleared his throat. "Is there some

problem with begetting an heir? I would think that would be the most enticing thing about a marriage."

"Of course you would say that."

Lucien laughed. Genuinely. Which was even more irritating. "What does that mean?"

"As if you aren't aware of your reputation."

"I have a reputation for enjoying sex? Why yes, I'm a breathing person. Don't most breathing persons enjoy sex?" The humor abruptly fell from his face. "Con? Do you...not enjoy sex?"

Constantine shot out of his chair. "Of course I do. Just not with my wife." Lucien opened his mouth to speak, but Constantine cut him off. "I shouldn't have come here. You have no notion of how things are between a husband and wife."

Lucien held up his hand in a calming motion. "That may be true, but I'm damn sure they have sex, and plenty of them enjoy it. If *you* like sex—and apparently you do—you should like sex with Lady Aldington."

"What if *she* doesn't like it?" Except after hearing her last night, Constantine wasn't even sure if that was true. It seemed *he* was the problem. With him, she was cold and aloof. Without him, she sounded quite...happy. He collapsed back into the chair and put his head in his hands.

"Con? Are you all right?"

"Fine." He stared at the carpet between his legs. The reds, golds, and browns blurred together, and he closed his eyes.

"I would like to help," Lucien offered softly. "If I can. Since you're here, you must think that's at least possible."

Constantine dropped his hands and lifted his head. "I have limited experience compared to you. I would like to find a way to...pleasure my wife without scaring the hell out of her." If he could. If she even wanted that from him. A child didn't require pleasure.

"Ah. Well. I'd ask if you considered spending time with a professional, but I know you did. I also know it didn't actually happen. Perhaps you should allow Barbara to...tutor you a bit."

"I know what to do," he snapped. He just didn't know how to do it with a woman—his wife—who shrank from him in the bedroom. Was it even possible to seduce a woman who didn't want you, who never had?

"I mean this with the greatest respect and kindness, but do you really?"

Constantine swore viciously.

"Christ, Con, I didn't know you could curse like that. Well done!" Lucien grinned at him. Upon receiving another glare, Lucien held up his hand once more. "My apologies. I'm just trying to bring some levity into this...situation. I really do think spending an evening or three with someone like Barbara could benefit you."

"When presented with the opportunity, I found it difficult to be unfaithful." Which was sad or comical—or both—since his wife didn't want him. Any other gentleman would have taken a mistress by now. "I think I was perhaps relieved when she and I came upon Overton and his ward."

Lucien's brow knitted, and he leaned back in his chair. "Then why did you seek Barbara out?"

Constantine shrugged. "It seemed like I should. I *do* like sex, and I don't have very much of it." He suddenly realized he was lonely. The revelation was distracting, as if he should have known and now wondered what in the hell was wrong with him.

"Why not?"

"It's...complicated. And awkward. You know our marriage was arranged."

"Yes, but I thought you wanted to marry her."

"I did." Until he'd learned she hadn't wanted to marry

him. The day before the wedding, his father had said the bride wished to cry off but that she would do her duty. Anything else would have been a scandal, which the duke would never have tolerated.

Learning she didn't want him, that she would have preferred to ruin herself than marry him had hurt more than he'd ever acknowledged. Not to himself and certainly not to anyone else.

"She was a demure, sheltered young lady when we married. She knew absolutely nothing on our wedding night other than that I would come to her bed." Which had made for a disastrous occasion in which he'd rushed through the act in an effort to get it over with as quickly as possible for her. She'd been absolutely terrified. He hadn't sought to share a bed with her again for months.

Lucien's eyes widened, and he sat straighter. "Shit, who's going to tell Cass about this sort of thing? That would have been Mama's responsibility."

Constantine stared at him. "I don't want to talk about our sister and sex!"

"Someone's going to have to speak with her. The duke expects her to marry by the end of the Season."

"Aunt Christina will do it." As the closest female relative, their father's sister was their younger sister Cassandra's sponsor for the Season.

Lucien snorted. "Will she? And if she does, can we trust her to do an adequate job, or will she bungle it as your mother-in-law did?"

"Can we address my crisis first?"

"It's a crisis now, is it?" Lucien wiped his hand over his brow and apologized again.

"You can't seem to keep yourself from making light of this, which is precisely why I was hesitant to come." A long-held frustration that had burned just below the surface finally boiled over in Constantine. "You taunt me at every turn. I know you don't understand my reticence and love of solitude, but you don't have to. You only need to accept me as I am and leave me the hell alone about it."

Lucien stared at him for a long moment during which Constantine's chest felt lighter than it had in years. Finally, he blinked. "I'm sorry." The words were soft and heartfelt. "You're right. I don't understand you—not entirely. You are too much like our father, who I rather dislike. Sometimes I allow that to affect my behavior toward you and I shouldn't."

"Thank you."

"However, I stand by my belief that you should relax and be less restrained. Bask in your solitude and avoid people as if they carried syphilis if you must but pursue the things that make your life whole and wonderful."

Constantine wasn't sure what those things were beyond his work, which, like his marriage, his father had pushed him into. That wasn't precisely true. "I have my racing club." He took great joy in that, actually.

Lucien cast him a gimlet eye, then stood and went to the cabinet with his liquor. A few moments later, he returned carrying two glasses. He handed one to Constantine before retaking his chair.

"Isn't it a bit early for this?" Constantine sniffed the liquid, thinking it looked like whisky. And yes, it was—likely smuggled—Scotch whisky.

"Is it?" The question was sardonic and completely rhetorical. Constantine sipped his whisky, grateful for his brother's hedonism for perhaps the first time. Perhaps he *should* loosen up.

"You said you wanted to marry Lady Aldington. You felt something for her then?"

Feel… Constantine didn't typically survey his emotions. "I thought she was the most beautiful woman in England. I still do." And objectively, she was—or at least one of the most beautiful. But something had shifted last night. The pull he felt toward her went beyond an appreciation for her beauty. She'd asked him about his work, and she spoke with an intelligence and confidence he hadn't known she possessed.

"That's a start," Lucien said encouragingly. "How did you envision your marriage?"

Irritation sparking, Constantine ran his hand through his hair. "I didn't." He'd just done the next duty on the list. "Can you stop asking me about our marriage and just tell me what to do?"

"I need to understand the problem—as do you—before we can fix it," Lucien said drily. "But fine, let's get to the important part. You need to have sex with your wife, and you'd like for both of you to enjoy it. However, you are hung up on something that's preventing you from just shagging her senseless, as you claim to know how to do."

"I never claimed any such thing. And there's no need to be crass." Except his brother was right. Her fear and agitation and the knowledge that she didn't want him made it nearly impossible for him to bed her, let alone make it pleasurable.

Lucien rolled his eyes in a thoroughly exaggerated fashion. "Jesus, Con, do not get distracted by the language I'm using. Do you know how to seduce her or not?"

"Not her, no. She's…different. I honestly don't even know where to begin. I'm trusting you not to make light of this."

"I won't. Not about this. Trust me." Lucien looked him in the eye, reminding Constantine of when they were boys and they'd promised each other to keep whatever mischief they'd gotten into from their nurse. Neither of them had ever broken one of those vows, not even when Lucien had broken a windowpane or when Constantine had picked all of their mother's favorite daisies.

"I'll try," was all Constantine could say. He didn't really

trust anyone, least of all himself. How could he, when his father had always told him what to do and how to act?

"I'll do everything in my power to show you that you can." Lucien took a long pull on his whisky, baring his teeth briefly as he lowered the glass. "You say Lady Aldington is different and you aren't sure how to seduce her. A woman with practical experience, someone like Barbara, could help. She could tutor you in how to ease Lady Aldington's apprehension while showing her there is pleasure in coming together. I could find someone to fill this role for you."

"You're going to hire someone to tutor me in how to seduce my wife?" Hopefully this woman would have expertise in seducing the unseduceable.

Hell, did he really think it was that hopeless? Clearly not, or he wouldn't have come to Lucien. His wife *was* seduceable, just maybe not by him. Still, he had to try since she'd demanded a baby. Which he needed in order to cross the next duty off the list.

"That's my recommendation, yes. And if you prefer, you don't have to actually have sex with her—then it's not being unfaithful, is it?" Lucien swirled the whisky in his glass. "I'd argue it's bloody altruistic since your entire goal is to pleasure your wife. She'll thank you in the end."

Constantine wasn't sure he agreed. He also wasn't sure he could do it. Wanting to let go of some of his rigidity didn't mean it would be easy. "I'll take it under consideration."

Lucien's gaze shot to his, and his mouth opened. But he snapped it closed and only nodded.

After tossing back the rest of his whisky, Constantine stood. "Thank you for your counsel." He went to place the empty glass on the cabinet.

Lucien deposited his glass on a small table near his chair and stood. "I'm glad you came to see me. I'm sorry we aren't always as brotherly as we should be. We are allies, I hope."

"I hope so too."

"I like Lady Aldington," Lucien said affably. "Even if you don't have a love match, I think you two could be quite compatible."

That assessment should have cheered Constantine or made him feel optimistic. But again, emotion seemed difficult. Or maybe it wasn't, for he suddenly felt a spike of annoyance. Compatible was so...boring. Just like him.

But not like her. He'd thought she was colorless, that they were a good match. Only she wasn't. She was strong and bold—hell, she'd asked him if he preferred men—and he was completely out of his element. Even so, he wasn't sure he could take his brother's advice.

"Will I see you at the Kipley rout on Tuesday?" Lucien asked. "I know you aren't fond of Society events, but you've been at least making an appearance at some for Cass's sake." It was their younger sister's debut Season, and the responsibility of playing escort had fallen almost entirely to Constantine. Their father couldn't be bothered, and while Aunt Christina accompanied her, she wasn't the most reliable chaperone. "On second thought, maybe you won't," Lucien said. "Since Father has hired Miss Lancaster as her new companion."

"Miss Lancaster?" Constantine recalled the name but not the face.

"She was companion to Miss Wingate—Overton's ward. But now that they are on their way to being married, she found herself in need of employment. Miss Wingate suggested the duke might hire her for Cass, and I was actually able to persuade him to do so."

Constantine blinked at him. "You were?"

"Once I told him that she'd seen Miss Wingate betrothed in a matter of weeks, he jumped at the prospect."

"Anything to achieve his ends." Constantine's shoulder twitched.

"Just so," Lucien agreed. "Well, if you decide to come to the rout, I'll see you there. Perhaps by then, you'll have an answer for me."

Perhaps he would. Or perhaps he'd find the courage and ability to bed his wife.

Hope did spring eternal. Too bad Constantine rarely had any.

CHAPTER 6

*L*ucien walked up the familiar stairs to Evie's drawing room, his mind churning. She was seated in her favorite chair near the hearth with a newspaper in her hand.

Gifting him with one of her glorious smiles, Evie never failed to dazzle him. She was one of the most beautiful women he'd ever known, and she possessed a rare ability to put anyone at ease. It was her skill for listening, he thought, something he valued very much.

"Good afternoon, Lucien. Come sit." She gestured with the newspaper to the chair facing hers as if it wasn't where he sat whenever he visited, which was often. After all, she only lived a short walk away, and they usually had Phoenix Club business to discuss. Plus, they were friends and had been for years.

She narrowed her eyes at him briefly. "You've a scheme in your head."

Lucien laughed as he settled himself in his chair. "You know me too well. I've a particularly sensitive situation to manage, and I need your help."

"I am always eager to assist in your endeavors." She set her newspaper on a small table next to her chair. "Who is in need this time?"

"My brother. And since you are already offering support to his wife, you are perfectly positioned."

Evie rested her elbow on the arm of her chair. "If this scheme of yours involves bringing them together, I will gladly help. I like Sabrina very much."

"I do too. I think she and my brother could actually be happy if they can get past themselves."

"What do you mean? I think I know, but I'd like to hear your opinion on the matter."

"It sounds as if their marriage is a disaster on all fronts, including in the bedchamber."

Surprise flickered in Evie's blue gaze. "Con confided this to you?"

"Reluctantly." Lucien let out a short laugh. "He is clearly desperate since he came to me for help. I think he would prefer to waltz across hot coals on his way to Almack's."

Evie's shoulders twitched as a smile drifted across her full lips. "Desperate indeed. Sabrina was also rather anxious for help. She's anxious about everything, really."

"She seems to be, and it sounds as if neither she nor Con can do what they must to meet each other in the middle. She's too apprehensive, and her fear has caused him to also be apprehensive. It's a bloody mess."

"I've been encouraging her to overcome her anxiety, particularly about sex." She clucked her tongue. "The poor thing has never had an orgasm."

Lucien shook his head. "Oh, Con."

"Don't blame him. As you said, it's a mess and neither of them is at fault."

"Or they both are."

She pursed her lips. "How about we don't assign blame

and just help them? Are you going to share your plan? It seems you have one."

"I do. Con had planned to finally take a mistress, but, as you know, the attempt was foiled." Lucien had told her about giving Constantine a key to a room in the Phoenix Club to meet with a courtesan. Because she was the manager of the women's side of the club, Lucien shared just about everything that involved the club with her. "I think spending time with someone who can help him be more commanding would be beneficial to his marriage. I suggested he see someone who can tutor him in seduction—specifically with his nervous, reticent wife. I don't suppose you can think of anyone who could help?"

The look she gave him could have frozen his balls off. He was glad it didn't. "I've overstepped," he said quietly. "I know it's been two years since you left that profession, but I thought you might be able to recommend someone."

Her brows, pitched in an angry V, did not relax. "As you *should* know, I completely cut myself off from that life when I left London to reinvent myself. I have not kept in touch with anyone at all, and I can't reach out to anyone now, not as Mrs. Renshaw."

Of course she couldn't, and he damn well should have known better. "My deepest apologies, Evie."

She exhaled and waved her hand, her features smoothing. Thankfully, she never stayed perturbed with him for long. "Honestly, it's too bad we can't lock Sabrina and Con alone together in a room. Naked. Perhaps with some helpful instruments."

Lucien grinned. "A dildo?"

"Can you imagine?" Her eyes glowed with mirth. "But no, that would be too much."

"Actually, I don't think it's a bad idea—the alone together in a room part anyway. And hopefully they would remove their clothing at some point." Lucien leaned his head back and stared up at the ceiling a moment. "This could work." He lowered his head and leveled a stare at Evie. "Sabrina could be the tutor."

Evie's eyes rounded, and she immediately shook her head. "That would never work. Sabrina lacks the confidence, let alone the knowledge."

"You said you've been encouraging her, including about sex. Surely you can tell her what she needs to know. This could really help them lower their inhibitions." Lucien was warming to this stratagem. But first he had to convince Con to meet with the tutor. And Evie had to persuade Sabrina. "I'm not sure I agree that Sabrina lacks the confidence. She only thinks she does. She's already come to London with the goal of taking Society by storm."

"I think you're exaggerating a bit," Evie said with a wry chuckle. "But you're right that she possesses a steel I don't think she's fully aware of—or used to. This could give them both the push they need to, as you say, meet in the middle." She frowned suddenly. "Except this is a major deception. Con would need to betray his wife, and Sabrina would deceive her husband."

He leaned forward slightly. "I don't agree. It's a *minor* deception for a much greater good—the benefit of their marriage. I fear that without some assistance, they are doomed to fail."

"Do you really think Con would do it?"

"I do, with a little more persuasion. I mentioned it yesterday, and he said he'd consider it. Do you think you can get Sabrina to agree?"

Evie blew out a breath. "I don't know her *that* well yet, but she's committed to making drastic changes to achieve what she wants. And what she wants most is a child."

"Then they need to get into bed."

"Perhaps this scenario will allow them to be more comfortable. Sabrina can pretend to be someone else and that could give her the confidence she needs, that she doesn't realize she already has."

"And Con can practice what he needs to do without the stress of performing in front of his anxious wife. He will also gain the confidence he needs to take charge and give them both what they want."

They fell silent for a few moments, both turning their heads toward the hearth as if they could divine answers and direction from the burning coals. Finally, Evie spoke. "This will take some coordination. Where do you envision this taking place?"

"The Phoenix Club's second floor." There were several bedchambers at the club, which Lucien had installed in case anyone needed a place to sleep. Or for something else. With the men and women mingling together on Tuesdays, Lucien had thought it prudent to have private spaces, even if the majority of members weren't aware they existed. Lucien and Evie—as well as the membership committee—knew they were there, and so far they'd proven helpful.

Evie nodded. "Of course. It's almost as if you knew they would provide a benefit." She winked at him, and he laughed softly. "Con will need to be blindfolded so he can't see that the tutor is Sabrina."

"She should also wear a mask, in case the blindfold slips."

"And the room must be as dark as possible—just a small, single candle."

Lucien arched a brow at his friend and, really, partner, at least in matters such as this. "It sounds as if we're moving forward with this stratagem?"

"It does seem as though it could work. *If* we can persuade them both to participate."

Lucien inhaled as he straightened his spine against the

back of the chair. "I have the utmost faith in our abilities. We're helping them achieve what they both desire."

She sent him a sly look that would once have driven him to sweep her into his arms. "It's your most daring act of assistance yet."

"It's my brother," he said simply. "I would do anything for him."

Her features softened. "That's the Lucien I know. You persuaded me to give up the only life I've ever known and become someone completely different. This will be no trouble for you. You've the best heart."

"Shh. That's best kept between us. Now, let us plot our brilliance as we drive Lord and Lady Aldington together."

"I think this calls for wine." Evie stood and moved toward a cabinet that held a variety of liquor.

"That new port, if you have any left." Lucien *did* love his brother, and he would see him happy. Con deserved nothing less.

⁓

There was a short line of coaches on North Audley Street, but Sabrina didn't mind waiting since this was her first foray into Society this season. She gently smoothed her hand over the cobalt gauze covering the silk of the same color, giddy with the beauty of her new gown. This was not a garment she would have chosen—the color was too vivid, the style too daring. The back sloped to a vee at the middle of her spine, exposing a generous expanse of flesh. She was glad for the embroidered wrap she'd brought for the coach ride, particularly since the sleeves didn't start until mid-shoulder.

While her costume wasn't what she typically wore, she had to admit it gave her a confidence she sorely needed in order to face tonight's rout. In it, she could believe that she was truly a self-assured countess worthy of respect. That a garment could ease her anxiety was astonishing. It was more than that, however. She just felt more prepared—more ready—to face Society now than she had two years earlier when she'd become betrothed to Aldington.

He hadn't arrived home from Westminster before she'd left, and she couldn't help but feel disappointed. He'd been polite the past few days—slightly warmer than usual but still distant, which was making it difficult to do as Evie had suggested. How could she get to know a man who kept a very high wall around him and let no one inside?

He hadn't come to her bedchamber since Saturday, when she'd advised him to wait until his hand was healed. Presumably, it was still troubling him. Only she wasn't sure she believed it was his hand, not when his behavior continued to reflect a keen lack of interest. She should have expected that nothing would change by her simply inviting him to visit her. It's not as if he could suddenly decide he was attracted to her. Perhaps this gown would help. If he even saw her in it.

She'd kept busy reacquainting herself with managing the London household. The servants were glad to have her in residence, and she'd spent time working with her new maid. Charity was turning out to be a lovely replacement, for which Sabrina was grateful. In particular, Charity possessed a magnificent talent for styling hair. Sabrina touched the back of her head where jeweled combs would sparkle beneath the candlelight once she was inside.

Aside from keeping busy with the household, Sabrina had studied the book Evie had given her. She had so many questions and though she would see Evie tonight, she wouldn't discuss such matters at a rout. Hopefully, they would arrange to meet soon.

In all honesty, she couldn't regret Aldington not visiting

her the past few nights, not when she'd been able to do what Evie had advised and learn her own body. Sabrina was now well-acquainted with the parts of her that enjoyed attention and the joy and satisfaction that resulted.

Her cheeks grew warm in the dark solitude of the coach, and a brief pang of need pulsed between her legs. Had she become a wanton? Would her husband think her one? That depended on if he ever came to her bed. She feared she was going to have to assert herself again, and then he most certainly would think her utterly brazen.

No, what she feared was not finding the same pleasure with her husband that she'd found on her own. She realized she wanted that—pleasure with Aldington. She'd come here wanting a child but now she hoped for something more. Something that seemed impossible, given her husband's indifference.

The door of the coach opened, and she stepped down from the vehicle with the groom's assistance. Clearing her mind to prepare for the coming onslaught of people and noise, she made her way up to the open door.

Sounds of laughter and glass clinking carried down into the wide entry hall. A footman took her wrap, and she followed the other guests up the stairs to the drawing room. The host and hostess stood at the top of the stairs, greeting people as they arrived.

Sabrina had met them before and particularly admired Lady Kipley. She was more reserved, like Sabrina, but was married to a gregarious baronet whose laughter filled every room he was in and who seemed to possess no fear when it came to commanding attention with a boisterous anecdote.

A fine sheen of sweat dappled Sir Cecil's wide brow as he welcomed Sabrina. "Lady Aldington, what a pleasure to see you here this evening. Did you just arrive in London?"

"A few days ago, yes," she answered.

"I told you that, dear," Lady Kipley playfully admonished him.

He laughed jubilantly. "You know I can't remember such things. Even about your friends." He lowered his voice, which Sabrina found surprising, and leaned toward Sabrina. "She counts you in that select group, so be sure to preen about it, though no one will know." He grinned, then winked at his wife, who shook her head with a warm smile.

Sabrina moved to Lady Kipley, who took her hand and gave it a gentle squeeze. "It's true. I'm so glad you've come to town. We need more people like us."

A look of confusion must have passed over Sabrina's face, for Lady Kipley added, "Those who are content to leave the spotlight for someone else." She flicked a glance toward her husband, who was now greeting the next guest.

"Yes, that is certainly me," Sabrina said. Though she was doing her best to at least step out of the shadows. The fact that she'd come on her own was something she would never have done before. Tonight would be the test to see if the courage she'd shown with Aldington would persevere.

Or wilt under the pressure of Society.

After promising to visit with Lady Kipley later, Sabrina made her way into the crowded drawing room. How she wished she wasn't alone. Although she doubted her husband's presence would have made her feel any less overwhelmed. In fact, it might have made her more nervous.

So why was she here?

Because this was part of her renaissance. Evie had adopted that word to describe what she'd originally called Sabrina's transformation. Sabrina rather liked the sound of having a renaissance.

Suddenly Evie was coming toward her, and much of the tension left Sabrina's shoulders. She exhaled and smiled, glad to see her new friend.

"Sabrina, you look absolutely stunning. I knew this color would be perfect for you, and I'm so glad Madame Dubois was able to complete the gown so quickly. It's an excellent choice for your first event. What did Aldington say?"

Sabrina continued to peruse the room, recognizing some people but not recognizing many more. While she'd spent most of last Season in London, she'd maybe gone to one event each week, usually a large ball where she could get lost among the throng. Her favorite places were corners, either in the ballroom or a quiet sitting room. She also quite enjoyed the retiring room.

However, she could not undergo a renaissance in the corner.

"Sabrina?" Evie prompted, reminding Sabrina she'd asked a question.

"Aldington was not at home."

"How disappointing," Evie murmured. "How have things been progressing?"

Sabrina pivoted toward her friend and kept her voice soft. "They have not. I have done what you, ah, recommended—for myself. And that has been most pleasant." Her cheeks burned, and she couldn't help but avert her gaze.

"Excellent. Nothing from the earl, however?"

"Not as of yet."

"Don't be discouraged. We've only just begun. I do wish he was here tonight." Evie looked about the drawing room. "You must come visit me tomorrow so we can strategize."

"I would like that very much, thank you." Sabrina had no idea what to do next. The concept of seduction wasn't just foreign, it was wholly intimidating.

Two young women came toward them. Sabrina knew one —it was her sister-in-law, Cassandra, who was marvelously gowned in peach silk—but did not recognize the other.

"Sabrina!" Cassandra greeted her. Of all the people in her

husband's family, his younger sister was by far the loveliest. She was also the only one Sabrina felt truly comfortable with. Although after her meeting with Lucien the other day, she'd changed her opinion of him.

Sabrina clasped her sister-in-law's hands. "Good evening, Cassandra. You look magnificent. How is your Season? You must have a trail of suitors following you about."

Cassandra laughed without humor. "Actually, no. I am beginning to think my father is just too fearsome. Allow me to introduce my new companion, Miss Prudence Lancaster. Pru is the best sort, and I am so fortunate her previous employer married quickly so that she could become my companion instead." She glanced toward her companion. "Pru, allow me to present Lady Aldington."

Golden-haired and pale-eyed, Miss Lancaster had a slightly ethereal quality to her. Her slender frame and alabaster complexion likely contributed to that. "I'm pleased to make your acquaintance, my lady." Miss Lancaster made an elegant curtsey.

"It's a pleasure to meet you, Miss Lancaster. I am so glad Cassandra has a companion of a similar age. She is hopelessly trapped with men in her family."

"I was until you came along," Cassandra said. "Though I'd hoped you would spend more time in London." She uttered the last with a wistful tone that carried no admonition. Still, Sabrina felt a pang of guilt. Cassandra had been ecstatic when her brother had wed, especially to someone so close to her in age. Sabrina was only a year older.

"I'm sorry," Sabrina murmured, looking into Cassandra's sherry-colored eyes. While Cassandra shared the same gender as Sabrina, that was about all they shared in common. Cassandra possessed a confidence and magnetism, like her brother Lucien, that had initially intimidated Sabrina. "I'm going to be more involved in this Season, so you must tell me how I can help you with your debut. Is your aunt still sponsoring you?"

"For what it's worth." Cassandra snorted softly. "You know how she is."

Yes, Sabrina did know. Flighty and unreliable.

"Perhaps I should take over as your sponsor," Sabrina mused aloud, surprising herself. She never would have had the thought before, let alone voiced it.

Cassandra's eyes lit. "That would be wonderful! *If* my father would allow it." She pressed her lips together and glanced toward Prudence, who only lifted a shoulder in response.

"I bet he can be persuaded," Evie said. "Speak with your brothers and gain their support."

Sabrina warmed to this idea. "Yes, we'll get Aldington to champion this cause, and the duke will have no quarrel with it. He grants Aldington everything."

Cassandra's brow arched. "You think so?"

Didn't he? It seemed that way to Sabrina. Aldington was the favorite son while Lucien was a dissolute scoundrel and Cassandra was somewhat ignored. That twinge of guilt intensified.

"Perhaps my perspective is not a very good one," Sabrina admitted.

"You aren't entirely wrong—Father *will* listen to Con more than he'll pay any heed to me or Lu."

"Then I will speak with Aldington about this as soon as possible," Sabrina said, even as she wondered what her husband would say—both about her initiative as well as acting as his sister's chaperone. She was certainly above reproach and would be far more engaged than their aunt.

Evie's eyes sparkled with enthusiasm as she glanced toward Sabrina. "What an excellent solution for everyone." Evidently, she thought this might help Sabrina's cause with

Aldington—or so it seemed. Sabrina would find out for sure when she spoke with Evie in a more private setting tomorrow.

Sabrina smiled at Miss Lancaster. "Have you been with Cassandra long?"

"Just a few days."

"She was previously companion to Miss Wingate—Overton's ward. But they are now on their way to Gretna Green. If I didn't adore Fiona so much, the romanticism of it would make me nauseated with envy." Cassandra let out an exaggerated sigh. "Honestly, I'm envious anyway. They are so very much in love."

Sabrina felt a flash of envy too. She'd had no expectations for her marriage but was coming to realize that perhaps she had nurtured a bit of hope for…something.

"They are also the most popular piece of gossip," Evie noted. "Some find their pairing scandalous, but since his grandmother has not only given her blessing but taken credit for the match, they are keeping their opinions quiet."

Cassandra's gaze darkened. "Still, you hear about them. Some people should mind their own business. Or better yet, go away. They won't be missed."

"Why the angry face, sister?" Lucien approached them, and he was not alone. Two gentlemen accompanied him, but Sabrina wasn't sure she'd met either of them.

"Just grumbling about busybodies. Good evening, Lu." Turning from her brother, Cassandra dipped a brief curtsey to the black-haired rogue—yes, rogue was the best description for his dashing good looks with piercing blue eyes and a slightly crooked nose—and then to the attractive almond-skinned gentleman with a captivating coffee-colored gaze flecked with gold. "Lord Wexford, Mr. MacNair."

"Good evening, Lady Cassandra." The rogue's Irish brogue lilted over them like a warm wool blanket. He bowed toward Sabrina. "You must be Lady Aldington. It is my distinct honor to make your acquaintance, my lady."

It was hard not to feel flattered by his charming language and the utterly beguiling twinkle in his eye. She curtsied. "Good evening, Lord Wexford. I'm pleased to meet you."

"Sabrina, allow me to also present Mr. Dougal MacNair. His father is the Earl of Stirling."

MacNair bowed just as elegantly as Wexford, but he made the addition of taking her hand. "Your beauty far exceeds your reputation, my lady. Lucien's brother is a fortunate man." He flashed a smile so bright and infectious that Sabrina couldn't help but smile in return.

"You are too kind, Mr. MacNair," she murmured as he released her hand.

Cassandra turned to her brother, touching his sleeve. "Lu, you and Con—mostly Con—are going to persuade Father that Sabrina should take over duties as my sponsor."

"Entirely Con," Lucien clarified benignly. "After my success in persuading him to hire Miss Lancaster, I'd best not push my luck. This is a brilliant idea and I wholly endorse it." He looked to Sabrina. "Are you up to the challenge?"

"Of course she is," Evie answered with a quick certainty. "She's more than capable of chaperoning the Season's brightest jewel." Which would put Sabrina in the center of attention. While she knew this was at least part of her goal, it now seemed terrifying.

Have confidence, Sabrina.

Lucien smiled at her with enough confidence for himself and Sabrina. "Yes, she is." His gaze moved over Sabrina's head toward the doorway. "If it isn't my brother."

Sabrina whipped around and silently cursed herself for reacting so quickly. Her heartbeat kicked up, and her insides seemed to float.

Dressed in dark, somber evening wear, Aldington was

even more handsome than she'd thought him to be. His tawny hair caressed his forehead as his gaze riveted on her. Though he stood several feet away, she felt his perusal and caught the subtle widening of his eyes. Had she caused offense?

Her anticipation took an anxious turn as he strode toward them. She offered him a tremulous smile as she silently cursed her sudden agitation.

"Good evening," he said as he arrived at their group. He took a position between Sabrina and MacNair. His gaze kept lingering on Sabrina.

"I'm glad you're here," Cassandra said. "I was just telling Lu that I need you both—primarily you—to convince Father that Sabrina should take over as my sponsor. It's already decided so we just need you to ensure Father approves the change."

Sabrina marveled at the way she spoke to her brother. She didn't ask, she asserted. Isn't that what Sabrina had done with Aldington when she'd arrived in London? She'd laid out her expectations quite plainly. For all the good it had done her.

"I see. I'm just to do your bidding then?" Aldington asked evenly. Sabrina couldn't tell what he thought of the plan.

"Yes, please." Cassandra flashed him a smile.

Aldington shook his head. "Fine. If you care about my opinion, it *is* a very good idea." He glanced toward Sabrina with a hint of curiosity in his gaze.

"I care," Sabrina whispered, though she didn't think he'd been addressing her. "Thank you."

Surprise replaced the curiosity, and he quickly averted his eyes from hers.

"Cass, let me take you for a spin around the room," Lucien offered. He looked to his brother. "You should take the countess around. There are likely plenty of people who'd like to speak with her since she's just arrived in town."

Looking at Aldington askance, Sabrina caught the brief scowl he sent Lucien. Why was he upset? Was she really that distasteful to him? She glanced down at her new gown and briefly touched the sapphire necklace adorning her throat. This was by far the most sophisticated she'd ever looked. If she couldn't entice him tonight, she doubted she ever could. But then, perhaps her appearance had nothing to do with his disdain.

She was about to open her mouth and say she was going to the retiring room, but he offered his arm. "Shall we?"

He was only doing this because to refuse would have been humiliating for both of them. Sabrina put her hand on his sleeve with a distinct lack of enthusiasm.

They started a circuit of the room, but he quickly led her into a corner. "My apologies, but I need a word with you before we're swept up with other people and mindless conversations." His gaze raked her, provoking a heat she wished she didn't feel. Now that her body knew how to respond, she felt that heat most profoundly in her sex.

"Why are you like this?" He licked his lower lip, and the simple act intensified the abrupt need within her.

"Like what?"

"Dressed like this, here at this rout, agreeing to be Cassandra's sponsor." His gaze met hers. "Who *are* you?"

CHAPTER 7

*A*s soon as the asinine question left his mouth, Constantine wished he could swallow it back. "I know who you are," he said lamely.

She'd stiffened and currently showed no signs of relaxing. "I should hope so."

"Still, you're different." He couldn't get over the cut of her gown and how the slope of pale flesh above the bodice made him want to rip the garment from her. "You look beautiful." He realized that sounded bad, as if she wasn't always the most gorgeous woman in the room. "But then you always do," he added softly.

"Thank you." She sounded...surprised? "I still don't understand. You say I'm different and seemed to indicate that was because I'm beautiful, but then said I always am, so how can that be different?"

When she put his words like that—with logic—he sounded like an absolute blockhead. "You're acting differently. You're more outgoing, dare I say assertive. I'm not used to that at all. You've always been shy. I was surprised when I arrived home tonight and learned you were here. I am shocked you weren't cowering in a corner." He inwardly winced at the word cowering even though it was accurate.

She drew a breath, which made him look toward her chest, something he didn't really need any prompting to do. "I'm not going to do that anymore. Does that bother you?"

"Er, no. But it will take some getting used to. Are you certain you wish to be Cassandra's sponsor? She likes to attend events and is very social."

"Yes, I think it's my duty, actually."

He couldn't argue with her there. "That's quite admirable of you. I appreciate your support of my sister. If you can manage to see her wed by the end of the Season—the sooner, the better—my father would be delighted."

"If I manage to facilitate a match of any kind, my hope is that it will delight Cassandra." There was an edge to her tone that made Constantine nervous. He still didn't recognize this woman. Yes, she was going to take a great deal of getting used to.

"Are you sure this"—she gestured down towards her gown as if it were the crux of his concern—"won't be a problem for you?"

"How you dress is no problem, provided you aren't showing too much flesh." His gaze once again strayed to the creamy skin above her bodice, and he remembered the amount of her back that was exposed. He'd glimpsed her from behind as soon as he entered, his attention drawn to the stunningly gowned woman before he realized he was ogling his wife. And now, when he thought of her shoulders, her neck, the tempting view of her upper back that was available to anyone who cared to look, he felt a sudden and staggering burst of possession.

Her brow knitted, her delicate, honey-gold brows pitching toward one another. "I wasn't just speaking of my attire, although it seems you are troubled by this gown."

Troubled was not the right word at all. He was bloody aroused.

"It is not what you typically wear. But then you are not at all the woman I thought I had married."

"How would you really know? It's not as if you've spent a great deal of time with me. The woman you see tonight is the woman I am. I suggest you reconcile yourself to that fact. Please excuse me." She brushed past him, her skirts swinging against his calf as she walked back toward the group they'd left. Only now, it was just the ladies—Cassandra, her companion, and Mrs. Renshaw.

Constantine stared for a long moment, realizing he'd offended her but not certain of exactly how. He hadn't spoken ill of her. He'd only told the truth—she *wasn't* the woman he thought he'd married.

But she had also spoken the truth: he hadn't spent much time with her and perhaps his idea of who she was and who she *actually* was were not the same thing. His head began to ache.

"That didn't seem to go very well."

Constantine turned at the sound of his brother's voice. "Where did you come from?"

"I'm everywhere," he said with a grin. "Isn't that what you used to say when we were at Oxford?"

"Because you *were* everywhere. And you still are."

"I am not at Westminster," Lucien said with a note of pride.

"You could be."

"I'll leave that to you. I am far too busy with my club and, as you said, being everywhere. But let us return to the matter at hand: your wife. What did you say to upset her?"

"She's not upset."

"Then why did she abandon you before your promenade?"

Constantine let out a pent-up, irritated breath. "You are a meddlesome troll."

"What a colorful insult. I quite like it, thank you. I thought I was helping you—that requires meddling."

"That doesn't mean I enjoy it." Constantine looked toward his wife. She laughed at something Mrs. Renshaw said, her pink lips parting to reveal her even white teeth. Joy made her even more lovely. "Just look at her," he murmured.

"I am. But mostly I'm watching you watch her."

Constantine snapped his attention to Lucien. "She's different, and she's trying to be. I don't understand why." He thought again of what she'd said—that he didn't know her.

"Perhaps she was lonely before."

After stealing another look at her, he glanced back to Lucien. "Have you spoken to her?"

"That would be odd, wouldn't it?" Lucien surveyed her. "She looks lovely this evening."

"Very."

"Have you made a decision about my suggestion?"

Mrs. Renshaw and the countess linked arms, then started to mingle with the other guests. Constantine watched in shock as his wife chatted with people. "She always stood or sat in the corner before."

"Wouldn't you rather she be anywhere else?" Lucien mused, a hint of disbelief in his tone.

Constantine didn't bother answering. He was too focused on her. And on the two gentlemen who were currently standing too close to her and allowing their gazes to linger too long on her bodice.

"Con, are you ready to meet with a tutor? I have just the person in mind to help you."

"No." He didn't divert his attention from his wife. A discomfiting realization washed over him. In addition to her being a completely different person, she'd adopted some sort of air. It wasn't just confidence. Whatever it was, Constantine felt intimidated. After working up the courage to visit her chamber last night, he'd heard her again, pleasuring herself—to great effect. She clearly knew what she was doing, and how in the hell had that happened? He'd wager Hampton Lodge that she hadn't known how to do that before.

Before what exactly? What had happened to prompt all this? He wanted to ask. He needed to ask. But as she'd so painfully pointed out, they did not discuss such personal things. They discussed almost nothing. To question her about this would open up a closeness—an intimacy—that would change the dynamics of their relationship forever.

"Con, you look as if you either want to run from the room or toss up your accounts in the corner."

Constantine barely heard him. He couldn't think past his wife at the moment. She was changing, and he had nothing to do with it. Anger and disappointment—in himself, if he were honest, and it was probably time he was—coursed through him.

"Do you think she's having an affair?" he whispered, the words dark and hollow sounding to his ears.

"You can't be serious," Lucien hissed, his voice a low burn near Constantine's ear.

"How else can you explain her newfound confidence, her —" He clapped his teeth and lips together. "Never mind."

"She would never," Lucien said with a certainty that drew Constantine's full attention.

"How would you know?"

Lucien stared at him, clearly aghast. "You mean to tell me that wouldn't shock you to your very bones?"

"Everything she does right now shocks me." Constantine turned his gaze toward her once more, but she'd moved on. Scanning the room, he found the vibrant blue of her gown.

She was talking to yet more gentlemen, one of whom he knew quite well and who was smiling and laughing with her as if they were old friends. Constantine didn't think they'd ever met.

And what did that say—that someone with whom he was well acquainted didn't know his wife? Constantine's abject failure as a husband was becoming distinctly and bitterly clear.

He'd tried to be a good husband. In doing his duty, he'd given her space and consideration, moving things along in the bedroom as quickly as possible, given her trepidation. He'd ensured she had a beautiful estate, which she could manage on her own without his father's interference—the duke never visited Hampton Lodge and had "given" it to Constantine to use as his primary residence when he'd wed. Furthermore, Constantine hadn't denied any of her requests for refurbishment or for the design of the garden. Indeed, he'd gone out of his way to support her. What more should he have done?

The answer seemed suddenly and painfully obvious. He needed to get to know this woman who was his wife. Only he didn't know how. "The wall between us is too great," he said, sounding rather like a frog. He coughed, trying to clear his throat.

"Don't let it be. Isn't it worth trying to breach it? It's not as if you can find another wife." He took a breath. "I suppose you could, but why, when it's very possible things could work out well between you and Sabrina."

Hearing his brother use her Christian name provoked something within Constantine. It wasn't jealousy, like he was feeling toward the men who were flirting with his wife, but it was similar. He felt the need to lay claim to her but didn't know how. And did she even want him to, or was all of this just to have a child?

"Who is this person you have in mind?" Constantine asked without looking at his brother.

"Someone who used to be a courtesan but isn't any longer."

Constantine jerked his head toward Lucien. "Why would she agree to this?"

"Because she enjoys sex. Plus, she has a very kind heart and is happy to help someone in need. Does this mean you've changed your mind?"

"No." But he was thinking about it. The longer he watched his wife, the more he realized he wasn't certain how to proceed. She *seemed* different and had invited his attention, but he couldn't shake the memory of the nervous bride who hadn't wanted to marry him and who couldn't wait for him to complete his "duty" and leave the bedchamber.

"Well, when you do, I am here to help you. Now stop glowering toward your wife and try to have fun. I'm going down to the card room. I'd invite you to join me, but I know you won't."

"Correct." Constantine tried to relax his attention toward the countess. She and Mrs. Renshaw had moved on, their heads bent together in what seemed to be close friendship. When had that happened? Hell, he really didn't know his wife at all.

Alone now that Lucien had gone, Constantine moved out of the corner. Only he didn't know where to go. He ought to rejoin his wife, but after their encounter, he didn't think she wanted to see him. He needed to work on that. They should try to make an entirely fresh start, as if he were courting her again.

Had he ever courted her? Their union had been inevitable.

However, their happiness, or at least their satisfaction,

was not. This must be a different kind of courtship, starting with seduction.

And given the state of their marriage, his lack of skill in seduction, and the uncertainty of his wife's interest in being seduced, how the hell did he start with *that?*

~

*S*abrina had wondered if Aldington would invite her to ride home with him from the rout, but he'd left at an early hour. After his departure, she and Evie had discussed his behavior, how he'd seemed irritated and generally discomfited by her appearance. Grinning, Evie had suggested he might be jealous. That seemed wholly impossible, but then Evie had pointed out that Sabrina had earned the attention of many people at the rout, including a good number of men, both married and unmarried.

Even now, as Sabrina pulled her favorite night rail over her head, she blushed. She had somewhat been the center of attention that evening, and she wasn't sure how she felt about that.

That alone was a problem, for if she meant to become her sister-in-law's sponsor, she would need to feel comfortable with being seen and heard. The prospect filled her with a thrilling dread.

Charity put away the last of Sabrina's clothing. "Will there be anything else, my lady?"

"No, thank you. I'll tidy my own hair." She gave Charity a smile, and the maid departed.

Sitting at the dressing table, Sabrina brushed out the long waves. There were curls buried in the mass, strands that Charity had styled with an iron as part of her style for the rout. Sabrina looked in the mirror and saw herself but didn't quite recognize the image.

The knock on the door nearly made her drop the brush. Sabrina's pulse sped as she set the implement down and slowly rose. Glancing toward the bed, she didn't have a dressing gown laid out. Because she'd told Charity it wasn't necessary. Sabrina had planned on retiring immediately. She hadn't expected a visitor.

Padding to the door on bare feet, she opened it to find, unsurprisingly, her husband. He wore a dark gray silk banyan over the black kerseymere pantaloons he'd worn to the rout. At least, she thought they were the same ones. Most of his clothing was black, gray, dark blue, or dark brown, and he presumably had multiples of everything.

How like her mind to fixate on such things when faced with an anxious situation. Such as her husband showing up at her door unexpectedly.

"Good evening." She hoped she didn't sound nervous. "Do you want to come in?"

"I thought I might." His voice was tight, and his words lacked certainty. Perhaps he was nervous too.

Sabrina opened the door wider and stepped to the side to allow him entry. His gaze briefly dipped over her. He didn't stare at her as when she'd worn the new pink dressing gown the other night.

When he moved into the room, she closed the door. He paused near the bed, pivoting toward her. "Did you enjoy yourself at the rout?"

"Yes. Did you? I noticed you left early."

"I went to White's."

She noted he didn't respond about whether he'd enjoyed himself. "I can understand wanting to find a haven after the crush of the rout. I am rather tired from it, I admit."

"Should I go?"

She wanted to say yes, because she hadn't prepared herself for this tonight. But that was silly. This was what she wanted, and she shouldn't have to work up her courage on a nightly basis. "No, you should stay. That is, um, the purpose of my being in London." Heat began to climb her throat, and she willed herself to remain calm.

"Shall we get to it then?" he asked tentatively. "We can go quickly as we've done before—just get through it."

As if it were a transaction, which she supposed their entire marriage was. A gaping sadness threatened to grip her chest.

"Might we go a *little* more slowly?" Pausing, she forced herself to say the next part even though humiliation burned her cheeks. "I'd like to have an orgasm."

His eyes widened for a second, and he turned his attention to the coals burning in the hearth. "Yes, that can certainly, ah, be accommodated. I apologize for not taking that into consideration before. I'd only meant to keep your distress to a minimum."

He still didn't look at her, and she couldn't blame him. Everything about their marriage had been forced and awkward. It *was* a bloody business transaction. The question was whether they wanted it to remain that way.

The only definite answer she had at the moment was that she wanted a child. And she preferred to go about it in a more pleasurable way.

"I appreciate your concern," she said softly. "I always have, even if I didn't say so. I apologize for being so anxious. I have never known what to expect."

He turned his gaze to hers, the green in his eyes vibrant in the candlelight. "Yet you now know about orgasms. This must be part of how you are trying to be *different*."

Sabrina fidgeted with her night rail, her fingers twisting into the cotton. Willing herself to relax, she dropped her hands to her sides and steeled her spine. "You certainly didn't tell me about them."

The sharp intake of his breath was satisfying. "No, I did not. As I said, I focused on trying to ease your discomfort. Perhaps I should have done things differently. I do wonder how you have become…educated."

The flame she'd felt when she'd said the word orgasm returned even hotter to her face. "I have a book. Should I get onto the bed?" That's what they'd done before.

"Since we want this to be different, no. I'm going to remove my banyan. Is that all right?"

Nodding, Sabrina held her breath. He untied the sash and shrugged out of the garment before draping it at the end of the bed.

There was a candle on the bedside table and the hearth was behind him. A brighter lantern sat on her dressing table. It was the most light in which she'd seen him without clothing. Typically, when they were at Hampton Lodge, he joined her in the bed, with the drapes drawn, while a single candle burned elsewhere in the chamber.

His chest was pale and muscled with a patch of brown hair between his nipples that narrowed as it trailed down his abdomen. She couldn't help but stare at him, enthralled with his form, as she wondered what it would feel like to run her fingertips across his nipples as she'd done to herself. Did that feel as good to a man as it did to her?

He inched toward her, and she instantly tensed, hoping he didn't notice. "May I remove your night rail?"

"I'll do it." Closing her eyes, she whipped it over her head before she lost all semblance of courage.

When she finally opened her eyes, it was to see him staring at her, his eyes slitted. She couldn't read his expression. Perhaps she should have let him take the garment off as he'd requested.

The urge to cover herself with her hands was great, but

she summoned the steel that Evie had said she possessed to stand straight. She might quiver, but she would not bend.

"May I touch you?" He'd asked her permission on every occasion. As with each time before, she murmured in the affirmative. Unlike their prior encounters, however, her shivers were not entirely due to apprehension. Now that her body knew there could be pleasure, there was a nudge of anticipation.

He touched her hair, his fingers gliding over the locks before he gently tugged on a curl. She hadn't expected that and let out a soft gasp.

"I've never seen your hair down." His voice was soft and captivating. It settled her a bit, and she wondered if this time might truly be different.

"I hadn't braided it yet."

"It's...lovely. *You're* lovely." His gaze dropped, leaving no question as to what he was looking at. Her. He was looking at *her*.

Again, she wanted to wrap a hand over her breasts, but she resisted. She did not, however, stop herself from moving one hand in front of her sex.

He met her eyes. "Are you certain you want me to stay?"

She moved her arm back to her side. "Yes."

There was a long moment in which they only looked at each other. She suspected he was waiting to see if she would change her mind. She had to be clear, to make a move.

Hardly any space separated them, but it was enough for her to take a small step. Her breasts didn't quite touch his chest, but her nipples tightened at his proximity.

He bent his head and kissed her cheek, his lips soft and gentle against her. Sabrina closed her eyes, both because it was easier and because she wanted to focus on the feel of him instead of the anxiety of what was to come.

His lips moved to her jaw before descending to her neck

with whisper-silk kisses that barely teased her flesh. He clasped her nape, his touch light, while his other hand skimmed from her shoulder down over her breast. When his palm stroked over her nipple, she bit her lower lip as sensation rippled through her and bloomed in her sex.

However, his hand didn't linger on her breast. He continued downward, grazing her belly, until his knuckles swept along her curls. Her breath snagged, and her muscles tensed. In the past, he'd stroked her there—soft, surface brushes before he positioned his sex at her opening.

But he was still clothed from the waist down, and they were standing up. Sabrina struggled to imagine what he would do in this position, but she'd seen drawings of couples having sex standing up in the book Evie had given her. Perhaps her lack of imagination was because her thoughts were consumed with the very real things that were happening right now instead of possibilities.

When his fingertips slid across her folds, she jerked. He withdrew his hands from her but didn't step back.

Sabrina opened her eyes. "I didn't mean to do that."

"I can stop." He'd offered that too on many occasions, and she'd never once asked him to.

She shook her head. "Please continue."

He didn't resume touching her. "Do you want to get on the bed?"

"Yes." Then she wouldn't be able to feel her legs shake. She went around to the side and slid onto the coverlet where she reclined against the pillows.

He joined her on the bed, his pantaloons still fastened, and moved between her legs. "Have I ever hurt you?" he asked, surprising her.

"No. I mean, the first time was uncomfortable, but that is to be expected."

"I know you wanted to go more slowly, but perhaps we

should move this along tonight. With an orgasm." A faint smile swept across his mouth, and she tried to relax her body into the mattress.

He was different too. He was always in control of himself —ruthlessly so—but she sensed something else. She just wasn't sure what it was. Perhaps it was the discussion of orgasms. A giggle threatened to burst forth, but she held it back.

Leaning down, he brushed his mouth over hers. Once, twice, a third time, and with each pass, she felt a tug of desire in her belly. He kissed down her throat again as his hand lightly caressed the outer edge of her breast.

The contact jolted her, making her gasp again. He hesitated, and she wished she could stop deterring him with the sounds she was making. Intent on staying quiet, she clamped her teeth together and gathered the coverlet in her hands, gripping the fabric.

He touched her again, stroking her in a circle, his fingertip barely touching her nipple. Sabrina squeezed her eyes closed.

She felt his hand between her legs again, sweeping against her thigh before finding her sheath. This was familiar, the gentle seeking of his fingertips. But since the last time he'd done this, she'd put her own fingers there.

Rotating her hips, she tried to capture the sensations she'd aroused in herself as he moved upon her. He used his thumb to tease her, and she gasped yet again. However, he didn't stop. She felt him unfasten his pantaloons and for the first time, she anticipated him—how he would feel as he filled her.

His finger slid inside her, then stroked back up to massage her clitoris. That was the spot she really loved. She could find release when she only touched that part of herself, but when she put her fingers inside, everything intensified.

Suddenly he was there—his sex nudging hers. This was the moment she always tensed, her body tightening as she braced for his invasion. Tonight, she willed herself to stay loose—as much as she could—and welcome him.

When he was fully inside, he didn't withdraw his hand. This was new. He kept it between them and went back to stroking her clitoris.

"Oh!" She failed again at keeping herself from making a sound and once more clamped her jaw shut. For good measure, she brought her hand up and put the back against her lips.

His hips moved in tandem with his hand, thrusting into her as he coaxed pleasure from her restless body. For the first time, she knew what was within reach, felt more than a vague desire.

He braced his hands on either side of her head and leaned down. "Lift your legs, put them around me," he whispered.

Yes, of course. The image from the book flashed behind her closed eyes. In it, the woman's legs were wrapped around the man's hips, her feet digging into his backside. Tentatively, she curled her legs around him. This opened her in a new way, allowing him to drive deeper. She pressed her hand into her mouth, her teeth grazing her flesh.

He moved faster, his hips thrusting between her legs, making her intensely aware of his body and what he was doing. To her.

The drawing from the book rose in her mind once more. The woman's head was cast back as the man kissed her throat. And her mouth was open.

Should she feel free to make sounds? It seemed so...primitive. Surely, he would be horrified. She tried to recall if he'd made noise during their previous encounters.

His hand was suddenly between them again, teasing and taunting her, provoking a deep, desperate pulse in her sex.

This was what she'd learned—this need for release. Only having him inside her was better. There was no discomfort, no uncertainty. On the contrary, this felt like the most natural, wonderful thing in the world.

"Come," he said urgently, his lips against her ear. He worked her clitoris with a frenzy, devoting his entire focus to that part of her. Her muscles clenched as the now familiar rush of impending orgasm raced toward her.

She dropped her hand to the side and sucked in air as he pumped into her hard and fast. *There.* Satisfaction flooded her—far longer and more acutely than when she'd been alone.

As her body began to return to its normal state, he let out a dark cry. She recognized his release. Had he made that sound before? She honestly didn't know.

His body rocked into hers several more times before he collapsed—gently—atop her. Would this be the time his seed finally rooted?

He didn't stay with her long before rolling to his side and then off the bed. A bare moment later, he set her night rail beside her.

"Thank you," she murmured, drawing it over her head.

"Are you all right?" He asked the same question every time after they finished.

"Yes." She always answered yes. "Quite," she added, looking over at him and feeling suddenly shy and embarrassed when his gaze locked with hers.

"Er, good." He'd fastened his pantaloons and now pulled his banyan on, covering his shoulders.

Which she hadn't managed to touch once. In fact, she hadn't touched him at all.

"Well, good night, then." He tied the sash at his waist on the way to the door and was gone.

Sabrina bolted upright. She should go after him. Tell him

she meant to touch him, that she was just woefully out of her element, despite demanding this.

Damn.

She'd thought that had gone better—it had certainly felt better. But she wasn't convinced that it was a great improvement. He still hadn't removed all his clothing, and he hadn't lingered more than was necessary. What did she expect when she couldn't seem to stop gasping and had failed to touch him? Whereas he'd asked her repeatedly if this was what she wanted. It seemed he was trying, and she was only slightly less reserved than she'd been before.

"I need more help," she said to no one as she stared at the ceiling. Evie would guide her. Sabrina just hoped she could act on it as well as she'd done with her solo enterprise.

Unless... What if she became pregnant tonight? She wouldn't know for weeks, so that was a moot issue. She needed to continue sharing her bed with Aldington, and dammit, she wanted it to be better than this.

The question was whether he wanted that too.

CHAPTER 8

$\mathcal{C}$onstantine didn't know how long he'd lain awake last night, his mind going over—and over—their coupling. Just when he convinced himself she'd enjoyed it, *finally*, doubt crept back in. Had she actually orgasmed? He wasn't entirely certain. It had felt like it, but his experience was admittedly thin.

She hadn't moaned or even touched him, aside from putting her legs around his waist, which he'd suggested she do. She'd made a few noises, but he'd also noted that she put her hand over her mouth. Had that been to keep herself from asking him to stop?

Then she'd done that thing with her hips—moving them in a…provocative way. Now he was back to believing she *had* enjoyed herself.

You could just bloody ask.

She would probably say she was doing what was necessary to have a child. That was, after all, why she'd come to London. If she could have an orgasm along the way, so much the better.

He couldn't spend all day worrying over this; he needed

to change for his racing meeting. Hopefully, he wouldn't encounter her in their sitting room when he went upstairs. They'd managed to avoid each other all day, which was typical and probably for the best.

As he stood from behind his desk, a dark gray…*something* dashed into the study and disappeared behind the blue drapes framing the window. Haddock stepped in through the half-open door. For the first time in Constantine's experience, the man looked harried.

"I beg your pardon, my lord, did, ah, something run in here?" The butler glanced about the room, his eyes darting wildly.

"Something, yes. What is going on, Haddock?"

"It's a cat, my lord. Where did he go?"

A cat? What the devil was a cat doing in the house? Constantine went toward the draperies. "He disappeared behind these." He grasped the thick fabric and pulled it aside only to see the same flash of gray take off back to the door.

Haddock turned and lunged forward. "Grayson!"

Grayson?

The butler's foot must have caught the doorframe, for he went sprawling forward onto the floor over the threshold into the parlor. Constantine had never seen the man in such an ignominious state.

"John!" The voice of Constantine's housekeeper was almost unrecognizable as the single word trilled at an impossibly high volume and pitch.

Mrs. Haddock rushed into the parlor and knelt beside her husband. In her late thirties, Mrs. Haddock possessed a small stature, which was at odds with her sense of command. She led the household with a firm but kind hand. She was also pretty, with an engaging smile and serene blue-green eyes that never failed to put one at ease. It was no wonder Haddock had married her three years ago.

"I'm fine," Haddock grumbled as he got to his feet with his wife's help.

Lady Aldington came into the parlor, her features a mask of concern beneath the brim of her bonnet, indicating she was on her way out. Her gaze went directly to the butler and housekeeper who stood together. Mrs. Haddock's arm was around her husband's waist.

"What happened?" the countess asked with alarm. "It sounded as if someone fell down."

"Haddock tripped," Constantine said. "There is a cat in the house." He turned his attention to the butler. "How did that happen exactly?"

The butler and housekeeper exchanged sheepish looks. "It's my cat," Mrs. Haddock said.

Haddock put his arm around his wife's shoulders and held her against his side. "It's *our* cat. We began feeding it a few months ago. It was just a wee kitten."

"And it was very cold outside," Mrs. Haddock put in, her features taut. "So we let him come in at night."

Constantine had never seen his butler and housekeeper like this. And it wasn't just because of the obvious affection they were displaying toward each other. They were united, facing a situation they knew could get them into trouble, or worse, terminated. Constantine glanced toward his wife and wondered if they would ever behave like that.

"We deeply apologize, my lord," Haddock said. "We will find Grayson with due haste and expel him from the house."

Mrs. Haddock's face paled, but she said nothing.

"You'll do no such thing," Lady Aldington said, coming farther into the room, her gloves clutched in one hand. She wore another ensemble Constantine had never seen before. This was a dark blue walking gown with a military-fashioned spencer sporting two vertical rows of gold buttons.

"There is no harm in having a cat. Did you say his name was Grayson?"

"He is gray, my lady," Mrs. Haddock said softly. "And he has been a bit like a son to us." She looked up at her husband, emotion glowing in her gaze.

"Well, that is just lovely," Lady Aldington whispered. She moved to stand near Constantine, close enough that he could smell her vanilla-apple scent. Suddenly, all he could think of was last night—the lush curve of her breast, the sweet clasp of her legs around him as he drove into her. "Allow them to keep the cat. Please."

Constantine blinked as he pulled his thoughts from distraction. "He must be managed—contained. At least at certain times. He can't run roughshod about the house when we have guests." They rarely ever had guests, and even then, it was only family. Still, his father and Lady Aldington's parents would likely be horrified to see an animal running about. The thought of it nearly made him laugh.

"Why are you smiling?" Lady Aldington asked, sounding bemused.

"No reason." Constantine coughed. "We must find this cat at once. I take it this is the first time he's run amok?"

"Yes, my lord," Haddock replied, taking his arm from his wife.

Mrs. Haddock slid her arm from her husband's waist and moved to the side. "I do apologize for this wholly inappropriate interlude."

"Nonsense," Lady Aldington said, surprising everyone in the room with her firm tone. "I'm glad you helped this poor kitten, and why shouldn't you welcome him into your family? Is there anything we can do to coax Grayson out? Does he have a favorite treat or a toy?"

Constantine stared at the woman who was taking charge of this situation. He kept repeating himself, but by God she *was* different. Meanwhile, all he could think was where did this cat live? Did the Haddocks carry him upstairs to their suite of rooms on the uppermost floor? If so, how did he get outside from there?

However, rather than demand answers to these questions, he decided perhaps he should change a bit too. Indeed, why *shouldn't* his married butler and housekeeper have a pet cat?

Because this isn't their house!

The response speared into his head in his father's voice, as most admonitions did. This one in particular pricked Constantine's ire. It may not be the Haddocks' house, but they effectively ran it. The household would be a shambles if not for them. So yes, they could have a bloody cat.

"I'll go down to the kitchen to fetch a kidney. Those are his favorite." Mrs. Haddock started toward the door.

"And I'll find the stuffed mouse Mrs. Haddock made for him." Haddock cocked his head to the side. 'It doesn't really look like a mouse, just a small stuffed...*thing*. We call it his mouse, however. He is rather good at catching the real ones, my lord. If that helps to soften your opinion." The butler gave him a feeble smile before departing.

"Does my opinion seem hard?" Constantine threw the query out to the room at large, but since only his wife remained, she was the one to respond.

"You always seem...cool. Not hard, though."

He turned toward her. "I thought you said I was dispassionate."

"And cool. Perhaps." Light swathes of pink flashed across her cheeks.

Dispassionate and cool were not wrong. That was who his father had schooled him to be. When Constantine thought of his siblings, those words didn't come to mind. But perhaps this was who he truly was. Except why then did he have a sudden urge to show the countess that he could be heated and…impassioned?

"Perhaps I will be different too," he murmured.

Her lips parted, and he wanted to kiss her in a thoroughly different fashion than he had last night. He'd never opened his mouth against hers or put his tongue inside or invited hers. Would she recoil if he attempted such a thing? She'd appeared to do that last night when he'd lightly touched her breast. But then she'd also seemed to enjoy his hand on her sex.

"There he is!" Sabrina dropped her gloves and flew after the gray streak as it dashed toward the bloody window draperies again.

"He loves drapes," Constantine muttered as he joined the chase. "Careful. Cats have sharp claws."

"Close the doors so he can't get out!" She pulled the draperies aside, and the cat ran out into the room.

Constantine dove for the doors that led to the dining room and then for the one that opened to the corridor from the stair hall, slamming them closed more quickly and loudly than he normally would.

"He's in your study again!" Lady Aldington called.

Turning on his heel, Constantine ran into the study and shut the door behind him. Lady Aldington was on her knees near the window.

"Is he hiding in the drapes again?" Constantine asked.

"Shh. I'm going to wait patiently. I think he's scared."

Constantine didn't have all day. He had a racing club meeting and needed to go upstairs to change. But then the view of his wife's backside could likely persuade him to ignore everything he had planned.

"I suppose we should fetch Haddock or Mrs. Haddock," she suggested. "Grayson will likely feel more comfortable with them." She looked back at Constantine over her shoulder. "You could go fetch one of them while I stay here."

There was something very wrong with him. Watching her in this position made him want to strip her bare and take her from behind in the most obscene way. He imagined the bare flesh of her back, exposed as it had been at the rout last night. Blood rushed to his cock. What was happening to him? He'd never fantasized about her like this, certainly not to the extent he was in the past quarter bloody hour.

Just then, the cat ran from the draperies, his trajectory aimed for the door. Constantine threw himself backward and grasped for the ball of gray fur. He plucked up the animal and held it tightly. Which Grayson did not appreciate, for he swiped at Constantine's chest.

He held the cat up. "No need to be rude. I'm only trying to help."

Grayson stared at him with wide yellow eyes. He really was still a kitten, certainly not an adult, with whiskers that were much too large for his face.

"You're a handsome lad," Constantine said softly, recalling the kittens that had lived at Woodbreak in his youth. His mother had loved to care for the litters every spring.

Without warning, Grayson lashed out at Constantine's chin with his paw.

"Ow!" Constantine dropped the cat and brought his hand to his chin.

"Oh no!" Lady Aldington stood and rushed to stand before him. "Did he scratch you?"

"Yes." The pain in his chin was sharp. "Apparently I offended him by calling him handsome."

"Cats are known to be particular."

"Where did he go?"

"Back under the draperies."

Constantine glared in that direction. "You're an unsightly, unrepentant miscreant! Is that more to your liking?"

The countess sucked in a breath. "That's not nice."

"It's a ploy," Constantine whispered. "If he doesn't like compliments, perhaps he prefers insults."

"Oh." Her eyes lit with mirth. She went back to the draperies and knelt once more. "Come out now, Grayson, you horrid little scamp."

"Scamp may be too nice," Constantine cautioned. He pulled his hand from his chin and saw that there was blood. Damn. Without a handkerchief, he pulled his cravat off and dabbed at the wound.

"Grayson, come on, you menace," she coaxed in a singsong voice that made Constantine smile. Suddenly, a dark nose appeared beneath the hem of the curtain. "There you are, you fiend."

A moment later, the cat crept carefully from the drape and sniffed at the countess. She held out her finger, which he practically inhaled in his efforts to conduct his olfactory investigation. The countess laid herself flat on the carpet and rolled to her side. "Is this better? Now I'm not lurking over you."

Constantine moved closer—slowly and quietly—to obtain a better view. He just managed to see Grayson put his paw on Lady Aldington's chest as if he were trying to push her onto her back. She must have thought the same thing, for she rolled to her back with a smile. "Is *this* better?"

In response, Grayson sniffed her some more before climbing onto her chest and sitting down as if he were a small loaf of dark gray bread.

Lady Aldington looked up at Constantine, her lips curling into the most charming smile he'd ever seen her wear. He was captivated. No, more than that. He simply couldn't look away. Nor could he not smile in return.

"Grayson prefers you to me. Smart cat."

A laugh escaped her lips, and Grayson started. The countess clapped her hand over her mouth, but her eyes still danced with amusement. Constantine started to laugh too, in spite of the still aching slash across his chin.

The door to the study opened, and Mrs. Haddock stood at the threshold. "Grayson! You naughty boy!"

The cat leapt off Lady Aldington and ran to his mama, who scooped him up with one arm. She held a small bowl of something—presumably kidney—in her other hand. "There you go," she murmured as the cat dipped his face into the bowl. "I'm so sorry, my lord," Mrs. Haddock said earnestly. "This will never happen again."

Constantine honestly didn't care if it did. The event had been the most entertaining and enlivening thing that had ever happened in this house. "So long as he stays out of sight when we have guests, Grayson is not a problem." He lowered the cravat from his chin.

Mrs. Haddock's jaw dropped. "Oh no, did he do that?"

"I'm afraid so," Constantine glanced at the blood stains on the white silk.

"My deepest apologies, my lord. If you want us to turn him out, we will at once." The housekeeper looked pained as she made the offer.

"Not at all. He's a cat, and Lady Aldington has reminded me that they are particular. It seems he prefers the countess to me."

"He also prefers me to Haddock," Mrs. Haddock said with a commiserative nod. "Which causes poor Haddock a bit of distress, I'm afraid. Don't tell him I told you." Grayson began to twitch in her grasp. "I'd best get him downstairs. Again, my apologies. And gratitude." After dipping a brief curtsey, she left, closing the door behind her, which Constantine found odd.

"See, Grayson does respond to insults," Lady Aldington noted from the floor. "Mrs. Haddock called him naughty, and he went right to her."

Constantine turned toward his wife as she rolled to her side. He crouched down to help her up. "I'm sorry to have left you down there."

As she stood, they were practically in his each other's arms, so close that he could lean down and kiss her as he'd thought of doing earlier.

"I'm quite all right." She smiled broadly. "That was certainly entertaining."

"I thought the same thing."

"Did you?" She seemed genuinely surprised. Then she did the most remarkable thing, she lifted her hand and gently caressed his chin. "Does it hurt?"

"A bit." He felt slightly off balance. This was not the behavior of someone who loathed him. Perhaps she was trying to make the best of their marriage, as he was hoping to do.

She glanced toward the open neck of his shirt, and he could have sworn she blushed the barest amount. "You should go upstairs and clean it. Perhaps apply some of the salve you used on your hand."

He was tempted to ask if she would help him, but that sounded rather like flirting, and he didn't flirt. But he wanted to. With her.

She lowered her hand, and he was unaccountably disappointed. "That was very kind of you to allow them to keep their cat, especially after he wounded you."

"Cats are cats. My mother used to let us tend the kittens at Woodbreak when we were children. I'd all but forgotten that."

"How lovely," she said softly, her eyes sparkling with warmth. Again, he was struck by her demeanor. How could he think she still hated him as she had in the beginning? "You like cats then?"

"I never gave it much thought—not in years. But I suppose I don't mind them."

"I love that he seems to be a family member for the Haddocks. I feel as if we caught a glimpse of who they really are today." She glanced away briefly. "It makes you think about how we all put up a façade for the roles we play, whether we are in service or peers of the realm."

She was talking about him. Did she see him as having a façade?

Or was she referring to herself? Was she now playing the role of happy countess in order to have a child?

Her gaze dipped to where her gloves lay on the floor. "I should be going."

Constantine went to retrieve the accessories. When he handed them to her, his fingers brushed her hand, and the connection raced through him, heating his blood and quickening his pulse. Ignoring the sensations, he asked, "Where are you off to?"

"I'm visiting the modiste to pick up a ball gown. Then I shall pay a call on Mrs. Renshaw."

"Do you have plans for this ball gown?" He wondered if it exposed as much of her back as last night's ensemble.

"I thought I might wear it to the Hargrove ball on Saturday. Are you planning to attend?"

"I will now that you are."

Another flash of surprise brightened her gaze. "Will we go together then?"

"I can't see why not. If I'd known you were going to the rout last night, I would have accompanied you." It was the courteous thing to do, and they were, for better or worse, married.

You want to go with her, a voice at the back of his mind whispered.

"I assumed you would be late at Westminster, as you so often are." The typical stiffness of their dialogue had crept back after the ease of their earlier conversation. Because of a cat. Perhaps he should have Haddock find another.

Could that conviviality extend to the bedchamber? Or would things continue to be tense? Last night had been a slight improvement, but Constantine still felt as though there was a canyon between them. Perhaps he *should* consult with Lucien's tutor. What harm could come from a meeting? As Lucien had said, they didn't need to have sexual intercourse for Constantine to learn what he needed to.

"I can make accommodations," he said with regard to accompanying her to events.

"Oh. I should not have assumed," she said softly. "I'll endeavor not to do that in future. Shall we make a point of sharing our social plans?"

"I think that would be beneficial. And don't apologize. I have been too busy, and perhaps I should not be. I should have accompanied you to the rout last night, and I should not have left."

She hesitated a moment, her eyes locked on him with perhaps a glimmer of disbelief in their depths. "I had Evie at my side."

Evie. Evangeline Renshaw. "You have become quite friendly with Mrs. Renshaw. I didn't even realize you knew each other. I will pay more attention to your friends and acquaintances."

She arched a brow at him. "Why? So you can decide if they are appropriate?"

His eyes widened briefly. "Heavens no, why would you think that?"

Her lips parted, and she glanced away. "My apologies. I

am used to my parents dictating everything I did, including who I could become friends with."

"I understand," he said wryly. "My father voices his opinion on nearly every aspect of my life."

"He still does that?" At his nod, she added, "Well, I'm... sorry. He should recognize you are your own man and don't require his opinion—or approval—about anything."

Her support lit something inside him, spreading an unfamiliar warmth. "Yes, he should."

"To answer your question, Mrs. Renshaw and I have only recently become acquainted. I like her a great deal. She's been very helpful, particularly with my new wardrobe."

"Then I shall thank her. The gown you wore last night was stunning. As is your walking costume." He glanced over her but didn't dare look too long lest he start undressing her in his head once more.

"I was afraid you didn't approve of my dress last night."

He heard the uneasiness underlying her tone and regretted his behavior at the rout. "I was surprised by it." *By you.* "I apologize if my comments made you upset or uncomfortable. You must wear what you wish."

"Even if it displays too much flesh?" The question was dangerously close to flirtatious.

Constantine still couldn't bring himself to flirt in return. Because what if she wasn't being coy? What if she was genuinely concerned? He wanted to alleviate any apprehension she may have. "I trust you to dress appropriately. I cannot, however, promise not to feel a strong possession if other gentlemen feast upon the display."

Possession.

Her attention dipped to his open neckline once more, provoking another flash of longing. "I'll keep that in mind," she murmured.

"I need to go change before my racing club meeting." He

said this in response to his state of undress and also to prompt himself to go. Strangely, that was proving difficult. "Afterward, I plan to call on my father to discuss your becoming Cassandra's sponsor."

Her red-gold brows rose. "Thank you."

"You're certain this is what you wish? You'll have to attend a great many events, and my father will be watching to see how Cassandra's Season progresses."

She hesitated, and he glimpsed conflict in her expression. "Yes, I'm sure. I want to do it."

"Very well. I'll speak with him and let you know what he says this evening. Shall we dine together then? I will not be at Westminster since it is Wednesday." His lungs squeezed as he awaited her response.

Exhaling, she smiled. "That would be lovely."

He breathed a sigh of relief. Mayhap she wasn't just seeking a child at any cost, and there was more behind her new behavior. "Excellent, I'll look forward to it." He stood aside and gestured to the door. "After you, my lady."

"Thank you." She didn't move for a moment, then took a final glance at his exposed neck and left the study.

Perhaps there was hope for them yet. Another reason to move things along with the help of a tutor. Constantine would send a note to Lucien immediately.

CHAPTER 9

*S*abrina sat across from Evie at a round table in her
drawing room. Her butler had placed a plate of
biscuits and a pot of tea between them. As Evie poured their
cups, Sabrina pulled an invitation from the Phoenix Club
from her reticule. She'd received it earlier that day but hadn't
mentioned it to Aldington. It wasn't that she'd planned to *not*
tell him, but she'd been nervous about his reaction. Plus, with
the Grayson situation, the issue hadn't come up.

She'd been too distracted. Pleasantly so.

"Is that what I think it is?" Evie asked, setting the pot
down.

"I think you know," Sabrina said with a smile. "You must
be the reason I received it. And Lucien, I should think."

"We did recommend you. Highly." Evie arched her brows
playfully as she moved a cup toward Sabrina. "I'm so pleased
the membership committee saw fit to extend the invitation,
but I am not surprised."

"Why? I realize I'm the wife of an earl, but he is not a
member." Even if he was the owner's brother.

"Unlike other clubs, status, like gender, has nothing to do

with whether one is welcome at the Phoenix Club. One's individual character is far more important. The Phoenix Club is a haven for those who are more concerned with finding a place where they feel welcome and comfortable. Where they can be their true selves and not what Society expects or demands them to be."

Sabrina hadn't known the club served such a purpose. And it was all her brother-in-law's doing. Why had she *ever* been intimidated by him? Because he was handsome and confident? That seemed so silly now. "Lucien possesses a surprisingly thoughtful nature."

"He goes out of his way to help anyone, but that's not what Society expects of him." Evie stirred her tea. "I think that's why he does it."

"I admire that he is confounding expectations."

"That's what you're doing too." Evie's mouth curved into a satisfied smile. "Aldington was rather flustered by you last night. Does he know about the invitation?"

Sabrina shook her head. "Since he is not a member, I assume he does not approve of the club. He's rarely mentioned it and when he has, it's been with disdain."

"He has never been invited. That may be the true source of his derision."

Now Sabrina was even more nervous about sharing the news with him. "How can I tell him I've been invited when he has not?"

"He can't hold it against you," Evie said firmly. "You've nothing to do with who is invited and who is not."

While that was true, her concern came from more than that. "I don't want to cause any strife between him and Lucien. They seem to struggle sometimes as it is, and I would hate to contribute to any difficulty."

"You can't feel responsible for their relationship. They'll get on fine—or not—with or without you. Besides, it seems they have reached an accord as of late. In any case, I hope you plan to accept the invitation. I'd love for you to join me at the assembly on Friday."

"I do, and I would enjoy that too." Even if she was apprehensive about her husband's reaction. The entire interlude with the Haddocks and the cat had been so lovely, as if he too wanted to find some harmony in their union. But then there was last night, which they'd rather neatly avoided talking about. "I shall have to think of a way to break the news to Aldington."

"He won't be angry, will he?"

Sabrina sampled her tea. "No, he doesn't typically get angry. Frustrated perhaps, especially since I've returned to town."

"Because he doesn't know what to make of you." Evie took a biscuit from the plate. "Oh, but his reaction at the rout was delicious. He hated that other men were flirting with you and perhaps that you seemed to enjoy it."

"You really think he was jealous?" Was that the reason he'd come to her chamber last night? Could it be that he actually wanted her? Or did he merely feel a sense of possession because she was his wife? He'd used that word earlier, and it had provoked a sharp, primal response within her.

"He certainly seemed to be, or perhaps he thought you were provoking him." Evie looked at her expectantly.

Sabrina certainly hadn't done so on purpose. "I wasn't flirting."

"No? You sparkled with vivacity and charm. What's more, you looked completely at ease."

She hadn't been. Inside, she'd been a tangle of anxiety. Laughing softly, she said, "Then I pulled off quite an act."

Evie cocked her head. "Are you saying that wasn't really you?"

"It was me. Rather, the new me. But it takes effort." She

realized it was akin to assuming a role on the stage, or what she imagined that might be like. It all took effort, and she was more than willing to do what was necessary to get what she wanted—a child. That was still her primary goal in all of this, and after last night, she needed more help. "Aldington visited my bedchamber last night," she said softly, not quite meeting Evie's gaze.

"My goodness, why didn't you tell me that straightaway?"

"I suppose I am still rather embarrassed—or at least self-conscious—about the matter." She winced inwardly as she recalled her behavior in bed, then grabbed a biscuit from the tray and took too large of a bite in order to avoid saying more.

Evie's brows pinched together. "You're feeling comfortable with yourself, yes? Your body, I mean."

"Er, I thought so." Sabrina frowned down at her teacup. "But when he was there and things were…happening, I was still incredibly nervous. I didn't know what to do with him. With my…reaction."

"What happened?"

Sabrina lifted her gaze. "I kept making noises, which seemed to bother him. Or at least surprise him. So I put my hand over my mouth to stop from doing it. And I didn't touch him, and I should have. I did, however, have an orgasm."

Evie didn't exactly frown, but her brow creased with concern. "Well, the last part is an improvement, isn't it?"

"Definitely, but it was still awkward. We seem to suffer from an inability to communicate our…desires." Why was this so unbelievably painful to discuss? And it was even more difficult to do so with her husband—Sabrina couldn't even summon the nerve!

"I think you may both benefit from a situation where

your reticence can be set aside. As it happens, Lucien and I have come up with a plan that will facilitate this."

Sabrina drank some tea to wash down the biscuit. Her mouth was suddenly drier than it was a moment ago. "I can't even begin to comprehend what that could be."

"Lucien has determined that Aldington has some sort of wall that he must break down with regard to you and sex. He's suggested that Aldington work with a tutor to breach that wall."

Sabrina was glad she hadn't taken another drink of tea, for she most definitely would have swallowed it down wrong. "A tutor? Who would do that?" His mistress, perhaps?

Evie gave her a sly look. "You, but Aldington won't know that."

"*Me*?" Sabrina gaped at Evie. "I could never. I hardly know what to do." As evidenced last night. "I'm an utter failure when it comes to him."

"But you haven't been in finding pleasure—you had an orgasm last night. This is progress! Now, you just need to allow yourself to respond. You must absolutely make whatever noises you want, *and* you should touch him. If he doesn't know you're you, would that make these things easier to do?"

The idea that she could act a role returned to her mind. When she'd put on the cobalt gown last night, she'd looked and felt like a confident, elegant countess, perhaps for the first time. It had helped her to actually have the confidence to not only attend the rout, but as Evie had said, *sparkle*. And when she'd donned the seductive dressing gown to entice Aldington, she'd looked like a woman who was eager for her husband to join her in the marriage bed, and again she'd felt more self-assured, even if it had been fleeting.

"He wouldn't know it's me, so I could be anyone…" Her mind chased that thought, conjuring things she might say—

or do—to him if he didn't know it was her. "Aldington agreed to this?"

Evie nodded. "I received a note from Lucien just before you arrived."

He must have decided today then. Apparently, he'd seen last night as a failure too. A new wave of anxiety threatened to overwhelm her, but she refused to succumb. She wanted a child, and this was how she was going to get it.

"Who does Aldington think this tutor will be?"

"A former courtesan who is eager to help someone. And who enjoys sex."

A laugh burst from Sabrina. "This will take quite a bit of playacting from me." She paused. "Why isn't his mistress performing this task?"

Evie shook her head. "He doesn't have one and apparently never has."

Sabrina was surprised to hear this. Why had he not ever taken a mistress? "But now he's willing to meet with a former courtesan?"

"Apparently he recognizes he needs help in how to seduce you. You needn't have sexual intercourse with him or touch each other at all, really. You must simply play the role of an expert in these matters."

Another laugh leapt from Sabrina. "*Simply.*" The wild scheme was beginning to take root in her mind. "You really believe I can do this?"

"I do." Evie's eyes glowed with conviction. "You have the book, you've discovered what you like, you even had an orgasm *with* your husband. Just focus on being assertive and letting down your guard."

She was to give him lessons in seduction. There was something strangely arousing about being with Aldington without him knowing who she was. "I'm still trying to determine how this will work. And whether I can summon the courage—and skills—necessary to behave like someone who enjoys sex."

"But you do," Evie said simply. "Or you will, when you have more of it. You've enjoyed having orgasms, have you not?"

"Well, yes." An unavoidable blush rose up her neck and into her face. "How is it he won't know my identity? Is it to be pitch dark?"

"Mostly. He will also be blindfolded, so there will be no chance for him to see you. Just in case, you must also wear a mask, in case the blindfold slips at all."

"I would have to disguise my voice, I would think."

"Yes, that's probably a good idea. Can you do that?"

"I think so. What if Aldington realizes it's me?"

"He won't, unless you think he might recognize your body when he touches you."

A laugh bubbled inside her, but Sabrina didn't let it out. "If he can, I'll be impressed. When is this to happen?" She needed plenty of time to prepare.

"Tomorrow night."

Sabrina had picked up her teacup and practically sloshed the remaining contents down her lap. Setting it back down with a clack, she gaped at Evie. "That's too soon!"

"You can be ready." She gave Sabrina an encouraging smile. "You've already done so much—you've been open to learning what you need to do, and you were brilliant at the rout. Just coming to London and demanding your marital rights was a massive leap."

Sabrina wasn't sure she agreed that she was ready, but she *had* come a long way. It would be foolish to not seize this opportunity, especially if Aldington was open to improving things, as it seemed he might be. "What is the plan?"

"Tomorrow evening—later, around eleven—Lucien will

show his brother to a private chamber on the second floor of the Phoenix Club."

Interrupting her, Sabrina asked, "Why the Phoenix Club?"

"Because there are bedchambers, and it offers discretion that an inn or other establishment might not. Both you and Aldington will be secreted upstairs wearing masks and cloaks, so there will be no chance of recognition. Aldington will be waiting in one of the chambers, blindfolded, and you will enter a few minutes later. A single candle will be lit so that you can see the surroundings. As I said, you'll retain your mask in case his blindfold is dislodged."

"You've thought of everything," Sabrina said in wonder. "What should I do when I arrive?"

"You should undress to the level of which you are comfortable. Most of all, you must be commanding and alluring. Everything you say must carry the weight of experience and sensuality. We'll practice this today, if you'd like."

Sabrina appreciated her friend's support and assistance, even if the thought of practicing seduction made her stomach knot. "I'm still not sure I'm capable of doing this."

Evie folded her hands in her lap and regarded Sabrina expectantly. "Are you an outgoing person fond of crowds?"

"Not at all. But I've already told you that." During their first meeting and again last night as exhaustion had begun to set in near the end of the rout.

"Yet you behaved last night as if you were both." Evie's expression dared Sabrina to argue. She could not. "You can do the same as the tutor. The only obstacle is you believing you can."

She had already done much more than she'd expected herself capable of just a few short weeks ago. A sudden calmness swept over her. "I can do it."

Evie beamed with pride. "I'm so glad. Now, let us finish our tea and begin your lesson." She waggled her brows.

Later, as Sabrina rode home in the coach, she couldn't help but think the scheme was utter folly. She was going to pretend to be a tutor of something at which she was woefully uneducated, and her husband was turning himself over to the care of a stranger. That he'd never taken a mistress and would now meet with a former courtesan—even if she was a fraud—to learn how to seduce his wife was somehow sweet. Would she feel differently, however, if the former courtesan was someone other than her? It was a moot question because it *was* her.

Her mind turned to what she would wear tomorrow evening—something she could remove and don without assistance. A corset would be an unnecessary bother. The idea of going without a corset was titillating—perhaps that was the right mindset she needed. Her cobalt gown last night had made her feel like a countess, so she would dress to summon the role of a former courtesan. And she would speak with a different tone. Lower, perhaps. Seductive. A tickle of anticipation danced over her flesh.

There was also a chill of uncertainty that had nothing to do with her self-doubt. This was a deceptive scheme. Though this would help their marriage, she couldn't ignore the troublesome flash of guilt when she acknowledged that it was still a betrayal. She hadn't even discussed this concern with Evie. The rest had been too overwhelming.

Since Aldington had agreed to meet with this stranger, he wasn't entirely blameless—not that it was a competition or that both of their behavior somehow canceled out the wrongness of it. But was it really wrong if they were both trying, however drastically, to save their marriage? If it meant the difference between a lifetime of loneliness and an intimate union they both enjoyed, Sabrina knew which she would choose. Whatever the cost.

$\backsim$

$\mathcal{F}$ollowing his racing club meeting, Constantine drove his phaeton to his father's house in Grosvenor Square. As he stepped down from the vehicle, he brushed his hand over the side, where a bright yellow sun, the official design of the Gentlemen's Phaeton Racing Club, was painted on the ivory lacquer. The name was perhaps unoriginal, but it perfectly stated their purpose. It was a club comprised of drivers of phaetons with two horses who raced to various locations.

Constantine looked to his pair of matched bays. They and the vehicle were his greatest pride, for this was the one activity he did for himself. His father hadn't suggested or asserted it, but he did support it.

With a deep, fortifying breath, Constantine turned and went up the steps to the house. The duke's stoic butler, Bender, greeted Constantine. "His Grace is in his study."

There was rarely any chitchat with Bender even though he'd occupied this position all of Constantine's life. Instead of just greeting him and walking past, Constantine asked, "How are you today, Bender?"

The lines around Bender's blue-gray eyes creased more deeply, the only indication he had a reaction to the question. "The same as any day, my lord."

"Then that's well, I suppose." Constantine handed the butler his hat and gloves before taking himself to his father's study, moving more quickly than perhaps was necessary.

The door was open, which meant the duke would allow interruption. Still, Constantine stood at the threshold and cleared his throat to announce his presence.

Seated behind his massive oak desk, the duke looked up from the papers he was reading. He set down the magnifying glass he employed and sat back slightly in the chair. "Aldington, come in. I'm pleased to see you, since you are my only rational and capable offspring. Sit."

It wasn't an invitation but a command.

Constantine took a chair near the hearth instead of the one next to the desk. It was a minor grasp for independence, but one he liked to take from time to time. "Lucien and Cassandra are both rational and capable."

"Your brother is a wastrel who squandered a promising military career, while your sister, who is arguably the prettiest young lady to grace Society in a number of years, has no suitors!" He slapped his hand on the desk to punctuate his frustration.

"As it happens, my errand today involves Cassandra. Lady Aldington has offered to take over as her sponsor, and I think it's a capital idea."

The duke's mouth opened as he stared at Constantine for a moment. "No. That's a terrible idea."

Suddenly, the notion that the duke was somehow behind the countess's return to town seemed utterly silly. Which meant she was acting entirely on her own. Constantine would contemplate that later. His father continued, "Lady Aldington is far too timid to assume that role. If she were a man, I'd call her a milksop."

Constantine frowned, a mild display of the reaction he felt. What he wanted was to tell his father to shut his insulting mouth. "I find your description of my wife ironic given you insisted I marry her."

"You are well aware that she had to be forced into it." His father wiped his hand over his eyes. "I regret that I chose poorly for you."

"Perhaps you should have let her cry off then," Constantine said frigidly.

"And suffer the scandal of it?" The duke shook his head.

"Never. Though, given that she hasn't been able to provide an heir, perhaps I should have considered it."

The anger simmering inside Constantine boiled into a fury. He should have expected this. His father had voiced his disappointment more than once.

"Do you suppose she's incapable?" The duke asked, seemingly unaware of Constantine's ire. "Her mother had six children who survived to adulthood, and her older sister has already birthed several babes. In fact, I think her younger sister, who wed last season, has also delivered a child. That would be most unfortunate if you ended up with the invalid."

Constantine gritted his teeth. "She is not an invalid. Furthermore, she's no longer timid. She is eager to act as Cassandra's sponsor, and she is up to the task." He would ensure she was. There was no way he would let her fail in his father's eyes. Which meant he supposed he couldn't let her fail in her duties either. He would bloody well give her a child.

"Why? She has no social skills. She'll do nothing to contribute to Cassandra's husband hunt."

"In fact, last night at the Kipley rout she was most scintillating. She's matured, Father, and you must admit that Aunt Christina has demonstrated a lack of ability when it comes to shepherding Cassandra."

The duke scowled. He had to be aware of his sister's foibles, and yet he didn't seem to care while picking everyone else apart for theirs.

"You aren't at the balls and routs," Constantine continued. "You don't see how Christina abandons Cassandra and barely pays her any mind."

"That's why she has a companion now."

"Is her companion to be facilitating dances with prominent gentlemen and encouraging promenades?"

The duke's cheeks hollowed as he sucked in a breath, and

the hand that had remained atop the desk fisted. "I will speak with my sister on this matter. Now explain to me why I am hearing murmurs that you may not be in support of the Importation Act."

It was as if Constantine was still a lad, defending his every decision, which his father had said was necessary so that he could ensure his heir was developing the appropriate capabilities. As an adult, he'd continued to answer his father's demands, but in this case, he would almost certainly disappoint the duke who was in favor of the law. The act would impose tariffs on foreign grain in an effort to maintain prices of domestic grain so as not to bankrupt English farmers. Those in opposition, such as Constantine's friend Brightly, argued the law would increase prices, which would hurt the laboring class.

Constantine was leaning toward voting with Brightly but wasn't going to tell his father that. "I have been focusing my energy on the apothecaries bill." His father should have been too, after what had happened to his wife.

"Well, divert your attention to the bloody Importation Act. It will be up for vote soon, and I expect you will support it."

"Just as I expect you to support Lady Aldington as Cassandra's sponsor. She will do an excellent job. Imagine what could happen under Christina's lack of supervision. What if Cassandra was lured into a compromising position?"

The duke's dark brows pitched into an angry V. "Then that would be your sister's fault, not Christina's. Bender!" He bellowed the last.

A moment later, the butler stepped into the study. "Yes, Your Grace?"

"Send for Lady Cassandra at once."

Too late, Constantine realized the trouble he'd caused. Goddammit. He turned to Bender. "Don't bother." Directing a glare at his father, Constantine clenched his jaw. "Cassandra hasn't done anything wrong, nor will she. This conversation is about your sister and her failure as a sponsor. Give Lady Aldington a chance, and if you are unsatisfied with her performance, by all means go back to Aunt Christina." Oh hell, Constantine had just set his wife up to be sharply scrutinized by the most demanding of men.

After sending a dismissive nod to Bender, the duke sat back in his chair, his eyes narrowing in irritated contemplation. "Why are you pressing this matter so hard? I didn't think you cared much for your wife, yet here you are acting like her champion."

Constantine almost asked why he would think he didn't care. However, the answer seemed obvious. To any outsider —hell, to his wife—it would seem as though that were the case.

Did she care about him? She'd come here and demanded an heir. If she despised him and was still willing to do her duty, for whatever reason, including her own desire to be a mother, he had to give her credit.

He ought to credit her for more than that, and not just because he was fairly sure she *didn't* despise him. Which was why he was fighting so hard for her to be Cassandra's sponsor. They may not be close, but he'd made vows to her and it was time he kept them.

Drawing a breath, he straightened his shoulders, adopting a stance as if he were facing down a pack of wolves. "You have raised me to be the duke when you are gone. It will be my responsibility to ensure the members of this family are taken care of. I take that duty very seriously, and I want what's best for Cassandra. Don't you wish to see her wed this Season? Lady Aldington is a better choice of sponsor to meet that end. Furthermore, you selected my wife based on a variety of factors, including her unimpeachability. That trait alone makes her a better sponsor. Whether you think she has the initiative or cleverness to navigate Cassandra's path doesn't particularly matter. I know her far better than you, and it's time you allow me to do what you've educated me for." Constantine nearly laughed. As if he knew her very well at all. Hopefully, that would change.

He truly hoped for that?

The duke's gaze simmered with a heavy contemplation without any indication as to what he would decide. "That was a pretty speech. You have been an excellent student. I will take your recommendation under advisement."

Constantine allowed himself to relax the barest amount, the tension in his body lightening but not disappearing. "Thank you."

"In the meantime, you'll consider very closely how you plan to vote on the Importation Act." The duke sat forward and picked up his magnifying glass, returning his attention to the papers on his desk. Constantine was dismissed, and it seemed a deal had been proposed: if he voted for the act, his father would appoint Lady Aldington as Cassandra's sponsor.

Constantine didn't want that arrangement. Turning on his heel, he stalked from the study. The comfort and relaxation he'd felt from his racing club meeting had been completely pulverized by his father's domineering autocracy.

Bender met him in the entry hall with his hat and gloves.

Constantine wondered if he should speak with Cassandra to inform her how the meeting went and that he'd inadvertently given their father the idea that a compromising situation was possible. But no, if he did that, the duke would find out and it wouldn't help their cause for Lady Aldington to be Cassandra's new sponsor. He would have to hope that his father would see reason.

Because Constantine sure as hell didn't want to vote for

that act. Especially now that his father had all but demanded he do so. Apparently, Constantine would prefer to be contrary.

Or perhaps he was ready to emerge from the duke's shadow.

CHAPTER 10

*W*hen Sabrina arrived in the dining room that evening, her husband was already there, standing in profile at the head of the twenty-foot table. The candlelight seemed to make his bright-white collar glisten against the stark black of his coat. A single emerald stick pin was the only color in his attire, sparkling amidst the snow of his cravat. She was a bit disappointed that his neck wasn't exposed as it had been that morning after Grayson had scratched him. Apparently, she rather enjoyed ogling his bare flesh.

He pivoted as she walked into the room, his gaze sweeping over her in a hooded fashion. She couldn't read anything about his reaction. Or if he even had one.

The head of the table was set as was the seat to his right. Sabrina moved to the chair and he, not a footman, held it for her.

"Thank you," she murmured. "Your chin looks to be improved." Though there was an inch-long, thin, red stripe.

"It is no longer bleeding, at least. I am not usually this prone to injury." He was of course referring to the cut to his hand on the night she'd arrived. Was that humor in his voice? She thought so. Perhaps they had turned a corner onto a new path earlier. Who knew a mischievous cat could do what they could not?

As she sat, his hand fleetingly grazed her shoulder. Though the contact was brief and slight, she felt it in the pit of her belly, where a mass of flittering butterflies tickled her in anticipation of the following evening. When she would be his tutor, of all things. The thought of it still sent her into a near panic, and she had to suppress the urge to let out a nervous laugh.

After Aldington was seated, the footman poured claret and the first course, white soup, was immediately placed before them, sending a pleasing aroma of veal and almond into the air.

Sabrina picked up her spoon amidst a tumult of anxiety. She needed to tell him about her invitation to the Phoenix Club. Instead, she said something completely inane. "I have missed Cook's white soup."

"She does make my favorite version," he said before sampling from his bowl.

They ate in silence for a few moments—well, outward silence. There was a cacophony in Sabrina's head as she contemplated how to tell him about the invitation, recalled everything she'd discussed with Evie that afternoon, *and* anticipated what was to come tomorrow evening.

She cast a glance in his direction, noting the sharp angle of his cheekbone and the lush sweep of his eyelashes. How had she never noticed how long they were?

Setting down her spoon, she sipped the claret, which reminded her of summer berries. Again, she stalled. "This is delicious. I don't drink wine very often at Hampton Lodge. I never know what to ask for. Perhaps you could provide me with some direction."

His brow pleated. "Dagnall should be able to help you with that."

Dagnall was the butler at Hampton Lodge. She preferred to have her husband's assistance. "I was rather hoping you could share your opinions," she said serenely before taking up her spoon and finishing her soup.

"I'll ask Haddock to put together a selection of wine for us to taste. You should form your own opinions instead of relying on mine."

"I'd like to hear yours all the same. Tasting them together sounds delightful." Something else to look forward to. The butterflies in Sabrina's belly rose to her chest.

A footman removed their dishes, and another replaced them with the next course, sole and green beans. Sabrina gathered her knife and fork. *Now. Mention the invitation now.*

The butterflies grew darker and moved more quickly, with a sickening effect. She forced a smile. "How was your racing club meeting?"

She was such a coward. And why? Telling him this was nothing compared to asking him if he preferred to sleep with men. He was also not her parents who typically found a way to make anything Sabrina found good into something bad. Aldington wouldn't do that. He hadn't ever.

"Quite the usual. We won't begin the actual racing season until the end of the month, but we do like to plan our excursions. Our season always begins with the jaunt to the Pickled Goose."

Sabrina recalled that was a tavern in Richmond. "Are wives ever allowed as guests?"

His fork, with a green bean speared upon it, was halfway to his mouth when his arm arrested. "We've never discussed it. Likely because half our members are unwed." As if that explained why it hadn't come up.

"I should be intrigued to join you some time, if it were

allowed." Sabrina set her utensils down. She couldn't—
shouldn't—avoid the subject any longer. She'd made it into
something far bigger than it was. "Earlier today, I received an
invitation to join the Phoenix Club."

He set his knife and fork down and reached for his wineglass. "I see." The words were flat, his gaze fixed on his wine
before he took a long drink. "And do you plan to accept it?"

"I do. In fact, I'm going to attend the assembly on Friday
with Mrs. Renshaw." She clasped her hands in her lap,
wringing them as her insides cartwheeled with unease. "Are
you angry?"

"Why should I be?" His entire demeanor had cooled.
They'd been sharing a pleasant meal until now. "I am
surprised."

"Because you haven't received an invitation?"

Now he looked surprised—and slightly irritated. "You
know that?"

"I, er, assumed," she lied, not wanting him to know she'd
discussed his membership, or lack thereof, with Evie. "But
maybe you did receive one and declined. That wouldn't
surprise me, since you seem to disdain the club."

"I haven't ever been invited, nor do I expect to be. How...
nice for you to be a member." He'd held onto his wineglass
throughout this conversation and now finished the contents.

"I would prefer that you were a member too. Perhaps
Lucien could see that you are invited."

"No." The clipped response landed hard, like a stone. "It's
his club. He would have invited me by now if he wanted to."
He set his empty glass down, and the footman moved to
refill it.

Plucking up his utensils, he pushed his food around his
plate. She could see he wasn't eating and hated that she'd
caused him distress.

"How was your meeting with the duke?" she asked softly.

As much as she wanted to know how it had gone, she was more concerned with filling the uncomfortable air.

Aldington's lip curled slightly, and she instantly thought the interview had gone poorly. "He is considering our request for you to replace Aunt Christina as Cassandra's sponsor."

Our request. Sabrina liked the sound of that, even if she didn't feel like they were an "our" or an "us." "That's better than an outright refusal."

"To be honest, denial was his initial response, but I told him that you were up to the challenge and would do a much better job than Aunt Christina."

Sabrina lifted her gaze to his, glad for his advocacy, though an old feeling of dread wriggled between her ribs. "I *am* up to the challenge."

Aldington instructed the footmen to leave them alone. The dismissal surprised Sabrina. He'd never done anything like that. When they were gone, he continued, "The person I saw last night at the rout and somewhat again earlier today—charming, outgoing, flirtatious even. Is that really who you are?"

"It's who I want to be," she answered softly, trying to convince herself as much as him.

"But it's not who you *were*. You've been different since you arrived. However, I still glimpse the cautious woman underneath. Are you certain you can be the woman you want to be? Are you, in fact, certain that's what you really want?"

"Yes, it is what I want. Just as I want a child."

"So I gathered," he said coolly. "And you shall have your child."

"Do you plan to visit my chamber again tonight?" She held her breath, wondering if he would, even as tomorrow night's "lesson" loomed.

He hesitated and, for a scant moment, the anticipation simmering inside her roiled.

"I have a meeting at White's and will likely be late." He stood quickly, making the chair wobble. "Oh, I nearly forgot. I purchased some books on horticulture for you and procured the latest issue of *Transactions*."

She blinked at him. "From the Horticultural Society?" The organization was little more than a decade old and produced a wonderful periodical with color plates of all manner of plants. "How exceedingly thoughtful of you."

Indeed, he'd never done anything of the sort. Not in two years. He'd gifted her something on her birthday and at Christmas—handkerchiefs or jewelry. Books about gardening, about which she was passionate, were far more personal.

"Please excuse me. I'll instruct the footmen to return so you may finish your dinner."

"I hope I didn't upset you. Thank you for the books and the periodical. I am very much looking forward to reading them."

"You didn't upset me. Have a pleasant evening." His gaze lingered on her a moment before he departed the room.

After finishing her dinner, she went to the library. There she found the latest issue of *Transactions* as well as three books. One stood out for its red Moroccan leather cover. It couldn't be... But it was. A design book by Humphry Repton himself emblazoned with "Repton's Plans for Hampton Lodge" in gold on the cover.

Sabrina sucked in a breath as she carefully opened the book and drank in the gorgeous watercolor before and after paintings. When he'd said he'd purchased books, she'd never imagined this. Repton was a renowned landscape designer—this was far more than a book.

When had Aldington commissioned this? Did he mean to fund such a sweeping revision to the landscape? Repton had included a narrow lake with a bridge as well as a folly nestled amongst a crescent of trees.

She was overwhelmed by Aldington's thoughtfulness, as well as his support of the thing that brought her the most joy. And he'd done it well before she'd come to town. Perhaps he *was* different too, and the change hadn't been provoked by her arrival.

Closing the book, she stared into nothing, her mind turning back to the dinner they'd just shared. He'd been reserved but not dispassionate, which was how she'd thought of him before arriving in London not even a week ago. It was progress, wasn't it?

Slow, incremental progress. Yes, he'd been upset about the invitation—whether he wanted to admit it or not—and had left abruptly. He was also championing her to his father, and he'd consented to meet with a courtesan in order to improve the sexual state of their marriage.

Another twinge of guilt stole over her, and she reminded herself that this was a benevolent betrayal, if there could be such a thing. It would be for their common good, and the deception wouldn't last forever.

This would bring them closer together, as well as give them the child they needed and wanted. That he was willing to go to such lengths told her he wanted things to change. As did the gifts he'd just given her. These were not the actions of a man who didn't care.

∾

The bedchamber at the Phoenix Club was smaller, more intimate, than the one Constantine had seen before. This one held just a bed with tables on either side and a chair near the hearth. The single candle burning on the mantel produced scant illumination, but that was the point.

In darkness there was mystery and anonymity. Constantine found it oddly soothing. As much as anything could be in this moment.

His mind warred with itself, caught between the beneficial outcome he was seeking from this desperate assignation and the guilt that he was doing this behind his wife's back. She'd invited him to her bed—nay, *demanded* he visit her there. Shouldn't he be in her chamber instead?

He'd tried that a few nights ago and while it had been better, it had still been awkward. Tonight, he would hopefully find the audacity to improve their bedsport. Hell, he just needed to find a way to *make* it bedsport instead of cold duty.

"The lady will arrive shortly," Lucien said. "You should probably prepare yourself."

Constantine had already removed his cloak, mask, hat, and gloves and placed them on a narrow bench at the end of the bed. "What else is there to do?" Besides overcome the doubt in his head.

"Er, you might want to doff your coat? Whatever makes you most comfortable."

"Not being here would make me most comfortable." And having a wife who wanted him, not just the child he could give her.

Lucien exhaled. "I suppose it's not too late to change your mind, but only if you can answer the following question in the affirmative."

"What's that?"

"Can you go home and shag your wife?"

Constantine clenched his jaw. He could, but he didn't want a repeat of the other night. He wanted his wife to *desire* him. Unfortunately, the stark truth of it all was that whatever he learned tonight might not change that. "Just send her in before I *do* change my mind."

"A few rules," Lucien said crisply, pulling a dark strip of

cloth from his coat. "You'll wear a blindfold so she can't be identified."

"What about her identifying me?"

"Your blindfold will obscure the upper portion of your face. She has agreed to direct her attention to education only. Don't worry that she'll spend time trying to determine who you are. Her goal is to help you—nothing more." Lucien stepped behind Constantine.

"Wait." Constantine removed his coat and draped it over the back of the chair. Then he sat and took off his boots, leaving his stockings on. Standing, he turned his back to Lucien. "I'm ready." The hell he was. His insides were in knots, and he was a breath away from calling the whole bloody thing off.

The moment the blindfold plunged him into obsidian night, uncertainty gripped him hard. He told himself to relax, that plenty of men took mistresses, not that he was even doing that. He was seeking advice of an intimate nature, nothing more.

"I'm trusting you, Lucien," he said, as though it were necessary that he say it out loud.

"I don't take that lightly." Lucien clasped his shoulder. "There is a bell on the bedside table. If at any moment, you want to end this, ring it. She will do the same. She won't touch you unless you ask her to, and you won't touch her unless she gives you permission. Those are the rest of the rules."

A blindfold, a bell, and consent. It all sounded very civilized and orderly. With a hint of carnality.

No, they would only talk. There would be no touching.

Lucien's hand left his shoulder. "I'm going now."

Constantine nodded and was glad he'd taken that long drink of his brother's smuggled whisky on the way upstairs. The snick of the door latching sounded like a pistol shot.

While he couldn't see anything, his other senses had become more, greater. He smelled the wax of the candle burning, and the gentle heat of the low fire in the hearth warmed him.

What in the hell was he doing? Did he really need this? What he needed was for this woman—or someone else—to sit down with his wife and talk to her about what happened in bed and how she ought to respond. Presuming she liked what was happening. Perhaps she didn't. Which meant he needed the damn tutor.

Swearing softly in frustration, he lifted his hands to the buttons of his waistcoat. The latch clicked, and he froze. His breath caught and held as he pivoted toward the door. It was a silly movement since he couldn't see anything.

The air in the chamber shifted, thickening and beguiling him with the scent of an exotic flower his father grew in the hothouse at Woodbreak.

"Good evening." He sounded foreign, as if there was a gravel-voiced stranger within him.

"Good evening." Her voice was soft and melodic, a vaguely southern Welsh accent, if he had to guess. Yes, his other senses were working very hard to compensate for his lack of sight.

He still didn't breathe, nor could he move, his body rooted in disbelief over what was happening. Or about to happen. "Why are you here?" He blurted the question despite Lucien telling him she only wanted to help. Why would she?

"I went to Lord Lucien in search of a discreet lover," she said simply and without hesitation. "He has a reputation for helping people."

Constantine finally exhaled. "Did you hope to become his mistress?"

"No, why?"

Because most women would. "He also has a reputation for, ah, libertine behavior."

"What about you?" She'd moved closer, the air moving again, as her tropical scent enveloped him. "You look to be a very attractive gentleman."

"I am not like Lord Lucien." There was just something about Lucien that attracted the fairer sex. Even when they'd been boys, the maids had doted upon him. Not that they'd ignored Constantine, but it was different. Lucien always smiled and charmed. For him, it was as easy as breathing— and Constantine was even having trouble with that at the moment.

"I can see that." She was behind him now, circling him, taking stock.

His muscles stretched taut, as if he were being pulled in multiple directions, drawn and about to be quartered. "This was a mistake." He reached up for the blindfold, intending to leave.

"You can't do that," she said quickly, the pitch of her voice rising. "The blindfold stays on. That's one of the rules."

"I can't leave if I can't see."

"Then I suppose you can't leave." She stood in front of him now, close enough that he could feel her heat. "Do you want me to go?"

Yes. But the word lodged somewhere on the way from his brain to his mouth, stuck in a battle now being waged between his mind and body—what he believed he should do and what he wanted to do.

"I am conflicted. You are not my wife, and that… distresses me."

"But you are here *for* your wife, are you not?"

"Yes." It was more than wanting her to desire him. He wanted to give her pleasure, to show her how passionate things could be between them. But he supposed he needed to believe that for himself. Until she'd arrived and done things like masturbate, he never would have imagined passion and pleasure between them was possible.

"She would understand, I think."

Would she? Perhaps one day he would tell her the drastic measures he'd resorted to in order to give them what he thought—or hoped—they both wanted. Or not. He didn't want her to feel bad, not when she was already so apprehensive about nearly everything.

"You were a courtesan?" he asked, taking a half step back to try to cool the air between them. He was too aware of her proximity.

"I was, but not for a few years now. I prefer my independence. I enjoy the ability to do some of the things that men do."

"Such as take a lover."

"Yes."

She wanted to have sex for the purpose of having sex. Not to have a child and not out of some sense of duty. And she was no longer a courtesan, so there was no financial incentive.

She'd moved closer again because he felt the whisper of her breath against his jaw. A shiver of need tripped up his spine, awakening his body. "Tell me about your wife. What do you think she would like?"

"I'm sure I don't know. I don't even know if she wants *me*. She wants a child, but that can be accomplished without, ah, fanfare."

"Fanfare? What an interesting way to describe it—pleasure, I think you mean?" She didn't wait for him to respond before continuing. "You could keep things simple and straightforward, lackluster, if you will, but if you were content to do that, you wouldn't be here. Have you spoken to her about what she wants now? Lord Lucien indicated you aren't newlyweds."

"Our relationship is a bit, er, strained."

"I gather that's why you're here."

"I'm here because apparently I've got the completely wrong idea of how to behave with my wife. In my defense, she is incredibly reserved and apprehensive. At least she used to be."

"She's not anymore?"

"She's trying not to be, but when it comes to the bedchamber, I have no idea. We, ah, shared a bed the other night and I *think* she orgasmed, but I can't be sure."

"Why not ask her?"

"She seemed alternately horrified and…responsive during the act. Honestly, it was incredibly confusing."

"Perhaps she simply didn't know what to do," she said softly. "That's possible, isn't it?"

It wasn't only possible, it was probable. He couldn't expect that her mother had discussed the matter with her. Who else would teach her then, but him? "I'm going to have to talk to her to make seduction work, aren't I?"

"I think you must, yes. Would that be so bad? Talking can be somewhat…arousing, can't it?"

"I hadn't considered it, actually. But I will, if it will help my wife relax."

"Oh my." She laughed softly. "If you wish your wife to relax, perhaps you should offer her a glass of sherry or port. And if a modicum of pleasure is all you desire, we can be finished in short order. I would assert, however, that you try for something more than a *modicum*. Why not aim for a satisfactory amount? Or, if you're feeling adventurous, you might even set your goal at, say, an *excess*." She hissed the last word, and another frisson of need danced across his flesh.

Constantine wanted an excess of pleasure. So much.

Her fingers grazed his hand, and she abruptly withdrew. "My apologies. May I take your hand?"

He wanted to say no, to deny the burgeoning desire igniting inside him. He did not. "Yes."

She curled her hand around his. "Sometimes it's nice to just touch someone like this. No expectations, only an intimate moment shared between two people. Perhaps you could hold your wife's hand."

Her flesh against his teased his senses, making the darkness even more profound as everything else worked to compensate. He didn't want this intimacy—not with her. He imagined his wife instead and immediately felt calmer.

"You could also stroke her arm as you sit together—in your coach, perhaps, as you ride somewhere. Your touch outside the bedchamber might ease her anxiety. Then, when you are alone together, you can caress her neck, her back…"

With the inability to see anything, Constantine's mind filled in the void. He recalled the alluring expanse of Lady Aldington's back. *Lady Aldington?* Her name was Sabrina. If he first-named her, that would certainly break down some of the wall, wouldn't it?

His hand lifted, without direction from him, and he imagined trailing his fingertip down Sabrina's spine. His finger met flesh, and the woman's soft gasp cloaked him, drawing him closer in thought, if not in actuality.

He pulled his hand back, realizing somewhat stupidly that this *wasn't* his wife. "I didn't mean to touch you. I didn't realize you were so close." He wondered what he'd touched. "Where did I—?" He cut himself off, thinking it best if they didn't discuss that. "Never mind."

"You touched me just above the bodice of my gown. If you'd been an inch lower, you would have found my breast."

He swallowed. This was becoming dangerous. He wished he *had* touched her breast. No, not hers, Sabrina's. "I tried to do that to my wife the other night. She didn't seem to like it."

"Perhaps she was merely startled. Try telling her what

you're going to do—that you want to caress and fondle her, to put your mouth on her there."

Lust pooled in his loins, a great thirst he feared couldn't be slaked. Not tonight anyway. He hadn't wanted to frighten Sabrina, so he'd taken things incredibly slowly. But he could have communicated to her what would happen, prepared her so as to alleviate her fear.

Regret cascaded through him in a torrent. "I'm sorry," he whispered before realizing, again, that this wasn't Sabrina. He was struggling to distinguish this woman before him from the one in his head.

"Don't be. Do you want to touch me? Show me how you would touch your wife. If you like."

He was almost desperate with wanting to touch her, but not her. He wanted Sabrina. He wanted to do as the tutor suggested—caress her neck, her back, her breasts. His cock, fully aroused now, strained in his smallclothes.

Would it be terrible if he took this woman to bed? Most other men in his position would do it without thought. Furthermore, if Sabrina didn't want him for more than having a child, would she even care?

"*Fuck.*"

"Excuse me?" She sounded shocked, which meant he'd said that aloud.

"My apologies. I didn't mean to say that. Outside of my head anyway. My wife only wants a child," he blurted as it seemed all his thoughts wanted to break free. "She's been very clear. Demanding, even. It was quite shocking," he added in a murmur. But maybe a little arousing too. A commanding woman, especially one's wife, was a heady thing.

"Then perhaps you should be demanding about what you want. Tell her what you desire."

The blindfold was suddenly constricting. He wanted to

throw it off and see this woman, to differentiate her from Sabrina. "What color is your hair?"

"Dark brown."

He relaxed slightly. "Your eyes?"

"Er, blue."

Damn. He'd hoped they would be brown instead of the same color as Sabrina's.

"If you're trying to conjure an image of how I look, why not touch me and let your hands inform you?"

The temptation was so great. He clenched his hands into tight fists at his sides lest he reach for her.

She exhaled softly, a sigh of disappointment. "I shall hope you touch your wife instead then. Stroke her and perhaps kiss her skin. Have you done that?" She hesitated a bare moment before adding, "Have you put your mouth on her?" This last question climbed, as if she were also aroused.

"No," he croaked.

"Then you should. She will likely enjoy your mouth on her breasts, at her sex—"

"*Stop.*" He couldn't endure another moment. "You need to leave."

"Why?"

"Because you should." His voice was tight, thin, as if he were being relentlessly squeezed.

"I'm not sure I've made any progress. You haven't touched me, and you haven't said how you plan to seduce your wife. Might I suggest you strip her clothing from her and ply your tongue along her breast—"

"Bloody hell, woman, if you don't go now, you're going to have to watch me frig myself." His hands were already on the buttons of his fall.

"I would like to." Now, her voice had dropped to an almost guttural level. The sound was as intoxicating as the notion that she would *watch* him.

"No." Though he refused her, his body yearned for him to say yes. He hesitated, his fall half open.

"Please, may I stay?"

He surrendered to his basest needs, barely whispering, "Yes."

"Show me what you want your wife to do." It was a soft but devastating command.

Mindless, he freed the last buttons and slid his cock from his smallclothes. Grasping the base, he let his head fall back as blood rushed straight to his prick.

He moved his hand up, slowly at first. Delicious sensation rocketed through him. His muscles tightened as pleasure ignited and built.

Her breathing rasped in the quiet of the room, the sound deepening his arousal. He could imagine her touching herself. Was she? He couldn't bring himself to ask.

His legs wobbled, and he reached out with his left hand for the bedpost for stability. Otherwise, he feared he might collapse, especially when he came.

"How tightly do you hold yourself?" The question jarred him, and his hand slipped.

He struggled to speak. "Not too tight, but not too loose either." He was tempted to show her, to ask her to finish him. But he'd already gone too far—doing this in front of her.

"Tell me how it feels. Practice so that you can tell your wife how it feels when she does this to you."

The thought of Sabrina holding his cock, of her driving him to rapture sent a new surge of lust into his cock. He stroked his hand faster, and the tutor's rapid, shallow breathing joined his in a reckless, sensual symphony. He imagined it was Sabrina, her sweet, soft hand cradling him, and he came undone.

Every muscle in his body clenched just before his release tore through him. He cried out, a low, awful sound he didn't think he'd ever made before. But then he didn't think he'd ever come that hard before either.

He cast his head back and gripped the bedpost as though his very life depended on him not letting go. It wasn't that dire, of course, but he was certain he'd collapse if not for the post.

At last, his orgasm subsided, and he fought to regain control over his body, taking deep breaths, as he tucked his slackening cock into his smallclothes. With shaking fingers, he rebuttoned his fall.

"My apologies," he said when his breeches were closed once more. "I should not have allowed you to watch."

"I enjoyed it," she said in a rather sunny tone. "I think your wife will too, especially if you let her touch you. Although, just watching is incredibly arousing."

He wasn't sure he agreed with her as to Sabrina enjoying it. "Did you...touch yourself?"

"No, but I should have. And I will. Next time, we can do that together."

"There will not be a next time." He shouldn't have allowed a first time, even if he thought it would help.

"If you change your mind, I'd be happy to see you again. In the meantime, I wish you luck with your wife."

"Thank you." He would take all the luck he could get.

"I hope this helped. I'm leaving now. Good night." The door clicked shut, indicating she'd gone. Constantine realized he was still clutching the bloody bedpost.

He released the post and shook out his hand, the muscles tight from clenching so hard. Swiping his hand over his face, he'd forgotten about the bloody blindfold. He untied it at the back of his head and pulled it away. Blinking, he stared into the near darkness, as if he could discern the woman's imprint before him. He could still smell her decadent tropical scent and would forever equate that with toe-curling bliss.

Trudging to the chair, he pulled his boots on. Could he seduce Sabrina as he must?

He thought of how she was trying to change and wondered if he should be doing the same. Perhaps he'd find the real Constantine buried somewhere beneath duty and expectation.

Was there a real Constantine other than who he was? When had his wife's arrival provoked some sort of existential dilemma?

I am who I am supposed to be.

But was that the husband he wanted to be?

CHAPTER 11

*S*abrina pushed the emerald through her earlobe and turned her head to watch the jewel sparkle in the candlelight. The matching necklace was heavy against her throat. She brushed her hand over the brilliant green gems. She certainly looked like a countess, even if she didn't completely feel like one yet.

Rising from the stool at the dressing table, she moved in front of the long glass and held still while Charity drew the green and gold ball gown over her head. Sabrina smoothed the garment over her waist and hips before Charity fastened the small row of buttons at the back.

"Beautiful, my lady," Charity said with a smile as she fetched the gloves.

"Only because of what you accomplished with my hair." Sabrina touched the back of her head, marveling at how sophisticated she looked with the jewels gleaming among the red-gold curls.

"I've so enjoyed learning how to dress hair. I believe it's my favorite part of becoming a lady's maid."

"You have a natural skill." Sabrina pulled on the gloves and took a final look in the mirror before pivoting.

"Your reticule." Charity went back to the dressing table to retrieve it and handed it to Sabrina.

"Thank you, Charity. I shall see you later. Enjoy your evening."

As Sabrina made her way downstairs, she wondered if she would encounter her husband. He'd been ever-present in her mind since last night. How could he not be? She'd been forever changed by their encounter, and he hadn't even known she was there.

That deception stuck in the back of her mind, as did everything she'd learned about what was wrong with their past attempts at coupling. Hearing his perspective about how the other night had gone between them, when they'd finally shared a bed, was eye-opening. She needed to learn to relax, to be comfortable with his touch. Last night had been a step in that direction, and for that reason alone, she couldn't regret it.

She'd made it to the bottom of the stairs, and there Aldington was standing in the threshold to the foyer. Aldington? She ought to think of him as Constantine, especially after last night.

His eyes locked on her, his lips parting as he slowly perused her. Sabrina couldn't move. It was as if he held her captive. Her breath snagged while she waited for him to speak.

At last he said, "You're going to the assembly?"

She hadn't realized she'd been hoping for a compliment until he didn't give her one. "Yes. I wish you were coming with me." She moved toward him across the marble floor of the stair hall. "Will you be up when I return?"

"I imagine you'll be late. These assemblies go on well past

midnight. Indeed, I may be out late myself, so you shouldn't expect me."

Sabrina closed the distance between them. Had she imagined the progress they'd been making? Perhaps she was giving too much credit to last night, which didn't even count since he hadn't known it was her. "You said you would fulfill my desire."

His nostrils flared as she whispered the last word.

"A child," she clarified.

His eyes darkened. "Why didn't you want to marry me?"

She blinked, surprised by his question. He'd known and married her anyway? Of course he had. He was nothing if not the embodiment of duty and responsibility. "I didn't realize you knew," she answered softly.

"My father informed me the day before the wedding. He said you'd wanted to cry off, but he refused to endure a scandal."

She was having trouble drawing a deep enough breath. "Would you have preferred the scandal of calling it off to marrying me?"

His brow furrowed into deep grooves. "Of course not."

That would have been unconscionable. Sabrina wrung her hands together, her palms moist inside her gloves. "I didn't want to marry anyone. I was so...anxious. About everything. Just the thought of having a Season, of going out in crowds, was nearly devastating to me." By the time she finished, she could barely hear her own words. Perhaps that was due to the blood rushing in her ears.

"Yet, you are going out into a very crowded assembly tonight," he noted.

"Yes, because I am working on overcoming my fears. I must. I am a countess, and I mean to behave like one. I didn't before now—certainly not when we wed, and not last Season either." She hadn't finished trying to explain herself to him.

But would he understand? Would he even try? "I've always struggled in large groups of people. I'm nervous and shy, and I want to stand in the shadows so no one will talk to me. No one will see my mistakes if they aren't paying attention."

His lips parted, but he didn't say anything, so she went on.

"It wasn't that I didn't want to marry *you*. I didn't want to marry anyone. I wanted to stay at my father's country estate and probably become a spinster." Now she took a breath, her heart speeding.

"That's why you love Hampton Lodge so much." He spoke with the measured words of someone who had just learned something. "You can hide there."

A lightness spread through her. Perhaps he was beginning to understand her. "I hadn't thought of it that way, but yes, I can hide there. Only, I can't hide anymore. I am a countess—your countess—and I have a duty. Someday, I will—hopefully—guide my own daughter through her Season. How can I do that if I don't gain the confidence I need to be successful?" She took another breath, her pulse finally slowing. "Anyway, you didn't want to marry me either."

His gaze turned sharp. "Why would you think that?"

"My parents said you didn't, that if I didn't improve my behavior, you were going to cry off."

He stared at her. The gold flecks she'd only just noticed in his hazel irises seemed to burn with incredulity. "That simply isn't true."

It shouldn't be a surprise that her parents had lied to her. They would have done anything to ensure she married Aldington. *Constantine.*

"Your parents sound incredibly cruel," he added.

"They are not kind. That is part of the reason I want to change. I don't want to be manipulated or viewed as malleable. I want to sponsor your sister, attend Phoenix Club assemblies, and host a ball of my own."

He arched a brow. "Do you?"

She'd been considering it, wondering if she had the courage. If she didn't, she'd find it. She had to. Notching her chin up, she looked him in the eye. "Future duchesses host balls. And they don't allow themselves to be handled."

"So, if I told you to stay home tonight, you wouldn't listen to me?"

Was he serious? She couldn't tell. "No, I would not. I like how I'm changing. And I-I hope you do too. Tonight, I want to go to a ball with my friend and come home to see my husband. Will you be here?"

"I guess you'll find out later." He brushed past her.

"I hope you will be," she called after him. If she kept pushing him off balance, he eventually had to fall in her direction, didn't he?

Sabrina watched him walk up the stairs and found herself appreciating the ripple of his shoulders as he moved, as well as the slope of his calf. She imagined his bare chest and hoped it wouldn't be too long until he revealed himself to her again.

Tonight, she'd talk to Lucien and plead with him to ensure Constantine received an invitation to join the club. Then, she intended to wait up for her husband.

～

*A*fter quickly changing his clothes, Constantine arrived at his brother's terraced house just as Lucien was stepping into the foyer from the stairs. The butler, Reynolds, was a terrifying figure—loomingly tall with a nasty red scar across his cheek. Despite his fearsome appearance, however, he was quite affable and always greeted Constantine warmly.

"You've arrived at an inopportune time, Con," Lucien said as he drew on his gloves. "I am just on my way to the club."

"The Phoenix Club. Of which my wife is a now a member, but I am not."

Lucien pressed his lips together and grimaced. "Indeed. Let us discuss the matter." He gestured for Constantine to follow him back to the library. On the way, he removed his freshly donned gloves, then tossed them onto a table before turning to face his brother. "You're angry."

"You're damned right." That had been Constantine's initial reaction, but he'd convinced himself he'd overreacted, that he didn't want to belong to Lucien's club anyway. But seeing Sabrina tonight and knowing he couldn't accompany her to the assembly had summoned his ire even more fiercely than when she'd told him about the invitation the other night. "How can my wife be a member while I'm not even invited?"

"Simple. The membership committee extended her an invitation." Lucien exhaled. "And not you. To be fair, your name has never been proposed for membership. To my knowledge," he added hastily.

Constantine rolled his eyes. "Spare me your rationale and your feeble attempts to make your position on the membership committee opaque. Everyone knows you sit at the top of the *Star Chamber*. It's your bloody club."

Lucien gaped at him. "First you roll your eyes—I can't remember the last time you did that. I think I was ten and you were twelve? Then you refer to the membership committee with that tawdry nickname? Since when did you become so enmeshed in the bon ton and their comical obsession with how members are selected for the Phoenix Club?"

Swiping his hand through the air, Constantine scoffed. "Don't try to avoid the issue."

"Fine, I *am* on the membership committee, but it might

surprise you to learn I am not a king—I do not have the final say as to who receives an invitation. We are a democratic group."

Constantine snorted. "You could have submitted my name for consideration, but *to your knowledge*, you have not."

"No, I have not." Lucien threw up his hands. "I didn't think you would accept, nor did I imagine you would even want the courtesy of receiving an invitation knowing it was only a formality because you would, in fact, decline."

"How do you know I would decline?" The truth was he would have. And why did he want so badly to become a member now? Because of some ancient custom that said a wife must share all things with her husband? It certainly didn't work the other way. If he wanted to invite Sabrina to White's, he'd be laughed at. Then probably expelled.

"Because I know you." Lucien fixed him with an unflinching stare. "You can try to deny it, but I think I know you better than anyone. Which is unfortunate. That should be your wife's job."

"I'm bloody working on that." Constantine paced to the window in a fit of agitation. "Can you get me an invitation?"

"Is it that important to you?"

Turning back to face his brother, Constantine gave a slight nod. "Apparently."

"I'll do my best. As I said, it's not entirely up to me." He cocked his head to the side and smiled. "You do rather fit our profile."

"There's a profile?"

"Don't all clubs have one? It's not as if Brooks's or White's will invite just anyone. Nor can everyone get a voucher to Almack's. Where's the importance if there's no exclusivity?"

"Except your club doesn't seem to follow the same rules. How many dukes do you count in your membership?"

Lucien's gaze flicked toward the ceiling as he thought for

a moment. "None, I believe." He grinned. "They don't need our club, and we don't need them."

"Does any club need anyone?"

"Certainly, if they wish to be relevant and provide a place for one to belong."

That single word—*belong*—drove an ache into Constantine's chest. He ignored it.

"I'll do my best, Con. I promise." Lucien retrieved his gloves. "You have not mentioned how the tutoring session went last night. I admit I've been dying to know."

"It's none of your bloody business." Honestly, it had left him feeling uncertain about his ability to seduce Sabrina. Could he set aside his preconceptions about her, when she'd only ever been petrified of him, to improve things between them?

"That doesn't sound as if it went well."

"I'd like for you to arrange for her to meet me tonight." The request tumbled from Constantine's lips before he realized what he meant to say.

Surprise dashed across Lucien's features. "It's rather late notice."

Constantine almost took it back. But he didn't. If he planned to visit his wife tonight, he needed to know he could do what he must. He could practice with the tutor, just pretend… "I'm sure you'll do your best," Con said evenly, using his brother's words.

Lucien snorted. "Always for you. I'll send word as soon as I can confirm the appointment. Where will you be?"

"At White's." Constantine left, bidding good evening to Reynolds, and went out to his coach. A few minutes later, he stepped into White's and waited for the familiar air to settle him.

It did not.

In fact, he bristled as Trowley came toward him with

single-minded intent. "Aldington, there is a wager in the book about your dear sister, I'm afraid." His features folded into what was likely meant to have been an expression of concern but in reality made the man look as if he'd stepped in horse manure.

"I pay no attention to the betting book," Constantine said with his haughtiest tone. "If you'll excuse me."

"The wager is that she will remain unwed at the end of the Season. A travesty, to be sure, but—" Trowley clamped his thick lips together and glanced about. Lowering his voice, he started once more, "But no one wants to court her for fear your father will eviscerate them. I, however, am not such a weak-minded sop, and as you know, I have been widowed these past three years. My children need—"

"Excuse me, Trowley." Constantine had located Brightly on the other side of the room and immediately took off through the throng.

Brightly saw him coming and waved him over, taking a seat at a small empty table. "Ho there, Aldington. You're a sight for a beleaguered gentleman. I was just about to pick up and head to Brooks's where there are kinder waters. Too many sharks here." He glanced about, then winked at Constantine.

This was better. The company of a friend. It was as if Constantine was seeing Brightly for the first time. Yes, they were friends, not just colleagues.

A footman came to the table with a tray offering port or claret. They both chose the latter and Brightly proposed a toast. "To defeating the Importation Act."

Constantine drank to the sentiment even while he was fairly certain defeat was impossible. Brightly would not be deterred, however. He never gave up on a fight.

"Your cause is rather outnumbered, Brightly." Constantine set his glass down, but kept his fingers curled around the stem.

"There is still time before the vote. I could use help in convincing others to join us."

"I haven't said how I will cast my vote. Is it wrong to want to prevent foreign imports from undercutting good English grain?"

Brightly sat forward, engaging potential debate with his entire body. "Not in theory. However, in practicality, it won't help the lower classes. Prices are too high, and their wages have not increased. We need to provide relief, such as lower rents."

"As you've done on your estate."

Brightly's estate in northern Essex was one of the most profitable in England, producing a great supply of barley and wheat.

"Precisely."

Brightly made a good argument. He'd lowered his rents a few years ago and had managed to increase his profits.

"I promise I'll come to a decision—my own—soon," Constantine said evenly.

Brightly offered a single nod. "I want you to know that no matter what you decide, I still support regulating the apothecaries."

"Thank you." Constantine wished he could offer the same assertion to Brightly about the importation law. That the other man pledged his support to Constantine's cause without demanding something in return was a rarity among those at Westminster.

Brightly grinned. "You'll come through on the Importation Act, even if it pricks your father's ire."

"It will do more than prick it," Constantine said darkly. "He'll be livid. I hope you're prepared for the effects of his wrath."

Brightly looked surprised. "How will that affect me?"

The duke's threat to have Brightly expelled from White's rose in Constantine's mind, though he doubted his father would actually follow through. He'd been trying to bend Constantine to his will.

Constantine quickly surveyed the large room for the familiar form of the duke but didn't see him. If he was sitting, he likely couldn't be seen. Constantine would hope he wasn't here. "Trust me, he will not forget that you not only championed the opposition of the act, but that you worked to obtain my support."

"You're concerned he'll seek revenge against me for winning you over?" Brightly laughed as he swept up his glass. "I appreciate you looking out for me, but I am not frightened of the Duke of Evesham." He sipped his claret and gave Constantine a devilish look over the rim of his glass.

Constantine admired the man's courage. It made Constantine wonder if *he* was afraid of the duke. Not afraid, but cautious. He'd had to be, lest he end up the subject of his disdain like Lucien, and sometimes Cassandra. Thinking of that only stirred the chaos swirling inside him. He took a long drink of claret.

"I understand Lady Aldington has come to town. Mrs. Brightly and I would be delighted if you would come to dinner next week. Would Wednesday suit you?"

Constantine hesitated. Should he make plans for her? What if she'd already committed to something else? He didn't want to reveal their uncoordinated relationship, so he responded the only way he could. "That would be brilliant. I know Lady Aldington will look forward to it."

Uncoordinated? What a woeful understatement to describe the status of their marriage.

"Mrs. Brightly will be thrilled. Cheers!" Brightly held up his glass and finished his wine. "Now, I must be off to

Brooks's. Still work to be done this eve." He grinned heartily, his blue eyes twinkling. "I'm glad I saw you this evening—always a high point. Night!" He stood and took himself off.

Constantine smiled in spite of how his evening had started. Brightly possessed an uncanny ability to spread good will wherever he went. It was a wonder he wasn't able to convince the entire House of Commons to vote with him.

Nursing his claret, Constantine chatted briefly with a gentleman who stopped to wish him good evening. As soon as he left, the duke sat down at the table, a frown creasing his entire face.

"Good evening, Father." Constantine gripped his wineglass.

"Why were you talking to that miscreant again? I thought we had an arrangement."

"You hinted at one, but yes, we do have an accord. I am going to vote in favor of the Importation Act, and you are going to appoint my wife as Cassandra's sponsor. Starting tomorrow."

The duke clutched a glass of port and lifted it to his lips. "I'll do it after the vote."

Fed up with his father's demands, Constantine leaned forward and spoke quietly but firmly. "That won't be for a fortnight at least. You'll make the change now, or I'll vote with Brightly."

"You wouldn't."

"Do you want to find out? Don't forget who raised me. I will not be manipulated." But he had been—his marriage was the prime example. "Not anymore."

The duke studied him a moment, his eyes glinting with something that might have been admiration, but Constantine couldn't be sure. "I see. I will speak with my sister tomorrow. You may inform Lady Aldington that her sponsorship will begin on Monday. She should come to confer with Cassandra as to her calendar."

"I'll make sure that she does." Victory sang in his blood as he sipped his claret.

A footman arrived at the table and handed Constantine a letter. "Lord Aldington, this was just delivered for you."

Anticipation gripped Constantine as he opened the parchment.

"Who is sending you notes here?" the duke demanded.

Constantine scanned the words. Lucien had set the appointment for one o'clock. That was still so many hours from now.

"No one of import." Constantine refolded the paper and tucked it into his coat. He glanced toward the center of the room and wondered if he could endure an entire evening here. Or perhaps he should follow Brightly to Brooks's.

Returning his attention to his father, he made the decision. He certainly didn't want to spend the evening with the duke. Not that his father would want to either. He would likely go home soon.

Constantine finished his claret. "If you'll excuse me, Father, I have another appointment."

The duke glanced toward Constantine's coat. "To do with that note?"

"Not directly, no." Constantine stood. "It's of no concern to you, in any case. You are not privy to my entire life, nor will you be. Good evening."

He turned and left without allowing the duke to respond. His father was likely seething—he hated not having the last word, and Constantine rarely spoke to him like that. When he did, uncertainty and regret often took hold. He didn't hate his father, and he actually understood why the man treated him with exacting expectation. He only wanted Constantine to be the best. He also demanded the same of Lucien and

Cassandra, except they apparently fell short in the duke's eyes. *That* bothered Constantine.

Walking to Brooks's, Constantine felt the note's presence in his coat, searing him as if it were heated. Or perhaps that was just his blood as he contemplated another meeting with the anonymous tutor. Who was she? And why was he looking forward to seeing her so much?

He realized he'd enjoyed their conversation. Some of it had been uncomfortable, but it had been necessary. He had to think of Sabrina differently, had to treat her differently.

That her anxiety and shyness had been so crippling for her was distressing. Along with the fact that her parents hadn't seemed to care. Why force a Season on a young woman who wasn't prepared? Let alone a marriage? Not even his father was that cruel. When Cassandra had asked to delay her Season, he'd allowed it. And she wasn't plagued by a paralyzing fear of people.

The fact that he was looking forward to his time with the tutor later picked at Constantine's mind. He shouldn't be anticipating it, and he wouldn't allow what had happened last night—they would *only* talk. Now that he knew Sabrina didn't actually loathe him, he could, perhaps, seduce her.

Hopefully the tutor could help him formulate a plan. Her purpose was to educate, and he was ready to learn.

CHAPTER 12

The moment Sabrina stepped inside the Phoenix Club, she felt an overwhelming sense of lightness. There was joy here—sparkling candlelight, laughter, warm and genial employees who greeted her and offered to take care of any need.

It was quite different than her previous visit the night before when she'd been secreted into a side door, ushered up the backstairs to Evie's office, and then taken through a hidden doorway to the gentlemen's side of the second floor.

She looked up at the massive painting of Circe with her nymphs as they seduced Odysseus's men. Some of them already sported snouts and hooves.

"Isn't that a magnificent piece?" Evie met her in the foyer.

"Quite."

"Lucien had it commissioned. It has a brother over on the men's side—Pan hosting a bacchanalia."

"How decadent."

Evie laughed softly. "That describes Lucien, actually. Or at least, the image he projects."

Sabrina thought of her brother-in-law's unassuming residence and wasn't sure she agreed with that assessment. "He strikes me as a rather economical person."

"To do with himself, yes. But when it comes to the club or others, he will spare no effort and no expense. He's an incredibly generous person."

He did seem that. She wondered how the Duke of Evesham had managed to rear such a child. But then she thought of all the ways in which Constantine had been generous—from ensuring she had a beautiful, comfortable residence to allowing her to claim it entirely and make it her own. The red-covered book detailing the plans for the renovation of the parkland was another instance of his generosity, as well as his thoughtfulness. While he may not say the things she wanted to hear, he'd certainly acted in ways that let her know he cared.

And what, exactly, did she hope he would say?

Thankfully, she wasn't able to chase that intrusive thought because a footman approached with a missive for Evie. "Lord Lucien bade me give this to you. I'm to wait to see if you have a response."

"Thank you, Dexter." Evie opened the parchment and read, her lips curling into her heart-stopping smile. "Aldington has requested a meeting with the tutor. Shall we say one o'clock so you have ample time to enjoy the ball?"

Constantine wanted to meet with her—rather, the tutor—again? He'd said he wouldn't. "I—" Her mind arrested, wondering what had provoked his request.

"I need to give Lucien a response," Evie urged.

"Yes, one o'clock is fine." Her mind swam. She'd had to prepare herself extensively for their last meeting. There would be no such luxury this time. Perhaps she would drink an extra glass—or ten—of champagne.

Evie gave their verbal response to the footman, who then

departed toward the gentlemen's side of the club. She offered her arm to Sabrina. "Don't be nervous."

"How can you tell I'm nervous?"

"Because though our friendship is young, I believe I've come to know you well. You require time to think about things and to muster your courage, particularly when it is a new or intimidating experience."

A lump rose in Sabrina's throat. "You *do* know me well. No one has ever understood that about me." She whispered the last, feeling as if she'd received the greatest gift.

Evie patted her forearm. "Thank you for sharing your true self with me. I hope you'll do the same with your husband."

Sabrina had, at least a little, that evening when she'd told him about her anxiety. There was so much she should have revealed about herself, things that could have helped their marriage be more successful.

"I wasn't ready to do that before," Sabrina said quietly. "But I am now." Her parents had pushed her into this union, and it had taken her this long to get to where she could feel a modicum of comfort.

"Marvelous," Evie said brightly. "Now, let us go into the assembly. You look stunning in this new ball gown, by the way. The blue-green suits you well."

Sabrina murmured her thanks as they moved past the cloakroom into the ballroom. The large space was really two spaces—each club had a ballroom—with doors that separated them. Locked at every other time, they were thrown open during assemblies to make one large ballroom. Gleaming chandeliers cast a glow over the brightly clothed ladies and the dashingly garbed gentlemen as they moved over the polished parquet floor.

"The dancing takes place on the gentlemen's side because it has the mezzanine for the musicians. Over here is where people mingle and take refreshment," Evie explained.

Tables ladened with food and drink beckoned the guests, and footmen carried trays of champagne. Music began to filter through the doorways—a waltz.

"Waltzing is allowed here?" Sabrina asked.

"Many things are allowed here that would not be else-where," Evie said with a triumphant nod. "You must come on Tuesday evening, for that is the one night each week when the female members are allowed to enter the gentlemen's side."

"And when are they invited to this side?"

Evie laughed. "Never. Other than assemblies, when only the ballroom and garden are available to them, they are firmly excluded. It's only fitting since there are so many places we may not go."

Sabrina could find no fault with that argument. Scanning the room, she looked for people she knew and realized there weren't very many. But then, she scarcely knew anyone really. Instead of feeling eager to make acquaintances and show everyone that she was not the meek countess they might remember—or perhaps, more accurately, who they didn't recall at all—she found herself thinking about her appointment later. Why had Constantine requested it?

Alas, the curiosity was bound to nibble at her all evening while she played the role that she'd accepted nearly two years ago. She gave her head a shake and told herself to focus on being the countess she needed to be. One who the Duke of Evesham would allow to sponsor his daughter. She realized she didn't see Cassandra there, but then she wasn't a member, and apparently couldn't be since she wasn't married.

"Perhaps you can explain who is here tonight," Sabrina said. "Only members?"

"Mostly, but you'll see plenty of young ladies on the Marriage Mart here. If one's sponsor is a member, they may attend the assemblies. We've also recently expanded the rules as to who may come to include family of members."

"Then my sister-in-law should be here, should she not?"

"She attended last week. However, it is my understanding that the duke does not want her to come to every assembly. In fact, I think he has said that last Friday was the only one she could attend." Evie grimaced. "He's so dictatorial, but then I suppose you know that."

"Yes," Sabrina murmured. "If I'm able to become her sponsor, I will try to persuade His Grace that she be allowed to come. This seems a far better place to meet someone than Almack's." Her shoulders twitched as she recalled the one time she'd visited that most auspicious place. She hadn't relaxed during the entire evening and had been more than grateful that her impending betrothal had prevented a second ordeal.

"I do hope that will come to pass." Evie looked about the room. "I keep trying to think of a suitable groom for Lady Cassandra, but so far I haven't discovered anyone who I think will keep her interest. Perhaps more importantly, I can't think of anyone who wants to take on the duke as a father-in-law." She flashed Sabrina a look of admiration. "You are quite the brave soul."

Laughter erupted from Sabrina with such force that she had to clap her hand over her mouth. "Not at all. The man terrifies me still and probably always will. I've always thought of him as the man who coldly arranged my marriage."

Evie gave her a look of sympathy. "I do hope you and Aldington will be able to find some measure of happiness."

"Until you introduced me to the possibility of a pleasing…physical relationship, I only wanted to have an amiable marriage—and a child."

"And now you want more?"

"I think I do." The thoughtful husband who gave her gifts and took drastic measures to improve the sexual nature of their marriage was someone she wanted. As desperately as she wanted a child, she *desired* her husband. "But I don't know if Aldington does."

"I don't think he would be meeting with a tutor for help if he didn't want something…more." Evie smiled encouragingly.

How Sabrina hoped her friend was right.

~

*B*ecause Sabrina had not known she would be playing the part of the tutor this evening, she was wearing far more clothing than the night before—she'd dressed for a ball, not seduction. But then, last night's meeting hadn't required her to be dressed, or not dressed, in any particular way. She rather assumed that tonight would be the same, but Evie convinced her to don a scarlet dressing gown she'd procured. Even though Aldington wouldn't see the garment, and it was likely unnecessary, the fitted gown helped Sabrina transition from elegant countess to tempting former courtesan.

As with last time, she waited in the chamber next to the one where Constantine was located. A knock on the door, just like the previous night, told her it was time. That he was ready.

Taking a deep breath, Sabrina stepped into the dim corridor. She knew Lucien was somewhere nearby, ensuring that no one happened upon them, particularly while she moved between rooms.

She hurried into Constantine's chamber, barely opening the door before slipping inside. The interior was even darker than the corridor had been, with only the single candle burning on the mantel.

Constantine stood where he had last night, near the bedpost, his eyes covered with a dark blindfold. She wished she could see his eyes for they were quite lovely with their long lashes and captivating hazel color. However, with them masked, the rest of his features commanded her attention. Despite the near darkness, she could make out the aquiline slope of his nose, as well as his lips, especially the lush, full lower one. She'd stared at it last night, wondering what it would be like to take it between her teeth.

"Good evening," she said, employing the Welsh lilt she'd used before and cutting herself off before she called him "my lord." It was difficult to remember she wasn't supposed to know his identity.

"Thank you for seeing me again." His voice seemed different too, lower and rougher. Arousing.

"I was surprised you asked. And so soon."

He took a step toward her. "I needed to see you. To…talk."

She watched his hands flex and his chest rise and fall with rapid breaths. Last night, he'd discarded his coat and boots. Tonight, he'd only removed his coat.

"Is that all you wish to do? Talk?"

It took him a long minute to answer, and when he did, he sounded strained. "Yes."

Constantine raked his hand through the front of his hair, tousling the light brown waves over his forehead. It made him look reckless. She liked it, then wondered if she might like it more if she'd been the one to do it. Oh, she was feeling quite audacious this evening.

She liked the sensation. She felt…powerful. Or as if she could be.

"I don't know how to begin with my wife." He pivoted toward the bed and reached out to grip the post. That had helped to steady him last night—she was sure of it. And that knowledge had filled her with a joyful satisfaction. She'd pushed him to the edge, and he'd stepped off it into wild abandon.

He continued, "She invited me to visit her bed later tonight, but I don't know what she actually wants. There is so much I don't understand about her." There was an agony in his tone that tore at her chest. "I wish she hadn't hidden herself from me."

No one regretted that more than Sabrina. She hadn't been able to see past her fear and anxiety to give this man—her husband—a chance. Moving toward him, she stopped just shy of touching him. "Is she hiding from you now?"

"No. I just wish I knew if she really wanted *me*." He let out a low, harsh laugh. "Don't we all want to be desired?"

"Is she desired?"

He let go of the post and faced her. She tried to imagine his gaze behind the blindfold. Did he keep his eyes closed, or was he staring at her, unseeing, through the fabric?

"Yes." The word was barely audible. He cleared his throat and said it again, this time with more volume and weight. "You have to help me. I don't know what to do. She suffers from some sort of affliction, I think, where she can't face people without great effort. I wish I'd known this when we wed. I would have—" He exhaled and dropped his head forward to massage the back of his neck. "I would have been more considerate."

"You might have guided her?" Sabrina asked, wishing they could go back and start over.

"I think so." He exhaled. "It's so hard to say. We both started with the absolute wrong expectations. But I am trying to set things right." Turning, he sat on the edge of the bed, moving cautiously and using his hands to find his way. "I mean to seduce her, as you suggested. However, I don't want to move too quickly. She is easily agitated."

Sabrina's chest expanded as she listened to him. Could this be her husband? She'd never estimated the depth of his thoughtfulness. "You seem to be such a generous person."

As soon as the word generous left her lips, her mouth went dry with fear. She'd said that to him earlier, as his wife. Gathering her dressing gown in her fists, she squeezed, worried that he would put everything together and determine her identity.

Best not to let him think about it.

"Why did you want to see me tonight?"

He licked his lips. "I thought I might…tell you what I would do."

"That is an excellent idea." Her body was already hungry with need, just from the prospect of hearing him *talk* about what he would do to her. "What you would do to your wife if she were here?"

The intake of his breath, sharp and sudden, fanned the desire smoldering within her. "That would depend on what she would allow."

"Pretend she would permit you anything. Would you kiss her? Caress her? Bring her release? Tell me."

"I would feast upon her with my eyes. She's the most beautiful woman I've ever known."

Sabrina's knees quaked under the aching sweetness of his words. "Tell me what you would do after you looked your fill of her. Imagine I am your wife."

She saw him swallow, his throat working. "She's nude," he rasped. "I would kiss her—with my lips and tongue, exploring every part of her mouth."

Heat pooled in Sabrina's sex and built, like a fire taking

hold from a flickering spark to an eager, hungry flame. "What then?"

"I would kiss along her neck," he continued, his voice deeply sensual, captivating her with each word. "She smells like vanilla and apples, so fresh and sweet. The scent is most potent between her breasts, I think. I would bury my face there, cupping her flesh before I took one of her nipples into my mouth."

In response, Sabrina's nipples hardened to stiff points. She'd never experienced quite this sensation, this aching fullness, desperate for his touch. And all of it came from just words. "Then what would you do?"

"I would use my tongue and perhaps my teeth—gently, of course—and I would suckle her. Hard. Until she cried out. I have to determine what she likes. Will she like me to pinch her, to torment her until she can no longer bear it?"

Sabrina pressed her thighs together to ease the pulsing ache between them. "I think she would like that. Tell me what else."

"I would stroke her sex and tease her until she was panting."

Sabrina's lips had parted, and she realized she was precariously close to doing exactly what he described.

Constantine went on, "When she could no longer bear the anticipation, I would press my finger into her."

Unable to suffer another moment, she perched beside him on the bed, careful not to touch him. She pressed her hand between her legs and stroked herself through the silk of the dressing gown. "*Please.* Don't stop. What else would you do?"

"I'd fill her with my fingers and make her come."

Sabrina longed to open the gown and do what he said. Actually, she wanted him to do it, but he couldn't. Not like this. She rubbed her clitoris, her hips moving gently.

"Are you...?" His unfinished question made her stop.

Filling her lungs, she moved her hand to her thigh. "Please, continue."

"I would marvel at her naked beauty, at the honeyed curls guarding the sweetest part of her. And then I would taste, softly at first. When she relaxed—*if* she relaxed—I'd claim her. She is *mine*." His breath caressed her ear. "You didn't have to stop. I won't touch you, but you can touch yourself."

"Will you?" Sabrina managed to ask. The notion of them together on this bed, pleasuring themselves in concert, was incredibly erotic. She was quivering at the thought.

"I wasn't going to, but I admit it's difficult when I imagine my wife splayed nude before me." He inhaled sharply. "It's a dream, and I don't know if it will ever come true."

"It will." Sabrina was so tempted to tell him who she was, to show him that his dream could come true. "I can't imagine your wife resisting or not reacting—with complete abandon —to this seduction. You can do this." She was desperate for him to try.

"I will...try what you suggest. It's difficult to imagine talking to her when she blushes at the slightest provocation."

Frustration rippled through Sabrina. She wasn't as pathetic as that, was she? She'd been assertive and straight-forward on several occasions since coming to town. Perhaps she needed to do more to invite him to talk to her, to reveal himself. To reveal his desires. "Think of her as a woman with wants and needs she hasn't discovered yet. Show her what she has been missing. Don't you think she will appreciate that?"

"When you put it like that, yes. I will start with talking to her and not necessarily just about this. We need to establish a level of comfort between us. An intimacy such that even friends share."

His words made her want to swoon. "That is an excellent way to begin."

"Would you mind going now?" he asked.

She stood from the bed, her knees weak from her unsatisfied desire. "Your wife is a lucky woman. I hope you show her how much soon."

She hurried from the room, taking care to glance about the corridor before she closed the door behind her. Even more quickly, she rushed to the chamber with her clothing. She rang a bellpull, and someone knew to summon Evie, who would help her dress.

While she waited, she went back over his every word and nearly succumbed to touching herself. She would wait, however, in case he visited her bedchamber later. If he didn't, she may become impatient and throw herself at him.

Anticipation danced along her flesh as she realized the stakes had changed. She wanted much more than just a child. She wanted a real marriage.

CHAPTER 13

"*D*o you approve, my lord?" Haddock asked from the other side of the dining room table.

Twelve wine glasses stood in two rows on the table at his chair and Sabrina's. Each glass held a small amount of a different wine. In the front row were three claret wines and three hock, while the rear glasses contained fortified wines. The type of wine and the year it was produced had been written on small pieces of parchment, which were placed at the base of Sabrina's glasses—because this was for her education.

"I do. You've outdone yourself, thank you."

Haddock smiled. He'd seemed to show a...livelier side since the incident with the cat. "It was my pleasure to arrange for this tasting. What a wonderful idea to introduce her ladyship to wine."

Constantine hoped it would be more than that. After last night's meeting with the tutor, he was committed to doing what he'd said. He meant to seduce his wife and not just in the bedchamber. That was why he hadn't visited her last night. They needed to establish a relationship if they meant to carry on.

Mrs. Haddock strode into the dining room. "Her ladyship will be down presently. I will fetch the accompaniments." She'd looked at Constantine as she'd spoken, but before she went to the door to the backstairs to the kitchen, she sent a glance toward her husband who reacted very slightly. Still, Constantine noticed. There was a lightening to Haddock's expression, an answering glow in his eyes.

Constantine wondered if he and Sabrina would ever exchange such looks.

He moved to the doorway to await his wife. A moment later, she appeared, as breathtakingly lovely as always. Her honey-gold hair was worked into a simple style, but a pearl comb nestled amongst the curls. It matched the pearls at her throat, which in turn complimented her rose and ivory floral gown. She looked fresh and alluring, as if she'd just walked in from outside and brought the sun with her.

Her slender brows arched, and her eyes widened as she took in the table. "My goodness, that's a great many wine-glasses."

"It is indeed. Today, you're going to taste a variety of wines so that you may decide what you prefer."

"You planned this?" She stared at him in wonder.

"Mostly Haddock did, but at my request." He dashed a grateful glance toward the butler.

"This is...marvelous." She shook her head, then pivoted to face him. "I am reminded that I didn't properly thank you for your other thoughtfulness—the red book from Repton. I still can't quite believe you had that done. I can't possibly express my gratitude. Or my delight." Her blue gaze met his with an openness he didn't think they'd ever held in his presence.

A surprising burst of joy spread through him, a splendid

heat that made him want to smile. So he did. "It was my pleasure to commission it. Did you like his design?"

"Very much. It's exactly what I would have wanted to do, but then I deeply admire Capability Brown's landscapes, which seems to have been the primary influence."

His brow puckered. *"Would have wanted...* Would you not like to have the work completed?

Her eyes goggled even wider this time. "You would support that?"

"Of course. Why have him make the book if we didn't plan to complete the work?"

"Oh." She pressed her lips together, and for a moment he was uncertain. She appeared agitated. Then her face lit with a smile, as if she were indeed carrying the sun in her pocket. "I would love to see it done. I am overwhelmed by your generosity."

That word—generosity—made him think of the tutor. She'd said something similar last night...

Mrs. Haddock came in bearing a tray of food to be sampled with the wine. There were biscuits, breads, and cheeses, as well as some fruit. As she set the tray down and began to arrange the dishes, Sabrina moved toward the table.

"This is enough food for a group," she noted.

"Perhaps we should invite the Haddocks to join us," Constantine offered genially.

Both the butler and the housekeeper stared at him, freezing in place for a moment.

"I am content to pour for you and her ladyship," Haddock said carefully.

Constantine hadn't meant to make them uncomfortable. "Yes, of course." He moved to Sabrina's chair and held it for her.

She murmured her thanks as she sat. Then she lifted her gaze to Mrs. Haddock. "How is Grayson?"

"He's quite well, my lady"

"Naughty as ever?" Sabrina asked with a smile that captivated Constantine's attention as he took his chair.

Mrs. Haddock chuckled. "He's slightly improved, as evidenced by his lack of gallivanting about the house." She grimaced toward Constantine. "I'm still so mortified by his behavior that day, my lord."

"I would say it's been forgotten, but I fear that's impossible. There is, however, nothing for you to feel mortified about. Now, please tell us about what you've arranged on the table."

As the housekeeper reviewed the cheeses in particular, Constantine watched the slope of his wife's neck as she nodded in response, the flutter of her lashes against her cheeks. He heard none of what was said as he lost himself in the simple beauty of the woman seated beside him.

"I thought you might begin with the red wines, my lord." Haddock's deep baritone pushed Constantine from his reverie.

"Very good."

"I've provided information about each wine for Lady Aldington." He looked toward Sabrina expectantly. "Perhaps you'd like to set aside the cards for your favorites so that we may take note. I can also communicate your preferences to Dagnall so that you may request specific wines at Hampton Lodge."

"What a brilliant idea. Thank you, Haddock."

The butler inclined his head. "Mrs. Haddock and I shall leave you to it."

The housekeeper started to turn as her husband came abreast of her, and it would have been easy, second nature even, for Haddock to gently touch her back as they departed. However, he didn't do that, nor did she move close enough to invite his attention. Because they couldn't, not while they were working. Why had Constantine never wondered about their marriage and how it might converge with their posts before?

"Haddock," Constantine called before they left.

The butler pivoted. "My lord?"

"When you and Mrs. Haddock have your next afternoon off, I want you to have your own wine tasting."

Haddock looked mildly horrified. "We could not."

"I insist. With the cheeses too." He smiled at Mrs. Haddock who looked completely bemused.

"Thank you, my lord," Haddock said, and this time they left without interruption.

Sabrina slid him a glance that was not unlike Mrs. Haddock's expression. "I think you shocked them."

"Did I surprise you too?"

"Yes. With the Repton book and now this."

"I am also surprising myself," he murmured. "Shall we sample the first claret?" He picked up his glass.

She did the same. "How am I to try all this without becoming frightfully inebriated? I have never been even a little bit drunk, but I hear the aftereffects can be most unpleasant."

"That is true. The first time I overimbibed, I was at Oxford. I couldn't hold my head up straight or keep food in my stomach for two days."

Again, her eyes rounded. It seemed he couldn't help but shock her repeatedly today. "I can't believe you would do that."

"It was many years ago, but yes. I haven't thought of that in a very long time." He sipped the claret and set the glass down. "If you take very small samples and nibble as you go along, you should be fine. The white wines have a lower alcohol content while the fortified wines in the back row have more."

"I see. Perhaps I won't even finish those. Or I will barely wet my lips with them."

Suddenly he was staring at her mouth, wishing he could wet her lips with his tongue. He took another drink of the claret. "Ah, what did you think of that one?"

"It was nice, I suppose. I should probably try the next one so that I have something to compare it to." She sampled the second glass, and Constantine did the same.

"Clarets are a blend of different grapes from the Burgundy region of France. The first two have been in the cellar for some time, but the third one, I admit, was smuggled last year."

She gave him a sly look. "I never would have guessed you would purchase smuggled wine. You are so very proper."

"Occasionally, I allow myself to indulge." He winked at her and couldn't remember the last time he'd done so. Had he ever winked at anyone before?

"This must be a very good wine." She plucked up the third glass and sipped. "Oh, that is lovely. I would describe it as velvety. It's very soft against my tongue."

Did she have any idea what her words were doing to him? He was half-erect already. Shifting in his chair, he took a drink, already knowing it was his favorite of the three reds. "Velvety is exactly the word I would use. I think we should have a few bites before we continue."

"Allow me. But first, let me set this card aside." She plucked up the third claret card and set it to the left of her place so that it was between them. Standing, she put together two plates of the various foods.

Constantine continued to take pleasure in watching her. This simple task she performed was incredibly domestic and somehow also incredibly arousing. Perhaps he should stop looking at her backside as she bent over the table. "I wanted to tell you that my father has agreed to allow you to assume the responsibilities of sponsor for my sister."

Sabrina dropped a wedge of apple on the tablecloth, her gaze snapping to Constantine's. "He did?"

"Aren't you pleased?" He couldn't tell, particularly since her eyes had darkened with what he thought was fear.

"I am, though I confess I am astonished that he agreed. I expected him to refuse." She picked up the apple and put it on the plate before setting it in front of Constantine.

He wouldn't tell her that he was also surprised or that he'd negotiated for it to happen. "The transition will take place Monday. In the meantime, you must call on Cassandra tomorrow to review her calendar and strategize."

The fear he'd glimpsed a moment ago flashed back. She busied herself finishing her plate. "The strategy is with regard to finding a husband?"

"That is my father's primary objective." And perhaps his only one, at least as far as Cassandra was concerned. With Constantine, the duke had wanted him wed, but, more importantly, he wanted him ready for the dukedom and weighted with the necessary sense of propriety and duty. His goals for Lucien were less concrete. Indeed, Constantine wasn't entirely sure what their father expected of his middle child.

What he did know, however, was that happiness or contentment didn't seem to be of interest to their father.

Sabrina retook her seat and picked up a piece of white cheese. "I will do my best to ensure Cassandra is settled with due haste. To her satisfaction, of course." She glanced toward him, her shoulders hunched, making her appear nervous.

"We are in agreement on that." He wanted to allay her concerns. There was no use in asking if she truly wanted to take this on. It was too late. The commitment had been made, and to withdraw now would only irritate his father. It would also confirm his low expectations, and Constantine would move heaven and earth to ensure Sabrina exceeded them. "I'm afraid it will be challenging to support Cassandra in the way you must while also adhering to my father's demands. We will all present a united front if trouble arises."

Her shoulders straightened, and he hoped that meant she felt better. "What sort of trouble?"

He swallowed a bite of cheese. "In the event Cassandra doesn't find anyone she wishes to marry this Season. I won't let him force her, not like he and your parents did with us."

Their eyes met, and in hers he saw gratitude and something else he couldn't precisely define. Warmth spread through him, and he abruptly returned his attention to the wine. "There are three kinds of white wines—all hock, which is from Germany. The first one is the youngest and will be the least sweet. The next one is sweeter and the last is the sweetest of all. As I said, they have a lower level of alcohol. So if you like them, you could rest easy that you could drink it throughout dinner and not become inebriated."

"No wonder so many ladies prefer it. I've tried it, of course, but I didn't realize there was a variation in sweetness. I don't know that I would have ever called it sweet based on my experience."

"If you've only ever had them with meals, you would likely have had the less sweet version." He smiled as he lifted the first of the hocks. "See what you think after you sample these."

After trying the first glass, she seemed to think for a moment, her lips pursed. "I'm not sure I like that. Perhaps it is better with food." She bit into an apple wedge. "That is preferable. In fact, I now think I've had this particular hock before at a dinner somewhere."

"Speaking of dinner, the Brightlys have invited us to dine

with them Wednesday evening. I hope you don't mind, but I accepted. If you have a conflicting engagement—"

He didn't have a chance to finish before she shook her head. "No, nothing. That sounds lovely. I so enjoy Mrs. Brightly."

"The sentiment is mutual. She is quite looking forward to it, according to Brightly." He finished the first glass of hock. "I suppose we should try to coordinate our social engagements."

Her brow creased, which was a usual occurrence during their acquaintance, but less, he noticed, since she'd come to town. "Because of last night? I notice you haven't asked me about the assembly."

No, he hadn't. In part, that was because he'd been too focused on what had happened later in the evening. "I should have done. Did you enjoy yourself?"

"I did. The club is beautiful."

Constantine didn't tell her he'd harangued his brother for an invitation. She didn't need to see the depth of his jealousy. The emotion reared its nasty head once more as he imagined her dancing beneath the sparkling chandeliers. He knew his brother had spared no expense with the club's decoration, a fact that drove their father mad with fury.

He drank the entirety of the middle hock in one swallow. "See if you like that one."

She sampled it but seemed preoccupied with him as her gaze kept straying in his direction. "That's very good. I hope you know that I regret we weren't able to go together last night. I'm attending another ball tonight. Will you be able to accompany me?"

There was a note of hope in her voice that drove the jealousy from his mind. "I'm afraid I have an appointment I can't miss, a strategizing session at a colleague's house."

"Of course. You are so very busy with important work."

She smiled briefly before tasting the third hock. "I rather like that. I could drink far more than would be necessary." The card went immediately to her left to join the claret card.

Constantine nearly laughed. "That is often the way with alcohol. Perhaps I can join you at the ball later? Where is it?"

"Lord and Lady Hargrove are hosting."

"I shall do my best. Starting next week, I will ensure I attend the same events as you and Cassandra. I have tried to appear alongside my sister, but now I have even more reason to do so."

She stared at him, and the air between them seemed to thicken. "Why, because I'm there?"

"Yes." He picked up the first wine in the back row. "This and the next are madeiras, then two sherries, a port, and lastly, a marsala."

She sampled the first madeira, doing what she'd said and taking a very small amount. Her eyes shuttered, and she took another, longer sip. When she opened her eyes, he saw joy. "Oh, that is very good." Off the card went into the pile of favorites.

"I think you might be in trouble," he said, smiling. "I'm afraid the next one is even better. At least in my opinion." He moved on to the second madeira.

Sabrina brought the second glass to her lips and took another tiny sip. Her brows flew up, and she sampled more. "Oh dear." Picking up the card, she set it neatly atop the growing stack to her left. "That really is splendid. I'd like to drink the rest of it, but I shan't. Perhaps I won't like the remaining wines and then I can come back to it."

Constantine suspected she was going to like all the fortified wines. It was hard not to. But like her, he was careful not to overindulge. This was yet another trait he owed to his father. Except sometimes he did like to indulge, as he'd told her earlier. Suddenly, he wanted to drink all the fortified wine and pour additional glasses of their favorites. He and Sabrina could become quite drunk, and he imagined their conversation—and perhaps their inhibitions—would become loose and open.

"I knew I liked madeira, but I haven't had it often," she said. "It's good to taste these like this. I'm able to differentiate between all of them, which will help me decide what to drink in the future. Everyone should do this before they enter Society."

Constantine tasted the first sherry, and she joined him. Her lips twisted briefly as she seemed to contemplate the taste.

"You don't like it?" he asked.

"I do, but not as much as the madeira." Her features relaxed into an easy smile. He realized he was becoming more used to this version of her, where smiles and conversation didn't seem laborious. "Thankfully."

"Onto the next then." He lifted the second sherry in a toast. "Sack was once considered the finest wine in the world."

Sabrina held up her glass and squinted at the amber liquid. "I wonder where the name sack came from." She tasted the wine and immediately took a longer sip. "Oh dear, that's quite lovely too."

"It derives from a Spanish word, I believe." Constantine took another sip because she was right. It was delicious. "Drake brought a great supply of it to Queen Elizabeth, and we've been in love with it ever since."

"Understandably." She moved the second sherry's card to the pile. "It seems I prefer the fortified wine to the regular." Her features had creased as if this were a problem.

"Does that trouble you?"

"Apparently, I prefer the higher alcohol content. Does that mean I wish to get drunk?"

Constantine laughed. "I think it's because it's sweeter overall. Most people prefer it. But yes, it also gives you a nice, warm feeling rather quickly, don't you think?"

She'd frozen, her hand hovering above the glass of port. "You've never done that before," she whispered.

He frowned, slightly alarmed by her expression and tone. "What?"

"Laughed."

"Of course I've laughed."

She shook her head gently. "Not with me." She lifted the glass of port and took the longest drink yet, as if she'd forgotten they were supposed to be tasting and not just drinking.

Constantine snatched up his port and downed the entire thing. It was his favorite port, and frankly, he needed a bit of fortification in that moment.

He'd never laughed with her. That should surprise him, disappoint him—and it did. But mostly it made him sad and angry at himself for being so damned uptight. For the first time, he understood why his brother harassed him about having a stick up his arse.

"What do you think of the port?" His voice sounded as if it had collected dust in an attic the past fifty years.

"I like it a great deal." Her gaze was fixed on his, and for a moment, he thought she meant him.

"It's my favorite," he murmured, wondering if he was referring to the wine or the incomparable woman before him. He may have married the woman his father chose, but he began to wonder if he might have selected her himself if they'd been given the chance to properly court.

That's what he was doing. This was courtship, not seduction. The latter would come, but the former was more important. It was why he didn't reach for her now.

"Is the port going into your pile then?"

She blinked and the spell, or whatever it was between them, faded. "Most definitely." She transferred the card. "Down to the last one, I suppose. Which is for the best, because I am feeling rather...warm, as you said. And tingly." She shook her shoulders and arms as if a great shiver had passed over her. Then she smiled, and he was utterly convinced the sun was not just in her pocket but at her command.

"Shall we finish then?" he asked, lifting his glass of marsala. "This is somewhat like a white grape version of port. Let's see which you prefer."

"This is the one wine on the table I have never had." She brought the glass to her mouth and took a very small amount. Perhaps just enough to wet her lips, as she'd indicated, because her tongue licked along them, capturing the wine and drawing it into her mouth. Constantine couldn't have looked away from her if his life depended on it. Rather, it felt as if his life, his livelihood, his very breath relied upon her lush pink lips.

He wanted nothing more than to put his mouth on hers and lose himself in her velvety softness. Instead, he drank the entire glass of marsala and looked to the sideboard where all the bottles and decanters stood. When he turned his head back toward Sabrina, it was to see her finishing the glass.

She moved the marsala card to the favorites pile and declared, "The best of the lot. I fear I'm ruined for other wines."

"Would you like more?" He was already out of his chair because, dammit, he was having more. In fact, he might polish off the bottle to keep himself from dragging his wife from her seat and carrying her upstairs.

Courtship now. Seduction later.

Yes, that was the right plan.

"Are you having more?" she asked.

He brought the bottle back to the table. "Yes." He looked at her in question as he began to pour into her glass.

"Thank you. Not too much."

He filled the glass a little more than halfway, then gave himself the same amount. "I'll convey your cards to Haddock so he may inform Dagnall."

"There's no hurry. I'm not rushing back to Hampton Lodge any time soon." She peered at him over her glass before taking a drink.

She was flirting with him again. He needed to respond in kind. How did he not know how to flirt? Because almost the entirety of his education, and certainly what he practiced, came from his father, who wouldn't know how to flirt if a peacock strutted around his bedroom every morning in an attempt to teach him the basic ways of nature.

Constantine may not be a peacock, but he could try. He leaned toward Sabrina and caught the scent of vanilla and apple. "Good. Because this wine tasting is just the beginning of this Season. Our Season."

Her lips parted, and it seemed her chest began to move more rapidly, as if her pulse had quickened. His had too, and he was now fully erect, his body eager for the next step.

Soon.

He held his glass toward her. "To the Season."

She tapped hers against his. "To the Season."

Starting with how in the hell he was going to ensure his meeting that night finished soon enough for him to join her at the ball.

CHAPTER 14

*A*s Sabrina stepped out of the coach in front of Evesham House in Grosvenor Square, she almost hoped she would turn her ankle so she could abort the visit and return home. Her chest felt tight, and her breathing was shallow as she worked to overcome her anxiety. The façade of the duke's residence rose tall and intimidating with four pillars at the entrance and gleaming windows stacked in perfect symmetry across the four visible stories.

Smoothing her hand over her hip, she took confidence in another of her new costumes. The smart walking dress was crafted from a bold, bright green and decorated with gold buttons and stitching. She chose to wear the color today to show the duke that she could be daring, that she was, without a doubt, the Countess of Aldington and the future Duchess of Evesham.

Constantine had said it was best if she went alone, and while she agreed, she was still nervous. Particularly since she'd felt a bit lethargic that morning. After yesterday's wine sampling, she'd emerged from her alcohol-infused giddiness feeling incredibly tired. So tired, in fact, that she'd left the ball rather early. Because of that, she'd already departed by the time Constantine was finally able to arrive.

She'd apologized to him earlier. He'd smiled warmly and assured her all was well, that it was he who should be sorry for not accompanying her in the first place. That was when she'd suggested he come along with her on this call. It wasn't that he hadn't wanted to. He'd argued that she'd gain more ground with the duke if she went on her own.

Lifting her lips into a smile she hoped would buoy her spirit, she went to the door, which a footman opened just as she arrived in front of it.

The butler stood in the center of the cavernous foyer. With its polished marble, sparkling gilt, and excess of eye-popping artwork, the space more resembled a museum instead of a home. She had this same thought every time she entered the duke's house and wondered what it had been like for Constantine to grow up in such a lavish place.

"Good afternoon, Lady Aldington," the butler intoned evenly. "His Grace is awaiting you upstairs in the drawing room."

Sabrina exhaled in relief. Constantine had thought she would be subjected to a more formal interview in his study. That's how he met with his sons, as if they were business associates instead of family. "Thank you."

She followed the butler into the staircase hall, which was every bit as grand as the foyer. The walls were covered in a dark wood paneling that matched the stairs. The atmosphere was masculine but also warm, warmer than the foyer at least. Here, she could imagine Constantine and Lucien chasing each other up or down the stairs. But then, she doubted they'd been allowed to do such things given the duke's disposition.

The duke was waiting for her in the drawing room, which was at the front of the house. He stood near the hearth, his dark gray brows drawn over his deep brown eyes that could have been borrowed from Lucien's face. Overall, he and Lucien looked quite a bit alike, while Constantine seemed to favor their mother, at least based on the portraits Sabrina had seen.

Sabrina sank into a curtsey. "Good afternoon, Your Grace."

"Come and sit, Countess." He indicated a chair, giving her no choice as to where she might sit.

When she was seated, he took a chair directly across from her, which seemed to put them in physical opposition. Or perhaps her mind was only looking for negativity.

She needed to be optimistic about this meeting. "Thank you for allowing me to sponsor Lady Cassandra. I am very much looking forward to guiding her this Season."

He squinted one eye at her as he rested his forearms on the sides of the chair. "That's amusing, isn't it? You guiding anyone through a Season when you have no experience. You could scarcely manage to suffer through yours."

She should have expected this. The man had never minced words. "I am older now. More mature."

A smirk twisted his lips, but he schooled his features quickly. "I should hope so. I am, in fact, counting on it. I will be watching you closely. Your primary objective is to see my daughter wed to an acceptable gentleman. You likely think I'm a hard and uncaring father, but I indulge my daughter past the point where most fathers would. I let her delay her Season, and I am giving her the opportunity to choose her husband."

"Which is more than you allowed your heir," she murmured. If he was going to speak plainly, so would she.

His brows shot up. "The kitten has claws? I never would have guessed." His demeanor altered slightly as he shifted in his chair and seemed to regard her with something akin to appreciation. Not admiration, however. That would be too much to hope for.

Still, Sabrina's chest expanded, and she sat a little taller. "I understand what you wish to happen, and I shall do my best to help Lady Cassandra find a match that is acceptable to her."

"Just know that if she does not, she will be wed to a man of my choosing."

Sabrina didn't doubt he was serious, even if he did have a habit of indulging Cassandra. "Have you already identified this man?"

He narrowed his eyes. "You are no longer a kitten but a cat. I shall bear that in mind. Enough of that discussion. There is one other matter I must address with you, and that is your failing role as countess. If you are to be Duchess of Evesham one day—and of course you shall, unless you happen to die—you must claim a larger role in Society."

Sabrina nearly choked as she swallowed. "I shall endeavor to cling to my mortal coil. What sort of role?" Her stomach knotted as she considered what he might have in mind. The thought of having any sort of "role" beyond that of countess made her want to retch.

"As countess and future duchess!" He glowered at her as if she were daft. "People look to you to be a leader—in fashion and entertaining." He blew out a breath as if he'd traversed dangerous terrain. "I am pleased to see you are dressed well today. It is a marked improvement."

Though it was a backhanded compliment, she would take it, given the source. "Thank you. I have an entirely new wardrobe for the Season."

"You may gain my confidence yet. However, to do so, you must do something else besides succeed as Cassandra's sponsor." He paused, and Sabrina wondered if it was to allow her gut to churn in anticipation for this mysterious task.

Whether that was his intent or not, her insides recoiled. "You and Aldington will host a ball on the twenty-third. The purpose will be to present Cassandra formally."

Sabrina *had* mentioned to Constantine that they should have a ball, she was still reluctant. It wasn't the planning or the execution, but rather fulfilling the requirements of a hostess at such an event. She'd have to greet everyone and ensure she exuded charm and poise for hours and hours amidst a clamoring crowd of some of the most judgmental people in London. Or not—she controlled the guest list, did she not? Perhaps she'd limit the invitation to members of the Phoenix Club. She'd never felt more comfortable amongst strangers than she had that night.

With more than a month to plan, she was certain that she could organize an outstanding event. "I'd been thinking of having a ball, but I'd thought to do so in May instead of April."

"April? No, the twenty-third of *March*."

Leaning forward, Sabrina practically fell out of her chair. "That's in ten days."

"Eleven, but no matter. There's no time to waste. Cassandra needs a groom, and the Season will be well underway by the twenty-third of April. Her Grace could have executed a ball here by Friday." His features softened briefly, but it was fleeting, and his austere expression returned.

Was he setting her up to fail? She longed to ask him that. "This is my first experience hosting anything," she said quietly. "I wouldn't want it to be lacking."

"Then don't allow it to be. You've proven yourself to possess more grit than I originally thought. I am certain you can meet this challenge." His eyes glittered expectantly. "Am I wrong?"

"No, Your Grace. I will rise to this occasion." She only hoped she didn't topple to the ground.

He abruptly stood. "Excellent. I shall look forward to my invitation. I'm certain your retainers will be up to the task, however if you require assistance, please feel free to consult Bender."

What would Constantine say if he'd heard his father practically insult his servants? Feeling particularly defensive about the wonderful people who ran Aldington House, she also stood and lifted her gaze to his. "Our butler and housekeeper are more than capable of managing everything that is required."

"My offer remains should you need it." His attention flicked to the doorway. "Here is my lovely daughter and her companion. I shall leave you trio to plot." He strode toward the door but paused at the threshold as Lady Cassandra and Miss Lancaster moved into the room. "Remember the goal, ladies. There will be a June wedding. You need only find the groom."

And with that, he departed, leaving a rather cold air swirling.

Lady Cassandra curled her lip toward the doorway and deposited herself onto a settee with a low grumble. Glaring toward the doorway, she pressed her lips together. "Pffft."

Even when she made a face and a silly sound, Lady Cassandra was beautiful. With her dark hair and eyes, she definitely took after her father and Lucien, but there was a golden quality to her eyes that the men didn't possess. In fact, if Sabrina had to describe the color, she would call them sherry. Or did she just want another glass of that excellent wine she'd tasted yesterday?

As the companion sat down beside her, Sabrina stood and went to take a chair closer to them in the center of the room. "Good afternoon, Lady Cassandra, Miss Lancaster."

Lady Cassandra straightened herself and smoothed her hands over her cheeks and across the sides of her head before folding them primly to her lap. "Why are you calling me *Lady* Cass*andra*? You should be calling me Cass as Lucien does and as Con does when he's feeling less priggish."

"Then you must call me Sabrina."

"I already do in my head. Does that count?" She grinned, and Sabrina laughed.

Sabrina looked hopefully between the two women before landing her gaze on Cass. "I don't suppose you've identified a potential suitor?"

"Not yet. I think they're all too afraid of my father to approach me anyway."

"Well, I can understand that," Sabrina said wryly. "However, that doesn't help you. Is he aware of that?"

"I've tried to tell him, but he says any gentleman worthy of my hand won't behave like an immature pup. He appears to enjoy making this difficult." Cass folded her arms across her chest and sat back against the settee.

"Perhaps your brothers should intervene."

"Lucien has tried to speak with him also—to no avail. I suppose Con could try, if you want to mention it to him."

"Actually, I meant that they could find a way to spread the word that potential suitors needn't be intimidated by His Grace, that the only person they need to impress is you."

Cass let out a laugh. "An auspicious idea, but I don't know if that's possible."

"It's worth trying," Miss Lancaster said.

Sabrina nodded. "I will speak to them. In the meantime, what are you attending this week?"

Cass rattled off a list of events, including a musicale on Tuesday, a rout on Thursday, and two balls on Friday and Saturday. Sabrina was glad she had nothing on Wednesday so that she could attend dinner at the Brightlys with

Constantine. The time they'd spent together yesterday had been magnificent, truly the best of their marriage. She hoped they'd moved to a new place in their relationship and that things would only continue to improve. She wondered how much she had the "tutor"—and Lucien and Evie—to thank for that.

"How shall we transport ourselves to these events?" Sabrina asked. "I can pick you up in Aldington's coach."

"Papa expects us to take one of his ducal coaches so that everyone will see the coat of arms on the door." Cass rolled her eyes. "He's rather insistent upon it. Which means we will fetch you on the way to the occasion."

"Lovely," Sabrina murmured. "I do promise to support *you*, not him, in whatever way I can. I made it clear to him that you will choose your husband. Or not."

Cass's dark eyes rounded. "You told him that?" At Sabrina's firm nod, she giggled. "How I wished I could have seen that. I always knew you were made of stronger stuff than you let on." She cast Sabrina an admiring glance before turning her head toward Miss Lancaster. "She will be an excellent ally."

"I agree," Miss Lancaster said. "It is always good to have allies."

Sabrina couldn't agree more, particularly since she'd never had one until Evie. Now she had two more. Perhaps it really wasn't too late for her wishes to come true.

~

*C*onstantine shot to his feet as Sabrina sailed into the parlor before dinner. He hadn't seen her since she'd returned from Evesham House and was pleased to discover that she appeared serene. And lovely. Honey-gold curls whispered against her temples as she moved into the room, and the hem of her cornflower blue gown swayed gently against the carpet.

"Good evening." He went and took her hand, bowing elegantly as if they were courting. Because they were. "You look beautiful."

"Thank you. You are quite handsome this evening."

He reluctantly released her hand and gestured toward the settee, hoping she might want to sit with him there instead of in separate chairs. "We have a little time before dinner. I am anxious to hear about your interview with my father."

Sabrina lowered herself elegantly to the pale yellow settee. "Anxious?"

Constantine sat beside her—close, but not too close. "Yes. You marched into the lion's den, and while you needed to go alone, I very much wanted to be with you."

"Thank you." Her gaze flicked down to his sleeve, where his hand rested on his lap. "I appreciate your support, and I think it gave me courage."

"Did it?" Constantine itched to touch her, to take her hand or stroke her bare shoulder. He curled his fingers against his thigh.

"Yes, and I shall need it because we are hosting a ball."

"You'd mentioned that, but what has that to do with the visit with my father?"

"He insisted we have it on the twenty-third. Of this month."

His jaw dropped. "He can't expect that from anyone, let alone—" He snapped his mouth closed and grimaced. "I didn't mean—"

"Even if you did, I wouldn't blame you. Why wouldn't you think I was unable to execute a ball in ten days' time. *I'm* not certain I can."

"It's still uncharitable. You deserve the opportunity to show what you can do. But I can't help feeling as though my father is hoping you will fail, just as he is with agreeing to let you sponsor Cassandra."

"I'm not at all sure that's his wish. He *wants* Cass to marry. I actually believe he wants me to succeed in pairing her off with an appropriate gentleman."

"Because it serves him." Constantine scoffed. "What does he get from us having a ball that is practically tomorrow?"

"He wants us to present Cass to Society. The ball in her honor will elevate her visibility and encourage more suitors. However, at present no one wants to court her because they are too intimidated by your father."

Constantine frowned. The ridiculous rumor he'd heard at White's was apparently not just a rumor. "No one? Are all of London's bachelors without fortitude? If they think the duke is frightening, they will not be satisfactory husbands for my sister. Furthermore, she can be just as intimidating." He muttered the last.

"Can she? I find her quite lovely." She gave him a coy look. "Perhaps she only shows that side to her older brothers when they deserve it."

"I had no idea you could be so saucy."

Her lids fluttered as she glanced away. "I didn't mean to be."

He reached for her hand and held it, the back against his palm. "I think you did, and I'm more than eager for it." He liked this side of her. Or this new part of her. Whatever it was, she was enticing and interesting, and he was bloody cursing all the wasted time they hadn't spent together.

Her lips curled into a slight, rather provocative smile. "Then I shall endeavor to increase my sauciness." She turned her hand over so that they were palm to palm. They sat like that for a moment in silence, their eyes locked. Though the touch was simple, it drove a keen yearning straight into the deepest part of him.

"Did you and Lucien ever run up and down the stairs at Evesham House?"

Constantine blinked at the non sequitur. "Why do you ask?"

"When I was there earlier, I imagined the two of you dashing about the stair hall. *Not* the foyer."

A chuckle escaped him. "We did in fact race up and down the stairs, and we even ran through the foyer." He put his finger to his lips—not the hand that was touching hers. He wasn't sure he'd ever move that one. "Don't tell the duke. It was one of many things our mother hid from him."

"I see. Your mother sounds wonderful. Were you close to her?"

His mother's brilliant green eyes and wide, infectious smile swam before him, her golden blonde hair a halo about her head. She'd been an angel on earth as she must certainly be in Heaven. "She was the best of mothers," he murmured. "Kind and sweet, never too busy to spend time with us. She was always reading us stories or taking us on walks. I swear she never stopped moving." Until she did. She'd fallen ill while Constantine was at school, and he'd never seen her again.

"How wonderful. I'm sorry I didn't have a chance to meet her."

His gaze met hers once more, and he could have drowned in the compassion that shone in her eyes. "I am too. She would have liked you. She said it would take a special woman to be my countess, someone with a softness who would dull my harder edges. I'm afraid that even as a child, I was driven."

"Was that because of your father?"

"I assume so. His expectations of me have always been high. A day didn't pass when I wasn't aware of my duty as heir."

"I wonder why your father was so exacting. *Is* so exacting," she amended. "I often try to puzzle why people are the way they are. I suppose that's because my own parents were so cold, and I never really understood why."

He clasped her hand, his fingers wrapping around hers. "How were they cold?" When she hesitated and averted her gaze, he gave her a squeeze. "You don't have to tell me," he whispered. But he hoped she would.

"I told you before about how I was so anxious about the Season, about going into crowds of people. I have always been nervous. As a child, I was easily startled by loud noises and I very much disliked change. My mother liked to tell the story of the first time they brought me to London. I was 'inconsolable and unmanageable' she said." She looked back at him, her mouth pressed into a sad line.

He stared at her as he suppressed a violent urge to visit her mother and demand she apologize. As if that would help. The pain in Sabrina's eyes was deep and old. "She *liked* to tell that story?"

"I think so. She certainly told it enough, and it wasn't as if my sisters and I weren't well aware. But I have no memory of that trip at all."

"Perhaps she fabricated the entire tale."

Sabrina shook her head. "I did struggle with change. I liked my routine. I do recall when I graduated from my nurse to the governess. I took ill to my chamber for nearly a fortnight. I just couldn't bear it."

He stroked the side of her hand with his thumb. "You were only a child. I can't tell you how sorry I am you were treated that way, that you were misunderstood."

"Nurse was wonderful. That's probably why I was so troubled when she left. The governess had less...patience for me. She did care for me and my sisters though."

Constantine wanted to wipe away all the dreadful memories. Since he could not, he was even more committed to providing her with new ones. "Well, you are going to show all of them how magnificent you are. We will spare no expense and no effort on this ball. Shall we meet with Haddock and Mrs. Haddock after dinner?"

She blushed, and now it was she who squeezed his hand. "You are so kind. I've already met with them, and, in fact, we will be working on the guest list and menu later. You are welcome to join us, of course."

"I shall." He wouldn't let her fail. His father, her parents, and anyone else who ever doubted her would be forced to recognize her for what she meant to be—a respected and capable countess. "What about the invitations? I can ensure they are printed tomorrow, and we will deliver them with the utmost haste."

"That would be brilliant. Do you really wish to make this an extravagant event?"

"I insist upon it." This was one area in which his father wholly endorsed spending money. It was imperative to demonstrate their primary place in the hierarchy of the ton.

"We may be working very late," she said, her eyes searching his. "You are welcome to stay the entire time, and then we can go up to bed…" Her invitation was clear even if she appeared to have reverted to her more shy self.

He leaned toward her and put his face next to hers, so that his lips were near her ear. "Lady Aldington, are you proposing I join you in your bedchamber?"

She turned her head slightly so their eyes could meet once more. "I am."

"There's my bold minx." He lightly pressed his lips to her jaw just in front of her ear. "Forgive me for declining, but I think it might be better if we continue to get to know each other, as we have been. I'm enjoying this time we're spending together. It feels like the courtship we never had."

Her sharp intake of breath was soft, and he felt it more than heard it. He also felt her pulse thrumming in her throat. "Aldington. You make me want to swoon."

"Then swoon. I shall catch you." He kissed her again, his lips lingering against the velvet of her skin.

"I can't swoon on a settee."

"Shall we test that theory?" God, how he wanted to seduce her, to see if he could tease her into such a lustful frenzy that she would indeed *swoon*.

Soon.

He sat back and willed his hungry body to calm itself. His cock did not understand why he was withdrawing.

"Would you care to ride with me tomorrow?" he asked. "Weather permitting, of course."

"That would be lovely. However, it will depend on what progress we make with the ball. I'm afraid this is rather pressing. Furthermore, I have several commitments this week with your sister. I am pleased to say she does not have anything planned for Wednesday, so I may still accompany you to dinner at the Brightlys."

His bloody father. Constantine ought to pay him a visit tomorrow and instruct him to leave his wife alone. He shoved his irritation with the duke away. "Splendid. You must tell me of the other events so I can meet you there. I assume you'll be going to them with Cassandra."

"Yes, and with her delightful companion, Miss Lancaster."

Haddock entered then and informed them that dinner was ready. He wore an odd expression as he regarded them together on the settee. It was almost as if he were pleased and was trying very much not to show it. His lips were pulled rather unnaturally tight, perhaps to avoid smiling.

Constantine found that rather nice.

With reluctance, he stood. However, he didn't release

Sabrina's hand. He held her fast as he guided her to her feet. "Shall we?"

"I am happy to go wherever you lead, my lord." She smiled up at him.

How he longed to hear her say Constantine instead of "my lord" or "Aldington." Hopefully that would come soon. After all, they were still only courting.

CHAPTER 15

*T*he previous two days had passed as if Sabrina had ridden through them at breakneck speed. Which of course she would never do. While she was a decent horsewoman, she did not enjoy racing.

Unfortunately, she hadn't been able to ride with Constantine on Monday, nor had she seen him much at all. They had dined together last night, but he'd had to rush off for another meeting. It was a busy time in the House of Commons.

In the meantime, she lay in bed at night, knowing he was right next door and imagining the pleasure they could share. She'd found satisfaction on her own, but where it had been a wonder a week ago, it was now a disappointment when she knew what she was missing with her husband. She longed to chastise her mother for filling her head with lies and nonsense. However, Sabrina was not *that* bold.

Besides, it didn't matter. What had gone before was in the past, and she must focus on the future. As well as the present. She couldn't stop thinking of what Constantine had said the other night, that this was the courtship they'd never had. Her heart still flipped over every time she recalled not just the words, but also the way he'd touched her…kissed her. She'd been certain he would come to her bed, but she understood why he did not. Yet. And blast it all if she wasn't falling in love with him for it.

"We're here," Cassandra said, looking past Sabrina out the window of the coach toward Mr. and Mrs. Markwith's house. "I must be honest. I find musicales dreadfully boring. What is your position on them, Sabrina?"

"I haven't attended a great many." Because she'd done her best to avoid these kinds of events and, more importantly, the people who attended them. She had to admit she was feeling much less agitated than in the past.

"Probably more than me since this is my first Season."

"I think I've been to three," Sabrina said.

"This is my third! You are clearly the expert then." Cassandra grinned. "In favor or against? We're not leaving the coach until you give your opinion." Her eyes sparkled with mirth.

"Mildly against," Sabrina murmured as she suppressed a laugh. Cassandra had such a warm and charming personality. She could improve anyone's disposition.

"Ha! That makes three of us." She glanced at Miss Lancaster who sat across from them on the rear-facing seat. "Pru won't reveal her opinion, but I *know*."

Miss Lancaster sat stone-faced, but there was a telltale twinkle in her eye.

They exited the coach and made their way inside between other guests. After exchanging greetings with their hosts, they climbed the stairs to the large drawing room where the musicale would be held.

"This is a great number of people for a musicale," Cassandra noted, glancing about the crowded room as people milled around the rows of chairs. The windows were thrown open, inviting the cool evening breeze, a welcome balm for the stuffiness of the air.

"Perhaps the musicians are particularly skilled." Sabrina surveyed the room and instantly wished she was anywhere else. The throng of people was overwhelming enough, but to add to her unease, her mother was coming straight for her. Thankfully, her oldest sister was with her. Peggy's presence should soften the encounter.

Before they arrived, however, Cassandra spotted someone across the room with whom she wished to speak. "Can I go alone, or do you both want to come with me?"

"I'll come," Miss Lancaster said. "That is my entire purpose, in fact."

"It's not your *entire* purpose," Cassandra said with a laugh. "Sabrina?"

"Er, my mother is coming this way." She would have much rather gone with Cass and Miss Lancaster. Indeed, she would have much rather jumped onto the dais and burst into song. *That* was how much she dreaded the coming encounter. She'd rather face her greatest fear—being the center of attention—than suffer her mother's company. No longer having to do so had been the brightest part of marrying a stranger.

Cass linked her arm through Miss Lancaster's as Sabrina's mother arrived. Shorter than Sabrina, she still had the ability to make Sabrina feel small.

"Good evening, Mother, Peggy." Sabrina pivoted toward Miss Lancaster. "Allow me to present Lady Cassandra's companion, Miss Lancaster."

Sabrina's mother and sister curtsied to Cass, from which Sabrina took a regrettable, perverse pleasure. Her sister-in-law outranked them, but then so did Sabrina. Her sisters' marriages might look more successful from the outside, given the fact that they'd produced offspring, but Sabrina had married the best of any of them since she would one day be a duchess. That still seemed unbelievable to Lady Tarleton, who never failed to seize an opportunity to comment on the fortune that had allowed Sabrina, of all her daughters, to marry so well.

"It's a pleasure to meet you, Miss Lancaster." Peggy gave her a bright smile before turning her attention to Sabrina. "You look well, Sabrina."

"Thank you."

"Please excuse us," Cass said. "I must speak with someone." She leaned toward Sabrina and whispered, "I'll find you again soon. Or you find me."

Sabrina nodded, and the two women left. Summoning the courage that was becoming easier to find, Sabrina faced her mother and sister with a serene expression, her hands clasped before her. "You also look well, Peggy."

Peggy always looked more than well. She possessed a vibrancy that had never failed to make Sabrina feel lacking, not that her sister had ever sought to do so. In fact, when they were young, Peggy had tried to coax Sabrina to relax and feel less anxious. Though Sabrina had tried, she could never come close to her charming and dazzling eldest sister. Her dark blonde hair was perfectly styled, and she wore a stunning gown of several hues of blue.

Sabrina caught sight of herself in one of the mirrors hanging around the room. Her hair looked elegant and pretty —Charity had done her usual brilliant work. And Sabrina's gown, another new confection of peacock blue and gold, made her look like the countess she was trying to be. The countess she *was*.

"Thank you." Peggy took a small step forward, her blue eyes alight. "I received your invitation to the ball. I'm eagerly anticipating it."

"If you invited Alicia, I doubt she will attend, since the

new babe is barely two months in the world." The viscountess's gaze dipped to Sabrina's belly. "I don't suppose you are expecting." It wasn't even a question.

Sabrina fluttered her hand briefly in front of herself. "It's certainly possible." In that moment, she realized it was. She and Constantine had lain together that one night last week. However, while possible, it was unlikely. They'd shared a bed on many occasions, and so far, she had nothing to show for it, unlike her sisters, Peggy and Alicia.

Her mother's eyes narrowed. "Well, that would be a miracle."

"Mother," Peggy murmured as she cast a frown in her direction.

Their mother clucked her tongue. "So late for your invitations to go out, Sabrina. You'll be lucky if even a fraction of who you've invited will attend." She paused a moment, likely for her words to land with their intended distress upon Sabrina. In response, Sabrina kept her features placid and worked not to squeeze her hands together.

The internal wobble that had been so much a part of Sabrina's youth and that made her feel as if she could crack into a hundred pieces at any given moment returned. Gritting her teeth, both against the unsettling sensation and her mother's obnoxiousness, she surprised herself by asking, "And how will you respond, Mother?"

The viscountess's eyes rounded, and a victorious surge beat down Sabrina's anxiety. "I haven't yet decided, to be honest. I can't imagine it will be well executed since you seem to be rushing to host it."

"Mother, you must come," Peggy pleaded. "Sabrina is going to be a duchess." That her sister had to use that argument to persuade her mother to attend her own daughter's first ball was incredibly sad.

Sabrina gave her mother a smile that should have peeled

the paint from the drawing room walls. "By all means, if you anticipate that the ball—that *I*—will be a failure, it's best if you don't come. When the duke asks where my parents are, I will explain they were too busy to attend."

Her mother's gasp was the most satisfying sound Sabrina had ever heard.

"There you are, my dear."

Sabrina pivoted to see her husband moving to her side. He set his hand against her back, eliciting a shiver along her spine. Had he ever touched her like that? Let alone in a social setting?

"Good evening, Lady Tarleton." Constantine inclined his head toward Sabrina's mother and then toward her sister. "Lady Stinton. How delightful to encounter you. It's so rare that we see you both, especially you, Lady Tarleton."

There was an acid to his tone that made Sabrina want to smile. Then hug him until he couldn't breathe.

"Good evening, Lord Aldington," Sabrina's mother said stiffly. "I'm not sure I recall the last time I saw you and my daughter in the same company."

"Well, it certainly wasn't at your house for dinner or even a visit." Constantine flashed her a smile that Sabrina hadn't even realized he possessed. Spectacularly handsome and deliciously taunting at the same time. Oh, yes, she was going to hug him at the earliest possible opportunity.

He presented his arm to Sabrina. "Come, lady wife, let us take a turn. Good evening, ladies."

The moment Sabrina put her hand on his arm, he steered her to the other side of the drawing room and into an adjoining room with tables of refreshments. He didn't pause to offer her anything. Instead, he guided her to a door and pushed it open. They stepped onto a small balcony, and he closed the door behind him.

Sabrina immediately chilled as gooseflesh rippled across

her bare shoulders. She suddenly realized they were alone. The balcony was small—perhaps one other couple could fit— and it overlooked the rear garden. Without pause, she threw her arms around him and squeezed him tightly. "Thank you," she said against his collar.

He clasped her back, his hands warm against her. "Are you all right?"

"I am now. What you did inside… What you said to my mother…" She drew back so she could look up into his eyes. The faint gold flecks seemed more brilliant tonight, despite the darkness on the balcony. "Thank you. No one has ever… rescued me like that."

A smile teased his lips. "I heard what you said before I interrupted. I'm not sure you needed rescuing, but I'm afraid I couldn't resist contributing." His fingertips stroked her spine, trailing upward until his glove met her flesh.

"It was marvelous," she whispered, leaning into him so her breasts pressed against his chest. The night air was cold, but he was so warm. Safe. Arousing.

His palm flattened over her skin, just below her nape. "You won't be a failure, and neither will your ball. I promise you that. We won't give any of them the satisfaction."

All Sabrina could think just then was the satisfaction she craved. What would it be like to kiss him? More than a chaste brush of lips, but a searing declaration of desire.

"Constantine…"

There was a flash of surprise in his eyes, but it was quickly replaced by something much fiercer. He curled his hand around her nape and lowered his head until his mouth touched hers. His other hand rested on her shoulder, his thumb sweeping gently across her collarbone.

She clasped his back, finally realizing how desperate she was for this connection. His lips plied hers, moving softly but purposely, coaxing her to kiss him back. It didn't take much. She wanted this and so much more.

Thinking of all Evie had told her and the book she'd provided, Sabrina slid her tongue tentatively along his lips. The press of his thumb on her intensified as he sealed his mouth to hers and met her tongue with his own. Angling his head, he deepened the kiss, giving her exactly what she desired. His hand cradled her head, holding her captive to his embrace, not that she wanted to be anywhere else.

Bliss raced through her, lifting her to a plateau she'd never even glimpsed. Heat and need pulsed in her sex and in her breasts, heavy against him. At last, they were on the precipice of rapture. On a balcony in the middle of a bloody musicale.

"Oh! I beg your pardon."

The masculine voice startled them apart. Sabrina turned her head away from the door, too humiliated to allow whoever it was to see her face.

"A moment please, Harkin." Constantine's voice was a deep rasp and did nothing to ease the ache inside her. If anything, it only sharpened her longing. The sound of the door, which she hadn't heard open, told her the man had left. "He's gone back inside," Constantine confirmed.

Sabrina let her body wilt against his. "That was horrifying."

"I wouldn't say it was *horrifying*," he said. "We are married, after all. It's not as if your reputation is ruined."

She looked up at him to see a frown flit across his features. "Yet you are troubled by it."

"Only because if my father hears of it, he *will* say it was horrifying. Once upon a time, I might have agreed with him."

"And now?"

He gave her an enigmatic smile. "Now, we must go inside before the musicale starts." As he guided her into the house, Sabrina was careful to look straight ahead and not make eye contact with Harkin. Did she even know who he was? She didn't think so, and she preferred to keep it that way, at least for tonight. And perhaps the rest of the Season.

"How was your evening before you had to deal with your mother?" Constantine asked as they strolled the perimeter of the drawing room.

"We hadn't been here long." Sabrina remembered that Cass had said she would find her. "Your sister is probably looking for me. I don't suppose you see any potential suitors for her here tonight?" She glanced up at him.

"I am not the best person to ask."

Sabrina's gaze fell on a tall, dark-haired Irishman she'd danced with during her Season and whom she'd talked with at the Phoenix Club assembly. "What about Lord Wexford?"

Constantine arched a shoulder. "I don't know him well. He's a friend of Lucien's if you'd like to determine if he's up to snuff."

"I'll speak with him." Sabrina scanned the drawing room to see if her brother-in-law was in attendance and found him near the doorway. She also noticed a gentleman waving his hand rather emphatically at Constantine. "Do you know that man?" She didn't recognize him.

"Yes, he's a colleague. Forgive me, but I must talk with him briefly. I will join you for the musicale." He took her hand and pressed a kiss to the back of her glove, his eyes glittering with promise.

Sabrina's insides fluttered as he moved away from her. She might have stood there mooning over her husband if Lucien hadn't approached her.

He bowed to her with a gallant flourish. "Good evening, Sabrina. How goes your sponsorship of our sister?"

"It's scarcely begun, but since you brought it up, I wonder

if you might tell me about Lord Wexford. Would he make a suitable husband for Cass?"

"Absolutely not." The answer came swift and hard. Lucien's usually jovial gaze had darkened to cinder.

"I thought you were friends."

"We are. Good friends, actually, but he is completely inappropriate for Cassandra."

"I see. Well, I'm glad I asked you. If there are any other gentlemen we should avoid, I hope you'll let me know." She moved closer to his side. "Have you been able to procure an invitation for Constantine to the Phoenix Club?"

One of his brows slanted. "Constantine? Dare I hope things are progressing well between the two of you?"

She couldn't help the blush that rushed to her cheeks. Probably because it was impossible to not keep thinking of their kiss on the balcony. "They are…progressing." Perhaps Constantine would come to her bed that night. Her pulse quickened at the thought.

Lucien grinned. "That must be why there have been no further requests for meetings with the tutor."

A wave of unease washed over Sabrina. She'd done a good job of ignoring the guilt she felt regarding her deception. It was easy when things were going so well between her and Constantine and when she was trying to look forward and not back. Should she even feel guilty given their newfound closeness? She hoped they would both see how the sessions had helped—and she was convinced they had.

"You should come to the club tonight," Lucien said, pulling her from her troubling thoughts. "It's Tuesday, so you can see the men's side."

"If my husband could come with me, I would." In truth, she wanted to go anyway. She was quite eager to see the inside of a gentleman's club.

"I'm working on it," he murmured. "But I can't tell you

anything about it. In fact, if you could come tonight, your presence and, frankly, your charm might persuade others to be in favor of inviting Con."

Her charm? "Are you mistaking me with someone else?"

He smiled at her. "Not at all. Lady Aldington has caused quite a stir since returning to town. Haven't you heard? She is no longer the shy wallflower countess. She's a coveted guest at any occasion, *and* she's a member of the Phoenix Club."

Sabrina had no idea she'd garnered so much attention. The old anxiety welled up inside her, but there was something else too—pride. "I will think about coming." It depended on Constantine and whether he had plans later. If he did, she would go to the club after dropping Cass and Miss Lancaster at Evesham House.

The host signaled that the musicale would shortly begin, and the guests should find their seats. Sabrina glanced about and finally saw Cass and Miss Lancaster. "Do you wish to sit with us?" she asked Lucien.

"I'm going to stand in the back. Hopefully, I'll see you later." His eyes twinkled mischievously, as they so often did, before he turned and strolled to the wall behind the last row of chairs.

As Sabrina made her way to Cass and Miss Lancaster near the front, she noted Constantine was still speaking with the same gentleman. His gaze met hers, and his brow briefly furrowed. He gave her a slight nod, which she thought was meant to reassure her that he would join her for the musicale.

She reached Cass, who apologized for not finding her earlier. "I'm afraid we got swept up in some drama with Miss Carrington."

"Oh dear, that doesn't sound good."

"She spilled ratafia on her gown," Cass explained. "You would have thought it was the end of days."

Miss Lancaster pursed her lips, and Sabrina couldn't quite tell if it was from exasperation or that she was trying not to laugh. They took their seats in the third row, with Cass between Miss Lancaster and Sabrina.

"I'm sorry that I wasn't attending you," Sabrina said. "I'm afraid Constantine distracted me." And still was, if she were honest. She looked in his direction and happened to catch his eye once more. He mouthed "sorry" and gave her a regretful stare. Then he and the gentlemen hastened from the room as the music began.

Disappointment curled in Sabrina's chest, but she shrugged it away. Her husband was an important and busy man. Still, he'd taken the time to come to the musicale where he'd rescued her before giving her a kiss she would never forget.

CHAPTER 16

When Sabrina emerged from the staircase hall in her evening finery—a stylish, sparkling headpiece that wound about her elegantly styled hair and a gown made of deep garnet silk—Constantine almost suggested they send word to the Brightlys that they were ill. However, he didn't think it was yet time to progress their burgeoning relationship to a more intimate level. They were getting closer, if last night's kiss was any indication.

Constantine stepped forward and took her hand, pressing a kiss to the back of her ivory glove. "You look radiant."

"Thank you. I apologize if I kept you waiting. I'm afraid we lost track of time with the preparations for the ball." She pulled the vibrant Kashmir shawl draped over her arm around her shoulders. Woven in vivid colors of red, blue, gold, and purple, the woolen garment perfectly complemented her gown.

"It was well worth the delay," he noted with a smile, his gaze sweeping over her once more. "We should be on our way, however."

He guided her outside, and she pulled her shawl up

around her shoulders to shield against the cool evening breeze. A few moments later, they were settled side by side in the coach, their thighs barely touching. It was both a provocation and a torture.

"I wanted to apologize for having to leave so abruptly last night," Constantine said. "It was imperative I meet with someone regarding the apothecaries bill."

She tipped her head toward him, and in the light of the lantern, her blue eyes shone like the surface of a lake on a bright summer day. "There's no need to apologize. I know how busy you are."

"You are very kind," he murmured.

"Was it a productive meeting?"

"I hope so, but it's hard to tell. This has been long in the making. For over twenty years, in fact." If something had been done much sooner, his mother might be alive today. "I'm trying to gain support for the bill and working to make sure there is a draft that is acceptable to all parties and can be passed. It's very difficult to get everyone to agree, but I believe, after all these years, we are finally getting close."

"What do you hope the bill will specifically accomplish?"

"Practitioners will need to complete certain education, be of a minimum age, and have received examination. There must be regulation in place to ensure the safety of our society. There are too many surgeons or apothecaries and the rest who should not be practicing." He realized his voice had climbed and his hands had moved animatedly as he'd spoken.

She gently placed her fingertips on his forearm. "This is an issue about which you care very much. Is there a particular reason?"

Constantine's throat constricted. He never discussed this with anyone. A week ago, he would have avoided answering the question. "My mother died at the hands of an inept surgeon. He should not have been practicing." He spoke softly, but the words cut like a rapid hail of arrows.

Her touch became a clasp, her hand closing around him. "I'm so sorry. I didn't realize."

"We don't discuss it. My father refuses. I've tried to speak with him about this bill, but he always finds another topic of conversation. I sometimes wonder if he feels guilt—he sent for the surgeon and trusted him."

"What happened?" Her gaze was so gentle, so encouraging. "You needn't tell me if you don't want to. I don't wish to press."

For the first time, he wanted to tell someone. The pain of losing his mother, of not being at her side, was a burden he'd never shared. "She had some sort of pain in her belly. It went on for several weeks and the surgeon insisted that bleeding, in addition to a regimen of unknown medicinals, would help. My mother didn't survive. I have always believed that if I had been home instead of at Oxford, I would have been able to prevent what happened."

Sabrina turned completely toward him and brought her hand up to his cheek. "You can't know that."

"That's the devil of it. I'll never know if I might have been able to save her."

"You mustn't blame yourself. She wouldn't want that."

He smiled sadly—because Sabrina was right and because he missed his mother so very much. "You are very wise for such a young, sheltered lady," he whispered.

"I don't know about that, but I see and hear the love you had for your mother, and I know she felt the same for you."

He stared at her, bemused by her understanding when her own mother hadn't demonstrated such emotion. "You *are* wise, against the odds, I will add, given what I know of your family." He put his hand over hers against his cheek.

She leaned forward and touched her lips to his. The

connection was a balm to his soul, easing an ache he'd thought could never be alleviated.

The coach stopped, and they abruptly parted. She withdrew her hand, and he let her go, though he wanted nothing more than to keep holding her in any way that he could. What was happening to him?

The door opened, and they exited the coach. They walked close together to the door, her arm entwined with his. A few moments later, they strolled into the Brightlys' parlor.

Mrs. Brightly, a cheerful woman approaching thirty with a heart-shaped face and round, brown eyes, dropped into a formal curtsey. "Good evening, my lord, my lady."

"Good evening, Mrs. Brightly," Sabrina responded with a smile. "We so appreciate your invitation to join you this evening."

"It is our honor." Mrs. Brightly stepped forward toward Sabrina. "Come, let us sit for a bit before dinner is served. Would you care for sherry or marsala, or something else?"

"What are you having?" Sabrina accompanied her to a large seating area.

Mrs. Brightly sat on a narrow settee, and Brightly joined her there. "The marsala. It's divine."

Sabrina took a seat on another wider settee covered in a rich, teal blue damask. Constantine followed and sat beside her, though not as close as their hosts were sitting. But then, the Brightlys' furnishing ensured a rather intimate proximity.

"Then that's what I shall have," Sabrina said to their hostess. "I find I'm distressingly partial to nearly all fortified wine. I only recently discovered this when his lordship arranged for me to taste several varieties so I could compare them."

"That sounds like such fun." Mrs. Brightly turned to her husband. "We must do that."

Brightly regarded her with a glowing expression. "Your wish is always my command, my love."

Already, Constantine felt the palpable connection between the Brightlys. It was always thus—it was no mystery how the couple felt about one another. Glancing toward Sabrina, he wondered if she noticed it. Both tonight and on their previous visits.

"Wilkes, four marsalas, if you please." Brightly looked to Constantine. "If that's all right with you? Keeps things simple, and it's a marvelous bottle, if I do say so."

"Brilliant," Constantine said, wondering if he ought to inch closer to Sabrina. He wanted to. Since she'd kissed him in the coach, perhaps she wanted the same.

The butler, who had lingered in the doorway after showing Constantine and Sabrina to the parlor, poured and distributed the wine. He then departed.

Brightly sipped his marsala before putting his arm along the back of the settee behind his wife. "I must tell you, Aldington, Mrs. Brightly and I received invitations to the Phoenix Club yesterday. I am rather shocked." He exchanged an excited look with Mrs. Brightly. They seemed to be suppressing, rather poorly, a sense of glee.

"This pleases you, I take it?" Constantine asked even as his insides felt as though he'd swallowed acid. Why was he not good enough for the club? A club run by his brother who claimed to be looking out for him.

"I'm quite thrilled," Mrs. Brightly said, her eyes dancing. "I understand I can visit the gentlemen's side on Tuesdays. And then there are the exclusive assemblies on Friday. It's all so decadent!"

"Lady Aldington is a member," Constantine said rather tightly. The press of Sabrina's thigh against his startled him. She'd moved closer. Her hand rested on her lap but was quite close to his. His pulse thrummed.

"How splendid!" Mrs. Brightly looked to Sabrina. "Were you there last night, Lady Aldington?"

Constantine felt her stiffen and knew her answer. Just as he knew she hadn't told him.

"Er, yes." She flicked a look toward Constantine. "It was my first opportunity to visit on a Tuesday, and Lord Lucien —Aldington's brother—showed me around."

"I hear the gaming room can be quite raucous," Brightly said.

"And the décor is reputed to be opulent." Mrs. Brightly lifted her marsala to take a drink.

Sabrina leaned her head toward Constantine's. "I was going to tell you," she whispered.

Mrs. Brightly looked to Constantine. "Lord Aldington, you can escort Horace while Lady Aldington does the same for me."

"I am not a member." Constantine took a long sip of the marsala, allowing the sweet wine to coat his tongue.

Mrs. Brightly paled, and Brightly moved his arm to her upper back. He squeezed her shoulder and gave Constantine a rather pained smile. "Apologies, Aldington."

"That isn't necessary. I'm sure many wonder why I am not a member of my brother's club. I do not presume to understand their membership practices, nor do I wish to. I am content with my other memberships. They certainly don't leave me wanting for more." He straightened, pushing his back against the settee. "Besides, I am delighted to be a founding member of the exclusive Gentlemen's Phaeton Racing Club."

Brightly lifted his glass. "Hear, hear!" Everyone took a drink before Brightly continued. "I can scarcely believe it's already time for our first excursion on Saturday."

"And I can scarcely believe wives are still not allowed to come." Mrs. Brightly gently nudged her husband in the ribs with her elbow. She grinned up at him, and they shared a moment in which it seemed they were the only people in the room.

Constantine was aware of Sabrina's hand brushing against his thigh. His head snapped toward hers as a jolt of heat shot through him.

Her eyes narrowed slightly, and her lashes fluttered in an expression that was at once demure and enticing. He struggled to take a breath.

"I asked Aldington the same thing," Sabrina said, her gaze reluctantly leaving his. "I was jesting, however. Are you doing the same?"

"Always. I understand the racing club is for gentlemen. Just as my needlework club is for ladies." Mrs. Brightly focused on Sabrina intently. "If you enjoy needlework, you should join us."

"Why thank you," Sabrina said politely. "I'll keep that in mind." Did she do needlework? Constantine had no idea. "Perhaps we should insist the gentlemen allow us to accompany them, just for this first excursion." She looked from Brightly to Constantine.

Mrs. Brightly's forehead creased as she pivoted toward her husband. "That's a splendid idea. Why not allow us to come on this first race? I can't see the harm in it."

Brightly's mouth opened but no words came out. He looked to Constantine, and his need for assistance was clear.

"We would have to obtain the agreement of the rest of the club," Constantine said. "We have a meeting tomorrow. I'll raise the issue."

Sabrina stared at him. "You will?"

"I'll support you in it," Brightly said. "I own it would be terribly diverting to have the wives along on a jaunt. Mrs. Brightly and I do love to drive together, though we don't do it as much as in the early days of our marriage."

"And when we were courting. You took me on that rather scandalous drive to Islington." She briefly grazed her hand against his leg and met his gaze, laughing.

Brightly chuckled. "We were already betrothed, so it wasn't *that* scandalous. I simply couldn't wait to be alone with you." He winked at her, and it was clear they had been a love match from the very beginning.

Mrs. Brightly turned her attention to Sabrina. "What sort of scandalous things did you and Aldington get up to before you were wed?"

"Nothing," Sabrina answered. "Our courtship was incredibly proper. I don't mean to imply that yours wasn't," she quickly added.

Constantine noted the faint flush at the base of her neck. "I'm afraid her ladyship and I are sticklers for propriety. Aren't we, dear?" He admired her profile before she turned her head.

"That, and we seem to enjoy anticipation." Her eyes glittered with heat, and Constantine feared his cock would embarrass him. For a woman who had never flirted with him before a week or so ago, she'd somehow become incredibly skilled.

Thankfully, the butler returned to announce that dinner was served, and Constantine was saved. He wondered if it was only a temporary reprieve, however. Because being in the presence of an affectionate couple in addition to wanting desperately to shag his wife could very well push him to the edge of his control.

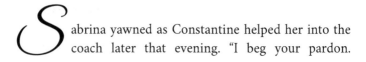

*S*abrina yawned as Constantine helped her into the coach later that evening. "I beg your pardon.

Between the preparations for the ball and this evening, I am exhausted."

That settled the debate that had been going on inside Constantine's head the past two hours: to take her to bed tonight or not. It seemed not. Despite the fact that his body was practically screaming for hers. Between the loving affection of the Brightlys, which for the first time seemed infectious, and the subtle flirtation from his wife, Constantine was at sixes and sevens.

"I enjoyed myself very much," Sabrina said as the coach moved forward. "Did you?"

"Yes. Horace is a good friend. I'm glad you and Mrs. Brightly get on so well."

"They are a devoted couple," she said softly. "I've always noticed that, of course, but tonight it felt…different to be around them."

Constantine tensed. She *had* noticed. "Different good or different bad?"

"Good, I think."

Constantine relaxed. But only slightly. "I'm glad their fondness doesn't make you uncomfortable."

"I think fondness is an inadequate word." She turned on the seat and faced him, stirring the air around him so that he was enveloped in her now-familiar scent. "Does this discussion make you uncomfortable? You seem anxious all of a sudden."

"I'm not anxious." He was bloody frustrated. But he could wait a little longer.

She took his hand between hers, then released him to discard her gloves, setting them on the seat on the other side of her. Carefully, she withdrew his glove, putting it aside with hers, so that they were flesh to flesh. "You feel warm."

He was burning. Entirely for her.

She stroked her fingertips along his hand and then up

beneath the cuff of his sleeve. He sucked in a breath, holding it, his entire body stretched taut as if on a rack. But this torture was sweet, and he wasn't sure he wanted it to end.

"I do like anticipation," he breathed, his gaze fixated on the pulse of her heartbeat in her pale throat.

"It seems prevalent of late," she murmured, her body swaying toward him. Perhaps she wasn't too tired...

He pulled off his other glove and cast it aside. "Yes." Lifting his hand, he gently touched that spot on her throat, dragging his thumb down over the satin of her flesh. Her chest rose and fell more rapidly as her lips parted.

The tutor's advice rose in Constantine's mind, that he should talk to Sabrina to allay her fears. "Are you nervous?"

She swallowed. "Perhaps a little."

"That's all right," he soothed, stilling his touch. "I will always go as slow as you ask. But I need you to ask. Can you do that?" He looked into her eyes and saw the apprehension recede.

"I can." She clasped his other hand—the one that wasn't resting against the base of her throat, splayed from the top of her bodice to her collarbone, which was disappointingly covered by the soft woolen shawl. "Now it is my turn to ask you... Why are you different?"

He wanted to say that he wasn't, but he knew that wasn't true. "Because I want to be. With you. As you have done with me. We didn't start off right."

"No, we did not."

They'd been pawns, steered by their parents for their own ends. Constantine understood Sabrina's parents' motivation, but what of the duke's? Why had he pushed Constantine to wed *this* woman?

It didn't matter because he was married to her, and he didn't regret being so. Not anymore. He realized in that moment that he *had* regretted it. Or perhaps resented it. A wave of guilt stole over him.

"I'm sorry for all the time before." He bent his head and kissed her, trying to go slowly while his body was urging him go faster, to demand more, to *take* more.

Perhaps she sensed that within him. She released his hand and put her palms against his chest, pressing briefly, before she clutched the lapels of his coat. Parting her lips, she met his tongue, and a heady rush of desire swept him from head to foot.

The shawl had fallen from her shoulders when she'd lifted her hands to his chest. He slid his hand along her collarbone and upper back. He cupped her nape, cradling the velvety softness of her skin.

She slipped one arm beneath his coat and wrapped it around his back, pulling him against her as she angled herself into the corner of the seat. Tentatively, she moved her other hand up along his chest and over his shoulder.

Constantine rotated, positioning himself over her and bringing one knee up while his other foot braced on the floor against the jostling of the coach. His hat tipped forward, and he tossed it away. Then she kissed him with an abandon he'd never thought possible, her lips and tongue tangling with his.

He kissed along her jaw and neck, savoring the flesh he'd long wanted to taste. Rapture flooded him. This was madness. This was bliss.

"Constantine, please, I would—"

He froze. Then he lifted his head to look down at her. Cheeks flushed, she opened her eyes.

"I love hearing you say my name."

"*Constantine.* Please. Touch me."

With a soft groan, he kissed her again, without any hint of gentleness this time. The connection was hard and desperate, the culmination of a deep longing. He pushed the shawl away from her completely and cupped her breast through the silk of her gown. It wasn't nearly enough to appease his desire, but she arched up, moaning softly.

Reaching down, he found the hem of her dress and pulled it up, exposing her legs. She gasped as he skimmed his hand along her inner thigh. Soft warmth greeted him, coaxing him higher where she was even softer and warmer. And wet.

Constantine stroked her sex, feeling how ready she was for him. Desperate to sink himself into her heat, he satisfied himself with using his fingers, sliding into her while he teased her clitoris.

Her hips moved to meet his thrusts as she clutched at his back and shoulder, her fingers digging into his clothing. Too damn much clothing. He wanted her nude and quivering, desperate with need as he was, beneath him.

The coach stopped. Lost in ecstasy, Constantine didn't think they could already be home. However, the sound of the coachman climbing down from his seat was unmistakable.

Constantine hurriedly withdrew his hand and brought her skirts down to cover her. "We're home." He helped her sit upright.

Her face was still flushed, and he could well imagine her frustration. He shared it, but she'd been close to release. Leaning into her, he pressed a kiss beneath her ear before whispering, "We'll finish this upstairs, where I will strip every bit of clothing from you and make you scream. I want to *hear* you come, Sabrina." He felt the quiver that danced across her shoulders as she drew in and held her breath.

He couldn't wait to get in the house.

The coachman opened the door, and Constantine climbed out. He reached up to help Sabrina down, then offered her his arm.

"You left these in the coach," she murmured, handing him his hat and gloves.

He guided her into the house. Haddock met them in the foyer, instantly taking Constantine's accessories from him. "Good evening, my lord, my lady." He pinned his attention to Constantine. "An urgent missive arrived while you were out."

Constantine could think of nothing more urgent than bedding his wife. "I'll read it in the morning."

Haddock grimaced. "The gentleman, Mr. Lambert, delivered it himself and said it was vitally important you read it tonight." *Bloody hell.* Lambert was one of the other MPs working on the apothecaries bill.

Pivoting to Sabrina, Constantine took her hands. "I just need a few minutes to read this letter and respond to it." That had to be the reason for the urgency—Lambert wanted a response tonight.

She gave him a warm, understanding smile. "It's all right." She leaned toward him and whispered, "I'll wait up."

His body, still teeming with unspent sexual energy, tightened with lust. He'd never felt more base, more primal. He ought to feel disgusted, but he felt...alive.

As she turned and went into the stair hall, Constantine couldn't help but stare at the curve of her backside, barely discernible beneath the sweep of her scarlet gown. He longed to see it—and all of her—bare.

Soon. *Very* soon.

"My apologies, my lord," Haddock said. "I hate to interrupt you and your ladyship. May I say it is nice to see you getting on so well."

Constantine snapped his attention to the butler, surprised by his words. Rather, surprised Haddock would utter them. Apparently, Haddock was too, for his cheeks bore tiny flags of pink.

"Yes, you may," Constantine said. "And thank you. Dare I say that you and Mrs. Haddock are an inspiration."

The pink in Haddock's cheeks deepened. "I am speech-less, my lord. You are too kind. The note is in your study."

Constantine turned, intent on concluding his business as quickly as possible. Upstairs, his future awaited.

CHAPTER 17

*P*acing the bedchamber as she awaited her husband's arrival was not new to Sabrina. Her emotions tonight were, however. Instead of wringing her hands with anxiety and plotting how she would suffer through the ordeal, she pulsed with excitement and anticipation.

Charity had helped her undress and brushed her hair out. As usual, she offered to braid it, but Sabrina nearly always did it herself. Tonight, she wouldn't do it at all. After Charity had left, Sabrina had tied it back with a simple ribbon, then brought the mass forward over her left shoulder.

She'd donned the dressing gown she'd worn to tempt him. Made of dark pink silk, it fastened beneath her breasts and the neckline plunged to a V at the top of them, allowing more than a glimpse of the valley between.

Her nerves were just as fraught as when she'd masqueraded as his tutor, but in a different way. She contemplated telling him the truth, revealing that they had already shared a pair of thrilling, revealing encounters.

Not tonight. She wanted this—needed this—moment for

them, for the marriage they were both working so hard to build. What they'd both done to get here had been necessary and understandable.

He seemed to be taking a long time. She paused, wondering if she should go downstairs and lure him up. No, he didn't need luring. He would come. She was sure of it.

Then she heard him in the sitting room—the sound of footsteps was unmistakable. As was the sound of his door opening and closing.

She frowned. That wasn't promising. Had he changed his mind? Did he think he'd taken too long and that she'd fallen asleep? No, she'd specifically told him she would wait up.

Sabrina resumed pacing, casting restless glances toward his room as her pace increased. Pausing, she went to the wall and leaned close, straining to hear what he was doing.

Oh, this was ridiculous! They both wanted this. She was sure of it. Just as she was sure she was done waiting.

She stalked to the door and went into the empty sitting room. His door was closed, but she marched right to it and knocked without hesitation.

A moment later, he answered, a lock of hair falling across his forehead as he tied the sash of his banyan. "I was just on my way," he said, brushing his hair back. "I wanted to change." His gaze swept over her. "I see you did too."

She reached up and pulled the errant lock back down. "I liked that. It makes you look more carefree. Maybe even a little bit wild."

One of his brows arched, which had happened more as of late. The expression gave him an air of humor and charm that made him incredibly attractive. She wanted to throw her arms around him and steer him back into his room. But no, he would insist on going to her chamber.

"Wild? I'm not sure I've ever been called that or ever behaved in a way that could be described thus."

"Not even when you drank too much at Oxford?"

His lips spread into a devastating smile. "Perhaps then."

She wanted wild. Now. Placing her palms on his chest, she pushed him gently and stepped over the threshold. "Show me."

His smiled faded as he sucked in a breath. "You want to stay here?"

"If you'll let me."

"Sabrina, I will let you do anything you desire." His gaze fixed on hers with an intensity that shot straight to her sex. Coupled with his intoxicating words, the look he gave her threatened to melt her into a puddle.

He took her hand and pulled her farther inside, then stepped behind her to close the door. "You are so beautiful." He touched the back of her neck, his fingers skimming along her flesh, then down over the silk fabric covering her spine. He paused at the top of her backside before splaying his hand across it and cupping her firmly. "Beautiful," he repeated, his lips against her neck.

Her backside tingled and her sex throbbed, but she didn't turn to face him. She'd been at the edge of orgasm when the coach had stopped. When he'd left her might have been the most frustrating moment of her entire life. Ever since, she'd been on a precipice, teetering. The urge to finish what he'd started was almost overwhelming, but she'd waited.

"I waited for you." She inhaled as his hand continued to caress her backside. Then his other hand came around her and closed over her breast, gently massaging her. "It was difficult."

"I imagine it was. How did you entertain yourself?"

Was he asking if she'd…? "I paced. Quickly."

His thumb and finger closed around her nipple, drawing on it and coaxing the flesh into a tight nub. Her breasts felt heavy and sensitive, desperate for his touch. He pinched, softly, then pulled sharply. She gasped, and he released her.

"Don't stop." She pressed back against him and felt his erection press into her backside.

His other hand swept over her hip and slid up to her other breast. He cupped them in tandem, repeating his caresses. Heat flooded her core, and she couldn't keep from whimpering. She was so close. Could she come just from what he was doing?

Suddenly, she wanted him to be on the brink, just as she was. And she knew how to get him there.

Spinning around, she placed her hands on his chest. "I'm alone out here on the edge, balancing between anticipation and satisfaction. I want you here with me." She dropped to her knees and untied the sash at his waist.

His entire body went rock hard. "What are you doing?" he rasped.

She parted the sides of his banyan and regarded his cock. Stiff and pale, cloaked at the base with a nest of brown curls, it seemed to stretch toward her, seeking. Recalling the images and descriptions in the book Evie had given her, Sabrina curled her hand around the base and stroked up toward the head.

He moaned and his hand clasped the back of her head. "*Sabrina.* This is not—"

She wasn't sure what he was going to say, but she didn't care. She'd touched her lips to the tip and found him to be velvety soft. There was also a bit of liquid. She licked at it with her tongue and was surprised to find it was rather salty.

"Dear God, Sabrina, you shouldn't do this."

"I should, and I will." She was emboldened by his reaction. Opening her mouth, she took him inside her, pressing her tongue on the underside of his shaft.

Stuttering words spilled from his mouth along with

desperate moans. He thrust his fingers into her hair. She moved her hand along with her mouth, swallowing his length and releasing him with increasing speed. His hips thrust forward, driving him toward the back of her throat. He pulled back with a muttered curse and an apology.

Grasping his hip, she held him fast and cupped the sac beneath his sex. He let out a guttural cry as she sucked.

Then he pulled at her shoulders. "Stop, please. If you wanted me on the edge, I am there. I am going to bloody fall off if you don't stop."

She rose, her knees shaking, and he picked her up. Squealing softly in surprise, she wrapped her hands around his neck as he carried her to the bed.

He laid her down on the coverlet. "How does this unfasten?" His voice was gruff, his features drawn tight.

Sabrina released the clasps beneath her breasts and spread the garment, revealing herself to him. He stared down at her, the candle on the table beside the bed casting its light over her. Apparently, that wasn't enough because he picked it up and held it over her, moving slowly from her neck to her feet.

"Roll over." The command came rough and unyielding, his face a mask of barely held control.

She did as he bade, removing her arms from the sleeves of the gown as she did so. He pulled the garment away, the silk fluttering across her back and tickling her thighs.

He set the candle down on the table, closer to the bed so there would be more light. "I want to see every part of you. Too much time has passed, and we won't suffer another night in the darkness."

Her body yearned for him, her limbs quivering and her sex pulsing. Pressed against the mattress, her breasts ached for his touch, for relief.

He caressed her back, his fingertips and palm skimming

over her sensitive flesh. When he reached her backside, his hand cupped her briefly before continuing down her leg. Then he ascended the other leg, his touch teasing and light as he moved to the inside of her thigh.

"Part your legs."

She spread her thighs, closing her eyes, as his hand swept up to her sex. Sensation sent sparks of light behind her lids as she gripped the coverlet with both hands. He massaged her clitoris, sending her right back to the coach when she'd been on the verge of her release.

Whimpering into the bed, she lifted her hips to give him more access. "Please, Constantine."

"Yes, that's perfect. Lift your hips and get on your knees."

She scrambled to do what he said, which was difficult given the way her body was quivering. But then his fingers drove into her and there was no difficulty. Nothing but bliss and pleasure building inside her.

His mouth was against her ear, pulling on her lobe and licking the outer rim. "Next time I'm going to put my mouth here." He thrust into her. "And you're going to come like never before. And the next time, I'm going to take you like this—from behind with you on your knees." His words enflamed her, sending a rush of wet heat to her sex. "Will you come for me now, Sabrina?"

"But I want you."

"You will have me. But now I want you to come. Do as I say." He withdrew his fingers and moved over her clitoris, driving her over the edge into the dark rapture she craved. Her orgasm exploded as he stroked his fingers into her once more. She moved with him, her desperate cries muffled by the mattress beneath her.

Her body was still shuddering with release when he flipped her back over. She cracked her eyes open, her breath coming hard and fast, and saw that he'd removed his banyan.

He climbed onto the bed and situated himself between her thighs. He pulled up her legs, bending them at the knees, then brushed his thumb over the sensitive folds of her sex.

Sabrina arched up, satisfied and yet not. He pitched forward and kissed her, his tongue driving deep into her mouth as he cupped her breast. She wrapped her legs around him and pressed her sex against his. The contact made her dig her fingernails into his shoulders.

He kissed down her throat and latched onto one of her breasts, licking and sucking as he gripped her flesh. Eyes closed, she cast her head back in wild abandon. Yes, wild. *This* was wild. This was everything she never knew she wanted.

"I need you now, Sabrina." His muddled voice broke through her rapturous haze as he stroked her sex and put his cock at her sheath. This was so different than every other time. There was no awkwardness, no shame, just breathtaking desire and overwhelming need.

"Yes, Constantine. I need you too." Her hand met his and, together, they joined their bodies in exultation. Finally.

He speared into her, hard and fast, filling and stretching her so that she was already on the brink of another orgasm. She tightened her legs around him, drawing a moan from his lips. He began to move, slowly at first, but she wanted more. Needed more.

"Faster," she urged, digging her feet into his backside as if she were a shameless wanton. Perhaps she was. He didn't seem to mind. But would he? Later?

Doubt crept in. Then he put his mouth on her breast once more, and the doubt fled beneath the weight of her passion. She threaded her fingers in his hair, holding him against her as she moved her hips with his. He kissed her, mouth and tongue dancing over her feverish flesh until he claimed her mouth, swallowing her whimpers as she climbed toward the pinnacle of pleasure.

He slipped his hand between them and stroked her clitoris. That was enough—more than enough—to pitch her into a soul-deep ecstasy that felt as if she'd been transported away from time and place.

She let out a low, deep cry that sounded as if it had come from a wild animal. Horrified, she clamped her mouth shut.

"*No.*" He tugged on her hair and gently bit her ear. "Let go, Sabrina. Let completely *go*. I want to hear you. Now. Give me *everything*." He thrust deep inside her, pushing her even farther into bliss. She cried out over and over again as her body seized with sensation.

A moment later, he met her on the other side, his body tensing as he came. Harsh, fevered sounds cloaked her as he unleashed his body. Eventually, he collapsed against her, his body slick and his chest heaving upon hers.

She floated in a dark euphoria, her body a mass of joy and fulfillment. She stroked her hand along his thigh, the curve of his backside, the dip at the base of his spine.

He kissed her cheek, her neck, before flipping to his back. She turned to her side and watched him. His eyes were closed, and he'd cast his arm up above his head on the pillow, his fingers pointing toward her. The rapid rise and fall of his chest slowed, and his slackened sex lay against his thigh. He called her beautiful, but so was he.

She wanted to trace her fingertips along the muscles of his chest, the deep planes of his belly, and the slope that ran from his abdomen past his groin to his hip. It was an alluring piece of the male anatomy, and in the end, she couldn't keep from touching him there.

"Sabrina?"

She looked up to see his eyes were now open, slitted, as he regarded her over the length of his torso. "Mmm?"

"Unless you want to arouse another, ah, interlude, you should perhaps go to sleep."

She thought a second "interlude" sounded rather wonderful. But she was too distracted by what he'd said about sleep. "You'll allow me to stay?"

His eyes opened more. "If you want to."

That he'd invited her into his chamber had been surprising enough, but to extend that invitation to spending the entire night was more than she'd expected. Then again, all of this was more than she'd ever expected.

Emotion bloomed and filled her heart. She pressed herself against him, her hand on his chest. Rising slightly, she kissed him gently, her lips sliding briefly over his. "I want to."

"Stay or have another go?" The look in his eyes was so hopeful and the smile teasing his lips so alluring that she had to swallow against the lump gathering in her throat. This was all too perfect.

She slid her hand up to his neck and gave him her sauciest grin. "Both."

"Minx." He pushed her to her back and kissed her, his hand skimming along her side.

Sleep, as it happened, was fleeting.

~

It was past midnight when Constantine arrived home the following evening, exhausted and frustrated, from Westminster. He instantly brightened as he saw his wife walking into the house.

Bounding from the coach with more energy than he'd possessed a moment before, he strode inside just as she was about to leave the foyer.

"Sabrina," he called, halting her progress.

She turned, her eyes alight as her lips curved into a warm,

welcoming smile that stirred his cock. "You're just getting home?"

He nodded. "It was a very long day. Would you care to take madeira with me in my study?"

"That would be lovely, thank you."

They walked together, their arms brushing, and Constantine could scarcely believe this was his marriage, his wife. "How was your evening?" he asked, looking askance at her aquamarine gown and thinking it made her eyes shimmer like the sea on a summer day.

"Quite pleasant, thank you, though I was rather tired." She sent him a provocative glance, and any plan he had of leaving her alone tonight to let her rest evaporated.

"Are you sure you wouldn't rather go upstairs?"

She laughed softly as they reached his study. "You can't mean in order to sleep."

"Actually, I did."

"Then you shouldn't be removing my clothing with your gaze."

Smiling, he shook his head as he crossed to the sideboard to pour the madeira. "How did you become so skilled at flirtation? I never would have imagined it when I met you."

"I don't know that I'm all that skilled. I look for ways to lighten the mood or to make you smile. I suppose that comes across as flirting."

He turned and found that she'd taken a seat in one of the chairs near the hearth. Delivering her wineglass, he tapped his against it before sitting opposite her.

"You try to make me smile?"

"I resolved to do so when I came to town. But don't give me credit for wanting to. My goal was to ease my nerves. If you smiled more, I hoped I could relax."

He grimaced, thinking he was a terrible, self-centered beast. "That you were in a position of discomfort because of me fills me with a remorse I can't adequately express." He clutched the wineglass and took a sip, hoping to calm the sudden roiling inside him.

"You mustn't take all the blame. Even if you'd been a cheerful sort, I likely would still have been afraid. It's taken me this much time to even want to try to emerge from the shadows." She looked down at her wine. "I don't think I was ready before."

"Then we must be grateful for this moment in time when we have met and joined together as we were meant to."

Her head lifted, her gaze meeting his. "That's a lovely sentiment." She lifted her glass. "To this moment in time."

He raised his madeira, then took another drink while she did the same. "I forget what you were doing tonight. My apologies."

She set her glass down on the hearth while she removed her gloves. "Another ball. And I am happy to report that your sister seemed to have a successful dance with Lord Glastonbury. She's been encouraging gentlemen to call—with great subtlety, of course—in the hope that if someone, or preferably a *few* someones, pays a call, your father will stop being such a nuisance. He nags her almost daily about securing a husband."

Constantine heard what she said, but he'd been far too fixated on the simple yet seductive act of her removing her gloves. By the time she draped them over the arm of the chair and retrieved her madeira, he was shifting in his seat to try to keep his erection at bay.

"Do you know Glastonbury?" she asked.

"Not well." Constantine was aware that the viscount was a pugilist and quite a good one. "He boxes at a club near Covent Garden, I believe."

"Will your father find him to be a satisfactory suitor?"

Blowing out a breath, Constantine lifted a shoulder. "That

is like trying to guess tomorrow's wind direction. I'll do some investigating."

"I would appreciate that, thank you."

Constantine sipped his madeira, his gaze trapped for a moment by the fire in the grate. How domestic and satisfying this was, sitting here discussing mundane issues that were actually not mundane. "How are the preparations for the ball?"

"They're going surprisingly well, considering the amount of time we've had to get everything finished."

"Good." Constantine wanted nothing more than his wife's first ball to be a rousing success. He didn't want anyone to doubt her, not his father or her family, and least of all herself.

"How are things at Westminster?" she asked. "You've been working awfully hard."

"I have." He pressed his lips together in a not-quite frown as he recalled the events of the day.

"Did something happen today? You seem...disappointed. When I mentioned Westminster," she clarified.

He sent her a look of mild surprise. "You can tell?"

"I think I'm coming to know you."

Yes, she was, and he was inordinately pleased by that revelation. He worked at focusing on that instead of today's potential setback. "The Apothecaries' Company exempted the druggists from the bill. While this prompted the druggists to withdraw their opposition, I am not certain it bodes well."

Her brow creased. "Because they should not be exempted?"

"Not in my opinion. We must find compromise, but exemption is not the answer. I suppose I shouldn't be disappointed—not yet anyway. However, I've seen how this endeavor has gone over the last many years, and it's hard not to feel defeated."

"Then you shall have to try to be optimistic. Sometimes believing in something is all we have."

"You are speaking from experience now?"

"If I hadn't believed I could come to London and face you, I wouldn't have done it. But then, my motivation was very strong."

To have a child. He thought of her demand as well as the fact that they hadn't discussed it of late. Perhaps last night they'd finally found success. He wouldn't be disappointed if they hadn't. That just meant he could keep trying, and he was wholeheartedly committed to that endeavor.

A small but nagging voice in the back of his mind asked if that was all she wanted. Would she simply return to her solitary life at Hampton Lodge once she was pregnant? She clearly enjoyed their newfound mutual pleasure, but that was still a means to an end.

"Constantine, you didn't tell me!" Her exclamation jolted him from his ruminations. She sprung out of her chair and flew to his desk, setting her glass down near a stack of papers as she plucked up a letter with a red wax seal.

Constantine had risen and moved toward the desk. "Is that a…phoenix in the seal?"

"Yes." Eyes gleaming with joy, she handed it to him. "Open it."

He turned the missive over and read the front: *The Most Honorable, the Earl of Aldington.* It was unmistakably for him. After setting his wine on the desk, his breath stalled in his lungs as he opened the seal. The words jumbled before him, and he had to blink before he could read them.

You are invited to join the Phoenix Club.
The Membership Committee believes your presence will be a boon and benefit.

*Please refer to the enclosed membership agreement and respond in
writing at your earliest convenience.*

$\mathcal{H}$e looked up from the parchment to see her watching him with unabashed delight. "Why now?"

"Why not?"

"I haven't been good enough to invite for the past year. Why am I suddenly—" He glanced back down at the invitation. "'A boon and a benefit'?" He knew why—because he'd asked Lucien to make it happen. Still, he couldn't quite believe his brother had actually done it.

"Does it matter why? I am just glad you are. Now we can attend the assemblies together. We can even spend Tuesday evenings *at the same club*. I never imagined that would be possible. Or that I'd want to."

That begged a question. "Why *did* you want to? I was shocked when you were invited, but perhaps even more when you accepted."

She averted her gaze and clasped her hands. His admission had provoked her anxiety. He was beginning to recognize the signs.

He set the letter down on his desk and took her hand. "I didn't mean to imply that you shouldn't have. I'm glad you did. And I was an ass about it. A jealous ass, specifically."

She smiled, and her shoulders relaxed. "It felt good to be included in something, especially a place that specifically includes those who feel excluded or ignored."

"Is that true?" Constantine hadn't known that. And why not? Because he'd shown no interest in his brother's club. He'd followed his father's lead of disdaining the entire enterprise.

She nodded. "Lucien hasn't told you?"

"Lucien and I don't discuss everything." They actually shared very little—until recently—and Constantine regretted that. "He should have told me. No, I should have asked." He would do just that at the earliest opportunity.

"Are you going to accept?" She sounded uncertain.

"You want me to."

"I do." Now, her voice was firm, and he admired her confidence in the matter. Probably because he didn't share it. He wanted to accept it. Hell, he'd made a rather delicious cake of himself to Lucien after Sabrina had received an invitation, behaving, as he'd just said, like a jealous ass.

Constantine glanced toward the fiery phoenix, its wings spread, on the seal. "My father won't like it." His father wouldn't like many things about his behavior lately. When the Importation Bill came to a vote, he was almost certainly going to enrage the duke.

"I know how much his opinion matters to you," she said quietly. "However, you must do what you think is right—for you."

"I'll take it under consideration. Know that your opinion matters to me too."

Perhaps more than that of his father. Isn't that how it should be with a marriage? His father would likely say no, but Constantine wasn't sure he could listen to him any longer on the topic of wives. Which befuddled him. His father hadn't seemed to be a bad husband. In fact, Constantine would have said his parents loved each other. Certainly, his mother had loved her husband. But then, she'd loved everyone.

"Does it?" She lifted her hands to his cravat and loosened the knot of silk. "For instance, I am of the opinion that you are wearing far too many clothes." She slid the snowy white length from his neck and dropped it to the floor.

"Is that right?"

She nodded slowly as she pushed his coat from his shoulders, again letting the garment slip to the carpet. "Mmm."

"What of all your clothes?" He slid his arms around her waist and backed her against the side of his desk. "The number of garments a woman is required to don is criminal."

"Lord Aldington, are you flirting with me finally?" She fluttered her lashes at him, a coy smirk curling her lips.

"Here I thought we'd progressed to first names."

"My apologies, *Constantine*." With one hand, she plucked the buttons of his waistcoat open and with the other, she stroked her hand down the front of his fall and pressed her palm against his rigid cock. "Still too many clothes."

"You have two choices." He shoved the items on his desk to the other side, heedless of what was there and what damage he might inflict, and lifted her onto the edge. "You can endure the clothing for a brief while and let me pleasure you here." He lifted her skirt and pressed his fingers against her sex, drawing a soft moan from her moistened lips. "Or you come upstairs with me where I will likely ruin your clothing in my haste to tear it from your delectable body."

"Delectable?" The word squeaked forth as she stared at him. "Me?"

He bent his head and kissed the flesh just above the edge of her bodice, cupping her breast through her ball gown and lifting, as if he could force her from the gown and expose her nipple to his greedy tongue.

She thrust her hand into his hair, her fingertips curling into his scalp. "I choose the first. Please."

That was all the urging he needed. Pushing her back on the desk, gently, he settled her skirts around her waist, revealing her sweet sex and her honey curls beckoning him.

"I told you what I would do next time." He spread her lips and licked her flesh, drawing a sharp cry. He looked up toward her face, but her head was cast back. He smiled. Then he noticed the bloody door was open.

Hurrying, he closed it firmly and threw the latch. "Privacy is important, lest we terrify the servants," he murmured as he returned to his delicious task. "Open your legs, Sabrina, so I can taste you."

She spread herself for him, one of her hands holding her skirts up out of his way. He stroked her slowly, teasing her clitoris and taunting her folds. Her breath came in pants as her hips arched to meet his touch. "Please, Constantine."

"Please what?" He was being quite terrible, but he was rather enjoying this side of his wife. Hell, this side of himself. He didn't even recognize the man standing between her legs and delivering torment upon her.

"Please, do what you started."

"With my mouth?" He slipped his finger into her wet sheath and had to close his eyes as a wave of lust surged over him. "Tell me, Sabrina."

"I want your mouth on me. Your tongue…*in* me. Please, Constantine."

"How can I refuse?" He literally could not. His body demanded he taste her. He bent again and spread her wide for his tongue, licking up into her with a calculated thrust.

She gripped his head again, her fingers tangling in his hair as she rose up. Nonsense sounds filled the air around him as she whimpered and moaned. He buried himself in her, using his mouth and fingers to wreak a beautiful chaos upon her.

Her muscles clenched around him, signaling she was about to come. Sucking on her clitoris, he speared two fingers inside and pressed up, finding that spot that would send her into sweet oblivion.

A high-pitched keen erupted from her lips as her sheath squeezed tight around him. Her legs quivered with the force of her orgasm. He massaged her thigh and kissed her flesh, carrying her through the storm until her body began to settle.

She opened her eyes and regarded him with a hazy stare. "Constantine, that was magnificent."

"Let me take you upstairs." He started to lower her skirts, but she held them fast.

"Don't you dare. I want you now. Inside me." She sat up and reached for his fall.

"We have a perfectly good bed," he reasoned. "Two, actually."

"And we'll use one—or both—later." She released his buttons and slipped her hand into his smallclothes. Cradling his cock, she wrapped her fingers around him. All argument left him.

"Come to the edge." He pulled her toward him. "Take me inside you."

Their eyes met, her blue gaze brimming with determination and erotic promise. She guided him to her sex, and he thrust into her. Her lids shuttered, and her lips parted.

"Yes," she hissed, wrapping her legs around him.

Constantine secured his arms around her—one on her back and one clutching her backside. "Forgive me, for I cannot go slow. Later, I'll take my time. But now—"

Now, he had no control. Nor did he want any. He surrendered completely to this blissful, spontaneous moment—the moment they'd toasted just a short while earlier. Gratitude and joy swept through him as he rocked into her. She clutched his shoulder and neck, pulling his head down to kiss him.

Her mouth was hot and wet, as greedy as he felt. Their bodies strained together, completely enraptured as they hurtled toward completion.

It came hard and fast for him. He managed to slip his

hand between them, to coax another release from her. She clenched around him, and he swore he'd never experienced such pure satisfaction. Since last night anyway.

Rising from the devastation of his release, he withdrew from her. "I don't have anything to tidy you…"

"Fortunately, I have a criminal number of garments with which to ameliorate the situation." She flashed him a smile as she tended to herself before sliding from the desk.

He hastened to help her, marveling at her brazenness. At her beauty. At her undeniable courage and fortitude. If not for her single-minded pursuit, they would not be here. She was astonishing.

And he was falling in love with her.

Two years wasted. Because he was such a reticent, self-involved *idiot*. He stroked his fingertips from her forehead down her cheek to her jaw. Then he kissed her, softly, reverently, dragging his thumb over her lips when he finished. "Now we can go upstairs."

She picked up her wineglass and finished the madeira. "And now, I am ready."

"I'll be along presently, after I pick up my clothing." He watched her go and hoped this was truly the start of something new, of something real.

If it wasn't, he didn't know what he was going to do. Because he couldn't go back to the way things were.

And if he thought about it, which he tried not to, he had the tutor to thank for everything that was happening. Without her giving him the courage to do and say what he ought with Sabrina, they might still be fumbling in the dark. Despite the inarguable benefit of her help, he was sorry it had been necessary. Although, he couldn't regret the progress they'd made, the intimacy they'd discovered. The tutor had been a help when they'd needed it, and he was grateful for what she'd provoked within him—the desire to court his wife, to give her the attention and consideration she deserved.

He retrieved his clothing, then his gaze fell on the invitation to the Phoenix Club. What the hell was that about? He couldn't deny the rush of joy—and relief—he'd felt when he'd read it. But the threat of his father's wrath had to be considered.

Or did it?

Perhaps it was time the duke altered his thinking when it came to his second son and his second son's incredibly worthwhile endeavor. More importantly, perhaps it was time his eldest son pushed him to that end.

CHAPTER 18

*R*eynolds, Lucien's butler, showed Constantine into his brother's library where Lucien sat at his small desk, his hand scratching a pen across parchment. He seemed rather intent on his task since he didn't react to their arrival.

"Lord Aldington is here to see you," Reynolds said, prompting Lucien to look up.

Lucien blinked, then wiped his hand over his face.

The butler left and Constantine moved toward the desk, which stood beside a window that looked out to the back garden. "Good morning, Lucien."

Lucien put his paper into a drawer and stood. "Another surprising visit. Can this be, what, the second in a fortnight?"

"Yes, I suppose it is." Constantine sat in one of the wing-back chairs near the hearth.

"Do you want a drink?" Lucien asked, taking a step toward his liquor cabinet.

"No, thank you. I can't stay long. Too much happening at Westminster this week."

"Ah yes, the Importation Bill?" At Constantine's nod, Lucien continued. "Have you decided how you will vote?"

"You sound like Father. Yes, and don't ask me about it. Please."

Lucien's brows climbed his forehead. "Such manners. And you're almost...smiley." He narrowed his eyes. "You seem happy. What's wrong?"

Constantine laughed.

"Dear God, you're *laughing*." Lucien strode to him and put his hand against Constantine's forehead. "Are you feverish?"

Swatting Lucien's hand away, Constantine pursed his mouth up at his brother. "Stop being an ass and sit down."

"*I've* been admonished." Lucien sat opposite him and straightened his waistcoat—he wasn't wearing a coat. "To what do I owe the pleasure of this highly entertaining call?" His eyes widened. "You and Lady Aldington have reached an accord."

"We weren't at odds." They just hadn't been...together. And now they were. Saturday's phaeton race to Richmond had been the best he'd ever undertaken and the fact that he'd arrived first wasn't the reason. It was his wife's company and perhaps the stop they'd made on the return that had involved a well-hidden tree and resulted in the loss of a button on his fall.

"Why are you smirking like that?" Lucien asked.

Constantine shook his head. "No reason."

"Liar. You're positively smitten. In fact, I would say you are glowing." Lucien leaned back in his chair, looking smug. "You're welcome."

Smitten? Yes, he was. He was tumbling headfirst into love with his wife, and the sensation was at once unsettling and delightful. He chose not to dwell upon it but to just enjoy her company and the time they spent together.

The last thing Lucien said finally sank into Constantine's brain. "I should thank you?"

"The tutor helped, did she not?"

"Yes, but I admit to feeling a sense of guilt about it."

Lucien's brows climbed in surprise. "Did you have sexual intercourse with her?"

Constantine ignored the heat that rose in his face. "No, but I should tell her about our meetings so that we can put all of it behind us."

"Don't." Lucien shook his head. "What would be the point? You aren't going to see the tutor again, she helped you when you needed it, and I daresay Sabrina is just as happy as you are to have gotten to where you are now. It would be a shame for you to mope about it."

"I'm not moping." Constantine narrowed his eyes at Lucien before deciding he would much rather bask in the newfound bliss he'd found with Sabrina than think of the tutor—or the past at all. "I came here to ask why I was invited to your club. Frankly, I'm surprised you didn't realize that."

Lucien exhaled as he rested his elbow on the arm of the chair. "I thought that was perhaps why, but I wanted you to bring it up. You were invited because the membership committee deemed you worthy."

"All it took was you recommending me?"

"I think the smiling and the laughing probably helped." The statement was mildly facetious and normally would have made Constantine scowl. Instead, he rolled his eyes.

Lucien leaned forward. "Did you just roll your eyes *again*?"

Constantine ignored his brother's inanity. "Sabrina says the purpose of the club is to provide a place for those who feel excluded elsewhere. Did you really not invite me before because I didn't want to join, or is it because I am included in Society?"

"That is the purpose, and yes, I didn't see you as someone who needed inclusion. I've changed my mind about that of late, however."

This grabbed Constantine's full attention. "Why?"

"Because I see you more clearly. You felt like an outsider in your own marriage. And when I think about how you interact in Society, you don't seem to enjoy it. You involve yourself because it's expected, particularly with Cass having her Season. Also, because of your work in the Commons, which actually means a great deal to you. All those things make you a good candidate for the Phoenix Club. I hope you'll accept the invitation. I think you'll find camaraderie there."

Constantine didn't have many friends. In fact, only Brightly and the other members of the racing club came to mind. "How did Horace Brightly and his wife qualify for membership?"

"Don't think of it as a qualification. The club seeks to grow its numbers by inviting people with good intentions and kind hearts, and in particular those in possession of qualities that are overlooked elsewhere—sometimes *because* of those traits."

Brightly was certainly good intentioned and had one of the kindest hearts Constantine knew. "And Sabrina?" he asked, despite thinking he already knew the answer.

Lucien looked at him as if he *should* know the answer. "Con, you know your wife. At least, I hope you do by now. She should have been invited a year ago, and the only reason she wasn't is because I knew you wouldn't support it."

That hurt. Constantine looked away, frowning. "She isn't comfortable in Society, but she's trying." She was sponsoring his sister and hosting a damn ball when both of those things would have made her hide under her bed a year ago.

"We are thrilled to have her as a member of the Phoenix Club," Lucien said.

Constantine met his brother's eyes. "I don't know that I'm a good candidate, actually."

"I disagree. The question is whether you want to be included. Do you?"

"I'm not sure it's for the right reasons. My wife is a member, so I feel I should be too. Plus, my brother owns the damn place, so it seems as though I should support his endeavor."

A wide grin split Lucien's face, reminding Constantine of how he looked when he found a stashed biscuit in their nursery. "I would love to have you in my club. Truly. I never imagined you'd even consider it. Please do—you're not the man you think you are," he added softly.

Constantine agreed with that much. If he'd learned anything since Sabrina had come to town, it was that she had the power to topple his strictly ordered life. The man he thought he was would be horrified and seek a return to order. Not that things were *dis*ordered, but they were different. Unexpected.

He stood, his errand completed, though he still hadn't reached a decision about the invitation. "Be sure to come to Sabrina's ball. I need for this to be a smashing success for her."

Lucien got to his feet, smiling. "You're turning into a rather caring husband. I shall have to believe in miracles after all. Oh, here it comes, another eye roll."

Constantine shook his head. "You're a provoking menace."

"I thought I was a troll."

"That too. Just be at the ball and be your most spectacular self. Everything you touch turns out wonderfully."

A darkness crept into Lucien's eyes, and the smile faded from his mouth. "That is hardly true. But I will do everything I can to ensure your wife is the most celebrated hostess in London come Saturday morning."

"Thank you." It felt good to be aligned with his brother. And it would feel even better when his wife's ball was the success of the Season.

~

The face staring back at Sabrina in the glass was the same one as the day before and the day before that. Yet, she looked different. There was a softness to her mouth and a sparkle in her gaze. She could attribute the change to the past week and the absolute joy it had brought.

Or perhaps it was because she was with child.

Sabrina's courses arrived every twenty-eight days without fail. She could set a clock to them, and as of today, she was two days beyond their arrival. It was difficult not to giggle with excitement and hope. She'd never, ever been late, not in twenty-two months of marriage.

But then she was certain that she and Constantine had engaged in more sex over the past week than in those prior twenty-one and three-quarters months. She did giggle then because she couldn't help herself. She'd come to London for a baby, but she'd gotten so much more.

Love for her husband swelled in her chest. She hadn't told him how she felt, but she would soon. Perhaps when she told him about the babe. Which she wouldn't do yet. It was far too early, even if she was all but certain.

There was something else she should confess—the deception of pretending to be his tutor.

A light rap on the door drew Sabrina to rise from the stool at her dressing table. Answering the door, Sabrina was pleased to see it was Evie. Her friend bustled in, her dark purple gown shimmering in the candlelight. "Sabrina, you are a vision! This is going to be the most wonderful ball."

Closing the door, Sabrina pivoted toward Evie, smoothing her hands over the gold and ivory gown. The thought behind it was to be a mix of debut, which was the ivory, and dazzling, which was the gauzy gold overskirt. Gold stitching and ribbon were worked into the ivory as a further complement.

"The pearls are an excellent choice." Evie inclined her head toward the necklace encircling Sabrina's throat. She also wore matching earbobs.

"They belonged to Constantine's mother. I've never been bold enough to wear them before. He insisted I do so tonight."

"I'm glad, for they are a brilliant accessory to your costume. I'm so happy for you and Aldington. I can't help thinking your inner happiness is giving you a special glow tonight."

Sabrina nearly blurted that it was perhaps due to carrying a child but diverted her thoughts to keep from spilling the secret before she was ready. "I think I'm going to tell Constantine that I was his tutor. Tonight—after the ball."

Evie blinked. "But this is such a wonderful occasion. Why darken it? In fact, do you need to tell him at all?"

"I think I must." Sabrina frowned. "He deserves the truth."

Evie took her hand and gave it a gentle squeeze. "You both benefitted, and I think you'd both agree it was worth every moment."

Was it worth keeping a lie? Sabrina wasn't sure she agreed, but she could see postponing her confession. "You're right that tonight is a singular occasion." After all, she had a lifetime to tell him the truth, though she wouldn't wait that long.

Letting go of Sabrina's hand, Evie smiled broadly. "Indeed, it is. You are going to be a triumph!"

Sabrina didn't share Evie's confidence, but she certainly appreciated it. While she'd made great progress in conquering her anxiety since returning to town, tonight would be an entirely new experience. She prayed all would go well and that the nervous tremors flitting throughout her body were for naught. She just needed to make sure that she sought quiet and solitude if she felt overwhelmed. As the hostess, that would be difficult, but she would try.

Constantine would also provide support. He made her feel like she really could conquer her trepidation. Just thinking of him settled her nerves and spread a calming warmth through her.

There was another knock, which Evie offered to answer while Sabrina donned her gloves. Cass and Miss Lancaster came into the room, the former bubbling with energy and the latter as cool and serene as ever.

Cass froze and stared at Sabrina, her gaze sweeping over her costume. "Oh, Sabrina, what an absolutely gorgeous gown. I am quite jealous."

Sabrina laughed. "Stop. Your wardrobe is stunning, and tonight's gown is no exception." As a young lady in her first Season, Cass would typically wear pale colors and white or ivory. However, her ball gowns, in particular, were often constructed of more vibrant colors. Tonight's was burgundy with silver accents. It was dramatic and eye-catching. Sabrina still didn't understand why gentlemen weren't knocking each other over to claim her hand.

Gloves in place, Sabrina took a final look in the glass. She took a deep breath and faced the other women. "I want to thank each of you for being so kind and wonderful since I returned to London this Season. I could not have managed this ball, or many other things, without your guidance and support, but most of all your friendship. I have never had friends before, and I can see that it was because I hadn't met you yet."

Miss Lancaster let out a rather loud sniff and immediately clapped her hand over her mouth and nose. The normally unruffled young woman's eyes rounded, and her cheeks flooded with color. "I beg your pardon," she murmured.

Cass moved to her side. "Everything all right, Pru?"

"Quite." She pinched her nose, then lowered her hand. "I was just trying not to sneeze is all."

Sabrina didn't think that was the case at all but would let the woman provide whatever excuse she wanted. She recognized and understood a person who wanted to stay out of the spotlight, who preferred to be completely unremarkable.

Another rap on the door drew their attention. This time it was Mrs. Haddock wearing a slightly harassed expression that drove a stake of cold fear straight into Sabrina's chest.

The housekeeper glanced toward the other ladies in the room before settling her attention on Sabrina. "There is a slight issue with the musicians, my lady. If you're ready, would you mind accompanying me to the drawing room?"

"I am ready, thank you." She glanced toward Evie. "Perhaps you should come along." Sabrina had learned it was quite acceptable to ask for help, and she had no problem doing so.

"Certainly." Evie accompanied her from the chamber, and they made their way to the drawing room where the musicians were setting up their instruments in the corner.

Sabrina could already see what was wrong. Because she could count, and one member was missing. Over the next five minutes, she listened patiently as the cellist explained that their missing member was sick, but that she would not notice their absence. Sabrina only hoped that was true.

"Don't fret," Evie said, touching Sabrina's arm. "This is a minor inconvenience."

"You're right. It's not as though the champagne is bad." Oh dear, what if the champagne or another beverage *was* bad? It wasn't as if she could sample every one of them, and even that wouldn't give her complete confidence.

"You mustn't worry." Evie's voice was soft and earnest, reassuring.

"I am doing my best." Sabrina saw her husband enter the drawing room and felt instantly calmer. "Pardon me." She walked toward him, and he stopped short, his gaze arresting on her.

Constantine's eyes slitted, seeming to smolder as he stared at her. "You are lovelier than you have ever been. My mother's pearls are perfect on you." He lifted her hand to his lips and kissed the inside of her gloved wrist. "I despise these gloves, however."

Smiling, Sabrina told him about the musicians. He surprised her by shrugging and saying if that was all that went amiss tonight, they should consider themselves fortunate.

Her good humor fled. "Are you saying you expect something else to go wrong?"

He squeezed her hand. "Not at all. It will be spectacular."

Haddock interrupted them, his brow creased. Sabrina tensed more than she already was.

The butler address Constantine. "I beg your pardon, my lord, but we had an accident with the champagne supply. I don't think we'll run out, but I wanted you to be aware of the situation."

"Thank you, Haddock. I'm sure it will be fine. We have plenty of other wines to drink."

"We do indeed. I will be positioning myself in the foyer in a few minutes and will see you downstairs." Inclining his head, the butler hurried off.

Constantine turned to her and brushed his fingertips against her cheek. "It's almost time. You will be brilliant. Everything will be brilliant." He leaned close and kissed her.

"You shouldn't do that in front of everyone." Everyone being the musicians, Evie, and a handful of maids and footmen.

"Perhaps, but I can't help myself. Honestly, Sabrina, you look good enough to eat." His gaze darkened with provocation, and she knew precisely what he meant.

Heat danced through her, and she felt better than she had a moment ago. She also realized he was wearing a gold waistcoat that complemented her gown. "You've never worn a waistcoat with color." She touched the gold brocade and fingered one of the pearl buttons.

"I wanted us to match, to present ourselves as a… I don't know. You like it?"

"As a couple who coordinate their costumes?" She smiled again, her good humor returning. "And yes, I like it—and you —very much." Beyond that. She loved him hopelessly and never more in that moment as he sought to allay her fears.

He presented his arm. "Let us take up our places in the foyer to greet our guests. I hope you are ready to spend the next hour talking and smiling so much your face will feel as though it will fall off."

The apprehension she was trying to keep at bay rose up in her throat. But she refused to succumb. The old Sabrina would never have had the courage to do this. New Sabrina might be nervous, but she would get through it. Especially with this man at her side.

∾

*I*t was near the end of the hour when Sabrina's parents arrived. Her eldest sister had already come through a short time before, and Sabrina was glad to have spoken with her without the dampening presence of their mother.

As Haddock announced the Viscount Tarleton and Lady Tarleton, Sabrina stiffened. Constantine's hand gently stroked the small of her back, and she relaxed slightly. She suddenly realized how all that had seemed impossible was now possible—due to the presence and support of her husband. With him at her side, she felt as though she could face anything.

Sabrina's father was tall and thin with an exceptionally angular face and sparse gray hair. He regarded her with one narrowed eye, assessing her from head to foot before turning his perusal on Constantine. "Aldington." He spared her one more fleeting glance. "Daughter."

"Good evening, Father," she said evenly. "I hope you've been well."

"Quite, thank you." He stepped forward, allowing Sabrina's mother to stand in front of her.

The viscountess's appraisal took longer and felt far more exacting. "What a bold gown, dear."

Constantine's fingers skimmed along her lower spine. "She looks stunning, doesn't she?"

"She seems a bit thin, honestly." The implication was clear —she couldn't possibly be increasing. Sabrina gently bit the inside of her mouth lest she blurt that she could, in fact, be expecting an heir.

Before Sabrina could summon a retort—and she doubted she could—Constantine clasped her waist. "I hope you have a pleasant evening, Lady Tarleton." He nodded toward the viscount. "Tarleton."

Dismissed, Sabrina's parents moved along toward the staircase hall. Though the downstairs was mostly open to guests, since the dining room contained the refreshments and the parlor held gaming tables, everyone funneled upstairs to the drawing room when they arrived.

Sabrina exhaled as her parents departed. She leaned her head toward Constantine. "Thank you."

"Ignore them," he whispered. "They are completely beneath your concern." The frigidity in his tone made her shiver. She'd once thought she was beneath his concern, or at least his notice, and that was a terrible place to be. It was, however, a deserving situation for her parents.

Shortly thereafter, they finished their duties in the foyer. Anyone arriving after they left would simply be admitted without a personal greeting.

"I'm going to do a circuit and see how things are going," Sabrina said. "Would you mind checking the parlor and seeing if the games are running smoothly?"

"I am at your command." He kissed the back of her hand, then winked at her before taking himself off.

Smiling with a contented sigh, Sabrina went first to the dining room. The sideboard, set with the first small wave of food, looked lovely, but there was an empty space. Something was missing. Scanning the room, Sabrina saw a footman in the corner and strode to him.

"Archer, did something happen to one of the dishes meant for the table?"

He grimaced just slightly before he schooled his features into a serene mask. "There was a problem with the lobster cakes, my lady. Two of the kitchen maids who sampled them this morning fell ill."

"Oh dear, are they all right?" Sabrina made a mental note to talk with Mrs. Haddock as soon as possible.

"I can't say."

"Well, at least the cakes didn't arrive on the table."

"Actually, they did, ma'am. The maids only became sick in the last half hour or so. Mrs. Haddock just had the cakes removed before you came in."

Sabrina wanted to ask if anyone had eaten them before they were taken from the table but was afraid to learn the answer. Offering him a tepid smile, she left the dining room on wooden legs. They were short a musician, the champagne supply was low, and they might have made a guest—or ten— ill from bad lobster cakes.

What more could go wrong?

Sabrina didn't want the answer to that either.

Her wishes didn't matter since not five minutes later, a footman informed her that the second delivery of ice hadn't arrived. After instructing him to make the current stock last as long as possible, she considered retreating to the second floor for the remainder of the evening.

She could not, of course, so she went to the drawing room and braced herself for yet another disaster. And there he was across the room scrutinizing her with narrowed eyes and a deep frown. The Duke of Evesham had apparently arrived while she was in the dining room. Blast, Sabrina had prayed, rather foolishly, that he'd decided not to come.

Hoping to avoid Constantine's father, at least for a short while, she went in search of Evie or Cassandra or Miss Lancaster—anyone but him. Or her parents. She found a great many people and spent the subsequent half hour or so conversing with guests until the next set of music began and dancers flocked to the dance floor.

As she made her way through the throng, she walked straight into her father-in-law. She ought to have known she couldn't avoid him forever. Was it too much to hope she could have evaded him tonight though?

"Your Grace, I hope you're enjoying yourself," she managed to say. "Is there anything you require?"

"A full complement of musicians would suffice. Or a glass of punch with a decent amount of ice. Everyone is complaining about the shortage of ice." He frowned at her, and she wished she could melt into the floor. "But all of that will fade from my memory when you find a suitor for my daughter. It's been nearly a fortnight and you've nothing to show for your efforts."

"That's not exactly true. Lord Glastonbury is a worthy candidate." She hoped so, but Constantine hadn't confirmed his viability as a potential husband.

The duke's brows shot up. "Glastonbury is in the mix?" He grunted softly, then narrowed his eyes at her, which seemed to be the way he typically preferred to regard her. "Until he pays a call, it's just your wishful thinking. You'll need to do better than this if you want to keep your position."

Sabrina's frustration and distress from the succession of troubles neared a boiling point. "What position is that? I am the future Duchess of Evesham," she said sweetly, feeling rather proud of her ability to stand up to him.

"As Cassandra's sponsor," the duke said sharply. "There is nothing I can do about your position in my family as Constantine's wife, but hopefully you will serve your purpose." His gaze flicked to her midsection, and it was clear he meant that she would bear her husband an heir.

"If you'll excuse me, Your Grace, I've a ball to oversee." She didn't bother trying to smile pleasantly or otherwise.

"Yes, you do. So far, it doesn't seem to be going well." Lines of disappointment creased around his mouth before he turned and left the drawing room.

Sabrina fought to take a breath. The heat of the air was cloying, and the stress of the evening was pressing down on her. As she walked into the hall, Constantine stepped from the stairs, his brow furrowed.

She hastened to meet him at the top of the stairs. "What's wrong now?"

His eyes flashed with surprise. "Wrong? Nothing. I just ran into my father and—" He shook his head. "Never mind. Why did you think something was wrong?"

"Because everything is. There's not enough champagne or ice or musicians. And we may have poisoned guests with the lobster cakes." Hysteria started to thicken her chest. She reached for the stair rail to steady herself.

Constantine clasped her elbow and drew her to the passage that led to the backstairs. Opening the door, he gently pushed her into the dim space at the top of the stairs, then sealed them into relatively quiet solitude.

"Breathe, Sabrina," he said softly, clasping her shoulders and running his hands down her arms. "It can't be as bad as all that."

"Everything I said is true, and your father also warned me to ensure your sister has a caller." Her voice had risen as she'd spoken, and her breath was coming in rapid pants.

Constantine took her in his arms and held her against his chest where the steady beat of his heart had an instantly soothing effect. "Don't fret. My father is an ass. Ignore him, please. The rest of it is beyond our control. The lobster cakes were removed, I hope?"

"Of course. However, I don't know if anyone ate any. I couldn't bear to ask." She shuddered against him. "I'm going to be known as the worst hostess in London's history."

"No, you won't. Everyone seems to be having a jolly time, especially in the gaming room."

She pulled back and looked up at him. "Truly?"

He smiled at her and stroked his thumb over her cheek. "You are flushed, and your heart is hammering. I would prefer to be the one to provoke this reaction." He lowered his head and kissed the spot just in front of her ear before flicking his tongue against her earlobe.

"If you're trying to distract me, it's working." She could not ignore the desire pooling in her belly, nor did she want to.

"Excellent." He cupped her nape and kissed her, his tongue tangling with hers. He tasted of hock—good hock— and smelled of cedar and spice. Her senses rejoiced at the familiarity of him, and she gave herself up to his embrace.

When he cupped her breast, she gasped against his mouth. "Constantine, we should probably return to the ball."

"Probably. But will we be missed for five minutes?" He pivoted with her, steering her toward the door that led into her dressing room, which the maid used when she came from the back stairs.

"Where are you taking me?"

He opened the door and moved them into the small chamber. "You know where this leads, so that can't be what you truly want to know. I think you want to know what I have planned."

"I can well imagine, you rogue. You will crumple my gown or mess my hair. Or both."

"What if I could avoid doing that?" He kissed along her throat. "Remember the other night when you were on your knees and I came into you from behind?"

A feverish heat broke over her skin and need pulsed between her legs. How could she forget that? She'd behaved like an utter wanton. "You want to go into the bedchamber?"

He lifted his gaze to hers and gently shook his head. "*That* would crumple your gown for certain. I want you to bend over the end of the chaise." He inclined his head past her to the chaise in the opposite corner.

She turned to look at the piece of furniture, the high end

of which was at about the level of her waist. This was madness. She ought to refuse him and march them back out to the ball. Her body did not agree, and so it was that she walked to the chaise as if carried by wings that didn't belong to her.

Standing at the high end of the chaise, she looked back at him over her shoulder. He came to her, his eyes slitted with desire, and kissed her again, hot and needy.

He hiked the back of her skirt up, and she bent at the waist, letting the chaise balance her. She put her arms before her onto the seat as he caressed her backside.

"Hurry," she breathed as his fingers slid into her crease, teasing her and setting her entire body aflame.

"I'm afraid I must. Not just because we can't take long, but because the sight of you in that gown has been taunting me all evening. And now, seeing you like this..." He thrust a finger into her sex, making her gasp.

"I wish we had more time." He put his cock against her backside, and she widened her stance, eager for him to enter her. "Later, we will, and then I will do everything I don't have time for at the moment. Until then—" He drove into her, pushing her against the chaise and creating friction against her clitoris.

He gripped her hips and let go, offering them both up to mindless sensation. She thought only of his touch and the delicious slide of his cock. After only a handful of strokes, her orgasm began to build. She pressed back against him, desperate to take him as deeply as possible. His fingers dug into her flesh as he buried himself to the hilt.

"Hurry, Constantine." She needed to come. Lights were already dancing behind her eyes.

Increasing his pace to a near frenzy, the sounds of their bodies filled the small space with an erotic symphony. He pushed her forward against the chaise, and she exploded, her sex clenching down around him as devastating shudders wracked her body.

She completely lost sense of time or place and didn't come back until he helped her straighten. Her gown fell over her legs, and she vaguely realized that he'd tidied her up.

"Thank you." She felt unsteady and wholly satiated at the same time. Her thighs quivered but the rest of her sang with joy and relief. "You have solved my problems, I think."

He laughed, then cupped her face. "Good. That is my job." He kissed her, but it was a brief touch as they were interrupted by a knock at the door they'd come through.

"My lady? Are you in there?" Charity's voice called.

Sabrina snapped her attention to Constantine. "Go through my bedroom."

He nodded and slipped from the dressing chamber, blowing a kiss to her on his way out.

Checking her appearance in the glass, Sabrina decided she would use the temperature of the drawing room to excuse her flushed complexion. She opened the door with as much composure as she could muster. "Yes, Charity?"

The maid's tawny eyes were wide with concern. "I'm so glad I found you. I'm afraid there's a…problem."

Sabrina's stomach dropped all the way down to the kitchen. "What?" The word was barely audible.

"Grayson has found his way into the drawing room during a reel. He was last seen in the dining room where he absconded with a piece of pheasant." The maid looked as if she wanted to cry, which was precisely how Sabrina felt.

CHAPTER 19

*W*hen Constantine had left Sabrina just a few moments earlier, she'd been bright-faced and smiling. As he encountered her in the hall at the top of the stairs, she was pale, her eyes wide with something akin to panic.

He rushed to her side. "What's happened?"

"It's the cat. We must find him before he can wreak more damage."

"Where is he?" Constantine whipped his head around as if he would see the animal racing by.

"He was last observed in the dining room stealing pheasant."

Constantine let out a soft curse. This was followed by a shriek from the bottom of the stairs.

Their eyes met as they silently communicated that they had found Grayson.

Starting down the stairs, Constantine nearly tripped as the cat ran by his feet. "Watch out!" he called, turning to make sure the animal didn't cause Sabrina to fall. Thankfully, she was still at the top of the stairs.

A footman dashed after Grayson, who veered left toward the drawing room, in pursuit. Haddock followed soon after, pausing just long enough to assure Constantine that he would have his resignation in the morning.

"The hell I will," Constantine muttered. He refused to lose a perfectly good butler over the antics of a cat.

Sabrina pivoted and hastened after the footman toward the drawing room. Constantine took the stairs two at a time as shouts and a crash signaled the cat's impact where the majority of the guests were gathered.

Arriving at the threshold, he surveyed the room. The musicians were no longer playing, and the dancers stood amidst the now-ruined chalk images that kept them from slipping on the floor, their gazes darting about, undoubtedly in search of a small gray terror.

"Where did he go?" Constantine asked loudly, commanding the attention of everyone in the room.

"We can't see him," Lord Wexford responded from the other side of the room. "It's possible that when Lady Fairweather ducked into the retiring room to avoid the animal, it slipped inside with her?" Lucien's friend grimaced, his eyes sympathetic.

Constantine started toward the door at the opposite end, noting Sabrina to his right as she joined him. A loud, sustained cry from inside the room spurred them faster, and Constantine indicated that Sabrina should look inside since the space was designated for ladies.

"Wait," Haddock said, coming abreast of Constantine. "Let me position myself to grab him when you open the door. He will likely dash out." He looked to Sabrina. "Open it a very small amount."

Sabrina nodded and Haddock crouched down right at the door. Exchanging a look with the butler, Sabrina did as he suggested and barely cracked the door. Haddock knew his cat, for the beast ran straight into the man's clutches. He stood and there was a resounding cheer from the drawing room as he carried the cat from the room.

Constantine's entire body slouched as the tension drained from him. Sabrina, however, did not look as if she was even slightly relieved.

"I'll go check on Lady Fairweather." She was pale, her eyes glazed with trepidation. This was a horrible situation for her. He struggled to find how to fix it.

Knowing the anxiety this must be causing her, he wanted to tell her to retire, that she needn't face this. But if she didn't, her absence would only further mar the event, which was fast becoming somewhat of a disaster. His heart ached. This was *not* how tonight was supposed to happen.

Sabrina slipped into the retiring room and closed the door. Pivoting, Constantine registered that all eyes were on him. This never happened unless he was delivering a speech in the Commons.

Wexford clapped him on the shoulder, grinning. "Well, that was certainly entertaining. I daresay no one will forget this ball!" He spoke loudly and laughed, then looked about. "I need a drink so I can make a toast."

A footman rushed over with a tray bearing punch with too little ice. Constantine clenched his jaw.

Snatching a glass from the tray, Wexford held it up as the footman rushed to deliver the remaining glasses and other footmen did the same. "To Lord and Lady Aldington and their wonderfully imperfect ball. It is as we all are—starting with the best intentions and making do with what happens along the way."

There was a satisfying—and perhaps surprising—chorus of "Hear hear!" Belatedly, Constantine realized he didn't have a drink. A footman pressed one into his hand. Thankfully, it was a brandy. Constantine sent the man a silent look of gratitude, then swallowed the entire contents. He was immediately glad he had, for the next crisis had already arrived.

His father was bearing down on him, his eyes practically black with anger. He spoke low so that no one would hear him but hard. "A word, Aldington. In your study." Without waiting for Constantine's response, he spun about and left the drawing room.

Honestly, Constantine couldn't believe it had taken him this long to seek him out. The confrontation had to happen. Constantine would ensure it was over quickly. Squaring his shoulders, he thanked Wexford for his words and delivered his empty glass to a footman before starting downstairs.

Just outside the drawing room, he ran into Mrs. Haddock, who looked as if she'd been crying. He paused and motioned for her to move to the side with him. "You mustn't feel upset about the cat. I refuse to accept your or Haddock's resignations. We must simply find a way to keep Grayson contained at certain times, and we can discuss that tomorrow. In the meantime, try to make sure he's locked away for the duration of the ball. Will you check on Lady Aldington in the ladies' retiring room? She is soothing Lady Fairweather, who seemed to be overly distressed by a small bundle of fur." He cracked a smile at the housekeeper, who dashed a hand over her eyes.

"You are the kindest of employers, my lord. I am so very sorry."

"It's all right, Mrs. Haddock. Just please take care of the countess."

"Right away." She took off down the corridor, avoiding the drawing room.

Exhaling, Constantine made his way downstairs, glad for the brandy now warming his insides. Lucien stopped him in the gaming room to ask if everything was all right. "I hear the cat has been caught," he said.

"Yes. The threat has been removed. Your friend Wexford gave a delightful toast upstairs. I thanked him, but please let him know how much I appreciate it."

"I will." Lucien flicked a glance toward Constantine's study. "Father just went in there. What's going on?"

"He's about to unleash his rage upon me." Constantine felt rather numb about the prospect, which normally would have upset him. He hated to disappoint his father. However, in this case, there was no help for it.

"Do you want me to come along?" Lucien asked quite soberly.

"No, but I appreciate the offer. I can withstand his anger." He continued on to the study and closed the door behind him.

The duke stood near the hearth, his arms crossed over his chest. "You voted against the act today."

"Yes." Constantine walked to the liquor cabinet and poured two glasses of brandy. He offered one to his father, who only narrowed his eyes further. Shrugging, Constantine returned the glass to the cabinet and sipped from the second.

"That's all you have to say for yourself?" the duke demanded.

"What else is there to say? The vote is done, the act has passed, which is what you wanted, so why do you care how I voted?"

"Because you told me you would vote for it. We had an *arrangement*."

Yes, they did, and that arrangement was the only thing that had given Constantine pause. Ultimately, he hadn't been able to vote for the act, even if it meant his father removed Sabrina as Cassandra's sponsor.

Constantine strode to the window, choosing his words

carefully. "Sometimes we must vote a certain way to gain political capital." He cast his father a perturbed glance. "I know you are aware of this from your vast experience. In this matter, it benefitted me to vote against the Importation Act in order to gain support for the Apothecaries Act."

"You're a fool because that is dead."

"No, it is not, and I won't let it die, as you did my mother." Constantine had *not* chosen those words. In fact, he couldn't believe he'd said them.

The duke's eyes widened to a seemingly impossible degree. "I did not—" He snapped his lips closed, pressing them so hard that they turned white with his fury.

"The Apothecaries Act is of the utmost importance to me, and I will do whatever is necessary to see regulation of medical practice in this country. If I have to vote against an act that was in no danger of failing in order to gain support for my efforts, so be it. I would have thought you would do the same. You taught me to be cunning and strategic." He glared ice at his father, daring him to find fault with what he'd done.

"You lied to *me*."

"I made a deal to get what I needed. The fact that you demanded such a thing for a matter as simple and uncontroversial as allowing *my wife* to act as my sister's sponsor says far more about you than it does me. Now, if you'll excuse me, I've a ball to manage." Constantine started toward the door, his body thrumming with anger and determination.

"You do that," the duke said coldly. "The bloody thing is a disaster as it is. Even if you hadn't deceived me, I'd have to reconsider the countess's role in Cassandra's Season."

Constantine looked back at his father. "You're going to remove her as Cass's sponsor, aren't you?"

"After tonight's failure? Of course I am."

A movement outside the window on the terrace drew

Constantine's attention. The light wasn't very bright, but he could make out the unmistakable gold and ivory gown of his wife and…a gentleman touching her in a way that was beyond the pale.

His father all but forgotten, Constantine threw the door open and stalked through the gaming room to the open doors leading out to the garden. The world seemed to glow red as he came upon the man whose arms were curled around Sabrina's struggling form. Before he could pull the miscreant away, he heard a grunt, which was followed by the man doubling over as Sabrina backed away from him.

The lantern hanging on the exterior of the house illuminated Sabrina. Instead of looking terrified, she appeared furious, her brows pitched into an angry V as her eyes seemed to glow with cobalt fire.

He rushed to her side. "What did you do?"

"I punched his groin."

"You what?" Constantine stared at her, utterly enthralled —and in love—with his wife.

She lifted a shoulder. "It's the only thing a woman can do when a scoundrel oversteps."

Overstep was a massive understatement as far as Constantine was concerned. Several gentlemen from the gaming room, and a few ladies, had swarmed onto the terrace, including Lucien.

"What happened?" Lucien moved past the man who was on his knees groaning.

"He was too forward," Sabrina said, brushing her hands together.

"Are you going to demand satisfaction?" someone called.

"There's no need," the man croaked, lifting his head to reveal his identity—Mr. Franklin Crimwell, a fellow member of Parliament who appeared to be well into his cups. Not that his state forgave his behavior in the slightest. "I offer my most sincere apologies. I did not realize this was Lady Aldington." The man's color was gray, his features squashed with pain and humiliation.

"That's true," Sabrina said quietly. "He kept calling me Mildred. I think he is out of his wits."

Lucien bent to help the man up. "Come, Crimwell, let's get you into a coach to your house." Looking toward the group of people, Lucien inclined his head toward one of his friends, Dougal MacNair, who quickly moved to lend assistance.

"Thank you," Constantine said, grateful for his brother's help.

When Crimwell disappeared into the house between Lucien and MacNair, conversation picked up as people filtered back into the gaming room.

It was at that moment that Cassandra rushed onto the terrace, straight for Sabrina, followed by her companion, Miss Lancaster. "My goodness, Sabrina, are you all right?"

A familiar scent washed over Constantine—a tropical fragrance that swept him into the darkness and overwhelmed him with sensation. He stepped toward his sister and sniffed. It *couldn't* be coming from her. Turning his head slightly, toward Miss Lancaster, he inhaled. And nearly staggered backward. It was her.

"That scent…"

"Oh, yes, my apologies," Cassandra said, looking toward Sabrina. "I'm afraid we helped ourselves to your fragrances before the ball. I forgot to don some at home, and this tropical scent is absolutely divine. Pru and I couldn't resist."

So the perfume didn't belong to Cassandra or Miss Lancaster, but to…Sabrina?

Constantine turned toward her, shock coursing through him. "It was you?"

Her eyes had lost their heat and were now round with distress. "Constantine, I can explain."

"Later," he ground out, his mind spinning at this astonishing revelation. His brain simply couldn't process this information—it didn't make any sense. Yet, he knew it was true. "We've a rather disastrous ball to oversee."

Whatever her explanation, it had to include Lucien. Constantine spun about and stalked inside, making his way to the entrance hall where Lucien was just walking back into the house. MacNair followed behind him.

"Crimwell is on his way home," Lucien said. "I believe MacNair and I have earned a drink."

Years of anger and frustration boiled to the surface in Constantine. "You've earned something." He strode forward and sent his fist into his brother's handsome face, knocking his head back.

Lucien staggered backward, his hand rising to his cheek. "Christ, Con! What the devil are you about?"

"I'm *about* fed up with your meddling and 'help.' It's past time you minded your own bloody business."

MacNair stepped toward Constantine, his gaze darting behind him and toward the stair hall. "Ah, Aldington, you may want to continue this in a more private location," he said quietly.

Constantine turned his head and muttered a curse. A small group of guests had gathered to watch him hit his brother. This would be the talk of the evening, far worse than a dearth of ice or a loose kitten running amok.

If the ball had been a disaster before, it was now a catastrophe.

∼

*C*assandra and Prudence had looked at Sabrina in question after Constantine had gone back into the house. After muttering something nonsensical and which she couldn't even remember a few minutes later, Sabrina had rushed inside and ducked up the backstairs to find a moment's peace.

She felt terrible about how Constantine had learned the truth. He'd looked so utterly shocked. Beyond that, however, she didn't know what he'd felt. Was he angry? Hurt? Disappointed?

She felt as if the world was squeezing in around her. No, she would not collapse. Taking long, deep breaths, she stood on the first floor landing and willed herself to remain calm. She just had to make it through the rest of the evening. And then she could face Constantine.

That did nothing to ease her mind or her anxiety.

Though she didn't feel much better, she couldn't disappear from the ball. She'd already done that earlier with Constantine when they'd shared that wonderful interlude in her dressing room. Had that been tonight instead of some long ago dream?

She stepped out of the stairwell and moved toward the drawing room. The rest of the evening would move swiftly and without incident. It had to. What more could go wrong?

Her mother walked from the drawing room and intercepted her. "There you are, Sabrina." She clucked her tongue disapprovingly. "This ball is an absolute tragedy. I fear you won't be able to hold your head up in Society."

Tragedy. Much to Sabrina's chagrin, she flinched.

"Have you nothing to say for yourself? Or your husband?"

Why would she include Constantine? "I realize you're quite used to denigrating me, but I won't allow you to insult my husband, especially not here in his home." *His* home. As if it weren't hers too.

"I wasn't insulting him. He's the one who created a scene by hitting his own brother."

What on earth had happened? Before the question even finished in her mind, she knew. Constantine was angry with him about the tutoring stratagem. And he had every right to be angry—with her too.

Except, shouldn't she be angry as well? He was the one who'd betrayed her with another woman. Another woman who was her. Sabrina's head began to throb. She massaged her fingertips against her temple. "Please excuse me, Mother."

Sabrina began to turn and felt her mother's hand on her arm.

"I wasn't finished speaking, Sabrina." The viscountess dropped her hand to her side.

"Well, I am finished listening," Sabrina hissed back at her. She'd managed to keep herself together all night, and she simply couldn't do it any longer. Stepping closer to her mother, she let anger and hurt meld into a vitriol she'd never felt before. "Not just tonight but forever. I don't wish to hear anything more you have to say about me, my behavior, or my husband. And I definitely don't want to hear anymore snide comments about my lack of a child or my failure as a countess. You've never understood me or even wanted to." Heart pounding and hands shaking, Sabrina moved past her toward the drawing room—she wasn't going to let her mother distract her from her duty.

Somehow, Sabrina made it through the rest of the ball without retreating to her room, suffering an attack of nerves, or seeing her husband for more than a fleeting moment. Whether Fate had decided to keep them apart for the remainder of the evening or Constantine had just been particularly adept at avoiding her, it wasn't until nearly three o'clock after the last guests had departed that she found him in their sitting room.

He sat near the hearth, his hand clutching a glass of something that wasn't wine. She would have guessed gin, given the lack of color, but she'd never known him to drink that. And why would she? A week or so of togetherness did not mean they were close.

"Have you been waiting for me?" she asked, clutching the gloves she'd removed as she'd climbed the stairs.

"Shouldn't I have been? You indicated that you had some explaining to do."

"I do, and I will." She moved toward him. "I heard about what happened with Lucien."

"All of London has heard by now." His lip curled before he took a sip of his drink. "There will be a hundred stories as to why." He looked up at her, his gaze inscrutable. "None of them will come close to the truth, however."

"I can't imagine they would." Sabrina slowly lowered herself into the chair facing his in front of the hearth. The usual twitter of anxiety rattled inside her. She clasped her hands together in case they started to quiver.

"It's a rather unusual situation." His voice carried an air of detachment. Sabrina couldn't tell at all how he was feeling. "My father has ended your sponsorship of Cassandra."

Though she wasn't surprised, Sabrina was still disappointed. "Because the ball was such a mess?"

He tipped his head in a slight nod. "And because I didn't hold up my end of a bargain we made." Before she could ask him about that, he asked, "Was the tutor stratagem your idea or Lucien's?"

Sabrina licked her suddenly very dry lips. "Lucien's. And Evie's. She suggested it to me."

Constantine's nostrils flared. "They worked together then."

"Yes."

He speared her with a dark stare. "With you."

"Yes. You were also involved," she added quietly, her gaze drifting to her lap.

"Of course I was involved—I was the mark."

She snapped her head up. "You weren't a mark."

"Wasn't I? You were all in on the ruse while I was the dupe." He wasn't wrong, and it was the aspect that had tortured the back of Sabrina's mind, even while they'd reaped the benefits of the deception.

"You weren't a dupe. At least, I never thought of you as such. I thought this would help matters, and it did, didn't it?"

He took another sip. "But I also thought it would help matters. Whether it did or not, perhaps you'll agree it wasn't the best idea." Now, she could see the emotion simmering just beneath the surface of his calm veneer.

"No, it was not. Still, it brought us here, didn't it?"

"To a place where secrets and lies are revealed and not because we shared them. We seem to suffer a lack of honesty and forthrightness. For myself, I have tried very hard—perhaps too hard—to protect you, to keep you from being overset. I resolve not to do that any longer. And you are going to have to find a way to speak your mind. I know you can do it, as evidenced from the very first night you arrived in London." The last part carried a hint of derision.

She understood what he meant. She'd had the courage and nerve to demand he bed her every night to have a child, but she hadn't been able to set aside her apprehension to facilitate that. Not until she'd become the tutor. Thinking about it from his perspective made her understand how he would feel—hurt, upset, perhaps even that she was afraid of *him*.

"I'm sorry for that," she said softly. "It took me a long time to gather the courage to come here, to…change, to be the countess I need to be." And so far, she'd utterly failed—from the ball tonight to sponsoring Cassandra, to being a wife.

Lines furrowed around his eyes, and suddenly he looked sad. "I'm sorry you saw me as such a fearsome person that you had to work so hard to approach me. I should have done more when we were first married to put you at ease. Perhaps we are not well suited after all. I am a focused…*dispassionate* person. You are easily upset, anxious." He finished his gin and stood, the empty glass dangling from his fingertips. "Let us hope you are with child by now so that we can put this unpleasantness behind us."

She stared up at him, words freezing on her tongue before she could utter them.

"I apologize for ruining your ball by hitting Lucien."

A humorless laugh spilled from her lips. "It was ruined before then. I'm sorry it all went so badly. I hope it won't reflect poorly on you."

"It will likely reflect poorly on both of us. It's a good thing neither one of us really cares for the social whirl." The emptiness in his eyes made her shiver. Was this the same man who'd run to her defense earlier? Who'd seduced her in her dressing chamber? Who'd shown her that love wasn't only real but that it was possible for her to feel?

He strode past her to the cabinet, swept up a bottle on the way to his chamber, and closed the door firmly behind him. She heard the lock catch.

Did he mean for them to go their separate ways? He'd certainly implied that by saying he hoped she was already with child. She smoothed her hand over her belly.

It was very late, and she was exhausted. There would be time for them to talk, to move past this…unpleasantness. Did he really think of it like that? The past days had been the happiest of her life, far surpassing pleasant.

She had to think they could find their way back to that. Unless he was right, that they weren't truly suited for one another.

Pressing her hand to her midsection, she thought, *at least I got what I came for*. Probably.

Only that was no longer enough.

$\mathcal{I}$n the past, White's had served Constantine as both a refuge and an opportunity, a place where he could relax and conduct business. It was not where he came to gamble or carouse, as most of the members did. Tonight, those activities seemed especially noisome as he sought out Horace Brightly.

After a fruitless search, during which far too many members queried him about his altercation with Lucien the night before, Constantine relegated himself to a table where he could see the door and hopefully catch Brightly as soon as he arrived. A footman delivered a glass of port, which Constantine accepted with gratitude, despite having over-imbibed the night before.

Thoughts of his wife crept into his brain, but he didn't want to think about the mess of their marriage. He didn't blame her for taking such drastic measures to ease the strife between them—he'd done the same bloody thing. That they'd both felt they had to betray and deceive in order to break down the walls between them made him distinctly uncomfortable. In fact, he preferred not to dwell on it. What had happened was in the past now, and he would continue on as he always had.

Taking a long drink of port, he refocused his mind on Brightly. They'd only briefly spoken about the passing of the Importation Act at the ball last night, and Constantine wanted to continue their conversation.

Perhaps, given their defeat yesterday, Brightly preferred to spend the evening at Brooks's. Or even the Phoenix Club.

Thinking of that establishment drove Constantine to drink more port. He'd actually thought his relationship with Lucien had improved due to the support he'd offered. All the while, his brother had deceived him as surely as Sabrina had. It was unconscionable. Constantine was glad he hadn't accepted the invitation to the Phoenix Club. He didn't want to be anywhere his brother was.

Another of their colleagues from the Commons walked by Constantine's table. He waved his hand toward the man. "Wilson, have you seen Brightly this evening?"

Wilson came to the table and took a chair, his expression intense. "Haven't you heard?" he asked in a low tone, as if he were about to impart a secret. Which begged the question, if it was secret, why would Constantine have heard about it?

"No." Constantine despised this sort of gossip nonsense.

"Brightly's been expelled. You won't find him here tonight. Or ever." He arched his brows, inhaling so that his chest puffed. He looked quite proud of himself for delivering the awful news.

"When did this happen?" Constantine lifted his glass for another much needed drink, thinking he was going to need a refill in a moment.

"Just today, I believe. I'm surprised you don't know. Rumor has it your father was behind the expulsion."

It hadn't been an empty threat. Or perhaps Constantine had provoked him to act by reneging on their agreement.

Fury spiraled through him. He hastily set his glass back on the table lest he break the stem and cut his hand open again. No, he would not think of that night when Sabrina had sauntered into town and changed everything.

He wanted his routine and his comfort back.

Wilson leaned toward Constantine, his eyes slightly narrowed as if he were hunting prey. "Is it true you may call Lord Lucien out?"

"No!" Constantine unleashed the word with an excess of contempt that he immediately regretted. He was angry with his brother, but dueling with him? "You really need to step away from the gossip, Wilson." Rising, he bid Wilson good night and left the club.

Outside, he looked in the direction of the Phoenix Club, situated so close that he could be there in a few short minutes. There was an assembly tonight, and though it was early yet, Sabrina would be there. Constantine could go, accept his membership on the spot, and whisk his wife upstairs where he'd blindfold her and show her what it felt like to be in the dark.

Scrubbing his hand over his face, he slammed on his hat and strode toward home. He hated that he felt like such a fool. He knew Sabrina, Lucien, and Mrs. Renshaw hadn't been laughing at him. They'd concocted the ridiculous stratagem to help him and Sabrina. That was what Lucien did—he helped people. Still, in this case, Constantine thought there had to have been another way to bring him and Sabrina together.

But was there?

She'd been so afraid, so nervous. Which had made him nervous. And uncertain. Perhaps there hadn't been another solution, and did it matter when what they'd done had ended up working in their favor?

It had led him to court her, to behave as he should have

done when they'd first married. Only, he'd thought she'd loathed him. He made a low, frustrated sound in his throat. This was all too damned complicated. He *did* want his orderly life back. It was easy and simple.

And completely…dispassionate.

"Lord Aldington! Lord Aldington!"

Constantine paused and slowly turned. A footman, running from White's, came to an abrupt stop just in front of him. "An urgent message was just delivered for you, my lord." He handed Constantine a folded piece of parchment.

Opening the note, Constantine quickly scanned the contents. His father was demanding he attend him immediately. Not tomorrow but *tonight*. This couldn't be good, but Constantine didn't care. He was furious with the duke about Brightly and eager to tell him so.

After thanking the footman, Constantine caught a hack. Anticipation thrummed in his veins. He could hardly wait to tell his father exactly what he thought.

～

Five minutes after arriving at the Phoenix Club assembly, Sabrina was ready to leave. She never should have come, though she'd wanted to show the ton that she was not cowed after her calamitous ball. Still, she was exhausted from last night. She'd barely slept after her conversation with Constantine. She should have said more, but once again her anxiety had gotten the better of her.

She should have fought. For him, for their marriage. To keep what they'd found.

And what was that exactly? She hadn't even told him she loved him, hadn't tried to find out if he might love her too.

"Sabrina, you look so pensive." Evie had approached her, and Sabrina hadn't even noticed.

Blinking, Sabrina recalled that she was in the Phoenix Club standing near the wide entry to the ballroom. "I think it was a mistake to come tonight. I'm still recovering from last night."

"I hope you aren't feeling bad about it. Didn't you see the evening paper? Lady Pickering declared your ball to be the Success of the Season."

That was almost enough to make Sabrina smile, but not quite. "I did not see that." She'd studiously avoided all the newspapers today.

"There were several other quotes from attendees. They all made the same point: that in spite of the challenges you suffered as a debut hostess, you are no longer the Wallflower Countess. They're calling you the *Renaissance Countess*."

Now Sabrina did smile. "You suggested that nickname to Lady Pickering."

Evie arched a brow, eyes sparkling. "I will neither confirm nor deny that. You are a rousing success and nothing else matters."

"I can't agree. I'm a complete and total failure." Just as her mother had said.

Evie's gaze darkened with distress as she stepped closer to Sabrina. "What's happened?"

"Constantine discovered I was his tutor. It was the perfume. When you and I left my chamber before the ball the other night, Cassandra and Miss Lancaster remained. They found the scent and applied it to themselves."

Deep lines splintered Evie's brow. "Aldington smelled it on them."

"I saw the moment he recognized the scent. He commented on it, and Cassandra revealed it was mine."

"I'm so sorry. Let us go up to my office." Evie ushered Sabrina through the retiring room to the backstairs that would take them up to the first floor where her office sat in the corner, just above the retiring room.

Sabrina had been to the office when she'd visited the club after the musicale. The space was as tastefully and beautifully appointed as Evie's house. Evie went directly to a cabinet and poured two glasses of hock.

"I take it Aldington is terribly angry," Evie said, handing Sabrina a glass before perching on the settee.

Sabrina didn't sit. There was too much energy coursing through her. "No, he isn't terribly angry." She thought of how he'd seemed after the ball—he'd reverted to his demeanor of detachment. Was that his true self? Not the passionate, caring man she'd come to recently know?

"We both agreed it was a terrible stratagem," Sabrina said, pacing toward the window that overlooked the back garden. "We never should have lied to each other, not when our entire marriage started with misunderstandings and assumptions."

She realized communication and honesty were their problems, not their ability to have sex. If they'd actually talked to each other—openly and without fear—the intimacy would have followed. In fact, that's what had happened. Constantine had courted her, wooed her, and she'd been not just receptive but eager for his attention. That's when everything had changed.

Turning from the window, Sabrina felt a surge of clarity, of calm. "I never should have gone to him as the courtesan tutor. I should have done so as his wife."

Evie set her glass down on a table near the settee and stood. "Perhaps I shouldn't have pushed you into the stratagem. But you were so apprehensive, and I so badly wanted to help you. I could see the persistence and strength inside you. The more you took on the role of countess and then of courtesan, you gained confidence."

"You're saying it took me being someone else to finally feel comfortable." Perhaps she *had* needed that. Still, she wanted to believe she could have faced Constantine in their bedchamber as herself, as his wife. The first time after she'd arrived in London had gone somewhat poorly, but it had been improvement. She should have given him—and herself—the time and patience to get where they'd needed to be. Instead, they'd both allowed others, Evie and Lucien, to meddle and manipulate. Given how their marriage had started in exactly the same fashion and had nearly been dead from the start, they both should have known better.

But they were who they were—a dispassionate earl bound to duty and a frightened shadow who didn't stand up for herself. "I think I might return to Hampton Lodge." There was no reason for her to stay.

Brow creasing, Evie strode toward her. "You can't do that. You and Aldington are so close. You'll work through this. Perhaps Lucien and I can—"

"Stop." The frightened shadow was who Sabrina had *been*. No longer. She took a long sip of hock, then straightened her spine. "I appreciate your friendship, but I don't want that sort of interference anymore. This is our marriage—Constantine's and mine. We will work this out together or not at all."

Evie's face fell. "I am so sorry. We should not have involved ourselves. The tutor stratagem was a desperate idea, born of Lucien's desire to help his brother and mine to help you. Though we'd just met, I felt such a kinship with you."

"Why?" Sabrina didn't understand how a sophisticated Society matron could have anything in common with her.

"Because you felt like an outsider. You wanted to find your place. Sometimes I feel like I'm still trying to do that," she added softly, her gaze dropping to the carpet. Sniffing, she jerked her head up. "But this is not about me. This is about you and how I meddled in your marriage. I should not have pushed you into the role of tutor. We—Lucien and I—just wanted to bring you and Aldington together, to give you the love and happiness you both deserve."

"That's incredibly kind of both of you, however neither of you can 'give' me or Constantine that. We had to find it for ourselves. And I do love him—so very much. Though I'm not sure he loves me." If he did, would he even allow himself to? If she thought she'd been playing roles, he'd been acting the grandest one of all, that of a dutiful heir with little inclination for emotion. Unless that's who he really was, but she didn't think so.

"He must," Evie said softly. "He would not have gone to such measures if he did not. It's clear to me that you love each other." She went back to the settee and sat. "Forgive me, Sabrina. It was far too easy for me to support a plan involving a courtesan, since that is what I know."

Sabrina slowly made her way to the settee and sat beside Evie. "Are you saying—"

"That I used to be a courtesan." Evie's lips pulled into a sad smile. "I reinvented myself a couple of years ago as Mrs. Renshaw. I've never even been married." She exhaled. "It feels good to unburden myself. I feel like a fraud every day, and it's nice when I don't have to around those I care about."

"I'm honored that you would share the truth with me."

"It's a very short list—people I care about. I realize we haven't been friends long, but I meant what I said about feeling a camaraderie with you. We have both taken unorthodox measures in the pursuit of happiness."

Sabrina understood what she was saying, even if their measures were somewhat incomparable. She took Evie's hand. "I feel the same closeness, and, of course, I forgive you."

"Thank goodness." Evie dashed her hand over her eyes, and Sabrina hugged her until they both laughed.

"I promise I'm not meddling," Evie said after wiping her

eyes again. "But you can't go back to Hampton Lodge. Not now."

"I know." Sabrina stiffened her spine and lifted her chin. "It's time I truly become the woman I want to be—not a dutiful countess or a courtesan tutor or even a biddable wife. I love my husband, and I want to be his partner." They'd navigated all the pitfalls last night so wonderfully—together. Right up until the deception between them had pushed them apart.

It was time for honesty and confession, an absolute baring of souls. Sabrina only hoped he would join her. For if he didn't, there was truly no hope.

CHAPTER 21

*A*rriving at the ducal residence, Constantine marched up the steps, eager for the coming interview. Bender admitted him inside, taking his hat and gloves, and Constantine went directly to his father's study. The duke was seated behind his desk, as usual.

The fury Constantine felt at learning his father was behind Brightly's expulsion from White's intensified. He was angry about so many things, including the duke's overall meddling and manipulation. "You're despicable," he muttered.

"What's that?" the duke barked.

Constantine straightened. A righteous wrath pulsed through him. "I am done working to please you. That's all I ever craved—to be the heir you wanted me to be, so you'd be proud. Every decision I made, every action I took was all to be the man I thought I had to be, the man you insisted I be." The words poured out of him, bringing a clarity he'd never experienced. "Then, as I grew older, I wanted to be sure I would never be on the receiving end of your disappointment and disdain, as Lucien was. As he *is*. I should have stood up for him. I should have shown him that not everyone is a callous, cruel autocrat like you."

"It seems I arrived at the perfect moment." Lucien sauntered into the room wearing a smug smile, but there was something beneath the surface—a thrumming, dangerous energy that belied his good humor. There was also a faint bruise on his cheek from where Constantine had struck him the night before. "Don't be hard on yourself, Con. If not for you pleasing the old man, it would have been much worse for all of us. I accepted long ago that our good son-bad son situation works to both our advantage." He took a position next to Constantine, facing their father's desk.

The duke stood, his jaw clenched in fury. If he was going to speak, he didn't get a chance, for Constantine had warmed to his ire.

He folded his arms over his chest. "I hear you had Brightly expelled from White's. I hope you're happy with that because I'm going to withdraw my membership as soon as I leave here. If it's not good enough for a man with as much integrity and generosity as Brightly, it certainly isn't the place for me."

"You wouldn't dare." The duke sputtered. "You can't. You're my heir."

Constantine shrugged. "Your heir will simply frequent Brooks's."

Their father's hands fisted at his sides, and his eyes narrowed with rage. "*Travesty.*"

"Or the Phoenix Club," Lucien suggested cheerfully.

In that moment, Constantine decided he would accept the invitation. Not just to irritate his father, though that was an enormous benefit, but to support his brother. Though Constantine was still quite angry with him for *his* meddling, he knew it came from Lucien's desire to help others. It was why he'd started the club with its particular purpose. It occurred to Constantine in that moment that there was likely a reason for Lucien's actions. He'd always seemed to have friends in excess, popularity among everyone, and an uncanny ability to charm and woo. But what if he'd felt isolated and alone because of their father, and even because of Constantine? What if he helped others in an effort to help himself?

A wave of understanding washed over Constantine, taking his breath away. He had accountability in his father's treatment of his brother, just as he did with his marriage. It was long past time he stepped out of his father's shadow, that he be the man he wanted to be. A man who wasn't dispassionate like their father. In fact, Constantine realized he was the opposite of that. He was passionate about his work, his racing, and, most of all, his wife.

"You can't leave White's," the duke declared, slicing his hand through the air. "I forbid it. Furthermore, I forbid you from coming to fisticuffs as you did at that catastrophe of a ball last night!"

Constantine exchanged an incredulous look with Lucien, who said, "We aren't children, Father."

The duke narrowed his eyes at Lucien. "Then stop acting as if you are. I can expect this sort of embarrassing behavior from you, but from Aldington?" He swung his angry gaze to Constantine. "I expect better from you."

"How sad that you don't expect the same things from your sons. You should. We were both raised by you." But the duke had treated them differently, and Constantine was only just beginning to see how much. "I realize this will be hard for you to comprehend, Father, but my decision to leave White's is not up for debate. You have no control over me, and your tutelage, or whatever this lifelong management has been, is over. I am my own man now. I will vote for—or against—things in the manner I choose, and I will allow my butler and his wife to have a cat in my house." The duke had admonished him for that later on during the ball. "And if I want to hit my brother when he behaves like you, I will." He glanced toward Lucien who mouthed the word "*Ouch.*"

Constantine continued, "I will also encourage my wife to assist my sister in any way she sees fit. She may not be her formal sponsor, but she will be there at Cassandra's side, steering her toward success and, more importantly, happiness." Constantine hoped she would anyway. There was so much he needed to say to her.

Lucien pivoted toward him and began to clap. "Bravo, brother. Bravo."

The duke's face pinched, and Constantine didn't think he'd ever seen his father look more uncomfortable. "Lucien, leave us," their father intoned. "Close the door on your way out."

Constantine flicked a glance at his brother, whose features registered surprise. He gave Constantine an encouraging look, then left.

Clearing his throat, the duke sat back down. He settled his gaze on some sport behind Constantine. "I'm going to tell you something, and I don't wish to discuss it. Just listen and go."

Alarm raced through Constantine, but he said nothing. He'd never seen his father so stoic—but there was also a steady pulse in his throat, indicating the duke was not at ease.

"I don't talk about your mother because I cannot. Loving her and losing her is the greatest pain I will ever know. You think I let her die, and sometimes I think that too. I summoned that surgeon. I allowed him to treat your mother over a period of time. I was blind with worry." His voice tightened. "Then she died. You blame the surgeon and me. I only blame myself."

A burning anguish sparked in Constantine's chest. "I don't—"

The duke's gaze darted toward Constantine, but only for a second. "You do and we aren't discussing this. If you speak again, I'll stop."

Constantine pressed his lips together and clasped his hands tightly behind his back.

"I chose Sabrina as your wife because she seemed a perfect match—good pedigree, beautiful, biddable, and utterly unremarkable in personality or passion. I thought it best you have a wife whom you would not love or be close to as I was with your mother. Having and losing that is a devastation I would never wish on my children." He coughed.

"I can see, however, that despite my best intentions, you are enamored of your wife. While this causes me distress, it is because I fear for you should you lose her. I shall pray that does not happen."

Constantine's throat constricted. He wanted to speak but wasn't sure he could even if he'd been allowed.

"I never meant to cause you pain. I was trying to save you from it. I am proud of you, even if I don't agree with your actions." The duke sniffed, and now his gaze found Constantine's. "This is between us. I ask—and expect—that you not share this with your brother or sister. It doesn't concern them in any way."

Constantine couldn't keep from asking, "Do you have the same hope for them, that they won't marry for love?"

The duke glowered at him, and Constantine knew the interview was finished. And his father would never acknowledge this conversation had ever occurred. Even if he tried to tell Lu and Cass, they probably wouldn't believe him. Constantine wasn't sure he believed it himself.

"Thank you," he murmured. "I love you, Father."

Turning, Constantine walked out of the study. In the

foyer, he retrieved his hat and gloves and bade Bender good evening.

Lucien was waiting for him outside.

Constantine sent him a perturbed stare. "I'm still annoyed with you." His gaze fixed on the god-awful cravat his brother was wearing. "That neckcloth is the color of goose shit."

"I know." Lucien grinned. "Isn't it wonderful?" He always wore an obnoxious cravat when visiting the duke. Wiping his hand over his mouth, he sobered. "You should be annoyed with me. But damn, did you have to say I acted like Father?"

"You were meddling and manipulating. Surely, you see the resemblance."

"Though it pains me to no small degree, yes. I truly only meant to help, not manipulate. Between your frigidity and your wife's terror, you were never going to find your way in marriage—or in bed. And you needed to."

"How do you know about Sabrina's anxiety? How did you even know to 'help' us in the first place?"

Lucien exhaled. "Your wife heard about my reputation for helping people and came to me—initially for help with obtaining a new wardrobe and making a splash this Season. I sent her to Mrs. Renshaw for assistance and, ah, Evie learned the true heart of the matter, that the countess wished to seduce you."

"Is that what Sabrina said?" Because wanting to seduce her husband wasn't the same as wanting a child, which is what she'd told him when she'd arrived in town. They could have accomplished the latter doing what they'd always done. But if she'd truly wanted seduction all along, they could have avoided a great many assumptions and misunderstandings. He realized *that* was the core of their discontent, not their inability to come together in bed.

"I don't exactly recall," Lucien responded. "You should know that she was reluctant at first."

"I wish we'd been able to talk to each other without your meddling," he whispered. "That we'd been able to be ourselves and not what others pushed us to be."

"Oh hell, Con." Lucien put his arms around him and hugged him tightly.

The action was shocking but incredibly necessary. Constantine hugged him back as years of stockpiled emotion loosened and flooded forth.

"I'm sorry," Lucien said, stepping back as Constantine blinked repeatedly. "But wasn't it worth it? You were both so happy. I thought you may have been in love."

"I was. I *am*. Desperately. Though, I'm afraid she may not return the emotion."

"I can't say for certain, but she looked like a woman in love to me. Watching you together at the ball when everything was going horribly wrong was wonderfully satisfying. You appeared as partners, and I was sure your marriage was saved."

"I thought so too, but then I fucked it up."

Lucien's jaw dropped in mock horror. "Such language! What are you going to do about it? About her?"

"I'm going home to my wife."

"An excellent plan." Lucien clapped him on the shoulder. "Let me know if I can be of any further help."

"You should stop with that," Constantine said. "It's one thing to help and another to meddle."

His eyes darkening, Lucien nodded. "Understood. I—we, Evie and I—overstepped here and I truly am sorry. I just need you to know that I only wanted your happiness."

"I know that, and I appreciate it." Constantine realized his brother and father weren't all that different in their motivation. Both wanted to ensure his happiness. Though in his father's case, he'd sought to do so by protecting Constantine's heart. The irony was that in trying to keep Constantine from misery, the duke had actually delivered him straight into the heart of it.

The true gift was that they'd pushed Constantine to acknowledge his true self—not a dutiful automaton who only wanted to please his father and not an emotionless dullard with a stick up his arse. He knew who he was, and he was desperate to tell the one person who needed to see him most of all: his wife.

"Lu, do I need to formally accept the Phoenix Club invitation, or can I just show up to the assembly tonight?"

Lucien grinned. "Aw, you called me Lu. Come on, we'll go together. On the way, you can tell me what Father said after I left."

"Actually, no, I can't. And please don't ask me to." There would probably come a time when Constantine would feel the need to break his father's confidence, but for now, he would keep the man's secrets.

As they made their way to the Phoenix Club, Constantine's chest threatened to burst with emotion. Unfortunately, when they arrived, it was to learn that Lady Aldington had already returned home.

"Go," Lucien said. "I look forward to when we can spend time together here at the club, but tonight is not that night."

"No, it is not." Constantine caught a hack and when they arrived on Curzon Street, he practically jumped from the vehicle. As they neared the house, he saw an unfamiliar gig outside.

Constantine bounded into the house where Haddock met him with a pinched expression.

"What's the matter?" Constantine demanded, his blood running inexplicably cold at the worry in Haddock's eyes. "Whose gig is that outside?"

"Her ladyship sent for a physician. He is upstairs with her now."

The world tilted sideways. Constantine couldn't breathe. He rushed upstairs, raced to their sitting room, and came face to face with her maid. "Where is Lady Aldington?" he demanded.

Charity paled as she pointed toward the closed door to her bedchamber. "She's in there with Dr. Montbourne."

Oh God, what if he was too late to stop whatever treatment the man had probably forced upon her? Who was this Dr. Montbourne anyway? Constantine didn't know him, had never heard of him. And holy hell, *why was his wife seeing a bloody doctor?*

Constantine stormed into the room to find Sabrina perched on her bed and the charlatan Dr. Montbourne standing beside her. The man was too handsome to have serious medical credentials and certainly didn't look old enough to have the requisite experience. Except none of that was regulated, which was why they needed the damn apothecaries bill.

"Back away from my wife," Constantine shouted. "Don't you dare touch her."

CHAPTER 22

S abrina almost didn't recognize the wild-eyed
gentleman who'd burst into her chamber. Constantine looked like some sort of beast, his teeth bared, his hands fisted at his sides as if he were going to launch himself at Dr. Montbourne and pummel him to bits.

"Er, good evening, Lord Aldington. I am Dr. Xavier Montbourne." Holding out his hand with an engaging smile, he stepped toward Constantine.

Glaring at the physician, Constantine moved around him and put himself between the man and Sabrina. "Get out."

"Constantine, stop. Please." Sabrina reached for his hand, but he jerked away from her.

"I said get out. Now." He advanced on the physician with a terrifying menace.

Sabrina jumped up from the bed and inserted herself in front of Dr. Montbourne. "Stop this nonsense right now. Dr. Montbourne was just leaving anyway. Even so, there's no call to be rude."

"Why is he here? What did he do to you?" The bleak

distress in his gaze at last prompted her understanding. Finding her with a doctor would be upsetting to him.

Sabrina moved closer and took his hand again, squeezing it tightly so he wouldn't let her go. This time, he did not. "Dr. Montbourne merely performed a simple examination. I experienced a few odd pains earlier, and I was hoping he would allay my concerns."

Constantine had watched her as she spoke, but now he sent a suspicious glance toward the physician. "What sort of pains?"

"The sort that normally accompany a woman who is likely with child. I'm fine. Dr. Montbourne is lovely. And since he will return at a later time to check my progress, you should apologize."

He stared at her, frozen for a long moment, so she squeezed his hand again and whispered his name. At last, he blinked and turned to face Dr. Montbourne.

"I apologize for my outburst. I require documentation of your education, your age, and how long you have practiced in your profession, and a list of no fewer than five—no, ten—references who can attest to your knowledge and expertise. References with medical backgrounds, from the Royal College and the like, not your neighbor or your mother."

He sounded so very cross but also concerned, and Sabrina wanted to ease all of his pain.

Dr. Montbourne inclined his head. "I would be pleased to provide this information, my lord."

"At the earliest opportunity," Constantine practically growled.

Sabrina let go of Constantine's hand. "I'll see you out, Dr. Montbourne." She led him from her bedchamber into the sitting room where Charity stood, her eyes wide.

"You may go, Charity," she said with a smile before turning to Dr. Montbourne.

"Please accept my deepest apologies for my husband's behavior. He lost his mother due to the care of an inept surgeon, and I'm afraid he has a grave distrust for medical practitioners."

"That is understandable. I shall do my best to alleviate his concerns." He took her hand and bowed. "Take good care, my lady. I'll see you soon."

"Thank you, Dr. Montbourne." She watched him depart the sitting room, then turned to see her husband standing in the doorway wearing an extremely disgruntled expression.

"You shouldn't tell him my personal history. It's none of his business."

Sabrina longed to smooth the worry from his forehead and from his very soul. "Why not, if it helps him understand his patients—you and me—better."

Constantine grunted. "He is not *my* physician. Nor is he yours yet."

She took a step toward him. "My dear Constantine, you must be willing to share things, to open up about your emotions—your fears and desires—if you want to get on in this life. I have only recently learned this lesson myself."

He ran his hand through his hair, exhaling. "That's why I'm here, actually." He started forward but stopped a few feet away, his gaze dropping to her belly. "Is it really true? That you're with child?"

She nodded, tears pricking the backs of her eyes and clogging her throat. "It seems so. My courses are extremely regular, and they are quite late. When I described my symptoms to Dr. Montbourne, he did a brief examination, and he believes that I am carrying. We will know for certain, of course, in the coming weeks." Was he happy? Shocked? Terrified?

"I can hardly believe it," he whispered. "What if something

goes wrong?" His gaze lifted to hers, and she realized he *was* terrified.

"We will face it together," she said. "I hope so anyway."

He blinked, his features opening as if he'd just remembered something vitally important. "Yes, together. I don't want to do anything without you. I thought I could go back to the way things were, that I preferred that—I think I even convinced myself that you wanted that too. But you came here looking for a change, determined to be someone different." He shook his head, a faint smile teasing his lips. "Not someone different, but *you*."

How had he come to understand her so perfectly? "*Exactly.* I've been who everyone wanted or expected me to be."

"Including me. I assumed you loathed me because you didn't want to marry me. I didn't give you a chance. I didn't give *us* a chance."

"And I assumed you would be autocratic and cold like your father."

"Haven't I been?" Constantine arched a sandy brow, and the effect of his self-deprecation and sly humor was devastating.

Sabrina rushed forward and clasped his hand between hers. "Yes, but that's not who you are."

"No, it's not. I didn't know who I was until you came to London to save me from myself. I know that was not your intent—you wanted a child—but that's what happened."

"Yes, I wanted a child, but I wanted you too."

He narrowed one eye at her. "I think it's important that we're completely honest with each other, that there are no more assumptions or half-truths or misunderstandings."

Heat rose up Sabrina's neck. "All right, perhaps at first I was fixated on a child. But as soon as I learned about the pleasurable side of marriage, I wanted that. With you.

Wanting you came very quickly—and easily. Even that first night when things were still so awkward between us, I wanted you. I just didn't know how to show it, and I was too afraid to say it."

He took his hand from hers and cupped her face, holding her as he stared into her eyes. "Promise you'll never be afraid of me again. I would never hurt you. I love you completely."

His words lit a brightness inside her that would never be diminished. For as long as she lived, she would remember this moment, this man, and this outpouring she'd never imagined to see from him. The tears she'd held back spilled forth, trailing down her cheeks and onto his hands.

"My love," he whispered before gently moving his lips over hers. "I wanted you even before we were wed. I was hurt when I learned you didn't want to marry me, but I think I always hoped we would find a connection. If only I'd told you so—"

"Shh. Don't look back." Sabrina clutched at his lapels and held him to her. "I love you too," she said, but she feared the words were lost against his mouth. She pulled away to look into his eyes. "I love you, Constantine."

His hands stroked down her neck and rested on her shoulders. "You came here to change, and in doing so, you changed me."

"I prefer to think we both discovered our truths—about ourselves and each other." She wrapped her arms around his waist. "I'm sorry it took an ill-conceived stratagem. If I could go back and change that, I would."

"It *was* ill-conceived, and yet we really can't complain about the results. I was desperate to do anything for you." His voice broke, and Sabrina's heart twisted.

She squeezed him tightly. "I treasured every moment of those encounters when you bared yourself to me in ways I don't think you realized. That's when I started to fall in love with you. Then you courted me, and I fell completely."

"You're right in that seeing the tutor helped me become myself, to strip away the artifice of being my father's son."

"Pretending to be a former courtesan allowed me to lose my inhibitions, to become your wife, not just your countess."

He laughed softly. "I suppose we should be thankful for the ruse after all. And to Lucien and Mrs. Renshaw for their meddling."

"Perhaps, but in the interest of speaking honestly, I must say I prefer to give the credit to us. You're the one who made me feel desirable, and ultimately that gave me the courage I needed."

"You are infinitely desirable." Constantine lowered his head and kissed her jaw, then her neck. "Perhaps you'd like me to demonstrate how much?" His lips and tongue elicited a shiver as need gathered inside her.

She moved one hand to the back of his neck, urging him to continue with his mouth. "May I make a request?"

"Anything," he whispered against her neck. "Make every request. I want to hear everything you are thinking from now on, no matter what."

"Everything? Well, then, I want you to blindfold me. I imagined that must have heightened your senses when I was the tutor, and I wanted to know what that felt like."

"Would you like me to be your tutor?" he asked huskily, provoking a flash of lust so hot and bright that Sabrina quivered in his arms.

"Yes, please. Tell me *exactly* what you want me to do."

He lifted his head and looked into her eyes. "Just love me."

"That's easy because I already do." She narrowed her eyes at him and tugged his hair. "You're going to have to be naughtier than that."

He swept her into his arms with a growl and strode to the

bed, depositing her carefully onto the mattress. After removing his boots, coat, and waistcoat, he returned to her as he stripped his cravat away. "Ready?"

She nodded, eager for this night and all the nights to come.

He paused, his eyes glistening as he looked at her. "I love you, Sabrina, with all of my cold, black heart."

She cupped his face and kissed him hard and fast. "Your heart is not cold, nor is it black. It is warm and kind and full of love. And it is *mine*."

EPILOGUE

April 1, London

"Why are you smiling?" Constantine asked his wife as their coach arrived in Portman Square, where they would attend a ball with Cassandra. While Sabrina was no longer her official sponsor, she and Constantine had agreed that they would continue to support his sister in her Season—if only to provide an additional defense against their father's meddling.

"I was just thinking of the new kitten and how Grayson already seems to adore him. I think he wanted a brother."

At both Sabrina and Constantine's insistence, Haddock had found another kitten the day before. Sabrina, with Constantine's full endorsement, had insisted both he and Grayson have the run of the house. The buff-colored kitten had slept on Sabrina's lap that morning as they'd breakfasted, and Constantine suspected that would become a regular occurrence. Both woman and cat had appeared quite content.

"I'm not at all sure the addition will calm Grayson, however," Constantine noted. The two liked to tussle, and it was rather amusing to watch.

Sabrina laughed softly. "No, I'm not sure it will either. But I don't mind, do you?"

"Surprisingly, no."

The coach had pulled abreast of the entrance to the house and a moment later, the groom opened the door. Constantine stepped out and helped Sabrina to the ground. She was even more stunning than normal due to the glow that Constantine was certain emanated from the child she carried.

Offering his arm, he guided her to the house, and they made their way through the receiving line and into the ballroom. "Shall we find Cass?" he asked, surveying the large space for his sister.

"Yes. I daresay your aunt has likely already abandoned her."

"Indeed, she has. Cass and Miss Lancaster are near that large potted palm." He led Sabrina through the crowd to where the two young women stood.

Cassandra's eyes lit as they approached. "Thank goodness you are here. I can't tell you how happy I was to receive your note, Sabrina." Sabrina had written to tell her that she would continue to act as a sponsor, even if she didn't officially carry that title.

"You look awfully relieved," Constantine said. "Has something happened with Aunt Christina?"

"Nothing outside of the usual." Cassandra glowered toward some distant point across the room. "She is mostly worthless as a sponsor, and why Father doesn't see that, I don't know." She turned her attention to Sabrina, her eyes narrowed in frustration. "I am still quite furious with him for removing you as my sponsor. I am so angry, in fact, that I've half a mind to marry the next man I see. We'll dash off to Gretna Green as my dear friend Fiona did."

"Did I hear my name?" A red-haired young woman stepped out from behind the potted palm. At her side was the Earl of Overton, her new husband. Constantine couldn't help but remember the very last time he'd seen them—some four weeks before. He could scarcely believe how much had changed in such a short time.

Cassandra had let out a delighted shriek, and she and Lady Overton were now embracing in a thoroughly inappropriate manner given their surroundings. Constantine was surprised to find he didn't care.

"Good evening, Overton," he said, hoping they could forget or at least ignore their encounter at the Phoenix Club those weeks ago. "May I offer my heartfelt congratulations to you and Lady Overton?"

Overton shook Constantine's hand, showing no indication he recalled their meeting. "Thank you, I am glad to have them." He introduced his new wife to Sabrina.

"I'm so pleased to meet Cassandra's good friend," Sabrina said.

Cassandra took Lady Overton's hand. "I can't tell you how glad I am that you're back. The last few weeks have been quite trying. There is so much to tell you. And, of course, I must hear all about your trip." She grinned. "You're a countess now!"

Lady Overton laughed. "Yes. It's rather bizarre," she added in a near whisper. "You didn't become betrothed while I was away, did you?"

"No, but it's not for my father's lack of pressure on the

matter. If I don't wed by June, he's threatened to marry me off to some indeterminate gentleman." Cassandra glanced toward Sabrina. "Isn't that right?"

"So he said," she exchanged a look with Constantine, and they silently communicated that they wouldn't allow that to happen.

Cassandra's gaze gleamed with determination. "I've decided I'm going to marry the next man I encounter. I hope he's especially roguish. Father will hate that."

"Overton, you've returned!" Lord Wexford came toward them, his handsome face bright with a wide grin. He clapped Overton on the shoulder. "Welcome home." He bowed to Lady Overton. "My lady, you are a vision of newlywed loveliness. My congratulations to you both."

Miss Lancaster leaned close to Cassandra and whispered something that made Cassandra laugh softly. She nodded in response before addressing Wexford.

"My lord, I think you should dance with me."

Overton pivoted toward her, his brow creasing. "Ah, perhaps you'd like to dance with me instead?"

Cassandra flashed him a smile. "Thank you, but I think it must be Wexford. In the meantime, let us take a turn, shall we?" She took the Irishman's arm, and they began a promenade about the room.

Constantine wondered what his sister was up to and wasn't entirely certain he wanted to know. A few hours later, he handed Sabrina into their coach and climbed in after her, his feet aching from dancing with her, which he hadn't done in ages. He kicked off his dancing slippers and wiggled his toes.

She stared at his stockinged feet. "Did you just take your shoes off?"

"I did."

"First you danced with me and now this. You continue to astonish me, my lord."

"You aren't supposed to address me like that anymore." He sounded cranky and immediately regretted his tone. "I meant that in jest, but that came out wrong. I suppose that's because I really do prefer that you call me by my name when we are alone."

She turned toward him on the seat and put her hand on his chest, her fingers diving beneath his waistcoat and pressing against him. "*Constantine*, I adore you so."

"Even when my haughtier nature comes out?"

"You have spent your entire life being the person your father wanted you to be. I imagine it will take time for you to settle into the man *you* want to be. I know the changes I have made will take time and effort. The ball tonight was easier, but I would have gladly left an hour ago." She smiled at him and leaned her head on his shoulder.

Constantine had sensed her fatigue and rising anxiety and taken her for a turn in the garden, which had given her the fortitude to stay the extra hour. He kissed her forehead and thought of all the change they'd undergone over the past several weeks. "Would you still describe me as dispassionate?"

She lifted her head and looked into his eyes. "Not at all. In fact, I would describe you as impassioned. I can't imagine a more attentive or devoted husband."

He slipped his arm around her waist and pivoted toward her. "With you captivating me at every moment, how can I not be?"

Sliding her hand up his chest, she tugged his cravat loose. "I promise to do all I can to keep you impassioned—and informed. Talking and sharing with each other is what brought us here, and I don't ever want to go back to my life without you."

"I promise you never will. You're mine, Sabrina. Now and forever."

Find out what happens next with Cassandra and Ruark! And find out what *already* happened... (how's that for a tease?). A romance between a young lady on the Marriage Mart and her brother's best friend is surely intolerable...

INTOLERABLE, the third book in the Phoenix Club series, coming October 2021!

Would you like to know when my next book is available and to hear about sales and deals? Sign up for my VIP newsletter, follow me on social media:

Facebook: https://facebook.com/DarcyBurkeFans
Twitter at @darcyburke
Instagram at darcyburkeauthor
Pinterest at darcyburkewrite

And follow me on Bookbub to receive updates on pre-orders, new releases, and deals!

Need more Regency romance? Check out my other historical series:

The Untouchables
Swoon over twelve of Society's most eligible and elusive bachelor peers and the bluestockings, wallflowers, and outcasts who bring them to their knees!

The Untouchables: The Spitfire Society
Meet the smart, independent women who've decided they

don't need Society's rules, their families' expectations, or, most importantly, a husband. But just because they don't need a man doesn't mean they might not *want* one…

The Untouchables: The Pretenders
Set in the captivating world of The Untouchables, follow the saga of a trio of siblings who excel at being something they're not. Can a dauntless Bow Street Runner, a devastated viscount, and a disillusioned Society miss unravel their secrets?

Wicked Dukes Club
Six books written by me and my BFF, NYT Bestselling Author Erica Ridley. Meet the unforgettable men of London's most notorious tavern, The Wicked Duke. Seductively handsome, with charm and wit to spare, one night with these rakes and rogues will never be enough…

Love is All Around
Heartwarming Regency-set retellings of classic Christmas stories (written after the Regency!) featuring a cozy village, three siblings, and the best gift of all: love.

Secrets and Scandals
Six epic stories set in London's glittering ballrooms and England's lush countryside.

Legendary Rogues
Five intrepid heroines and adventurous heroes embark on exciting quests across the Georgian Highlands and Regency England and Wales!

If you like contemporary romance, I hope you'll check out

my **Ribbon Ridge** series available from Avon Impulse, and the continuation of Ribbon Ridge in **So Hot**.

I hope you'll consider leaving a review at your favorite online vendor or networking site!

I appreciate my readers so much. Thank you, thank you, *thank you*.

ALSO BY DARCY BURKE

Historical Romance

The Phoenix Club

Invitation (newsletter exclusive)

Improper

Impassioned

Intolerable

Indecent

The Untouchables

The Bachelor Earl

The Forbidden Duke

The Duke of Daring

The Duke of Deception

The Duke of Desire

The Duke of Defiance

The Duke of Danger

The Duke of Ice

The Duke of Ruin

The Duke of Lies

The Duke of Seduction

The Duke of Kisses

The Duke of Distraction

One Night of Scandal by Darcy Burke
One Night to Remember by Erica Ridley
One Night of Temptation by Darcy Burke

Secrets and Scandals

Her Wicked Ways
His Wicked Heart
To Seduce a Scoundrel
To Love a Thief (a novella)
Never Love a Scoundrel
Scoundrel Ever After

Contemporary Romance

Ribbon Ridge

Where the Heart Is (a prequel novella)
Only in My Dreams
Yours to Hold
When Love Happens
The Idea of You
When We Kiss
You're Still the One

Ribbon Ridge: So Hot

So Good
So Right
So Wrong

ABOUT THE AUTHOR

Darcy Burke is the USA Today Bestselling Author of sexy, emotional historical and contemporary romance. Darcy wrote her first book at age 11, a happily ever after about a swan addicted to magic and the female swan who loved him, with exceedingly poor illustrations. Join her Reader Club newsletter for the latest updates from Darcy.

A native Oregonian, Darcy lives on the edge of wine country with her guitar-strumming husband, incredibly talented artist daughter, and imaginative son who will almost certainly out-write her one day (that may be tomorrow). They're a crazy cat family with two Bengal cats, a small, fame-seeking cat named after a fruit, an older rescue Maine Coon with attitude to spare, an adorable former stray who wandered onto their deck and into their hearts, and two bonded boys who used to belong to (separate) neighbors but chose them instead. You can find Darcy at a winery, in her comfy writing chair balancing her laptop and a cat or three, folding laundry (which she loves), or binge-watching TV with the family. Her happy places are Disneyland, Labor Day weekend at the Gorge, Denmark, and anywhere in the UK— so long as her family is there too. Visit Darcy online at www. darcyburke.com and follow her on social media.

facebook.com/DarcyBurkeFans

twitter.com/darcyburke

instagram.com/darcyburkeauthor

pinterest.com/darcyburkewrites

goodreads.com/darcyburke

bookbub.com/authors/darcy-burke

amazon.com/author/darcyburke

Printed in Great Britain
by Amazon

25526704R00187